THE TEMPLARS' RETURN

THE TEMPLARS' RETURN

Book One of Touched by Freia

DOUG WILSON

iUniverse, Inc.
Bloomington

The Templars' Return
Book One of Touched by Freia

This is a work of fiction. All of the characters, names, incidents, organizations, and dialogue in this novel are either the products of the author's imagination or are used fictitiously.

iUniverse books may be ordered through booksellers or by contacting:

iUniverse
1663 Liberty Drive
Bloomington, IN 47403
www.iuniverse.com
1-800-Authors (1-800-288-4677)

ISBN: 978-1-4759-4269-9 (sc)
ISBN: 978-1-4759-4271-2 (hc)
ISBN: 978-1-4759-4270-5 (e)

Library of Congress Control Number: 2012914309

Printed in the United States of America

iUniverse rev. date: 9/4/2012

A Wrong Turn

The windshield cracked in a spiderweb pattern and then folded into the car. A branch, shoving its way in through the hole, cut a furrow across Martin's scalp before tearing a path through the headliner. He saw more than felt the wheel well as it pushed its way into the passenger foot space. He unwillingly clapped his hands straight out in front of him when the seatbelt jerked him to a stop.

He flopped back into the seat. He listened briefly to the utter silence, not thinking or feeling, just listening. Hours or seconds passed. He didn't know which. Then came that horrific crack. It smashed at his ears, causing ice picks of pain to shoot briefly through his temples. He felt his weight shift, first up and then back. Time sped up. He lost track of up and down amid the flapping arms, slapping twigs, creaks and crashes. The seatback gave way when he slammed back into it. It saved his life.

Lying with his head on his arms, facedown inside on the roof the car, Martin felt the button of his Pendleton shirt pressing into his cheek. Sticky with blood, the sleeve and button clung to his face momentarily as he raised his head. He turned slowly, afraid of what he might see.

He looked at the driver. He could make out only the back of Amy's head. He called her name, but she didn't move or acknowledge him. She was bent awkwardly between the seats. Her seatback pressed against the roof. Her hair was fanned out below her, draped in a pool of blood.

It took the pain in his legs quite some time to intrude, but when it finally got his attention, the throbbing was a steady, ever-present companion gleefully torturing him. He looked around inside the car.

The scene around him was like a surreal dream or a Dali painting, full of normal shapes that were bent and twisted in cruel and useless ways.

Shattered glass was everywhere, broken into the little cubes they show on television and sparkling in the morning sunlight. A pop can, overturned in a dark puddle of liquid, was lying by the dashboard. It was difficult to comprehend the interior of the little Honda. Some parts, like the backseat, were pristine, looking like they had yesterday. Others, like the passenger door, with its white foam stuffing exposed and broken plastic trim everywhere, looked more like an aborted space project than the car he knew so well. None of the windows had survived. The compression of the roof had crushed them as it closed each opening. He tested his elbow to make sure it would hold his weight, and then, reaching up, he unclasped his belt. He dropped to the roof, screaming as his legs shifted in the small space, and then curled into a ball and panted out the spasm of pain.

Martin didn't want to move, but he couldn't reach Amy from where he'd fallen. Every inch of movement sparked a cascade of screaming nerves, each testifying to the million abuses he'd suffered. Eventually the pain eased enough for him to try to move again. He stretched out toward Amy, hoping against hope she was all right. He could barely reach her. When he did, she was cold. He heard a sound, a distant sobbing. It reverberated through the small car. He realized it was the sound of his own voice. Tears poured down his face as he called her name again and again. He dragged himself closer to her. Her eyes were open.

He screamed. He cursed God and himself. He cursed her. After a while his screaming quieted into low moans. He lay there for a long time, holding her hand and crying.

At some point the pain in his legs clawed its way through his sorrow and reminded him that he was still in trouble. He decided in that moment that he didn't want to live without her. He would just lie there and die beside her. But the pain had other ideas. It tore at him, implacable and ceaseless. It washed over him in great waves that ripped all other thoughts from his mind.

Panting and lying very still helped him through the long waves of pain.

Part of him felt like he deserved this agony for not dying with Amy when he had the chance.

But another part of him, one he wasn't proud of, wanted to live. It wanted to stop the throbbing in his legs and crawl out of this dead car and away from his dead fiancée and live, dammit!

And that part of him was getting stronger by the second. He struggled with it, feeling guilty and remorseful and hateful. But the part of him that wanted to live finally won out.

With some effort, and no small amount of misery, he hauled himself through a gap in the back passenger window that hadn't been completely pinched closed. The shards of glass jutting from the window frame tore at his clothes and skin but let him through. To extract his ruined legs he was reduced to hooking both hands under each knee and pulling them out one at a time. He lay on the ground near the rear window of the car for a while, gasping for breath while the pain in his legs once again kept his full attention.

He started to lie back on the ground, only to find that his first victimizer, the tree branch that had cut his face, had ended their mutual descent inside the back of his shirt.

For a few brief moments it had been his savior, holding the car up. Then it was his enemy, letting him fall. As a last insult, it bit him even after its death. When he reached back and pulled it over his head, it dug a new gouge across his shoulder blade before coming free. He threw it as far down the hill as he could manage. The movement sent a new spasm up from his legs through the rest of his body. When it passed, he came back to the present moment.

Digging his hands into the pine needles, rocks, and mud of the slope, he pulled himself away from the car a bit and looked back. It was a mess. The front passenger corner was gone, giving the impression that some huge beast had taken a bite out of it. A deep trench ran up that same side, buckling the front door and exposing the hinge.

Amy had frequently talked about how cute the tiny Honda was, with its shiny black paint and fancy alloy wheels. Now, with the two wheels that were still attached pointing up in the air and the roof caved in, it looked more like a squashed beetle than a car. Even the personalized license plate, AMYSTOY, was gone—ripped off by a stray branch, no doubt.

He turned his attention to the tree they had hit. It looked to have received nearly as much damage as the car. If it survived, the tree would be deeply scarred too. The near side of it had been nearly stripped of branches for the first twenty feet or so. Looking past it, he saw that it was the last thing between them and a hundred-foot drop.

He had no idea how to get back up the nearly vertical hillside to the road. He turned back to the car, hoping to see something that could help him. Shattered glass and twisted metal were of no use. The car's trunk was crushed closed. All four doors were smashed. Miraculously, Amy's bottle of strawberry-kiwi Snapple was lying, unbroken, in the pine needles next to the car. He scanned the area for the easiest route to the top. He was lying propped on an elbow, partway down a long, densely treed hillside. The road looked to be at least fifty feet up. Interstate 26. The weather had been dry as a bone. It was, after all, late May. But even in May the mountains get cold at night. He now realized the shadows had probably hidden black ice on the road.

As near as he could tell, they had shot off of the road at the sharp curve and slammed into the tree, up high but still below the middle of the trunk. The car had tumbled from the tree, crunching rear-first into the ground and flopping onto its back like a dying tortoise.

He looked up the slope again. Small scrub brush, some variation of holly with red-tipped leaves and red berries, dotted the hillside. Saplings with soft, flexible trunks and bright green needles grew in patches. The hillside was mostly semisoft dirt covered by pine needles. At random, large rocks thrust up through that carpet of needles. It was steep, but the ground was soft enough to dig his fingers into.

It seemed like the climb would be possible for a healthy, athletic man. But even uninjured, Martin had never been athletic. Now with his extra weight and twisted legs, he felt more like a grub than a person. While he was looking over the hillside and debating whether to crawl and die or lie there and die, a small, bright object caught his attention.

The box was tiny, no bigger than a gumball, and oddly shaped. It had eleven sides, no right angles and no openings. It had cost him a month's salary, but he'd had to have it. He didn't know what was so appealing about it any more than he could explain to Amy why he'd spent the money on it. But something about the box had demanded his attention. It tickled at his mind, whispering, "Pick me up. Buy me. Take me home." The old lady in the store hadn't had a clue what it was. Martin hadn't either, but he knew it was special.

He crawled over and picked it up, not realizing until much later that upon seeing it, he had decided to stay and die. He propped himself up against a rock that jutted out from the hillside and pondered the box. As he looked at it, it calmed him. He had spent many hours looking at the box and wondering where it had come from. Who had made it and how? It wasn't much to look at, neither attractive nor ugly. It was seamless and hard and obviously hollow.

Something shifted inside when he moved it suddenly. Martin fleetingly considered opening the trunk to see if he could get to the tools inside. But the thought of looking at Amy's face while he scrabbled for the keys was too much to bear. And he didn't think he could get the trunk open anyway.

He rubbed the box, unconsciously humming something tuneless and flat. Without thinking about it, he put it between his teeth and bit it hard: nothing. He dropped it from his mouth back into his hands and started stroking the sides with his fingers. While he was looking at the largest side and rubbing the sides above and below it, the box opened. He dropped it, sucking in a quick, sharp breath.

It had never opened before, and he was certain he had done the exact same thing on a number of occasions. The box landed on the ground and tumbled down the hillside a few feet before fetching up against a small sapling, open side directed at Martin. Starting as just a crack between two sides, the lid slowly lifted, revealing its hidden treasure. Completely filling the box was a bubble, golden and iridescent. It looked almost exactly like the soap bubbles he had blown as a kid. Colors swirled in a chaotic dance across the bubble's surface.

It took almost five minutes, but eventually the lid opened completely. The bubble grew. It plopped out of the box and hung suspended a couple of inches above the ground. It expanded rapidly: fist-sized, cantaloupe-sized, watermelon-sized. He was sure his eyes grew right along with the bubble.

He expected it to pop, but it didn't. It just kept getting bigger, hovering near the ground, never touching. That it didn't fly away, even in the stiff breeze, was something of a mystery as well. When it was slightly larger than man-sized, the bubble stopped growing.

It slowly floated toward him, against the wind. In a matter of moments it was within arm's reach. He could hear it. It made a rumble, not unlike a furnace. As he held his hands out to it, he could feel heat. Like an oven door, it wasn't hot on its own but gave evidence of immense heat below the surface.

He tentatively poked a finger into it, as if it were the Pillsbury Dough Boy. Instead of giggling, it bent inward. He pulled his hand back, but the dent stayed. It grew. Slowly, the side nearest him melted into the sphere. When it touched the other side, a hole formed, creating a torus, looking more like a giant glistening donut than a ball. The hole widened. Soon it looked more like a hula-hoop than a donut.

Looking through the hoop, he expected to see a sloping hillside, more trees, and bits of wreckage; instead, he saw something completely different. Framed within the hoop was an image. It was a ranch house with a large, covered front porch. He could smell flowers and grass. He leaned closer to see more. As he did, the hoop moved closer too. Whenever he moved, the image seen through the hoop moved, as if he was looking through a window.

He shifted over to get a better look and lost traction on the hill. He started slipping down and bounced a shin against a tree, sending shards of pain through his leg. Hitting the tree slowed him but sent him spinning. He dropped his shoulder and rolled head down through the hoop. He landed in the fetal position on hard, rocky soil, bounced, rolled, slid a few feet, and fetched up against a hard stone step.

He screamed in agony. Fire raced up his legs. The world spun as a wave of dizziness washed over him. He thought he might throw up. He hoped he might die. Instead of doing either, he laid his head down on the spikey gravel, looked up at the roof of the covered porch, and struggled to stay conscious.

"Oh my, you're early," came a man's voice from somewhere above him. Footsteps drew near. A blurry face slid into his view. "And you're hurt too! Raneal, help me get him inside." Martin felt arms lifting him. He screamed as his legs were shifted. "Oh dear. This won't do at all," were the last words he heard for quite some time.

— Tony Finds Some Friends —

The sleek black RX7 glided slowly and silently to a stop. After a few minutes the door opened and a man stepped out. Six feet three inches tall, he was thin, muscular, and imposing. He wore brown, well-traveled and comfortable but not ready to retire cowboy boots, peg-leg Levi's, a red and blue Pendleton shirt, and a black leather jacket. Reaching into the car he pulled a black cowboy hat from the passenger seat and arranged it on his head, covering his short-cropped red hair. He walked to the back of the car. His walk was distinct: heel-first impacts that snapped on the bizarre metallic roadway. Opening the hatch, he grabbed a duffel bag and threw it back over his shoulder. He slammed the hatch, checked that the doors were locked, and strode off down the road, reliving the events of the past hour.

His sports car hummed along, not minding the blistering pace at all. It had been gobbling nearly two miles a minute and seemed hungry for more.

Unfortunately, even at a hundred miles an hour the Mojave Desert takes forever to cross. The desert was just the first leg of a sixteen-hour trip, and already he'd been a victim of his creeping enemy. He'd passed the time by daydreaming about his latest Runequest *game design and listening to Robert Plant wail out "Black Dog," "Misty Mountain Hop," and "Stairway to Heaven."*

Tony caught a glimpse of something out of the corner of his eye. It was ball of light three inches across and filled with a squiggle of black ink that twisted, curled, and squirmed inside the ball. As it passed the side window and became visible through the windshield, the ball of light popped, releasing the squiggle, which sprang out into a large hoop, flying vertically in front of the car.

He slammed on the brakes. As the car dived he clenched the steering wheel in a death grip. The car had excellent brakes and bled speed rapidly. They dragged the car from a hundred miles an hour to a complete stop in fewer than three hundred feet. It was not quick enough. Just as Tony pounded on the brakes, the hoop stopped. The car was still traveling at more than ninety miles per hour when it passed through.

The change in road surface was immediately obvious. Normally his RX7 provided nearly perfect tactile feedback of the road. Suddenly, at the worst possible time, all sensation through the steering wheel was gone. With intense concentration and skill, Tony kept the tiny car from locking the wheels, but just barely. As the car slowed he searched for the feedback he should be feeling but couldn't find it. There was almost no resistance to turning. He managed to keep the car traveling in a straight line, and within a few seconds it came to a rest, settling back on its shocks.

Tony took a few seconds to let his heart slow down again. Then he got out of the car. He was greeted with a waft of tire rubber and brakes. And his first feel of the road. It was perfectly smooth, like cut marble, but it was resilient, like extremely hard rubber. Thankfully it wasn't slick or his hard braking would have ended very differently.

Where featureless, brown Mojave Desert horizon had existed moments before, a mountain range now stood. He slowly turned in a complete circle, seeing a new land for the first time. Low hills dominated the horizon on all sides. The ground around him was flat to the foothills, forming a large plain covered with low, brown grass. It reminded him of the Salt Lake Basin, but not as large and with more trees. They were scattered around the plain but began in earnest in the foothills. Those on the flat looked deciduous, but in the foothills he could make out evergreens. He noticed a herd of animals some distance away. They were the color of the grass, and had horns similar to an antelope. As he'd looked at them, he knew somehow they were "wrong". Their horns were long, twisted spikes. North American antelopes had short, curved prongs for horns.

He contemplated his situation for some time. He was obviously not where he was supposed to be. He'd given himself three options. First, he might be dreaming. Second, he might have lost his mind. Third, he'd somehow been transported somewhere. Option one would take care of itself. If he was dreaming, he would eventually wake up and all would be well. Option two would also take care of itself. If he had lost his mind, then it didn't really matter what he did here and now as he would have no control over what happened in the "real" world. That left option number three. He'd been a science fiction and fantasy fan since first learning to read, so this concept wasn't completely beyond the realm of possibility.

Tony had traveled through most of the west and had never seen a valley like this before. The road was a slash across the plain. Otherwise there was no sign of human habitation. Years of military duty had taught him to make a decision and take action. In the end, given few other choices, he decided to continue in the direction he'd been going.

He had driven on for another hour, drawing nearer to the foothills. Now, out of gas and forced to walk, he did not question his earlier choice but kept going in the same direction.

At first his frustration over the situation dominated his thoughts, but resignation soon replaced it. As the day wore on, twinges of fear crept into his mind. He denied feeling them, but they kept coming back. Was he going to die out here? How would he get home? Where was he? These worries and others briefly crossed his mind during the next few hours.

With a steady pace and long legs, he made good time. The black car quickly receded into the distance. Slowly a dark line appeared in the grass some distance in front of him. It cut across the plain north to south, perpendicular to the road he was using. As he got closer he could make out a cut in the ground. It looked to be about thirty feet across, and deep enough that he couldn't immediately see the bottom.

He was nearly on top of it before he saw the small stream, ten feet wide, churning across the plain. He saw a narrow bank on either side. Suddenly he was struck by an all-consuming thirst. He scrambled the twenty feet down the steep bank, dropping his duffel bag and hat when he got to the bottom. The small river rocks crunched under his boots and dug into his knees as he dropped to drink.

After a time, he sat back, catching his breath. He looked across the stream, noting the depth of the shadow on the other side. Judging by the shadow, it was late afternoon. He had left early in the morning. He could account for only about six hours, so it should be midday. He dragged the back of his hand across his mouth and contemplated the lost time.

During his walk he had noticed a couple of details he had found interesting. First, the sun was farther to the south than it should be. Originally when he noticed it he thought he had gotten turned southeast, the morning sun high on his side. But as the sun moved, it crawled down the sky in front of him.

The sun was definitely farther south. And it was quite a bit cooler than it should have been. He'd put on a heavy shirt against the cool desert morning air, intending to switch to a T-shirt when it warmed up. But it couldn't be more than sixty degrees on the road above and was considerably cooler down near the stream. He decide he must be somewhere north. Maybe up near the Canadian border.

He looked around at the surroundings. Excepting the grass that covered the valley floor, most of the vegetation surrounding him had been distant. Trees and low scrub were visible but so far away that identification was impossible. Down in the creek bed there was an abundance of foliage. Small bushes, between one and two feet across, grew up through the river rock in bunches, with bright red teardrop leaves and small white berry bundles. Farther from shore, saplings grew. They had small, tightly packed leaves, bright green with a yellow rim. Fewer than ten feet tall, they were shorter than the height of the cut. He wondered why they weren't taller. In fact, all the plants on both sides of the creek were new starts. He guessed that the creek was actually a wash, flooding every spring as the winter snows melted on the mountains around him. The banks were soft enough to let go of the plants under the pressure of the torrent. They would have to start over each year. One mystery solved.

The creek looked to be no more than two or three feet deep and flowed rapidly away from the road. Looking down through the crystal clear water, Tony saw tiny iridescent fish darting about. He looked across at the opposite bank. It looked much the same as this side, with the exception of several large boulders.

As his eyes moved along the creek, he noticed the underside of the roadway. Expecting to see trusses and abutments, he was surprised nothing supported the road. The ground simply fell away on each side. The creek had undercut the road. Judging from the river rocks and sediment, this creek had been flowing here for several years. With no support, the road should have collapsed into the water, but it held fast. He walked over to examine the material, getting his first true look at the edge of it. He rubbed his hand along as he looked. Like the top, it was smooth and hard as glass, with the same vague texture of rubber. The bottom was as smooth as the top. He dug at it with his thumbnail and then pulled out his small Swiss army pocketknife and sliced at it. Neither action had any effect. The thing it reminded him of most was extruded plastic, only much harder.

He moved in under the roadway, closer to the point where it met the ground. He used his knife to scratch away some ground. Dirt, sand, and chunks of rock broke free. He worked at the curve of a rock that was pressed up against the bottom of the road. After a couple of tries he wrenched it out. It squirted free and shot over his left shoulder. It smacked into Tony's palm, its momentary freedom cut short.

He was suddenly twisted at the waist, his left hand stretched out behind him. That was weird. He knew he was fast. But that was scary fast. He didn't know he could move *that* fast.

Tony examined the stone. River rock. It had been chipped into an egg-like shape by thousands of years of pounding during the trip down river. But it wasn't whole. Instead of the rough symmetry of most river rocks, this one was flat on one side. The side against the road had been cut and polished smooth before being laid into the foundation for the road. Tony had paid for college by working through the summer with the California road crew. He'd spent hundreds of hot, sweaty hours laying foundations for roads. They were usually laid down as layer after layer of crushed rock and sand. The foundation created a smooth, stable surface for the roadway. This one was strange. It seemed to be primarily dirt with some stones. Almost like the roadway was poured directly onto the ground. But why place only an occasional stone? And why polish it first?

"I'm done in. That's as far as I can go." A man's voice drifted down from above on the roadway. "It looks like you'll have to go the rest of the way home. Can you make it that far?"

"Sure, Dad, no problem," came the reply in a young girl's voice.

Tony heard their feet scrabbling in the grass as they moved to the embankment. Boots, large and thick-soled crunched the rocks and scrub down a few feet from the edge of the roadway.

"Let me help you," the man told his companion. The boots swiveled in their spaces. Two more boots, much smaller, sent a second cascade down the hillside to the rocky river's edge below.

The boots moved cautiously down the hillside, obviously taking care not to misstep. Their owners were slowly revealed: brown woolen trousers, dark belts, and brightly colored shirts that looked heavy and warm. The man's head came into view first, facing away from Tony. He was looking back and holding the hand of a teenage girl. They were nearly opposite in appearance. He had black hair and olive skin. She was fair, with blonde hair, blue eyes, and bright white teeth. Teeth Tony noticed when she started screaming.

Tony jumped. His head smacked into the roadway. Everything momentarily lit up. He closed his eyes and grabbed his head with both hands, dropping both the rock and knife. He groaned. He opened his eyes and saw the pair had backed up. The man was in front, shielding the girl and brandishing a rock of his own. He glanced briefly at the roadway, obviously weighing his chances of making it there before Tony could get to them.

"Wait, wait"—Tony held out a hand. "I'm not going to hurt you." He shuffled down the hill a bit so he could move out from under the bridge.

"Yeah, sure!" The man checked to make sure he was in the best possible position to defend himself and the girl. "Then why are you hiding under this bridge?"

Tony rubbed his head. A lump was starting to form. He slouched there, looking at them for a minute before speaking. "I wasn't hiding. I was looking at the bridge. It's not like any I've ever seen before."

The man was looking him up and down, apparently trying to decide how dangerous Tony was. Whatever the estimate, it would have been too low.

"I guess you missed the one half a mile up, eh?" the man replied, still suspicious.

Tony put his hands down and stood to his full height. "Look, I'm not looking for trouble. My car ran out of gas up the road a ways and I'm trying to get to a gas station. You're the first people I've seen all day, so there's obviously not much traffic on this road. Can you give me a lift?"

"What's a gas station?" the man responded, black eyes narrowed.

At first Tony didn't grasp the question. It was so unexpected he couldn't get his mind around it. "What?"

"What's a gas station? You said you had to get to a gas station. How could I take you to one if I don't know what it is?"

Tony started laughing. This was the last straw. He bent down, put his hands on his knees, and roared. After a minute the laughing fit passed and Tony looked back at the nervous pair. "Okay. I get it. Good joke." When most people grin, it's a sign of humor. With Tony it meant something much more dangerous. "So how did you get here?"

"We brought our wagon," the man replied, pointing up to the road.

Tony turned and looked at the roadway. Sitting just off of the bridge was a large, boxy vehicle. It looked like no other car Tony had ever seen. The hairs on the back of his neck stood up.

He moved left and spun, shooting his hand out as he turned. He snatched the rock out of the air like a pro ball player. It smacked into his palm. The man straightened from his throwing position, eyes wide and mouth agape.

"*Why did you do that?*" Tony exploded. "*I told you I wasn't going to hurt you. What's* wrong *with you?*" A loud crack punctuated his question. He lifted his hand and looked into it. The stone had shattered, the sharp chunks digging into his palm. He tipped his hand, letting the fragments fall. He raised his eyes to the pair.

"Where do you get fuel for that?" He pointed in the direction of their truck.

"Fuel? What fuel? What are you talking about?" the man asked, obviously confused. "Did you escape from an asylum somewhere, is that it?"

"*No!* I did *not* escape from any asylum!" With effort, Tony controlled his anger and calmed his voice. "I told you, I ran out of gas back there." He pointed in the direction he had come from. "I walked this far, stopped at the stream for some water, and you showed up, quaking and accusing. Now all I want to know is if you can take me to a gas station so I can get some gas for my car. Do you think you can do that?"

The man looked at Tony with concern and fear on his face. The girl touched his arm and whispered in his ear. He looked at the ground, took a deep breath, and looked back at Tony, this time with less fear. "Look, I'm sorry I overreacted. We've been on the road for a long time and I'm tired. You caught me off-guard." He held his arms spread, palms out, as a peace gesture. Then he stepped forward slowly and extended his right hand. "My name is Jakub."

Tony leaned forward, eyes narrowed, and shook the man's hand. "I'm Tony."

When they released hands, the man glanced at the girl and then gestured to her. "This is my daughter, Dinaala."

Tony and Dinaala exchanged nods and hellos.

The man continued. "Now, I can see you have a problem. As I said before,

I don't know what a gas station is. I've never heard the phrase before. I'm not trying to be difficult."

Tony replied, "This is bizarre. Gas stations are all over the place. How can you not know what one is? How do you keep your car running?"

"What's a car?" The man looked confused.

Tony's frustration was building. He almost railed at the man again when he caught a glimpse of his daughter. She was as confused as Jakub was. Somehow that made it real for Tony. These people had no idea what he was talking about.

He decided to try another tack and see if it got better results. He turned and looked in the direction of their vehicle. "What do you call that?"

"A wagon."

"Okay, how does the wagon run?"

"How does it run? Oh, you mean how does it work?"

Tony nodded.

"I don't have a clue. One of us feeds it and it moves. We direct it and it turns right or left and goes forward or back. Micah tried to explain how it works to me one time, but I think you have to see it through his eyes to truly get it."

Tony seized on the concept. "Aha! What do you feed it?"

Jakub furrowed his brow "Well, the same thing you feed everything else. You use the Touch and you feed it."

"What?" Tony responded.

"What, what?"

Tony rubbed his temples, knowing this was going to end in a vicious headache. He took two deep breaths and asked a question that he knew would only make matters worse. "What are you talking about?"

Jakub thought for a moment. "It seems like we have a language barrier. Maybe we're talking about the same thing but don't know it. What is gas? I mean in really basic terms."

Tony, still rubbing his temples, closed his eyes and tipped his head down for a moment. "Gas—gasoline—is fuel for engines, like the one in a car. It's a pink liquid. Gas stations store it in big tanks under the ground and dispense it from pumps. You pump the fluid into a tank in your car. It travels to the engine, where it's burned. As it burns the gas, the engine turns a driveline that spins the tires, making the car go."

"So a car is sort of like our wagon, right?" Jakub asked.

"Yeah," Tony responded. "Mine looks different, but it's basically the same."

"Ok, let's go look at my wagon and compare it to your car," Jakub suggested, heading back up the embankment, followed closely by his daughter. Since the conversation began she hadn't said more than hello. She would glance at him occasionally and then look everywhere else for a while, clearly trying hard not to be obvious about looking at him.

Tony followed the pair to the road.

"Now, where would this engine be on your car?" Jakub asked, gesturing to the vehicle.

Tony looked at the wagon. It resembled a flat-nosed van, sort of like a Volkswagen Microbus, only much larger. It had four doors toward the front. The back half was windowless, except for a small window into the cab that he noticed as he got closer. He looked into the driver's area. The bench seats were covered in gray plastic, with bright lines in a wavy pattern running up and down, denoting passenger spots, three across on each bench. He was looking for the engine housing. There was no telltale hump. Instead, he saw an unbroken bench closely matching the one at the rear of the cab. He guessed that the vehicle was rear-engined, like the Microbus. He turned and headed toward the back of the bus to look, when suddenly it struck him. *There was no steering wheel.* He turned back to the driver's compartment. The dashboard extended symmetrically across the front of the vehicle. Like most vehicles, the dashboard was a wedge of plastic that hung over the passenger's legs. It was about two and a half feet deep and six or eight inches tall. On the left side the dashboard had a glass plate set into it. It was about ten inches wide and took up most of the dash's six-inch height.

He turned and looked at Jakub. "How do you steer? You know, change directions?"

Jakub walked up and opened the closest door. "It travels straight unless you press on the grid." He indicated the glass section of the dashboard.

Tony had taken it to be an instrument panel. He looked at it closer. It was flawless ebony. Yet it had a depth to it, like a black diamond. The one visible distortion was a single line etched into the surface, dividing the panel in half, east from west. He looked over the rest of the interior.

"There are no seatbelts," he commented, knowing the response before it was spoken.

"What's a seatbelt?"

"Never mind. How do you roll down the windows?"

"If by 'roll down the windows' you mean 'take down the screens,' then you press on the grid in the door." Jakub pointed to a smaller black glass grid mounted in each door. These grids were sliced into north and south sections. Tony rubbed his finger over the smooth glass, feeling the line.

Jakub watched for a few moments before saying, "Of course, you have to feed it for it to work." He reached out, touching the grid, and the window slid silently down.

"How did you do that?" Tony touched the grid again. The window stubbornly remained down.

"I just fed it." Jakub shrugged. "You know—fed it."

"Maybe you can explain that one to me later." Tony looked back at the wagon. Still curious, he looked over the exterior. The wheels were oddly contrived. The rim was some sort of metal, sixteen or seventeen inches in diameter—pretty standard for a car, but they were shod not with tires but simply a strip of rubber less than an inch thick. The rim had no lip around it. In fact, the rubber strip was wider than the rim, allowing an inch or so to overhang. He poked it and prodded it to be sure it was rubber. It was solid and unforgiving but definitely felt like rubber. The wheels nearly filled the wheel wells. Tony bent, and placing his eye right next to the wagon, looked down the side. There was a slight bulge at each wheel, where the rubber extended a millimeter or two out from under the wagon's skin. He stood back up and looked at the side again, analyzing the engineering of the vehicle. No air in the tires, no room for shock absorption between the tire and the car. If this thing hit a bump, it would hammer anyone inside.

"I guess I don't have to know how this thing works. Do you think you could just take me to town and I can talk to someone about my car?"

Jakub looked down the road in the direction Tony had come. "Sorry, but town is too far to reach in one day. With us fully loaded, Dinaala can't make it that far and I'm used up." He looked back the way they had come. "She could take us back to Burrows, but I'm positive no one there could help you. There are a couple of regulators, but I doubt they could figure out what's wrong with your car." He turned back in the direction they had been traveling. "We can take you to Wilderburn Village. That's not too far from our house. Maybe someone there can help you." He looked at his daughter. "What do you think, Dinaala?"

She bit her lip and looked Tony up and down. "I think we should talk to Mom and Micah. Maybe Mom will have an idea, or Micah can help. No one in Wilderburn will be able to help him. Micah is the only fixer for a hundred miles, and he's the strongest inside five hundred. If the thing is dead, he can prob'ly fix it. We can pick him up and bring him back here after we unload and get some rest."

Jakub looked at her for a minute. He turned back to Tony, brows furrowed. "I need your word that you won't harm my family." His eyes burned into Tony's and his hands were clenched into fists, ready to fight if necessary. "I'll not help you if you won't give your word."

Tony looked at him for a moment. "I don't give my word lightly." He turned and walked a few steps before turning back. "What assurance do I have that you won't try something? You already tried to bean me with a rock. If I promise not to hurt you and you attack me ..." He trailed off. He raised his hand to his lip, thinking. "Well, I guess I'm at your mercy anyway." He looked into Jakub's eyes and put his hand on his heart. "I promise that to the best of my ability, I will avoid any action that may bring harm to your family."

Jakub returned his stare for a few seconds and then placed his own hand on his heart. "I promise that I and my family will do our best to aid you on your way." He then held out his right hand. Tony shook it.

Dinaala smiled and jumped in the wagon. "Let's go."

Jakub walked around to the other side and got in up front. But Tony turned and headed back off of the road.

"Hang on!" he called back to them. He climbed back down the embankment to retrieve his duffel bag and hat from under the bridge. After securing the hat on his head, he picked up the duffel bag and marched back up the hill. He reached for the door nearest him, touching a small glass block he found below the window. It did absolutely nothing. Dinaala reached back and tapped a glass block below the window button on the inside of the rear door. The door opened. Tony threw in the bag and climbed in behind Dinaala.

Tony watched Dinaala carefully. She made no movement, no gesture. Yet the wagon began to move. There were no lurches, stumbles, or even the gentle pause of a gearshift. Just smooth, powerful acceleration. Within a few seconds the wagon stopped accelerating and settled into a nice fifty to sixty mile per hour pace that Tony could appreciate.

Within a few minutes, Tony saw his car on the horizon.

"Is that your car?" Dinaala asked.

Tony scowled at the dead bug of a car. "Yes, it is."

"Do you need anything out of it?" Jakub asked.

"Nope, I've got everything I need with me."

They had been gaining rapidly on the car during the interchange, and they slid past it on the right.

"Maybe when we get Micah to fix it, you can take me for a ride ..." Dinaala trailed off.

"Yeah, maybe so," Tony responded, looking out the window.

They traveled in silence for some time, watching the trees pass in the distance. Tony was amazed at how comfortable the ride was. The only noise was made by the wind hammering against the boxy cab and there was no road vibration at all. The smooth road paid off.

"How far did you say it was to your house?" Tony asked.

"Not much further. It's just over that next rise in the road." Jakub pointed out the front of the wagon at the horizon, somewhat to the left of the road.

They made their way up the slight incline, slowing near the top. As they crested the low hill a farmstead or ranch came into view some distance from the main highway. They slowed even more. Dinaala reached out and touched the left side of the control panel. The wagon made a precise left-hand turn onto the only side road Tony had seen the entire trip. At this point the road was elevated slightly above the plane of the land, so the big wagon rolled down a long hill and into a wide circle of buildings surrounding a large patch of the mysterious road surface.

The wagon was completely silent during the decent. The woman who rushed from one of the buildings had to have been watching for it. She was carrying a large and heavy bundle in her arms.

Jakub and Dinaala leaped from the wagon and ran toward her, leaving Tony the undignified option of climbing over the seat as his only means of getting out. Before he could start over the seatback, he heard the new woman's strained voice. Tony looked out the car window at the small group.

"Oh Jakub, Jakub ..." the woman moaned, "it's Micah. He's been stung by a duur wasp." Tears streamed down her face. The bundle in her arms shifted, whimpering.

"Let me see!" Jakub exclaimed, as he hurried to her side.

She pulled back the blanket to reveal a small boy's legs. One was swollen to twice its normal size and fire engine red with a large black bruise on the side of the calf.

"When did this happen?" Jakub asked, grabbing the boy and sprinting back to the wagon.

"Almost an hour ago." The woman ran beside Jakub, reaching for the boy even after letting Jakub carry him.

Jakub reached the wagon, his family in tow, popped the rear door open, and signaled for his the woman to get in.

"Are you sure it was a duur wasp?" he asked.

"I … I think so. It's right over there. Micah stomped on it just after it stung him. I saw it happen. Oh Micah, my baby …" She cried as Jakub handed the boy in to her. She placed him gently on her lap.

"Tony, I'll have to ask you to ride up front with Dinaala." Jakub pointed to the seat he had vacated only a few minutes earlier. Tony climbed into the front seat and watched Jakub run to the spot the woman had indicated. He bent down, looked closely for a moment, and then picked up the wasp and headed back to the wagon.

When he came back he was carrying the ugliest bug Tony had ever seen. It only vaguely resembled a wasp. Its wings, head, and thorax were similar to any other wasp, but it had an extra abdomen and three sets of eyes, two on the head and one on the extra abdomen. It also had ten legs, two of which had lobster-like claws on them. Tony could make out all of these details because the beast was at least eight inches long. One wing, three legs, and the abdomen were crushed, but the thorax looked like it was intact and had a wicked, inch-long stinger attached to it.

"This isn't a duur wasp!" Jakub jumped into the backseat. "It's the wrong color and the venom sack is way too big. This is something else. We have to take it with us." He set the crushed body on the floor of the wagon and slammed the door closed.

"Dinaala," he said, "baby, how are you doing? Can you make it to Jesik's? Raneal is the only one around here who can help Micah." He leaned forward and put his hand on her shoulder.

When she turned to look back at her dad, Tony saw her face for the first time since the wagon had stopped. He was shocked. Her eyes were deep set and rimmed in black. She looked like she hadn't slept in days. She nodded and turned back to the front. Touching the left side of the panel, she did whatever it was that made the wagon move. The wagon made a tight U-turn and headed back up the ramp and onto the road. Dinaala turned left and accelerated.

This trip was entirely different than the pleasure cruise they had taken from the stream. Tony was crushed back into the seat as the wagon leaped forward. He had been in planes that didn't accelerate that fast.

"Dinaala!" Jakub shouted from the backseat. "Don't burn yourself out, baby! It's a long way to Jesik's house."

"I won't, Daddy" was her only response. She didn't slow in the least. The wind buffeted the wagon as it hammered the air out of the way. If forced to guess, Tony would have said they were going at least a hundred miles an hour.

Once they had gotten rolling, Jakub introduced the new woman as his wife, Beka, and the boy as his son, Micah. They traveled on in silence, each keeping to his or her own thoughts for the time being. Tony spent his time watching the landscape fly past the car.

Twice in the space of a few minutes they flew over creeks that had cut under the road, similar to the one at which they had met. As they progressed the trees got closer to the road. Not long after the second creek they started up a long, sloping hill. The trees were now common on each side of the road. It wasn't exactly a dense forest, but the trees were getting tighter together.

Suddenly Tony felt a tingling sensation between his shoulder blades. The hair stood up on the back of his neck. He felt like he was about to be struck by lightning. Without knowing why, he cried out, "Stop!"

"What?" Jakub asked, perking up in the backseat.

"We have to stop." The tingling was getting stronger.

"We can't stop. We have to get to Raneal!"

"*Stop! Now!*"

Dinaala flinched back from the outburst. Despite her father's protests, she slowed the wagon and came to a stop.

"What the hell are you doing?!" Jakub demanded.

"Look." Tony turned around. "I can't explain it. But I can tell you, if we went over that hill just now, we'd all be dead. I guarantee it." He extended his hand. "Can you hand me my bag? It's there on the floor."

Jakub handed the bag over, obviously furious at the delay. Tony could understand. The man's son was in jeopardy. While he could empathize with Jakub, Tony knew he was doing the right thing. Even though he didn't know why it was the right thing.

He rummaged in his bag for a minute, coming up with the set of Bosch binoculars his mother had given him one year for Christmas. He pushed at his door for a few seconds before Dinaala reached across and tapped on a small glass block. The door popped open. Tony climbed out of the wagon, dropped his hat on the seat, and slowly made his way up the hill. As he approached the top, he started slouching lower with every step. By the time he had crested the hill, he was crawling on all fours. When he could see the downward slope of the road, he lay prone and put the binoculars to his eyes.

A couple hundred feet down the road a dozen figures moved around a huge mound of brush and branches that was piled across the road. Tony's heart skipped a beat when he saw the creatures. They were hideous on a scale he'd never experienced, abominations that should not exist outside a mad science lab. A couple of them looked like giant beetles, walking on two legs with long, segmented arms and claws. A couple of the others were vaguely mammalian with triple-jointed arms and lupine faces. The rest stretched his mind's ability to rationalize them into recognizable shapes. They were random limbs attached to bulbous or arachnid or reptilian bodies. All of them were covered in a patchwork of fur and chitin-like exoskeleton. He unconsciously shuddered as if he could shake the image of the creatures from his mind.

As he watched, one of the monstrosities stepped off the road, wrapped four or five of its arms around a nearby tree, and wrenched it from the ground, roots and all. It then carried the tree over to the pile and tossed it on top.

Tony inched back from the hilltop and then sat and thought for a minute before making his way back down to the wagon. "There's an ambush up ahead," he said when he was near enough to be heard without having to shout. "About a dozen of the ugliest looking things I've ever seen have stacked a pile of trees across the road." He pointed at the wasp. "They make that thing look downright pretty."

"What do they look like?" Jakub asked.

Tony couldn't put what he'd seen into words. "Come and see for yourself."

He set down the binoculars and began digging in his duffel bag once again. This time he retrieved a small wooden box and a long thin bundle of gray cloth tied in three places with black cords. With the bundle under one arm and the box in his hand, he picked up the binoculars and headed back up the road. Jakub and Dinaala hurried to catch up. As they came to the top, Tony signaled them to keep quiet and to crouch down. With his guidance, they came to the crest together and looked down on the ambush.

"Chinon d'k Tal," Jakub whispered. "But why are they here?"

"Over there," Dinaala whispered back, pointing. "A Regulator. See him? He's standing on that stump."

Tony could see a lone man in a brown, hooded cloak standing on a large stump. His arm was extended toward the pile, but he was unmoving. Two other men in cloaks stood nearby, but they were oddly inactive, simply standing and watching the creatures work. Surrounding the three men were rippling heat waves, as if they were standing in frying pan.

"He's not very strong," Dinaala said. "He has two Activators. Between 'em they can feed almost as much as I can, but he can't use it very well. He's binding the pile. He also seems to have an affinity for the Chinon d'k Tal because he isn't using much Touch on them. That's not much drain for him to require two strong Activators. If I gave Micah that much power at one time, he could move the house."

"What are you talking about?" Tony asked.

"I'm strong enough that I can see the Touch when it is being used," Dinaala explained, as if the words actually meant something.

"Look, as you may have guessed, I'm not from around here. Talk to me like I'm six. What do you mean, he's 'binding the pile,' and how is he touching the chino things?"

Both Dinaala and Jakub looked at him for a minute, as if to gauge whether or not he was serious.

Jakub began. "The Touch is how we describe the power that everyone lives and breathes."

Tony stared blankly at them.

"Don't you have power where you come from?" Jakub asked.

"What power are you talking about?" Tony asked, sure they weren't talking about electricity.

"Look down there." Jakub pointed to the Regulator. "That man is using the Touch, a kind of power, to tie all of those trees in the pile together. He is also using that same power to control the Chinon d'k Tal, those ugly things."

"Most people can't see the Touch, but really powerful people, Activators or Regulators, *can* see it," Dinaala said. "I'm strong enough to see it."

"Touch, huh?" Tony looked back at the figures below. "And you can see it."

"Yes," Jakub and Dinaala replied in unison.

"You mean like those heat waves down there?" Tony pointed down the hill.

"Heat waves?" Jakub asked.

"Yeah," Tony replied. "They're all around down there."

"You can see that?" Dinaala asked.

"Well, sure. Anybody can see heat waves."

"How hot is it out here?" Jakub asked. "Hot enough to make heat waves?"

"No," Tony frowned, "I guess not. I guess I just never thought about it."

"Well, those heat waves are the Touch in use. You must be pretty strong if you can see them. Those are weak. Those over there"—Dinaala pointed toward Stump Man—"are kind of strong. Can you see those?"

With a renewed perspective, Tony could easily see the flowing waves. They made the background ripple and twist, just a bit. Dinaala was right. This batch of waves was much more apparent than those near the Big Uglies.

"Why didn't I see them when you were driving?" he asked.

"Maybe you weren't looking for them."

"What's a Regulator?" Tony asked.

"A Regulator is a person who can manipulate the Touch and make it do things like control the Chinon d'k Tal, lift things, or change things. An Activator is a person who can control the flow of the Touch, directing it into a Regulator for manipulation. One can't work without the other," Dinaala explained.

"But you drove the car. There was only one of you." Tony scrambled to get a grasp on the concept.

"That's not quite the same. The wagon is a machine, built by really powerful men thousands of years ago. They're kind of like automatic Regulators that do whatever they were designed to do, no more, no less. Activators feed them and they work. That's it." This time Dinaala's explanation made some sense.

"Can we save the lessons for some other time?" Jakub asked. "What are we going to do about this?"

They all looked down the hill for a moment. Jakub sighed. "I guess we'll have to go around. That could take hours. With you so tired, Dinaala, I don't know if we can make it." He looked at Tony. "Maybe you could take a turn. If you are as strong as Dinaala thinks, you could probably get us to Jesik's place."

"Daddy, we can't go around. Micah won't last for two more hours. He might not even last one."

"If we try to go through that, they'll tear us apart. Those things are vicious killers with no mercy." Jakub looked back down the hill. "I just wish I knew what they wanted."

"They want your boy," Tony said, completely accepting that he knew this truth without understanding how he knew it.

"What?" Jakub and Dinaala both jerked their heads toward Tony, talking as one. "Why would they want Micah?"

As he talked it through, his training in tactics pieced together the puzzle that his intuition had grabbed onto. "Look, we've been driving on this road for more than an hour and we haven't seen a soul."

"That's 'cause no one else lives out here." Dinaala gestured to the land around them.

"Right, so it stands to reason these guys were waiting for *you*, right?" Tony continued. Jakub and Dinaala nodded.

"If they were waiting for you specifically, they must know you. They know who you are and that you have something of value. Why would they be waiting here? If they wanted your goods, they could have taken them back somewhere before you met me. You wouldn't have been home yet, so you'd be tired. And if I've got this right, you would be pretty defenseless without Micah anyway, right?" They nodded as his spoken thoughts began to make sense to them.

"So they could have easily gotten the stuff from you up there. Instead, they waited down here. They must have known you would come this way. They must have *planned* for you to come this way. You came this way because your boy got stung by a kind of wasp you've never seen before. That guy can control those things down there, so maybe he can control a wasp too."

"If we'd have come over that hill into the barricade, we'd have been at their mercy. They would have killed us all and taken Micah." Jakub was thunderstruck.

"What do you bet that worthless slug right there has anti-venom for that kind of wasp?" Tony pointed to the hooded man.

Tony scooted back from the edge. He picked up the bundle and untied it, laying out the gray cloth on the ground like an ad-hoc picnic. On the center of the blanket he laid Shinyuu, his thirty-inch long, elegantly carved katana. He did so gently, with reverence. Then he picked up his box. Opening it, he took the Ghost from its velvet-lined resting place. He felt the heft of the big, nickel-plated Colt. Old as it was, it still felt like security in his hand. He set the big heirloom in his lap. He left the Darkness where it was, instinct telling him that one pistol was enough for this encounter. From another pocket set into the velvet liner, he took a small cardboard box.

"How certain are you they would have killed you if you had run into them?" Tony asked, pulling six small silver and bronze cartridges out of the box.

"Positive," Jakub replied. "I've never heard of anyone who has ever met up with the Chinon d'k Tal and lived. I know someone that saw one of them wipe out a group of travelers. From the way he described it, it wasn't a pretty sight."

"Do they have any missile weapons?" Tony asked. He set the half empty box down and started slipping the cartridges into the revolving chamber on the Colt.

"Missile weapons?" Jakub asked.

"You know, guns, bows and arrows, that sort of thing. Anything that can kill you from a distance."

"Oh … guns. No, I'm sure they don't have any guns. Those are far too valuable to give to this bunch. The Chinon d'k Tal don't need to kill from a distance. They can run down a deer, are strong as an ox, and are really hard to kill. But that guy"—Jakub pointed to the Regulator—"he might be able to kill you from a distance with the Touch."

"What about those other two?" Tony closed the revolver with a snap.

"Oh, they're just Activators. They can't do anything without a Regulator," Jakub said. "What are you going to do?"

"Kill them." Tony stood up and then bent and picked up Shinyuu. He turned and headed toward the top of the hill.

"What are you doing?" Jakub whispered fiercely.

"Wait here." Tony walked over the crest. "I'll be right back."

It never occurred to him to question what he was seeing. Since deciding that this was another land, he had equipped himself to accept whatever came up. His familiar gait was back. Heel-toe, heel-toe, his boots thunked with each step. Ten, twenty, thirty yards down the hill he walked. He was noticed but disregarded by both the creatures and the cloaked man on the stump.

From forty yards away he raised the big Colt. *Bam! Bam! Bam!* The cloaked man's head flopped forward as his dead body was blown backward off the stump. Instinct directed Tony's shots. The most dangerous opponents get the gun. The one Tony took to be the captain was second. Spasms racked a body that was no longer granted the use of a brain. It crumpled to the ground, six arms flailing an odd assortment of weapons. The second creature had a bug's head and arms. He killed it more out of disgust than tactics.

Bam! Bam! Bam! Three more fell. Five seconds had gone by and the enemy force was reduced by half.

He kneeled and set the smoking pistol gently on the ground. He held Shinyuu in both hands, at arm's length, straight out in front of him. The remaining monsters, freed from the Regulator's control, nearly leaped up the road at him. They came *fast*. He waited.

When they were close enough, he uncoiled from the ground. In one smooth motion he stood, stepped forward, ducked an incoming blow, and pulled thirty inches of Damascus steel from its *saya*, the long wooden sheath that housed a samurai sword. The long, slim blade flicked across the closest monstrosity, spilling out its insides.

Tony glided through them, delivering another killing blow as they passed. His hand went numb as the blade vibrated from the impact. The thing's chitin resisted but couldn't stop the razor-sharp samurai sword. Four remained. Unlike in the movies, the beasts didn't wait their turn to attack. They rushed in at random, striking with extra limbs and long, hooked, and barbed weapons. Tony dodged, rolled, and kicked and slid his blade between two chitin plates and deep into one of their bodies. Shinyuu stuck when the creature doubled over. Tony had to abandon the sword. Using fists, feet, and the saya, he crushed the others one after the other. Without an edged weapon, it took longer than he had hoped.

When he was done with the creatures, he made his way over to the Regulator. He searched him and the surrounding area but found no anti-venom. Then he made his way back to the pile of bug-like corpses and tossed the bodies around until he found the one with Shinyuu in it. Wrenching the weapon free, he checked Shinyuu quickly for nicks or marks. He dragged the blade across the fur of one of the victims to clean the ichor off and then slid Shinyuu back into his saya. He turned and walked back up the hill, stopping only to retrieve his Colt.

Jakub and Dinaala were standing wide-eyed and speechless when he got to the top. He turned and looked back down to where Stump Man had been standing.

"The Activators ran off as soon as you killed the Regulator." Dinaala answered his unspoken question.

"There was no anti-venom down there," Tony told them.

"That's not surprising." Jakub shook his head. "The Regulator probably would have used the Touch to heal Micah, rather than anti-venom. It's much harder to get than a good healer."

"So, he would have used this Touch thing to heal Micah, but you can't do that because none of you are Regulators, right?" They both nodded. "Ok. Can your rig break through that barricade now that the binding is off it?" He moved over to his little picnic and carefully rewrapped Shinyuu. Then he flicked open the gate on the revolver and took the spent shell casings out one by one. After a moment's thought he decided not to toss them away, instead putting them back in their box. He might be able to find someone to reload them.

"Let's drive down there and take a closer look." Tony started back to the vehicle. Dinaala and Jakub fell in behind him. Though they whispered quietly to each other, he could still hear them.

"He used the Touch to fight those things!" Dinaala whispered to her dad.

"Did you feed him?" Jakub whispered back.

"No, did you?"

"How could I? I haven't rested yet. That's why you're driving, remember?"

Tony could feel his face heating up as they continued their whispered discussion.

"Then how could he use the Touch?" Dinaala asked. "He'd have to be a Regulator to use it in a fight, but he didn't have any Activators …"

"Then he must be a Templar," Jakub replied.

"A Templar? Are you kidding me? I thought those were just horror stories."

"So did I. What have we gotten ourselves into?"

They walked for a few seconds in silence. Then Jakub whispered, "Maybe we should run … just jump in the wagon and head the other way."

"Dad! We can't do that. Micah will die if we don't get him to Jesik and Raneal!"

"Would that really be so bad? How much worse will it be for all of us, if a Templar has us in his grasp?"

"Wait! Let's not do anything rash. Look, he can't be a Templar. There haven't been any for thousands of years. Besides, his eyes aren't full of fire. His skin doesn't crackle when he walks. And he hasn't done anything to harm us, right? There must be some other explanation."

"Shhh!" Jakub scolded. "We're almost at the wagon."

Tony held his tongue through their entire conversation. Obviously they didn't know he had such good hearing. He stepped to the front door of the wagon. His jaw was clenched. While he was angry over what he'd heard, he realized he couldn't blame these people for their suspicion. They didn't know him any more than he knew them, after all. Besides, he had just wiped out a dozen Big Uglies right in front of them in fewer than five minutes. He took three deep breaths and then climbed into the front seat, setting his bundle and box on the seat beside him.

Jakub and Dinaala got in as well. Jakub shushed his wife before she could ask any questions. The wagon slowly moved forward. It crested the hill and started down the other side. Beka sucked in her breath when the bodies came into view. The wagon slowed to a stop some thirty feet from the barricade.

"Is there something you want to ask me?" Tony asked, his frustration at the situation and the day pushing him to speak. He pointed out the window at the corpses. "These things wanted you dead. I took care of them. We need to get this boy some help. We also need to get me some help, right? So what's your problem?"

No one responded. They wouldn't even look at him.

"Look, the only thing about me that has changed in the last twenty minutes is your perception. I'm still the same guy I was when you picked me up. If I was trustworthy then, what makes you think I would hurt you now?"

Jakub and Dinaala kept their eyes down. Beka looked at Tony, though. Then she looked at her husband and daughter. Her eyes burned with passion. "I don't care if this man is Andrus himself!" Both Jakub and Dinaala winced at that. "He helped us! Now Micah is dying. Either do something, or get out and this man and I will go on!"

"You're right, Beka. We'll go on. Dinaala, nudge the wagon up against the trunks and see if you can push your way through, okay?"

Dinaala nodded. The wagon inched forward until the branches of the barricade were smashed against the windshield. The wagon stopped. Branches snapped and creaked, but the wagon didn't move. Sweat beaded on Dinaala's forehead. Suddenly, she exhaled explosively. "It's no use. I can't budge this pile. In fact, I may have used myself up trying."

"Wait one minute," Tony said, reaching for the door. He paused, looking expectantly at it. Dinaala reached across and opened the door. Tony stepped out of the wagon.

Moving to a relatively clear spot, he stepped into the pile and positioned himself under one of the tree trunks. Not really thinking about it, he pushed the trunk up. He felt energized in a way he'd never felt before. The tree, and several that had been thrown on top of it, lifted up. He stepped forward, pushing the trees along with him. With every step, the load lightened. He felt like he was bristling with energy. By shrugging his shoulders and leaning to one side, he let the stack collapse on his left, out of the way of the wagon.

He turned back to the wagon, concerned about what he had heard Jakub and Dinaala say earlier. They could easily drive off while he was out here moving the refuse out of the way. He wouldn't blame them if they did.

It was the fear that would drive them away, if anything did. He knew that, even if he didn't know why they were afraid of him. He just hoped they would be kind enough to drop his stuff a little ways up the road so he wouldn't have to follow them too far to get it back.

He was mildly surprised to find them waiting when he had cleared enough brush for the wagon to move. He walked over to it and got in. He didn't thank them for waiting, and they didn't thank him for clearing the road.

"Let's go." Jakub looked at Dinaala.

"I can't," Dinaala replied, looking down at her hands. "I'm too far gone to get the wagon moving."

"No ... oh, Dinaala, what happened? You should have plenty left to get us to Jesik's place," Jakub moaned.

"I guess I burned myself up trying to push this thing through all those trees. I'm sorry, Daddy. I'm sorry, Micah ..." She burst into tears.

Because she was so mature, Tony had nearly forgotten that she was little more than a child. He turned back to Jakub. The man was looking at his wife. Tears were streaming down his face, but he was making no sound. His wife looked up, catching his gaze. She shook her head.

"I've been feeding Micah to keep him alive. I can't move this thing, either. I can barely keep up with him. He's burning up ..."

"Can I do something?" Tony asked, feeling totally useless but unwilling to give up and let the boy die.

Dinaala sniffed loudly and looked at him. She blinked a couple of times and then wiped the tears from her face. She stared at him. Tony grew uncomfortable under the intense and overly familiar scrutiny.

"I think he can ..." She turned back to her father. "Daddy, I think he can do it. He can feed the wagon."

"Wait a minute." Tony held his hands out in front of him. "I'll help in any way I can, but I don't have any idea how to do what you guys are doing. I'm not even sure I believe it *can* be done."

Dinaala looked at him, intently studying his face. "I can feed you a little, so you will know what it feels like."

She reached out her hand. A wide band of heat waves slowly stretched out from her hand, crawling through the space between them. The air was rippling, distorting everything seen through it, like the effect a rock has on a stream.

"It's a little like trying to use your stomach. I don't mean the muscles or anything. I mean actually making your stomach work. It's kind of hard at first, but once you figure it out, it seems so natural. Like, 'Why couldn't I do this all along?'" She watched the stream of power cross the gulf between them.

He watched it come, concerned, even a little afraid, but fascinated. It touched him and he knew joy. The power that flowed into him was awesome. When he thought about it later, it felt like filling his belly with air, but not in an unpleasant way.

She cut the stream off after only a few seconds, but Tony felt like he could move mountains. The energy was spreading throughout his body. He felt "full" for the first time in his life. He looked at his hands, spreading his fingers. He expected to see little crackling bursts of lightning between the tips and was a little disappointed when they weren't there.

"Now, do the opposite," Dinaala explained. "Aim it at the wagon and push it back out again."

Tony pointed his hand at the dashboard. He concentrated, pushing with different muscles in his belly and chest, and he felt like a maternity patient practicing Kegel exercises.

"No, no. It's not a muscle you have to push. Think of it like breathing. When you breathe, you just fill your lungs. You don't move the muscles in your chest, right? Don't push with your body, push with your mind."

Tony decided to think about it like martial arts. His master had shown him how to focus his spirit, his *ki,* and release it during strokes as a means of increasing the power of his blows. Maybe that same concept would work here. He stopped trying and simply sat, thinking about nothing. He worked through a quick relaxation technique his master had taught him, aligning his mind and spirit. He reached out his hand again and pushed his *ki* out through his fingertips.

His concentration was lost, however, when he was crushed backward into the seat as the wagon leaped forward. Dinaala's teeth clapped together with a loud snap. Beka let out a short scream. Jakub, facing his wife, lost his balance, crashed into the seatback, and rebounded onto the floor.

"Wow! Settle down, man!" Dinaala cried. "Don't push so hard!"

"I *didn't* push hard." Tony clenched his teeth. Usually in control, he was extremely uncomfortable this far out of his element.

Dinaala circled her head around on her neck a couple of times. "I'll feel that tomorrow. Look, you need to clamp down on the flow so that it doesn't all come out at once."

Tony looked out the window. With just the briefest instant of power, the wagon had been launched though the remaining branches. Momentum carried it another thirty yards down the road.

He looked back at Dinaala. "I don't think I can 'clamp it down' any more than I did."

"Well, let's try it again; you'll get the hang of it." Dinaala smiled at him.

Tony, with some reluctance, raised his hand again, pointing at the dashboard. He mentally prepared himself, then let out his ki again. This time he concentrated on limiting the flow. The wagon leaped forward. Where the first attempt was like a popped clutch on a formula dragster, this one was like a steady application of gas into a jet engine. The occupants were thrust back into their seats. Tony struggled to keep his head up. He turned and saw that Dinaala was having the same struggle. Through her window, he could see they were rapidly approaching the speed that had brought them this far. Within seconds they surpassed it. Wind buffeted the cab.

Dinaala, struggling against the weight crushing her into the seat, used both hands on the steering pad to keep the wagon on the road. "*Stop!*" she hollered.

Tony immediately cut off his ki. The speed dropped off quickly in the face of the wind. Even so, it took a few minutes before the wind noise had dropped enough to allow for conversation.

"Wow! That's power!" Jakub said from the backseat.

"Don't encourage him, Dad!" Dinaala snapped. "You've *got* to control that. There is no way I can steer this thing with you pushing it that hard."

"I can't. That's as tight as I can make it."

They slowly coasted to a stop.

Tony thought for a second. "Look, here's what we'll do. You keep steering. I'll push us up to speed and then let go. We coast down to a reasonable speed. Then I'll push us back up again. It won't be comfortable, but at least we'll get there."

Dinaala looked dubious. "Okay. Let's try it."

Within a few minutes they worked out a rhythm that was like inverting heavy acceleration from a stoplight. The wagon would occasionally lurch forward, but most of the time it coasted. With little bursts of power Tony could keep the wagon at a high rate of speed without blasting past Dinaala's ability to control it.

Forty minutes later they were approaching a new side road that Dinaala identified as Jesik's.

A few tense moments passed while Tony tried to slow them down without smashing them all into the windshield. Fortunately they knew the road was coming, so he didn't have to slow the rig much. Once on the narrow side road, he accelerated again. Ten minutes later they coasted onto the paved area in front of Jesik's house.

Jakub dived from the wagon before it came to a stop and sprinted to the door. He pounded with both fists, screaming for Jesik and Raneal. He lost his balance when the door opened.

The man who opened the door stepped back, eyes wide, when he saw the look on Jakub's face. "Jakub, my friend, what is it?" the man asked. A woman's head appeared over the man's shoulder.

"Jesik! Thank the Maker! It's Micah!" Jakub burst out, turning and running back toward the wagon. "He's been stung!" Jakub threw the last comment back over his shoulder.

The man, who Tony assumed was Jesik, sprinted from the house, robes flapping behind him. He overtook Jakub in a few strides and flew past him to the wagon, rounding it to Beka's side. With calm efficiency he slowed and gently opened the door.

"Hello, Beka." He looked at Micah's leg. He reached in and rested his palm on the child's face, feeling the heat there. He turned to Beka, wiping a tear from her face. "Don't cry, child. He's here now. Living or dying is up to the Maker, but he is with us. Raneal will make sure Micah has every chance to recover. Let me have him now."

With extreme care Jesik extracted Micah from his mother's grasp and carried him to the house, where the woman waited just inside the door.

Jakub and Beka followed close on his heels. Tony and Dinaala trailed a little behind.

"I just know he'll be okay," Dinaala murmured as they stepped through the door. It closed behind them with a click.

Thom Lays Low

Thom judged the door was solid enough, though it was chipped and cracked enough to make the question a good one. He slipped a chair under the handle, its back feet wedged between a couple of the floorboards.

He sat on the bed and pulled a small bag from his hip pouch. From an inner pocket of his cloak he pulled an ornately carved pipe. Packing it deftly, he had it prepared for action in a matter of seconds. He bit the pull string, tugging the bag closed. He tucked it back into the pouch and then scooted to the head of the bed. When he was comfortable—legs crossed in front of him and a pillow behind his head—he concentrated on the bowl of the pipe, feeding it a gentle stream. The bowl began to glow. He cut the feed when a small tendril of smoke rose from the crushed leaves. He put the pipe in his mouth and leaned back, breathing in the delicious blend he had picked up in the market a few days ago.

There were a few things about Freia that Thom liked better than Earth. Obviously, the Touch was really cool. He could do things on Freia that were simply not possible on Earth. On top of the Touch, though, he loved the tobacco. They didn't call it tobacco, of course. They called it something that sounded like a cross between gagging and a hiccup. But it was tobacco just the same. And here they didn't doctor it up with a bunch of chemicals. It was just plain old tobacco, dried and shredded by a Regulator.

He briefly glanced at the light, sending a small feed into it. It went dark. He closed his eyes and waited. He didn't have to wait long. The door knob turned slowly and quietly.

He cursed to himself that no one had any decency left. At least they could have waited until he'd finished a bowl before they came to take him.

The door shifted slightly, pressing against the chair. Thom took a couple of deep puffs from the pipe before dumping it into the ashtray Barton had provided. The door shifted again, more firmly this time. Whispered conversation in the hallway told him there were at least three men outside.

He tucked the pipe back into his cloak, climbed off the bed, and crossed the room to the coat rack that held his belt, pack, and scabbards. His soft, flexible boots made almost no noise as he stepped on the wooden floor. He slid his sword and dagger out, knowing they would be required before he could rest. The sword was long and gently curved. The pommel was long enough to allow a two-handed grasp but could be controlled with one, if need be. That is, if the wielder had sufficient strength and training in its use. Thom had both in abundance. The blade had an intricate pattern of runes engraved down its length. They began to glow dimly as he fed power into them. He held the dagger point down along his forearm.

The mumbling in the hallway grew in volume as the thugs discovered that the door was barred. Apparently they decided stealth was not going to work and turned to a more direct means of entry.

The door shuddered from a thunderous impact. It held. Another crushing blow popped the top hinge. The door had done its job. On the third impact the last two hinges popped, opening a six-inch gap up and down the right side of the doorframe.

Thom was relaxed. He let the tip of his sword drop to the ground, taking some of the weight. He knew he might get tired if things went badly, so he conserved his strength whenever possible.

Thick, hairy fingers slipped in through the crack and gripped the door. The door slid to the right a few inches, just enough to let the latch pull loose. Another set of thick fingers gripped that side of the door. A pair of tree trunk-like legs appeared as the door rotated out through the opening. The chair rattled to the ground as its support was suddenly removed. Thom watched the door sail over the handrail on the landing and out into the main hall of the inn. It seemed like minutes passed before it crashed into something below.

In the opening where the door had been, a giant stood. It wasn't really a giant, Thom told himself. He had seen real giants since arriving here. No, this one wasn't from that clan. It was, however, only loosely related to the human race. The Monster, as he was immediately and permanently dubbed, ducked under the doorframe and stepped into the room.

His companion was much smaller and slightly stooped. Fate had a sense of humor. Igor drew a thin, wicked-looking dagger. The blade was about ten inches long and black as night.

Rather than Igor, it was the Monster who spoke, demonstrating that fate would carry a joke only so far. "The Duke would like to renegotiate."

The hairs on Thom's neck stood up. Something was wrong. "Tell the Duke I'd be happy to come back at the end of the contract's term to negotiate a new one," Thom replied. "I'm sure the Baron would be willing to talk about alternatives then."

The Monster turned to his left and took a step into the room, talking in a reasonable tone. He spread his hands for emphasis. Unarmed as he was, he looked the height of diplomacy and reason. "The Duke is not an unreasonable man. He doesn't want us to kill you. He just feels like you took advantage of him."

"Hmmm … many people feel that way at the conclusion of a business transaction," Thom replied, bending his knees slightly. He centered his weight on the balls of his feet.

Apparently, the Monster did not feel a need for weapons. He had none. On his arms he wore massive bands of leather with intricate steel tracings. Thom spied the telltale lumps of chain mail under his shirt. He wondered briefly how much it would cost to outfit an eight-foot tall man.

Igor moved slightly, sidestepping left and crouching a bit. His eyes narrowed.

"It's an unfortunate aspect of business. I could suggest a couple of counselors, if he needs help getting over it," Thom said brightly, and then whipped around to his right, slashing out at a new, third attacker who had crept in behind Thom through the open window.

The blade, runes glowing white hot, came up in a steep, sweeping arc. Just before it hit its mark it jerked down, almost jumping out of Thom's hand. Thom had been expecting it and flowed smoothly through the change in direction. The blade slid into its victim's chest. After passing between two bands of his leather armor, it turned up again, slicing through a lung.

The whip-thin kid was totally unprepared for the attack. His blade, a long, jagged dirk, was held high and tight, ready to come around Thom's neck. It tumbled from his hand. "Ooooohhhh ..." The moan ended in a wheeze.

Thom's blade continued its progress, slipping quietly out through the boy's breastbone. Thom continued to spin. A bright red fan of blood splashed in an arc across the wall over the bed.

Igor, to his credit, reacted fast enough to get his dagger in front of the blade. The impact sent the sword high over his head. Unfortunately for him, this left him open to Thom's smaller blade. It punched between Igor's ribs, just under his armpit. Thom left it. Even if Igor could function with only one lung, he'd still be hampered by the handle under his arm.

Thom let his spin carry him back to position in front of the Monster. It took fewer than three seconds.

"I know a good one not too far from the palace, on Malaka Lane." Thom grinned. He heard the Whip drop to his knees. Igor's blade clattered to the ground. He didn't look at either of them.

"Is that a Kitarni blade?" the Monster asked. He hadn't moved from his spot.

First mumbling and then loud cursing sounded from the main room below.

"Yes, it is." Thom was still grinning. "It's called Meat Seeker." The Monster looked blankly at him. No one ever got the joke. That's the trouble with going to a new planet. No one ever gets your jokes.

"Your friends look ill." Thom nodded to the downed men. "Maybe you should get them to a healer."

"The Duke will not be happy." The Monster frowned. "I'm sure we'll see each other again." Keeping his hands out to his sides, he stepped to Thom's right and collected the Whip. He scooped him up under his arm like a sack of grain. The Whip cried out but got no sympathy from anyone. The Monster continued his circuit of the room. He tucked Igor under his other arm.

"He can keep my knife. I'll just trade him for that one." Thom pointed at the black blade on the ground.

"What the hell is going on here?" Barton bellowed from the doorway. Thom and the Monster glanced at him. Barton turned white. He backed out of the way as the Monster edged his way through the door. His companions flopped like bags of meat when he stepped past the innkeeper.

"I believe I'm ready to move to that better room now, Barton." Thom moved through the door to stand next to Barton, slipping his sword and new dagger back in place.

"Uh … yes, sir," Barton replied. "Right away, sir."

As Thom stepped past the innkeeper, he pressed a large gold coin into the man's hand. "It'll save you cleaning and maintenance bills if no one else learns that I'm here."

"Y-y-yes, sir." Barton looked back at the blood splashed on the wall. He turned and hustled after Thom.

The trees rattle in the wind. The horses whinny and shy away from the group. Thom looks, first at the horses and then at the trees on the opposite side of the fire. Something moves behind the huge old oak that dominates that edge of the clearing. He can make out a shape, a blackness moving behind the trees. It suddenly looms larger. It shoots straight up, disappearing into the upper branches of the oak. Snapping and crackling in the branches. Athon pulls out his long sword. It pings like a single plucked string as it comes free. He steps around the fire and looks up into the tree. Branches explode into the encampment. Ripping its way out of the woods, a demon drops out of the night and into their clearing.

Over Athon's head, Thom can clearly see the creature's face. Horns, bull's head, fangs, and huge wings. It's a thing of art. Dante's Inferno *come to life.*

It howls. Thom feels the blood leave his face. It strides purposefully toward Athon. Sweat drips from Thom's hair. Athon stands before the creature. It stops. It looks him up and down. It bellows, a whole body investment, bent forward at the waist. Athon seizes the opportunity and slashes at the beast. The creature catches Athon's sword in its left hand and rips him in half with the other. Thom's bladder lets go.

He stands transfixed. The beast throws Athon's top half away. Somehow that simple motion is enough to get Thom moving. He pulls Meat Seeker out of her scabbard. She sings and glows as he feeds her. She is like a fire in his hands. He knows instinctively that running won't work. This thing would chase them until it killed them all. He takes two steps toward the beast. Jesik hollers something. Martin is bent over, clutching his stomach. The horses are screaming. Time slows. The beast leaps straight up and spreads its massive wings. It floats down toward him. The ground shakes when it lands, threatening to cast Thom to the dirt. He gets his feet under him and swings. Meat Seeker bucks in his hands as he drags her across the beast's ribs. The demon bellows in rage. Hot blood splashes Thom's face and neck, and his face is on fire. He is flying through the air. Backward. The wind blasts out of him by a monstrous impact. He can't breathe. He can't move. He looks down. A branch is lying in his lap. He reaches for it. He is confused. The branch won't move. It's attached to a tree. The tree is behind him. The branch is sticking out of his belly. Left side, just above the hip. He screams himself awake.

Thom's shoulder and left arm were numb when he finally came fully awake. Disoriented, he rolled from his side onto his back, hearing a thump as his shoulder blade hit the hard wooden planks. He sat up. A large droplet of sweat fell from soaked bangs onto his eyebrow. It rolled into his eye without any consideration or care, stinging with authority. Thom sucked wind. He didn't care about the sweat, the hard floor, or his dignity. He cared about sucking wind. He cared about being *able* to suck wind. He cared about not puking his guts out. He cared a great deal about that.

Knock-knock …

In fact, he cared so much about not puking that he thought he might succeed. As long as he sucked wind. The dream faded, taking with it the chills and cramps. It left the sweat behind, almost as a reminder to Thom: *Don't fuck with me, boy. I've got your number. I've got it right here in my pocket.*

Knock-knock.

Someone wanted his attention.

Knock-knock.

"Mr. Kassidy, are you all right?" Barton's voice, muffled by the door, was almost gentle and quiet, a stark contrast to his usual booming basso.

Thom groaned. He grabbed the bed to pull himself up. His left arm refused to help, but he managed the job with his right. His left hip and knee were also worthless. He tested the leg. Shaky, but it held. He limped to the door and drew back the bolt.

In his apron and brown, rough-spun wool clothes, Barton was an intimidating fellow. In his night clothes, hair askew, and eyes bloodshot, he was frightful and comical at the same time.

"Are you all right, Mr. Kassidy?" His big head bobbed and weaved as he tried to peer into the room behind Thom. "No more trouble, I hope?"

"No, no, Barton." Thom sighed heavily. "Nothing like that. I just had a bad dream."

"You know, Mr. Kassidy, I like you and all." Barton looked down at his feet as he spoke. "I'm happy to have you at my place. But … the missus … she don't like all the fuss. Plus, sir, the other guests are startin' ta complain about all the noise." He looked back at Thom's face. "I appreciate your paying for the other damage and all."

His brow scrunched down. "I know it weren't yer fault; them other fellas came in here rough and tumble like. In fact, you ain't the only one's had trouble of that sort lately, so it's no problem. But this other, sir, it won't sit."

His brow went from scrunched to pleading. "I can't have all my guests 'fraid to go to bed, sir. That howlin' … it's just too much. It cuts right through a fella. I'm sure when I git downstairs in the mornin' all my milk'll be curdled."

"Howling?" Thom asked.

"Yessir. Dincha hear it?" Barton's face opened up a bit as his curiosity came up for a peek. "It came outa yer room. Woke durn near the whole town up."

Barton's eyes widened and became unfocused. "It was horrible. Unnatur'l. At first, just wailin' and moanin'. Then the shrieks started." He paled and looked down at his feet. "The wife pushed me to get me goin'. I told her it weren't none o' my business. I was scared to my bones and sweatin' pretty fierce. Evenchully I got my courage up. Maker's honest truth …" Barton paused, looking at Thom again. "I only come up 'cause it'd stopped already."

He peered deeper into the room. "By time I got up here, I tol' myself a story that a tinder cat come in your window and caught you unawares. You dealin' it some damage was what caused the ruckus." He moved his big round head from side to side, looking into the corners of the room.

"Barton, please …" Thom began, placing a hand on the big man's shoulder. "Rest easy. I assure you there will be no further howling or any other loud noises from this room tonight."

Thom allowed a small trickle of the Touch to flow from his hand into Barton. "I have some business to attend to in the morning. By about noon tomorrow, I should be safely on my way. Does that suit you?"

Barton nodded, smiling. "Yessir. Thank you for bein' so understandin.'" He ducked his head and backed out onto the landing. Thom closed the door. He sighed. The worst part about having a talent like his was using it on people who didn't deserve it.

He shook his head and turned back to his bed, piling the pillows up against the wall to support his back. He turned to the coat rack by the door. He rummaged through his vest until he found his pipe and tobacco. He walked back to the bed, sat down, and packed himself a bowl. As he lit it, he decided it would be better not to sleep in town again. At least for a while. He Touched the bowl again, bringing on the familiar, white glowing runes. He leaned back and watched the slow curl of smoke as it made its way up to the ceiling.

Three hours later, sunlight streamed in through his window. He tapped out the remains of his latest bowl. The dish he was using for this purpose had quite a pile in it. He shuffled across the mattress and stood up. His bones popped and crackled as he stretched, catlike, toward the floor. His belly got in the way, but slightly spreading his legs allowed him room to lay his palms flat on the floor. People who looked at him, at least those who wanted trouble, often jumped to conclusions based on what they saw. *He's slow. He's uncoordinated. He's lazy. He's not very flexible. He's not very bright.* It gave him another edge. In his line of work, he needed all the edges he could get.

He pulled his vest off the coat rack and slipped his pipe and tobacco back into the inside pocket before tugging the vest on. He clasped his belt around his waist, checking the position of each weapon before buckling it. Last, he grabbed his cloak and saddlebags.

The door opened onto the earliest murmurings on the ground floor. The first shift of workers was up and preparing the main hall for the first wave of guests. Barton was sitting at one of the tables, bent over a tally sheet. A short, ferret-faced man stood behind him, watching with nervous eyes that darted from Barton to the sheet. Time to pay Barton for last night.

"Ho, Barton," Thom called from the balcony as he walked toward the stairs.

Barton looked up from his tally. "Oh … good mornin', Mr. Kassidy." Barton smiled, genuine and open.

"Thank you for the excellent accommodations." Thom smiled back. His stride was purposeful and quickly carried him around the open area to the stairs. His boot heels clacked loudly on the hard wooden steps. He put his hand on the rail, smoothed over the years by many guests, though the rough-hewn texture could still be felt.

As he cleared the bottom step he turned and crossed to where Barton was sitting. He clapped the man's broad shoulder. "A great rest, indeed." Thom let a cloud darken his face for a moment. "I trust there were no other problems last night?"

"Oh, no, sir!" Barton responded with a smile. "It was quiet as a church for the rest of the night."

"Good, good …" Thom trailed off. He pointedly looked at the smaller man. Barton took the hint.

"Uh, this 'ere's Kister Bedanst, my main supplier."

Thom extended his hand. He cocked his head to the side. "What an unusual name. Did you say 'Kissed Or Be Danced'?"

The small man smiled at the joke, almost as if he hadn't heard it a hundred times before. He took Thom's hand. His grip was dry and strong. His fingers felt strange. Long and oddly bent. Thom held the handshake long enough to send a brief trickle of Touch through the contact. He smiled as he released the man's hand.

"Barton, I'd like to buy this man a drink." Thom turned to the innkeeper.

"But … Mr. Kassidy … it's not yet six o'clock in the morning …" Barton began.

Thom held up his hand and looked down. "Now, Barton, I didn't say it had to be ale. Maybe this gent would like a nice cup of coffee with a bit of Langdon White in it. Now that sounds nice, doesn't it, Mr. Bedanst?"

"Uh, yes, I guess it does …" he replied, looking somewhat confused. "But I don't drink much. I don't like the taste, y'see."

"Well, it's rare to find a completely honest man. Especially in these parts. I'd thought Barton here was the only one left in all of Duncester."

Barton beamed at the compliment, looking from Thom to Kister.

Thom dropped a silver piece on the table. Then he pulled the saddlebags off of his shoulder and laid them on the table as well.

"Barton, I need to run a quick errand. Can you keep your eyes on this for me? I won't be longer than an hour or so."

"O' course, Mr. Kassidy." He stood up, taking the bags with him as he walked toward the bar. "I'll just lock them up in my office. They should be safe enough there."

Thom stood and made small talk with Kister for a few minutes. Barton came back with a steaming cup that smelled of strong coffee and even stronger spirits. Kister sniffed it before taking a small sip. His eyes went from beady to bugged for just a few seconds. Then a slow smile lit up his face.

"There now ..." Thom grinned back. "There's no time of day that can't be dressed up a bit, if you're creative about it." He turned to Barton. "*I'll be back.*"

He said it with a very serious expression and a slight Austrian accent. He looked at them expectantly for a few seconds, then gave a heavy sigh, shook his head, and strode out the door.

One hour and sixteen minutes later, Thom walked back in. His side hurt ferociously where a new trauma was making itself known. He limped a bit and grimaced a lot on his way to a seat at one of the tables near the big stone fireplace that took up the center of the room. He sat facing the fireplace, his back to the door. He could Touch, even with this nagging injury affecting his concentration. He did it. When he let go, he felt much better about his situation. His injury wasn't life threatening and the weave he'd laid down on the floor would help him keep track of everyone in the room. No one could sneak up behind him across that weave, unless he or she could fly. He sat back, took out his pipe, and started packing the bowl.

Having the local gangs as involved as they were was unexpected. He'd been so sure they would hold back. They were on the fringe and never seemed interested in local politics. Then again, local politics could dramatically affect their business. Make a few things legal and their business could be wiped out. A small, swirling stream of smoke curled up from his pipe. He watched it make lazy curls.

Besides, it probably wasn't politics that spurred the Outlanders. It was greed. Pure and simple. They wanted what he had because someone would pay for it. And pay dearly. If not the Duke, then one of his enemies. A brief blast of cold air scattered the mesmerizing stream of smoke. Behind him, the door leading to the street thumped closed. He didn't turn. The smoke resumed its course.

What could he do about it? Did he need to do anything? Good questions, both. If he took further action against the gangs, he risked exposing himself. Exposing himself had never been his thing. He saw himself standing on a street corner in a long overcoat held open like wings. Nope, not interested. His weave registered movement. Someone was walking on it.

His face twitched ever so slightly. He focused all thought and perception on the person walking across the weave. Small feet, fairly light. A woman or a child. Strides too long for a child. Purposeful. Booted feet. Not heading directly toward him. Probably not a threat.

She strode into his peripheral vision. Tall and skinny. A long, dark gray overcoat hung to her knees. Black leather pants and riding boots poked out below it. A wide-brimmed cowboy hat covered her head. She looked like Sharon Stone in *The Quick and the Dead.* She clumped across the floor to the back bar. He lost her when she passed behind the huge fireplace. But he could still feel her on his weave as she pulled out a chair and sat at a table near the bar.

He closed his eyes. In his mind he watched the stream of smoke rise to the ceiling. He had to hang around for a while longer and let the seeds he'd planted take root. Fazha would take the bait. Unless he was already working for someone, that is. With a reputation like Fazha's, a guy could find work anytime he wanted it.

At least the gang didn't know exactly where he was. He'd made sure no one followed him back to the inn after the scuffle.

Heavy footfalls crossed his weave from the back bar to the woman's table. She mumbled. Barton's baritone voice rumbled back. She laughed, full-bodied and heartfelt. The footfalls retreated.

Maybe he could have Barton front-end the conversation with Fazha. That thought rolled around in his head for a few minutes.

The woman stood and walked toward him, circling the fireplace on the side nearest him. He felt her every step. Just before she came into view around the fireplace, he turned slightly away. Best not to let her know he was monitoring her progress.

He needn't have bothered. As she rounded the fireplace, she strode directly to his table. He looked up when she pulled out a chair. He didn't gawk. He didn't stop breathing. He did nothing but look curiously at this intruder. Only his years as a negotiator gave him the self-control necessary. She was without question the most magnificent creature he had ever seen. She sat herself and her coffee cup simultaneously. He still thought of them as coffee cups even though the brown syrup these people drank was more of a glucose tolerance test than it was coffee.

Her hat and coat had been left behind. Her long, straight, sandy-blonde hair disappeared down her back. Her eyes looked like chocolate drops and carved into him. For the first time in years he was nervous and dry-mouthed during a conversation.

"Are you Price?" she asked, almost casually.

"Hmmm?" He watched as her brow clenched above those marvelous eyes.

"Is your name Price?" She spoke slowly, as if to a child.

"No, should it be?" He pulled the pipe from his mouth.

She took a drink, looking at him over the cup. "Hmm … my mistake."

She pushed back her chair and stood up. "Someone told me a man name Price needed my services. It seems I was misinformed."

His hand shot out, lightning fast, covering hers. The Touch was light, but she stopped moving. The briefest Touch sent a chill up his spine. Instantly his perspective changed. He had to be very careful, but he had to move ahead.

"Wait." He pulled his hand back. "Please, sit down."

She stared at him for what seemed like years and then sat again.

He collected his thoughts. "I am, of course, Price. I can't be too careful."

"Good grief!" She rolled her eyes "This is a little too cliché for me. A clandestine meeting at an inn on the edge of town, for cryin' out loud. Have you read every book by Joutak, or just the ones with Pandy Karsh in them?"

He laughed. He couldn't help himself. "All right. I guess you're right. Then again, you don't know the whole story, do you?" He paused for effect, as if sizing her up. "Look, I'm sorry I didn't respond at first. I was expecting Fazha to be a man."

"Most people do." She eyed him over her cup. "How about if we get beyond the chauvinism and talk about what it is you want?"

"All right …" He sensed that, with her, it was best to get directly to the point. "Are you and your crew available for a few weeks' work?"

"It depends on the job. The amount of money you were waving in town was enough to get my attention, but I'm no fool. If you've got a war to fight, we'll be there. If you want something stolen or someone killed, we're not interested. We're not assassins or thieves. If you're crossing the Duke, we're done talking. I got my reputation by taking on jobs I can live through."

"Look, it's nothing like that. I just need a bodyguard. Things are a little hot for me right now. I'd rather not talk about why. Suffice it to say I've stolen nothing and killed no one. Yet. However, what I am carrying is extremely valuable. The Duke wants it very badly. On the flipside, your reputation is very good. Maybe you can keep me alive long enough to deliver it to the appropriate recipient."

"Hmmm. How much are you willing to pay?"

"I'll need you to travel with me for about two weeks. I'll pay three gold pieces for adequate protection."

She raised her eyebrows at the hefty offer.

Another cold blast of air hit him in the back. This one lasted longer before the door closed. Two pair of feet stepped onto his weave. One pair, large and heavy, moved to the end of the front bar. The second pair, lighter but about the same size, stopped a bit shorter. Bar stools scratched backward across the floor. He didn't turn from Fazha but followed their conversation through his weave.

"Whoooo, can't tell me spring is here." Mr. Heavy had a kid's voice.

"I say the Dark's coming back," Thin Guy responded.

Mr. Heavy laughed. A mean sort of laugh. Unpleasant and condescending.

"What are you on about? The Dark?" he squeaked. "Whadda you know about it? You're dumb as a rock."

"All's I'm sayin' is, it's been getting a lot colder over the last coupla years. And ain't nobody can explain it."

Fazha, not privy to the other conversation Thom was following, spoke over the Thin Guy. "You must be expecting pretty heavy trouble to throw down that kind of money."

"I'll consider it cheap, if you can do the job." He looked at her for a few seconds. "Speaking of which, I only know you by reputation. How do I know you can do it?"

Fazha slid her chair back from the table, dragging Thom's full attention back to his guest. She stood up and walked to the front bar. Thom turned and watched her graceful stride. Tilli, Barton's son, was still setting up glasses and cups behind the bar for the morning crowd that would soon be coming in. Fazha strode up to the bar and said something to him, nodding toward the wide array of bottles standing on the sideboard. Tilli grabbed a pitcher off of a warming plate, poured coffee and some amber liquid from one of the bottles into a cup, and handed it to Fazha.

The two gentlemen at the bar sat openly eyeing her. Mr. Heavy leaned over and whispered into Thin Guy's ear and then leaned back and laughed.

Fazha set down her cup and stepped around behind the two men. "Hi, guys." Her voice carried over to where Tom sat waiting. "I have a problem. Maybe you guys could help me."

"Uh, maybe," Thin Guy replied, obviously confused about the situation.

"See that guy over there?" She pointed at Thom. Both men looked over their left shoulders. She put her hand between them. "Spread out a bit."

Thin Guy grabbed his stool and scooted sideways, making room for her. She stepped up between them. She mumbled something. They looked at Thom again. They both shook their heads.

"Not interested." Mr. Heavy's response was loud enough for Thom to hear. "But maybe I got somethin' you can do instead …" He leaned out and looked her body over, noting every curve. He reached out and patted one of them.

"Yeah," added Thin Guy. "We can take care of you ourselves. Eliminate the middle-man, I always say."

Her head turned first to one man and then to the other.

The sudden flurry of activity was difficult to follow.

Fazha dropped straight down, like a trap door had opened under her. The stools flew sideways out from under the two men. Thin Guy's chin smashed down against the bar, snapping his head back. He crumpled to the ground. Mr. Heavy got a foot down and grabbed the bar, keeping himself upright. Unfortunately for him he was now at optimal height for a devastating blow to the groin. He too crumpled to the ground. The lady used the bar to pull herself up from the splits she had dropped into.

Thin Guy shook his head and stood up. "Oh, you *bitch*!" he screamed, stepping toward the lady. She stood facing him, no fear on her face. He tensed up, pulling his arm back for a mighty blow. The lady dropped to one knee and hammered his belly with her left fist. As he folded over the impact, she rushed upward, crushing his nose with her right elbow. He went over backward, landing hard.

She stood up and turned away from him. Taking her cup, she turned back toward Thom. A few strides later she was back beside him. She set the cup on the table. "Ten gold for two weeks," she said.

Thom looked over at the two men. They were moving. But it was slow and careful movement. The movement of someone just recovering after being very ill.

"Ten gold." He turned back to her. "Hmmmm … does that ten gold also cover your two friends, or will you leave them here in town?"

She looked at him for a minute without responding. Then she smiled. Thom's heart fluttered a bit at that. But his face showed no emotion whatsoever. "You're pretty sharp. What tipped it?"

"Thin Guy, there …"

"Spider."

"Ok, Spider," he continued, "is much better than he lets on. I'm guessin' the average Joe wouldn't know he was telegraphing on purpose. But it was pretty obvious for anyone with some time behind a blade."

Thom looked at the other "victim." He nodded. "Mr. Heavy …"

"Karf."

"He probably hurts like hell about now. I'm guessing you didn't pull your punch any. But if you wanted to do serious damage, you wouldn't have hit him in the thigh."

"You've got a good eye." Her smile faded. "Maybe too good." She sat down. "If you're that good, whadda ya need me for?"

He just looked at her.

"In fact, big money on the street says you're Thom Kassidy. I don't know if I believe that. What's a big gun like Thom Kassidy doin' in a place like this? It's decent enough for mercs and low travelers. But a guy like that? He could be stayin' in the palace, or some big shot's mansion. Diker's or Ktang's, maybe."

Her eyes pierced him. "That's not what really bugs me, though. Hey, maybe he's slummin'. Maybe he likes a little dirt and rough talk with his salty beef and watery beer. No, what gets me is—and this is a *much* better question—what's he doing out on the street, lookin' for muscle? I mean, this guy's got access to at least two different armies, right? Baron Rajka's and the Duke's? Couldn't he get as many guards as he needs? Why's he lookin' for rough and tumble when he could have finesse and training?"

He sat, silently eyeing her. She was smart. But damned if he didn't have a hard time concentrating on what she was saying. He liked her eyes. He was beginning to think it was a bad idea to try working with her.

"So maybe," she continued, "he's got some problem with the Duke and the Baron. Maybe Mr. Big Negotiator has a trick or two up his sleeve. Maybe he's playing one against the other. Letting each of 'em think they're getting the better of the deal, when in fact it's little Thom who's gettin' the goodies."

Nope, not a bad idea. A Bad Idea. Maybe even a BAD IDEA. It was time for Thom to get the upper hand. "Look, never mind." He slid back his chair to stand up. "This was a bad idea."

Her hand shot out and covered his. His heart skipped a beat, but his face didn't. He frowned down at her hand.

"Wait." A small smile graced her lips. "There's no sense in you goin' off in a huff. They were just questions. I didn't say I cared much about the answers."

He looked at her for a minute and then slid his chair back under the table. "Let's get a couple of things straight. First, who I am doesn't matter. What I want does. Second, I'm gonna have to sleep around you, so I want to know I can trust you. So far you've lied to me about who those two are, put on a show, and asked some pretty dangerous questions."

She sucked in a breath. Good. Equilibrium restored. She was quiet for a minute. She rubbed her forehead. "All right. Come clean with me and I'll come clean with you." She grinned. "I'll even go first … as a sign of good faith.

"My name is Fazha Dufrezne. It used to be Aing Kesst. For a brief period, I was a member of the Captain's Guard. We protected the Duke whenever he traveled. It was a tough job, especially for a woman. I had to be faster, tougher, and smarter than everyone else just to be considered equal. But I enjoyed it and did it well.

"As it turned out, some folks in the palace thought that a bit uppity of me. One of them, a great ugly slug of a man with one drooping eye and no table manners came on to me. I turned him down. He was powerful and had the Duke's ear, but he was also married. He couldn't make a public spectacle, so he decided to take care of me secretly.

"He arranged for some entertainment. I was out on patrol with Spider, Karf, and a couple of other guys. All of us were good. Unfortunately, the gang that slammed us was good too. And there were a lot more of them. Spider took a blade in the back. Karf took a club to the head. He should've been dead, but he's too stubborn. The rest … I don't know and Karf won't tell me."

She stopped, looking down and swallowing hard. It hurt him to watch.

"When they were done with me, they opened me up. Karf came to before I bled to death. He got me to a healer and then fed her while she healed me. When he went back for the others, Spider was the only one still alive. Karf brought him. We were all down for a while. When we surfaced, Aing was dead. At least as far as the palace was concerned.

"Karf and Spider helped me establish Fazha's identity. With their help, I hunted down and killed every last one of the bastards who did it." A single tear rolled down her cheek.

"Why do you stay around here?" Thom asked.

Her soft look disappeared, replaced by steel. "I haven't dealt with Hexa yet. I want to look in his drooping eye as I cut off his manhood. But he's careful. I can't seem to get close enough."

She looked down again. "In the meantime, we've been takin' the odd job, comin' and goin'. Frankly, mercs make good money. And I hang with classier people than I did at the palace. Real people, not courtesans and dignitaries with their noses in the air. When they're not up some politician's bum, that is. Mum and Daddy wouldn't be too proud, but then again, who cares? They didn't care about me any."

Thom looked at her for a couple of moments. The silence stretched on, she in her thoughts, he in his. Finally she came to herself. Looking up, she said, "Now it's your turn."

"Okay." Thom leaned back in his chair. "I can't tell you everything …"

She started to protest, but he held up his hand.

"Until we get on the road and away from prying ears. My name, as you guessed, is Thom Kassidy. I'm a Negotiator. I'm here representing Baron Rajka in a contract negotiation with the Duke. The negotiation is over. The contract is signed and ready to go back to the Baron.

"For reasons of my own, I don't want to travel by wagon and I don't want any escort the Duke might provide. I expect the round trip to take a couple of weeks. We may run into trouble along the way. I'd like to have your friends along and will pay extra for them. When we're done with this trip, I'll help you with your problem."

"What?"

He looked at her, smiling. "I'll help you get your hands on Hexa. I've had some dealings with him. What you plan to do couldn't happen to a more deserving fella."

"But what can you do? You're just a Negotiator. You don't even live here." She looked shocked.

"I've known him for a year or so. Our paths occasionally cross. I know some of his weaknesses." He winked at her. "Besides, he's afraid of me. I'm sure we can work something out. Do we have a deal?"

"Hell, yes!" She grinned back and stuck out her hand.

Shaking it was the hardest thing he had done in a very long time.

ADRIFT

Aleks tossed and turned. Moonlight rolled lazy circles around his head. He counted its passing like jumping sheep. Eighty-eight, eighty-nine, ninety. He shifted position again, knowing he should get up but refusing. A gentle slap, slap, slap drifted in through the doorway. The argument played over in his mind again and again.

"We can't afford any more crap for that boat!" Georgia screams at him. "We're barely makin' it as it is! Now you wanna go spend more *money on that stinkin' thing? I'm sick of it." She stomps down hard on the sticky, honey-colored linoleum to make her point. She has tears in her eyes as she looks at him. He is silent.*

"Dammit, Aleks, you know business hasn't gone well this year." She walks across the kitchen, her thighs rubbing together under the seam of the Lycra shorts she's taken to wearing recently. As she gets near, she smacks her hand on the table.

"How many projects have you done since January? Ten, fifteen max? Last year by this time we had at least thirty projects. We can't spend any more money! If we don't get more projects pretty quick, we're gonna have a real problem. Ralph says we can get some of Big Jake's stuff, if we just hook up with Marty and Gus."

"Marty and Gus are liars and cheats. They've ripped off nearly everyone they've ever built for. And Ralph? What the hell does Ralph know? He'd sell his mother for a quick buck." Aleks looks away from her. "He doesn't care about the business or the people. Yesterday he screamed at Mrs. Taylor."

"That old bitty? She doesn't have a clue what she wants, can't ever make up her mind. I'd yell at her too."

"Look, I don't care how many times she changes her mind. She's paying us to build her a house. What she wants, she gets."

"Ralph says—"

"Ralph's been doing a lot of sayin' *lately, hasn't he?"*

"What's that s'posed to mean?"

"Nothin'. I just wonder how you've been hearing so much from Ralph lately."

"Don't you change the subject on me! This isn't about Ralph. It's about us. We live on these projects and you aren't getting them anymore. But you keep spending money on that damn boat. What the hell good is that? You've never even put it into the water. How much is in that stupid thing, a hundred grand? One-fifty? Shit, we should sell it and cover some of our bills."

"We are not selling my boat!"

A whisper tickled his perception. The bright colors of the comforter cast the room in a crazy purple-green glow. He crunched the pale yellow pillow against his cheek and pinched his eyes closed. He could almost hear her screeching.

He stands up and walks toward the kitchen door, his boots thunking and snicking with each step.

"You bastard, you don't care one whit for me or the kids! All you care about is that boat*!"*

He whirls on her. "How long have you been talkin' to Ralph, anyway? And who was it before him? Oh yeah, that kid from the fairgrounds, Mufty or whatever the hell his name was. Who was it before that?"

Blood rushes into her face, turning it bright purple. She steps over and slaps him, rocking his head back. He grabs her by the shoulders and pushes her away.

"You've got no room to talk about caring for someone, Sugar! You haven't spent two weeks faithful to me since our honeymoon. You don't care about me. You never loved me. You care about my paycheck. You love your clothes and your rings and your Lexus. And since you brought 'em up, let's talk about the kids. Damned spoiled brats get whatever they want, eh? God forbid you should say no to 'em about anything. And why is it they don't look anything like me?"

"Aaaaaaggggghhhhh!" She snatches the nearest thing at hand and hurls it hard at his head. Aleks ducks as the ceramic "Cadillac of coffee cups" explodes on impact against the door jam behind his right ear. He walks out the door. Behind him, footsteps and a grunt tell him to duck again. A grinning Santa hands a

child a candy cane for a split second before the scene disintegrates into a shower of miniscule white shrapnel. Fire lances his left cheek. He darts through the family room and out onto the patio. The boat is already loaded. He jogs to the truck, ignoring her trailing profanities.

The whisper had become a dull roar. The gently slapping waves were gone. Suddenly the world tipped. He slid spread eagle across the bed as the bottom fell out of the world on the starboard side. He saw stars when his head fetched up against the frame where the side of the hull met the bow deck. What the hell was going on? He dragged himself out of the pile of pillows and blankets and staggered through the galley and up into the cockpit.

His view made little sense. His first look over the starboard windscreen was nearly straight down into a torrent of water. The water was sliding around and under the big Hustler and cascading through a hole in space. It pounded down a ten-foot drop into a lake that Aleks could see through. Sunlight was pouring out of the hole, lighting up his boat and the surrounding water. Looking forward, Aleks saw that the "hole" was actually a thin, golden ring about twenty-five feet in diameter. The bow and stern of the boat were pinned against the ring. As he watched, the ring grew. Oh shit. The ring was rapidly approaching the tip of the bow. A quick glance down confirmed it.

Aleks scrambled to the wheel and cranked the huge triples to life. The five hundred horsepower Mercruiser motors spat and thundered. He edged into reverse, afraid the screws would cavitate over the building waterfall, sending the boat backward over the drop. The low stern and heavy engines would drag the boat under if they hit first. A loud pop sounded as the prow slid past the ring and shot starboard. Aleks jammed the throttle, hoping to back out of the flow. Easily 40 percent of the boat was hanging in free space. Water was beginning to pour over the stern. No time for indecision. If it toppled now it would knife into the lake and sink. He dropped power, popped through neutral into forward, and hammered it again within a second. The forty-foot Hustler weighed almost twelve thousand pounds, but fifteen hundred horses gave it plenty of incentive. It launched itself through the hole, out into space. Aleks backed off the throttle and hung on as the boat dropped the ten feet to the lake's surface. *Boom.* Picture-perfect landing. His teeth rattled. He bounced off the throttle pod, deeply bruising his right thigh.

He shut down the motors and let the boat drift while he gathered himself. Silence. He looked astern. The hole, waterfall, night sky, and Pacific Ocean were all gone. All he could see behind him was a rippling lake bordered by a snow-capped mountain range. He slowly turned around. The mountains continued around the full loop. A couple of peaks stood out, toward what the compass said was westward. The GPS was blank. He was completely alone. He flipped on the bilge pump and sat down to think about what to do next.

One minute he was asleep—admittedly it had been a fitful sleep, but sleep nonetheless—and the next he was scrabbling around trying to keep his boat afloat. What the *hell* was that thing? By the look of the sky it was mid afternoon, maybe three o'clock. Feeble clouds, high and thin, drifted overhead. He looked at his watch: 2:27 a.m. *Son of a bitch!*

He looked down into the water. The green Pacific seawater that had come through the hole with him was dispersing into the lake. As it faded away the lake water cleared to crystal with a hint of blue. He could see the bottom. No idea how far down it was. The boat rocked gently in the small ripples that roamed the lake's surface. A school of small fish flashed by under the boat, darting left and right in search of whatever small fish searched for.

He got up and went to the fridge. He wasn't hungry, but his hands needed something to do while he thought through things. He opened the door and grabbed one of the sandwiches he had passed over at dinner. He pulled it out of the ziplock baggie, pulled the halves apart, and bit the corner off one of the triangles. He'd spent hours on the ham, slow-roasting it, basting, basting, basting. It was tender and juicy and rich with hints of molasses, brown sugar, and mustard. The cheddar was sharp and perfectly offset the taste and texture of the meat. And he still wasn't hungry. He spit the bite out into the lake, watching it sink slowly into the deep. A few seconds into its decent the school of fish came back. One or two snapped at the piece of sandwich, darting in for a nibble, then dashing back away again. But then something weird happened. The fish started darting in faster and faster. In seconds, the water was boiling as more and more fish fought to reach the sinking morsel.

At the edge of his consciousness, Aleks heard a new sound. One he hadn't heard in two days. A human voice. He turned, looking over the portside of the boat, to see a man jumping and waving his arms. The man was hollering something. His words carried the distance, but the boiling water drowned them out. Suddenly the noise stopped. He glanced at the school of fish, or at least the spot they had occupied. They were gone.

"*Get off the water!*"

The waving man's voice finally made sense. What a relief. The man looked even more animated than he had before, waving frantically and gesturing for Aleks to come toward him.

"*You must get off the water!*"

BOOMP. The boat shifted as something bumped up against it. Aleks looked down at a long, thin log that had thumped against the boat. It was black and slick from time spent in its watery grave and looked like no other wood he'd ever seen. It must have led a hard life. It was warped and had been twisted by wind and storms. The far end dipped down into the water at a fairly sharp angle. It extended under the boat and connected to a roiling mass of other logs and a huge eye. An iris, slit like a triangle, opened wide as his shadow covered it. He dropped back into the driver's seat, and for the second time in two hours he prayed the triples would start.

The log made a slurping sound as it lifted out of the water. The boat tipped as the log-tentacle slapped down on the gunnel. The Mercs cleared their throats. Aleks looked back to see the end of the tentacle split into sixths, blooming like a Satanic rose into a horror of hooks and barbs surrounding a wretched esophagus. He pounded the throttle forward. The boat lurched. His head snapped back and then forward. He turned back to see that a second tentacle had joined the first from the other side of the boat. Both were hanging deep into the stern of the boat, holding it in place. Well, technically speaking they were being dragged by the boat, but either way it was bad. Aleks cranked the wheel. The Hustler rolled to starboard in response. The big port screw lifted, biting into the tentacle on that side of the boat. Both tentacles jerked up and over, back into the water with syncopated slaps. The boat leaped to attention. Thirty, forty, fifty knots. Behind him a dark shape gave pursuit. It slowly fell behind.

The waving man was at least half a mile away, but the Hustler closed the gap in a hurry. He was fairly confident of his escape, so he took the time to make a pass near the shore to check out the beach before he turned straight in and slowed to a crawl, driving the big boat onto the sand and pebbles. They'd play havoc with his clearcoat, but it was better than getting out into the water and swimming to shore. New clearcoat—new fiberglass, for that matter—was a hell of a lot cheaper than a new set of arms or legs.

At the last second he shut down the motors and lifted the drives to protect them from the ground.

The man on the shore continued to flail about during the procedure. He rushed over when the boat came to a rest. It was tipped steeply to port and Aleks had to climb down from the seat to get out. He dropped to the sand and scampered away from the water line as the other man approached.

He was an odd-looking, cadaverous man in a ragged, loose-fitting gray shirt and torn up gray leggings. He looked like a bundle of sticks, tied together and covered with not quite enough skin, stretched tight to make a good seal.

"We should be all right here," the man said when he got close enough to talk with Aleks. "The Kraken can't come close enough to shore to reach this far or the crabsters will get her. They can't kill her, of course, but they can tear up her outer layers pretty quickly, if she gets too close." He stuck out his nearly meatless hand as a gesture of good will. "I'm Donte. Jesik sent me to get you."

Aleks hesitated and then wrapped his hand around the "loose sticks" but found they were callused and strong. The hands of a working man. The grip was nearly painful at first but loosened as the man pumped his arm.

"Mister, I appreciate your getting me off the lake and all, but I don't know Jesik from Adam and I sure as hell don't know you." He turned in a circle. "Shit, I don't even know where in the hell I am, for that matter."

Donte furrowed his brow for a few seconds before responding. "You are Aleksander Volovniev, aren't you?"

Aleks took a small step back from the man. "How do you know my name?"

"As I said, Jesik sent me to retrieve you." The man looked down, and almost to himself, said, "Of course, he couldn't tell me exactly *when* you'd be here, so I've been waiting for quite a while. But, no matter." He looked up and grinned. It was a dead-rock-star-junky grin. Too many and too-large teeth, lips too thin and drawn back too far. Horrifying. "We should get moving."

With that he turned and crunched off through the stiff, dry sand toward a grassy hillside that edged the beach. Aleks looked back at the boat once and then quickly around the lake. Not a soul in sight. It would appear that if he wanted answers, he'd have to follow the old man. He turned around and followed.

As he crested the hill the trees whose tops he had been seeing all along loomed up before him, large and ancient and mysterious. They reached skyward, great, leafless, gray-green claws on monstrous, gnarled trunks. They seemed poised to snatch any would-be Icarus from the sky. Even across a mile-wide sea of low scrub bushes, they were ominous. He could almost hear them breathing.

Donte led Aleks out into the scrub, along a game trail that meandered back and forth. The bushes were unfamiliar, with burgundy heart-shaped leaves and long, needle-sharp thorns. His jeans were snagged more than once by the vicious little buggers. Each time he was rewarded with a poke or scratch on his ankles.

"Mind the cotie." Donte tossed the comment back over his shoulder as he trudged ahead. "They're not really dangerous, but they have a light poison that itches like mad."

Great, now he tells me.

Aleks started focusing more on the placement of each step. It was almost a relief to look down instead of at the oppressive woods in the distance. They traveled on in silence for quite some time. Aleks looked back across the sea of bushes. It was at least a mile to the hill they had climbed up from the lakeside. Ahead was a similar distance to the woods. They seemed to have gotten no closer. A wave of despair swept over him as he looked at the trees.

What the hell is going on? Where am I and how did I get here? What am I going to do? "Aaauuggggghhh! Dammit!"

Aleks looked down at a long branch that was wrapped completely around his left ankle. The thorns bit deep, through his jeans, digging a long furrow across his shin.

"Are you all right?" Donte asked, stepping back toward Aleks.

"These damn bushes keep scratching my legs. Ow!" Aleks was trying to peel the unruly tendril from his pant leg without drawing new blood. "Damn!" As the plant came away from his leg, he stepped away and let the branch snap back. It swayed briefly, a floral cobra, lying in wait for a new victim. Aleks slowly rolled up his pant leg, revealing dozens of short scratches, marked by angry, red welts. The highest scratches were the longest: six ugly rips running across his shins. They were just beginning to swell. The itching started almost as soon as he saw the welts.

Donte grabbed Aleks's wrist. Aleks had subconsciously reached down to scratch at the newly raging itch. Donte's hand was slightly loose and disjointed, like a bag of marbles, but his grip was incredible. Aleks felt the bones of his wrist painfully come together under the pressure of Donte's bony fingers.

"You don't want to scratch those, my friend," Donte said with a cadaverous grin. His face turned serious. With sunken eyes and sallow cheeks, it looked more serious than most. "They could get infected. I'm not that good a healer." He let go of Aleks's hand. Kneeling in the spongy soil of the game trail, Donte gently placed a hand on each of Aleks's ankles. He closed his eyes and concentrated.

Aleks could feel Donte's hands getting colder. Like milk into tea, the cold flowed from Donte into Aleks. Aleks moaned and closed his eyes. He was repulsed but couldn't raise a finger. His bones ached. He shivered uncontrollably. He suddenly knew what his grave would feel like. He wanted to scream, "What the hell are you doing to me?" but could only manage that one soft moan. Then it was over.

Donte stood up. Aleks wanted to grab him and demand to know what he had done, what was going on, who the hell he was, and what this place was. Instead he stood there and concentrated on not falling onto the thorny bushes. Slowly his energy returned. He began to feel revitalized. He looked down at his wounded ankles. Instead of angry red welts, he saw tiny pink scars. He knelt and looked more closely at his leg, rubbing his fingertips across the wounds. They felt like any of the other hundred-odd scars he had.

"How'd you do that?" he asked.

"Do what?" Donte replied. His face flushed and his eyebrows came together.

"Heal my leg!" Aleks stared at it in amazement. "How'd you do it?"

Relief spread across Donte's face. "I don't know the technical term for it. It's just the way I've always done it." Donte glanced down at Aleks's leg. "I didn't mean any harm. Since you didn't heal it yourself, I assumed you were an Activator." He rubbed his hands together. "I just tapped your Touch and healed your leg as best I could. I didn't mean any harm, sir."

Aleks looked up at Donte's abashed face. "You *healed* me."

"Yes?" Confusion was written across Donte's face. "It seemed like the right thing to do. Was it terribly wrong of me to be so presumptuous? I'm sorry ..."

"What? No, you didn't do anything wrong ... I just don't understand what happened." Aleks stood up but continued to look at his leg.

Suddenly, Donte's face cleared. "You're not from here."

"Apparently." *And thank you for stating the obvious.*

"We'd better get moving again," Donte glanced nervously at the horizon. "We need to be inside before the lopers come out."

Donte was so agitated that Aleks decided to not to ask any more questions. He could wait until they were at Donte's cabin to find out what a loper was. "Lead on."

Donte nodded, turned, and headed out at a brisk pace. Aleks glanced briefly at the man's feet to see how he avoided injury. He moved with an odd cadence. His stride was not consistent. His foot placement was strange. In some cases, he put his foot down almost within a plant. In other cases, he avoided a clear spot. Aleks gave up trying to figure out the pattern and set off after Donte, trying to step only where Donte stepped.

Now that he was paying more attention to his feet, something caught his eye. The branches moved in odd ways. A light breeze blew from left to right across his face. As he stepped, the branches moved toward his leg, *against the wind.*

"Donte, can you hold up for a second?"

"Hmm?"

"I want to look at these bushes."

"I don't think …" Donte began, looking back over his shoulder.

Aleks, having stopped in a wide space on the trail, crouched down. He peered at those branches nearest his feet. The branches waved back and forth, as any would in a gentle breeze. As he watched, the branches inched in toward his legs. The plants must be meat eaters, just like a Venus flytrap.

"We really need to keep moving." Donte looked around with concern. "The lopers will be out soon." He edged further along the trail. Aleks reluctantly gave up on his study of the plants and followed.

Eeeeeeiiiiiiiyiyiyiyiyiyieeeeeee.

Aleks's skin crawled, trying to get away from the mournful wail. It sounded like a possessed mariachi band.

"Come on!" Donte yelled back over his shoulder. "We have to go now!"

Aleks started after him.

Eeeeeeiiiiiiiyiyiyiyiyiyieeeeeee.

A second wail pierced the air, closer than the first. Aleks moved faster. Running now, his breathing settled into that rhythmic runner's chuff. He watched his feet to make sure he didn't step into a gopher hole. If this place even had gophers. It probably did, but they would be mutant gorilla gophers from hell, with monstrous fangs dripping with venom.

He was jogging along thinking these strange thoughts when he looked up to check on Donte's progress. Donte was already a football field away and running as hard as he could.

Must be pretty serious.

Something on the horizon caught his eye. A shadow against the sunset. It was long and thick. Coming toward him. And moving fast. *Incredibly fast. "Holy shit" fast.*

Aleks ran. He ran as fast as he had ever run in his life. The bushes flew by. The gap between him and Donte started to shrink.

Up ahead the trees were finally getting closer. He could see, nestled against them, a small house or shack.

He glanced back. Glowing orange against the darkness, malevolent eyes tracked him. The thing was coming fast. Damn, it was *fast.* Two hundred yards to the house. Would he make it? One seventy-five. It was closer now. Nope. Wouldn't make it. Almost feeling breath on his back. Don't look. Count six, 125 yards. Five. Pump your arms. Four. Breathe. Three. Jump the bush. Two. Seventy-five yards. One. Dive!

A massive snap of teeth cracked over his shoulder as he flew sideways over the bushes. He tucked down the shoulder he'd almost lost, rolling as he hit the ground. Ball up. Summersault. Back on his feet. Boom! He almost went down as the thing's tail slammed into his back.

He kept his balance and ran.

The creature didn't turn but ran on after Donte. Aleks ran after them both. What he'd do when he caught up to the monstrosity he had no idea. But instinct told him to get his hands on it.

It leaped. Donte went down under a pile of flesh, teeth, and claws. The thrashing bodies looked like boiling water.

Aleks reached them. It took him miserable seconds to see where to grab. All the while, a confused part of his mind was saying, *What the fuck are you doing?*

Despite the voice, he stood his ground. Suddenly, clarity settled over him. His hand darted out and snatched on to a monstrous claw that was dug into the ground. The creature's skin was lizard-like but covered in spines that bit into his palm. What abomination from hell was this?

The grab, the thought, and the pain lasted no more than an eye blink. The part of him that talked of grabbing the beast now told him to let go. Not of the beast, but of himself. Fear was remarkably absent. Or at least was screaming quietly to itself.

The crystal clarity told him to let go of the rational. Open his mind to the possible. Time stopped.

He closed his eyes. Shapes, images, geometric impossibilities flowed behind his eyelids. Flashing, blinding, wailing, the colors ran together, separated, and came together again.

In that infinite instant, life flowed from him, power, energy, love, hate in a whole body orgasm that turned him inside out. Time started again. In his hand he felt soft fur where the lizard skin had been. He opened his eyes. Donte was lying on his side, gasping for breath. It came in squishy, liquid wheezes that bubbled on his shattered chest. Tangled up with him, panting hard, was a giant black and brown dog.

Aleks did his best to pull the dog off of the fallen man. Donte murmured something. Aleks bent low over the man's face, to better hear.

"Run, *sleesh,* you fool, *sleesh,*" Donte squirted out through clenched teeth.

Eeeeeeiiiiiiiyiyiyiyiyiyieeeeeee.

More howls. Coming from three sides. Not the woods. Aleks turned in a quick circle. They were coming. Sixty yards to the house. He could just make it if he ran.

Instead, he stooped and picked up Donte.

"Aaaaagghh … *sleesh.*"

At least he was still breathing. Over Aleks's shoulder the light and boney bramble man went. Now he ran. Oh, how he ran.

Clarity was still there, shining through the fear.

It said to turn and stand, eyes closed, free hand outstretched. The creatures came. But so did the lights. He almost fell when the flood left him, like the greatest orgasm ever. Straight out through the palm of his hand. Time shattered. The mariachi voices moaned. Then whined. Then fell silent. Dead. He knew it without looking.

Opening his eyes, he found the bodies of five more dogs scattered around.

The same black and brown breed as the one he'd changed a few seconds earlier.

He turned and walked toward the house. He grew weaker as he neared it. Oh, so tired. Just put one foot in front of the other. He knew he couldn't take another onslaught if it came. Twenty-five yards.

Eeeeeeiiiiiiiyiyiyiyiyiyieeeeeee.

He put his head down and walked. Fifteen yards. Ten yards. It took everything he had to take that next step. Then he did it again. Five yards.

Eeeeeeiiiiiiiyiyiyiyiyiyieeeeeee.

Closer.

His feet scuffed along the ground. His breath came in ragged bursts, chuffing out great clouds of steam in the chilling air.

Whump.

A massive weight slammed into him, smashing him to the ground, with Donte sprawled across his back. His air was gone. Like a caught fish, his mouth opened and closed spasmodically, but no air came in or out. The crushing weight shifted back and forth. Branches lashed out at his face. He thrashed his head. One daring branch flipped into his gaping mouth and latched onto the inside of his cheek with its inch-long thorns. Aleks jerked his head back at the sharp pain. But the branch was strong and the bush well rooted. It dug deeper into his cheek. He bit down. Hard. A coppery taste flooded his mouth. The branch came free but rabidly thrashed around inside his mouth. A thousand pinpricks landed in his cheeks, gums, and tongue.

He bit down again, trying to pin the little bastard until he could get it out. Pain started in all over his body. His legs and sides were being ripped and thrashed. The weight was pinning him nearly immobile in a field of man-eating daisies. Damn. He was going to die right here.

Suddenly the weight shifted off him. A great blast of air smashed the bushes flat around him. He sucked in a great, huge breath, ripped his arms free from the branches, tore the little bastard out of his mouth, and stood up. His pants shredded under the strain. He turned to look for Donte. A monstrous, six-legged leather vulture was flapping powerfully into the sky, dragging Donte with it.

Boom!

A giant arrow sprouted in the thing's chest, right between the first two legs. It threw its head back on an impossibly long neck and screamed. It flapped again.

Eeeeeeiiiiiiiyiyiyiyiyiyieeeeeee.

The loper's cry was different, more plaintive and moving away.

Boom! Another arrow. Donte fell. It was a short fall as these things go. No more than fifteen feet. But he fell like a rag doll, arms and legs flopping.

"Praise the Maker!" The voice came from behind Aleks. "Grab him! Quick!"

Aleks ran. He threw Donte's bag of bones over his shoulder and ran back to the house.

The voice that had called to him belonged to a slender blonde. "Get him inside." She pointed a wicked-looking crossbow at something in the distance.

Aleks stepped through the open doorway. The girl followed him into the house, slamming the door behind them.

"Good thing the palkin showed up." She put the weapon down by the door. "I don't think I could have hit one of the lopers from there. They're just too fast. Now let's see what we have."

She moved to the spot next to Aleks as he slid Donte to the floor. Aleks laid him on the only carpet in the main room of the small house. Not much larger than Donte, it served to cover the cracks between the ancient floorboards that were letting cool air into the room.

Wall sconces, holding three glowing stones spaced around the room, provided plenty of light.

Donte was even worse off than the last time Aleks had seen him. He now had a large piece of one cheek and most of his right hand missing. Blood was slowly easing out and pooling around various wounds. The one exception was his ravaged hand. The damage there was massive. Blood pumped freely from the wound.

Aleks ripped his belt off. The blonde woman stood up from her inspection of the dying man and moved quickly across the room. Aleks took her place, kneeling beside the torn limb. He looped his belt through the buckle and slipped it up Donte's arm, just past his wrist. He pulled the loop tight. The blood slowed immediately.

The woman was mumbling as she came back. "I knew he had a jar. I just hope he refilled … what are you doing?" She rushed over. "Get that thing off his arm. Do you want him to lose his hand?"

Aleks snapped back. "Better his hand than his life!"

She looked at him for the briefest of seconds. "What's your name?"

"Aleks." Without letting go of the tourniquet, he asked, "What's yours?"

All of the blood drained from her face. She knelt beside the wounded man. "Did you say Aleks?" Her voice was quiet.

"Yeah." He watched the hand to make sure the bleeding was controlled. "You should grab a towel and apply some pressure to his chest wound."

"Aleks …"

"Yes! Ah, that's got it. It's slowing down now."

"My lord!" She dropped to her knees. "If I had known it was you, I would never have been so impertinent."

He had moved from the arm to the chest wound.

"Please accept my apology, my lord. I meant no slight by my comments."

"Will you stop blathering and get another towel? We have to get this stopped or he'll bleed out." He finally looked at her; bowed head and hands clasped before her, she was pleading with him. "What are you doing?"

A tear rolled down her cheek. "My lord, please accept my apology. I did not know it was you. If you do not forgive me, all my struggles will be for naught." She shook her head and mumbled to herself. "Stop it, stop it, stop it … you'll ruin everything."

"Hey"—he turned from Donte, cupped her face in his hand, and turned it up, looking deeply into her hazel eyes. "It's okay. Donte is hurt very badly. I don't know if we can save him, but I'm doing my best. I'm not going to let him die without a fight. You haven't done anything wrong." She was younger than he had thought at first, maybe early twenties. And she looked like she had been traveling hard. Her clothes were worn and dirty. He had no time for such thoughts. He turned back to Donte.

"Thank you, my lord. I have heard tales of your great pity and kindness. I pray now that you extend them to me."

"What tales? What the hell are you talking about?"

"You, my lord, the Great Builder."

He took her by the elbows and raised her from her knees. "Look, I don't know what you're on, but right now we need to help Donte or he's going to die. So you gotta stop this nonsense and help me."

"Will you not simply raise him again?"

"What?" He looked at her for a few seconds before shaking his head. "You really are cracked, lady." He looked around the little one-room shack.

"Do you have a phone?" he asked.

"Fone?" she asked back, trying the word on like a new pair of shoes. "What is a fone?"

"A telephone! You know, telephone?" He mimicked holding a handset and dialing. He searched her face for recognition and found none. "Who the hell are you, Backwoods Betty? You've never heard of a phone?" He mimicked throwing it. Somehow that helped him feel a little better.

"I'm sorry, my lord. This is not my house. If Donte has such a thing, I do not know where it would be." She bowed her head in contrition.

Aleks took a deep breath and let it out very slowly. "Okay, no phone." He looked around the room. "What about a first-aid kit?"

"What is a first-aid kit, my lord?" She looked bewildered.

"Okay, knock that shit off! I've had enough games for one day."

"I beg your pardon, my lord. I meant no offense and play at no games. I thought perhaps it was you who was jesting. Why do you not simply heal him and be done with it?"

"How am I supposed to do that with no supplies at all?"

"Why do you not simply lay hands on him?" She looked closely at him, doubt flickering behind her eyes. Suddenly a dawning realization made her face glow.

"Oh, I understand!" She grabbed his hand. "You turned the lopers! You must be exhausted." She walked over to Donte and laid a hand on his side. She held her other hand in front of her, open and palm up. Resting in the center of her hand was a small figurine, shaped like a crude bear. It started vibrating, slowly at first, but picked up speed. Soon it was hard for Aleks to focus on it. It hummed and buzzed.

Aleks pulled his eyes from the figurine and watched the rest of the girl's ritual. The hand she had placed on Donte's chest slowly rose and fell with each of his bubbling breaths. Soon the bubbling stopped.

Through closed eyes, she spoke to Aleks. "The jar was full, but he's really hurt bad. I can't do much more than stop him from dying." She turned and looked at Aleks. "What about you? Do you have any Touch left in there?"

"What are you talking about?" He guessed she meant the weird way

Donte had healed him earlier. She appeared to be doing the same sort of thing to Donte.

"Please stop playing games," she begged. "He needs help right now! Could you please stop wasting time so he can stop suffering and either live or die. Please."

Her crying cut through Aleks's confusion and forced him to put aside his logical mind. He let go of his preconceived notions of reality and opened up to the possibility that he could do something about Donte's injuries. He relived that moment of healing. It seemed an eternity ago. Closing his eyes, he sought the energy, the life force—whatever it was that had filled him up. He found it soon enough, once he'd started looking. It was a lake in his mind, cool and clear.

"Maybe I can help." He reached out his hand and took hers. The bear was warm against his palm. In his mind he dipped his free hand into the lake and gently dribbled the water over their clasped hands. He felt a small and subtle release. It was the lift-off of a midnight moth compared to the body-gasm he'd had with the lopers. In his mind, he put a hose in the lake. Attached to the hose was a large valve. Aleks spun the valve open.

"Unnnnnh … too much. Too much, *too much! Aaaaagh!*" She lurched to her feet, stumbled to her left, and crumpled to the floor against the rough-cut wall.

Aleks rushed over. She was still breathing but unresponsive. He turned back to the higher urgency victim. He felt that strong urging again: *touch him.*

Almost against his own will he reached out his hand, just as the girl had. This time when he opened the valve he did it slowly, gently, allowing only a small trickle to pass into Donte. Closing his eyes, he followed his instincts. In his mind, he flowed with the Touch into Donte's ravaged form. Carrying him through skin, muscle, and bone, the Touch was now a vehicle. He moved through Donte, seeking smooth passage. Wounds were barriers, stopping his flow. He closed them. Bruises were swamps, bogging him down. He drained them. Broken bones were fallen bridges. He rebuilt them. Ruptured organs, crushed and pulpy, were collapsed houses. He raised them.

He had no clue how he accomplished these things. But like breathing, he didn't need to know how it worked in order to do it. Soon he was moving freely forward and back along each sinew, nerve, and fiber. At last, Aleks moved on to Donte's brain.

The structure was damaged. Like a city after a raging fire, some parts were intact but others were severely damaged. Aleks moved through the damaged areas, stabilizing the structure, repairing the damage, easing the flow of blood. He set things right. Soon it felt healthy. Blood flowed smoothly. Donte was whole once again.

Aleks withdrew, pulling back into himself. The room tilted at an odd angle. A bright flash of pain blasted through his face. The floor was cold against his cheek. He lay there for a few seconds. Breathe in. Breathe out.

Seconds passed. The room rolled relentlessly back and forth. Behind his eyes he felt a pressure building, like his head was too small for all that it contained. His eyes watered. Breathe in. Breathe out. More seconds passed.

In time—he never knew how much—the room slowed. It didn't stop, but he felt like he could roll over onto his knees without falling off the ground. He stayed on hands and knees for a few seconds, fighting the urge to throw up with everything he had. He lost. His one consolation was that he turned away from Donte before he let fly. When he was done, he wiped his mouth with the back of his hand. Breathe in. Breathe out. Seconds passed.

He turned back to Donte. The man's clothes were a tattered mess. But his color was better and he was breathing easily. Aleks crawled. Tremors ran up and down his thighs. His head started pounding. But he crawled. Around Donte, he made his way with deliberate slowness over to the girl.

She was lying on her side near a pool of vomit. Aleks carefully raised her head. Her eyes were open, glassy, lifeless. As her hair fell away from her face, he could see a small trickle of blood leaking from her ear. He gently laid her down on her back. Once again he grabbed Nirvana. This time when it came, it was noticeably weaker. The well was almost dry. As with all other aspects of the bizarre ritual, his instinct talked to him: *don't use it all.*

He didn't know what would happen if he did, but he knew it would be bad. He followed the flow of life into the girl.

She had a completely different feel than Donte. It was like writing with his left hand. He moved into her brain.

He almost lost control when he felt the damage. Donte's brain had been crushed in places and torn in others. This girl's brain was devastated. Everywhere throughout the brain, large patches of flesh were pulped. One huge section was completely missing. For the first time since his arrival in this place, Aleks felt despair. How was she even alive?

He put that aside and started in on the damage. He took the smallest wound first. He tried the technique he had used on Donte, not even sure what he was doing. But with Donte, the brain had been damaged but mostly intact. The framework had been there as a foundation for the repairs. Here there was nothing.

He went deeper, into the structure of her brain. Laid out before him was a vast, interconnected civilization. It reminded him of a photo he'd seen as a child. Taken from space, it was a picture of Los Angeles at night, tiny lines running everywhere. Only this time they were dark. He still could not see a pathway to healing. He went deeper still, into the very cells of her brain. There! A strand of DNA.

The only thing Aleks knew about DNA was how to spell it. And that was from watching *CSI*. But he was driving by instinct here. He grabbed on to the DNA and looked at it. Like a giant blueprint, it opened before him, revealing who this girl was. No. It was revealing who this girl could have been. Here in the blueprint of her body he found what he needed. He didn't understand it, but he could feel it.

He went to work. Very slowly, painstakingly slowly, he reassembled her brain. He drew upon the pulped tissue for raw materials and built a foundation. He laid down piece after piece. It was taking too long. Already on the edge, Aleks knew he would pass out from exhaustion long before he could put all this damage right. He paused in his work. He knew the building blocks were there. This brain was a powerful machine. It could work wonders. Maybe it could do some of this work for him.

He focused on a small area of damage. He drew material into contact with it and coaxed the nearby cells to absorb it, extend it into the free space, match it to the blueprint, and rebuild itself. Slowly at first, but with increasing speed, her brain began to heal itself. Aleks pulled himself back and watched as the greatest machine ever made went to work.

The structure began to reform. He watched and coaxed for a time. Then, as her brain learned its business, he just watched. Eventually it was done.

As he pulled himself back from her, he gasped in pain. His strength gave out. He collapsed face-first into her spew. Unable to raise himself from the stinking mess, he moaned. Darkness closed over him.

Battle Testing

Swick, chunk. The weapon bit deep into the wood. Its wielder jerked it free and brought it back for another swing. *Swick, chunk.* The blade slid even deeper into the small block of wood, cracking the bonds that held the block together. It split in two, each half spinning off in a lazy arc. Tony bent and picked up another block of wood from a nearby pile. The wood was some kind of pine, soft and filled with knots. It had taken nearly a day to take the tree down, trim the branches, and chop the trunk into sections for splitting. The hard physical work had kept him busy while the others tended to Micah.

While he worked, he thought back over the previous evening. The frantic trip and horrific battle behind them, the evening had taken on a distinctly dark tone. Jesik took a few minutes to welcome him and show him the kitchen, sleeping chamber, and bathroom and then rushed back to help with the boy.

Tony had followed at first, but standing and watching the mysterious Touch-based healing was not only unenlightening, but also oppressive. The hardest part wasn't his ignorance; it was the knowledge that he could do nothing to help. Uncomfortable, confused, and frustrated, he had decided to make better use of his time. He'd stomped off to the kitchen in search of food. Pickings were slim, but he'd found part of a large loaf of bread and some hard cheese. His stomach filled in a surprisingly short time.

After his makeshift meal he headed off to his chamber to catch some sleep. The long day full of shocks had left him drained. He hadn't bothered looking the room over. Instead, he walked directly to the bed, a thin mattress resting on a stone pedestal. It was surprisingly comfortable. He'd slept hard, and short.

Now, nearly another full day behind him, he had a large pile of wood waiting to be split and stacked. He paused for a minute to wipe his brow and catch his breath. Putting his foot on the stump of the tree, he started to lean on his tool of choice. He changed his mind as he glanced again at the odd weapon.

There was no doubt this was a weapon rather than a working tool. But even that use seemed unlikely. Not only was the blade poorly shaped, but it wasn't particularly sharp. And his early attempts to sharpen it had proven fruitless. In fact, his whetstone had had absolutely no effect on the black substance the axe was formed from. Like the road, it was somewhat metallic. But beyond that it was unlike any metal he had ever seen. It was impossibly hard but felt like plastic in his hands. It weighed next to nothing. In fact, that was part of the problem with the thing. Unlike a normal axe, with some mass at the head to drive the blade into the wood, this thing required pure muscle power.

To go along with the odd material, the shape was even stranger. It more resembled a fancy letter T with serifs than anything else. Instead of an oval shaft wedged into a blade, the shaft of this wicked thing was a blade. If it weren't so dull, the only place it could be touched was its two-handed grip. The axe head was eighteen inches long and very narrow. In the last inch, it widened into a six-inch-long edge.

Instead of leaning on it, he chunked the weapon into the stump. He pulled off his John Deere cap and wiped his brow with his sleeve. He cast his eyes upon the horizon. His instinct, rarely wrong, told him he was looking west. He struggled with the concept. The sun was sinking slowly at his back. He entertained, for the barest of moments, a heartfelt desperation.

Suddenly, despite his recent efforts and the warm sun on his back, Tony shivered. Something tickled—

He's coming

—at his mind. It was just past the edge of his perception, like a mouse scratching in the walls. A scent briefly snatched, unrecognized, that passed on the wind. No scent, this, but sour nonetheless. The feeling itched—

All will burn

—at the back of his mind.

"That's a pretty rude use of such a powerful weapon."

Tony jumped at Jesik's comment. He turned to see the man's tall, thin form striding up the hill.

"After using it all day, I'd guess it was more ornamental than powerful," Tony replied.

"Oh no. This is a very special weapon." Jesik pulled the axe from the stump and looked it over. "She was made more than four thousand years ago by a very powerful Templar named Kitarni for Citula Marn, queen of Banta. Her name is K'tichnam. Oh, she's strong-willed. In fact, she'll only work for the most controlled minds. And she's a wicked vixen. If you're a man, she's as likely to hit you as your intended target. But …" He raised the axe over his head with his left hand. "If you've got a small bit of Touch to feed her and the strength of mind to guide her …" Ornate patterns started glowing all along the blade and head of the axe. Suddenly, a horrific, keening wail ripped the air. Tony grabbed his ears as he was rattled to the very fiber of his being. The axe made a white-red arc. The ground shuddered with the blow. The stump split and spread, ripping roots and great clods from the ground. As abruptly as it started, the wailing went silent. The sudden cessation of sound was almost deafening in itself.

"She can do terrible things."

Tony stared in utter disbelief at the now quiescent axe.

"Very few men can stand against a woman wielding this weapon."

Tony suddenly shivered. For the second time in as many days, a tingling rose between his shoulder blades. He felt the hair on the back of his neck stand up again. Something unpleasant was happening somewhere nearby.

Unwilling to comply but unable to resist, he turned back toward the house. His eyesight was good, possibly great, and yet the house was a matchbox in the distance. How far away? Two, maybe three miles? He knew he could huff it back there easily, even after the morning's exertions. But could he get there in time?

In time for what? Battle. How he knew, he had no idea. But he knew. Someone was fighting.

Then he saw them. Four small dots defied gravity over the house. More like butterflies than birds, they bobbed and weaved in the air.

Tony snatched the axe from Jesik and started running. As he ran, his stride lengthened. Somehow he knew that his usual loping run wouldn't be enough. His pace quickened. Within a few strides, he was sprinting full out. His eyes shifted frequently from the ground ahead to the dots over the house. Their movement slowed to a crawl.

The rough terrain made his sprint dangerous. Stepping in a gopher or snake hole would break his ankle. He sprinted anyway. His feet dragged through the small, scrabbly bushes that dotted the stretch of land sloping up from Jesik's house, each impact sparking a fresh explosion of seed-pods, sticks, and insects.

As he closed on the scene, he began making out the shapes of the creatures flying over the house. They were the size of small elephants, with long, sinuous necks and tails. Four massive legs dangled beneath, and impossibly large bat wings flapped up and down in giant, lazy, arcing sweeps. The body of each beast bobbed up and down with the wing beats, giving them crazed butterfly movements. Their tails ended in a massive ball, spiked with horns or ridges. Their heads were great flat wedges with four eyes and horns on top. Two smaller arms sprouted at the base of the neck. Mounted on each beast was a pair of figures. Tiny compared to the massive creatures, they wore the same robes as the ambush party from the day before.

Tony had never run this far or this fast before, but somehow he had the energy to keep going. He also had the weird sensation that everything around him was moving in slow motion.

Bam. Something slammed into his psyche.

He stumbled but caught himself. He felt a sharp pain. Not physical but emotional pain. He could feel the battle. Someone had died. Someone close. Someone he knew. He ran faster.

Bam. This time he was better prepared, not missing a step. He was closing on the house. The front door opened and a robed figure emerged. It slowly loped across the grass to a waiting beast. The robed creature handed a bundle to the beast and crawled up its leg to its back. The two small arms on the beast cradled the bundle against its chest.

Tony didn't break stride when leaping the hedge, he simply stretched his leg over it.

The monster spread its massive wings and gave a powerful, slow-motion down stroke that drove it and its riders into the air.

Two steps, a stride onto the wagon, and a leap into the air and Tony swept the axe in a great arc. The beast's snake-like neck flowed into a long curve.

Its head ponderously twisted toward the new threat. The head was four feet across. It split into a massive mouth with hundreds of shark teeth.

Tony's leap was long. Very long. But not long enough. He was going to pass below the beast. He stretched up with all of his reach. The robed figures clutched at their heads as K'tichnam's scream assaulted them. K'tichnam was just long enough. She shuddered as she bit into the neck. The giant mouth snapped once as the head spun away. The beast's body thrashed, and all its limbs flung out at full extension. The bundle fell free.

Tony rolled with his landing, set his feet, and leaped back under the plummeting body, snatching the bundle out of harm's way. The ground shook with the beast's impact. Both passengers were crushed.

Tony looked at the bundle. Micah lay in his arms, wrapped in a blanket. He was limp, flushed, and covered in sweat. A shriek from the sky echoed off the distant hillside, drawing his attention skyward.

The remaining beasts, five in all, had been departing. They began circling back. The closest opened its mouth and repeated the cry. It was just how he imagined a harpy would sound. He guessed that he just had time to lay the boy down by the house before they would get there. He laid the boy by the door and darted back to the monsters.

He didn't recall dropping the mystical weapon, but K'tichnam was no longer in his hand. He scanned the field and spied her handle poking out from beneath the beast's body. He grabbed at it, but the weight holding it down was immense. For the second time in as many minutes, he let his Touch flow into the weapon. It sliced effortlessly through the beast's tough hide and came free.

He turned to see one of the riders throw a cloaked arm forward. Fire flared out of the sleeve. It streaked toward him, like a flamethrower. On instinct, he raised his hand. The flame splashed away on all sides, starting small fires on the sandy soil. His hand was warm but unharmed. He had no time to wonder about it, though. The creatures were on him.

For a time, all he knew was dodge, parry, and attack. K'tichnam was marvelous, hacking with ease through beastly limbs, necks, and riders. Neither teeth, claws, nor spiked tails could touch him. Flames, ice, water, and air all pounded at him. Each was turned aside.

At some point during the battle Jesik joined him, tossing small crystals at the creatures. One exploded on impact, blowing off the riders and a chunk of the beast. One opened into a ring. Through the ring, Tony could see a boiling mass of bright red. The beast, unable to stop, flew through it into whatever lay beyond.

Suddenly, only one beast remained. It flapped and bobbed just out of Tony's reach. Frustrated, he flooded the axe with power and threw it at the beast's chest. Glowing white-hot, the axe punched through both the beast and the riders. The ground shook with a final tremor as the trio collapsed in a heap.

Like a boomerang, the axe spun slowly in a wide circle, coming right back to him. As he watched the axe, that weird slow motion feeling was still there, as strong as ever. K'tichnam's handle still glowed lightly as it slowly rotated toward him. He snatched it from the air.

Tony looked at the mass of ruined flesh around him. This was going to be a large cleanup project. He turned back toward Jesik. Tony felt a jarring shift in reality when he saw Jesik move. While Tony was watching, Jesik accelerated. He moved from the odd, slow-motion gait he had been using for the entire battle to a more normal running stride. Jesik rushed to the bundle, scooping it up. He looked very intensely at the child in his arms for a moment or two and then moved quickly to the door of the house. Tony followed, dreading what they would find inside.

Cleanup Crew

Martin pulled his leg over the pommel and slid down to the ground with a graceless thump. He needed some time out of the saddle to soothe his aching pride. Or he would have, if he had any pride left. After all his failures over the last few months, pride was one of the things he had in least supply.

Thinking about his failures always brought back the images from the last time he'd seen Amy, hanging upside down from the seatbelt of their little Honda, with her head at an awkward angle and her blonde hair fanned out in a pool of her own blood. Her eyes had been open and staring. He could see the accusation in them.

You didn't save me, did you, you fat, lazy pig? If you'd been a real *man, I'd be alive right now.*

As true as the sentiment might be, it wasn't fair at all. Amy had never been mean. She'd always been sweet. He did her a disservice imagining those thoughts in her kind mind. But then again, what could you expect from a loser like him?

He grabbed his belt loops and hitched up his pants. He could continue to call himself a fat pig, but in the months that he'd been on Freia, his pants had gotten much looser. Despite their slipping down all the time, he still preferred to wear the Wrangler jeans and Black Sabbath T-shirt he'd come over in whenever he could. Jesik had provided some local pants and shirts, cut down a few inches to fit Martin's smaller stature. But the fabric wasn't substantial enough for him and the wrap-around, parachute style didn't appeal to him at all.

He really should have been more appreciative of the things Jesik had offered him. Jesik and Raneal had been very kind to him since he'd arrived, offering him clothes, food, and a place to stay. Jesik had spent hours in conversation with him, his tiny, round glasses bobbing up and down and his blue eyes shining as he got animated about some topic or another. He was definitely a funny duck. Jesik was just over six feet tall with a full beard, handlebar mustache, and long blond hair pulled back into a ponytail. He talked with equal passion and abandon about the science of Freia, the Prophecies, and Crunch, a game similar to chess but included an additional row of pieces that made it hell to follow.

And Raneal—sweet, sweet Raneal. She was curvy and strong and stood nearly eye-to-eye with Martin. She had long, raven hair and dark eyes rimmed in blue. She was smart and funny. But her most endearing trait was that she would crawl through a hundred yards of barbed wire to help a hurt child.

And she saw something in him he couldn't see. Not only did she not turn away from him in disgust, but she actually wanted to be around him. No. She didn't just want to be around him. She wanted to be *with* him. She wanted him to love her like she loved him. Screwed up as *that* was. Her love almost made him think he wasn't a complete loser. Or a monster. Almost.

But he knew at the core of his being that he was unworthy of that love. He was an abject failure. A loser. A monster. He had survived the car wreck that killed Amy and was brought to this planet for only one purpose. It wasn't because he was a nice man with a good heart. It was because he could summon the power of Freia like no one else. Ever. He had survived the wreck and been brought here because he could kill like no one had ever been able to kill. He could kill the Dark One. At least that's what the Prophecy Jesik always harped on about said.

Most people tapped into Freia's power like someone in wool socks storing up a static charge to zap their friends. He didn't store Touch. He just tapped directly into Freia, like plugging a blender into a nuclear power plant. And he controlled it just about as well as that, with equally messy results. When it worked at all. Athon had died waiting for him to get plugged in. And the Dark One had just laughed when Martin had tried to avoid global bloodshed and kill the Dark One directly. With Athon, the flood had come late, but it had come. With the Dark One, he'd had performance anxiety. The flood never came at all.

His time with the Dark One was something of a blur. It had started pleasantly enough, after the terrifying fall from the cliff side and the wet climb up to the balcony. He'd had a lovely meal and an interesting conversation with the Dark One. Not long after that everything sort of fogged out. He remembered being horrified at something he'd seen. And feeling an almost unbearable urge to flee. He remembered a vast sea of creatures that made his bowels shake.

And he remembered body parts. Lots of body parts.

But he couldn't put any of these things into context. His already traumatized psyche simply couldn't rationalize it.

There was one thing he did know for sure. He'd failed. He'd gone to the castle to confront the Dark One and end this battle before those thousands of people got killed. But he couldn't manifest his Touch. He remembered trying to call it up. But it wouldn't come. And now that he thought about it, he even recalled the Dark One offering to stand completely still and let Martin blast away at him. But Martin couldn't do it. He was a failure. The Dark One would sweep down from the north. And Jesik's pet murderer had let it happen.

And now he was standing on the side of the road that would take him back to Jesik's house, back to Raneal. Back to her beautiful, loving, misguided eyes.

Her eyes were open and her hair was fanned out in a pool of blood.

The memory came and went in a flash. Those painful memories had been coming for months now. And they still held the same pain he'd felt when they were being made. They were like tearing a scab off his heart.

And they were a reminder that he was unworthy of anyone's love, let alone someone like Raneal. She just didn't know him well enough to understand that.

He knew that she, like Jesik, was ancient by even Freian standards. From what they'd said over the last few months he'd guess them to be more than four hundred years old. But even that kind of age and experience didn't make a person infallible. She loved him and she was wrong to do it. He couldn't return her love. He was broken and confused and lost in a world that was not his own. And so very alone.

Martin decided that his internal conversation wasn't getting him anywhere, so he climbed back into the saddle, turned his horse toward Jesik's house, and started her walking. It took him most of an hour to get to the crest of the low hill that ran in front of Jesik's house. What he saw when he crested the hill nearly stopped his heart. There were monstrous bodies strewn across the yard. He feared the worst and kicked the horse into a gallop toward the mess. But as he got closer, he saw that none of his friends were among the dead, so he slowed her down to a trot.

He wasn't a skilled enough horseman to take the mare over the small picket fence that bordered the road in front of Jesik's place, so he guided her down the large circular driveway, slipped from the saddle again, and swatted the mare on her flank. She trotted across the drive and through the open barn door, heading back to her stall and the food in her manger. Martin watched her go and then turned and cautiously made his way into the carnage. It looked like flying beasts—the Dark One had called them *palkin*—and cloaked humanoids had been chopped up and tossed in a grisly salad.

A low moaning came from underneath one of the dead palkin. Martin looked around the grassy yard that was covered in gore and death. Some distance away he saw one of the giant beasts, its neck bent unnaturally below the body, resting atop its rider. The palkin rider's torso, head, and left arm were visible beneath the right center leg of the steed.

The rider was a lost cause. While technically not dead yet, it soon would be, crushed as it was by the mass of the palkin lying on top of it. Touch or not, the rider could not have been saved.

Yet, as was Martin's way, he bent near to comfort the dying thing. He recoiled for just a few seconds as he pulled the rider's cloak back. Suddenly exposed to the sun, the puffy white face squinted its four beady red eyes. The eyes weren't bloodshot but instead had great round irises the color of blood. In the center of each was a black slit, cut vertically across the eye. The creature opened its mouth and dragged in a short, ragged breath. It began pleading for mercy. Its voice was odd. Somehow it was both baritone and soprano. Not like a highly flexible voice, traveling the range of sound, but like a two-part harmony.

"Please," the odd voice twittered and rumbled, "please help me. It hurts … it hurts …" The creature raised an arm toward Martin. It was bent awkwardly between the wrist and elbow. Compassion welled within him. He gently took the creature's hand. It moaned at the contact.

"Stand up and slowly turn around!"

The booming voice nearly unhinged Martin. The rider wailed as Martin jumped at the sound. He gently released the rider's hand. Looking down at the creature, he slowly stood.

Her hair was fanned out below her, draped in a pool of blood.

He crushed his eyes closed, as if that could hide the hideous image he had seen once and a hundred times. He turned with his eyes still closed and a low moan in his throat, once again praying for control of the savage memories. He stood completely still for several seconds.

"Let me see your hands!"

He opened his eyes. What they brought him was surreal. In a world of monsters and magic, a tall, skinny cowboy didn't fit. This one, decked out in a Pendleton shirt, Levi's, and cowboy boots had a huge pistol in each hand. The left one, black as night, was pointed at the ground. The right one, shining silver in the sun, was pointed at Martin's head. He stood perfectly still, waiting for this new delusion to pass.

"I said show me your hands!" the cowboy repeated, not disappearing in the least. As Martin lifted his hands, Jesik appeared in the doorway of his cabin. He hustled over to the cowboy. He talked rapidly and motioned several times toward Martin. The tall man lowered his weapon but kept a steely eye on Martin. Jesik, with a pained look on his face, walked slowly toward him, hand outstretched.

"Hello, Martin. It's very good to see you, even in this sad time." He took Martin's hand. Still shaking Jesik's hand, Martin looked down at the palkin rider.

Her hair was fanned out below her, draped in a pool of blood.

"What happened here?" Martin asked.

"These palkin were sent to attack us and take Micah to the Dark One." Jesik pointed at the mass of torn flesh in the yard. "This is Tony. He fought and killed these beasts."

Tony, his guns now holstered, came up beside Jesik and extended a long-fingered hand. His grip was firm. His hands were bloodstained.

"Unfortunately, we were away when they first attacked. Jakub and Beka were killed." Jesik looked at the ground.

"Jakub and Beka are dead?" Martin asked. He closed his eyes against the sudden pain of this new loss.

Her hair was fanned out below her, draped in a pool of blood.

"They were good people." Martin swallowed hard.

Jesik swallowed as well as he looked back up at Martin. "Dinaala and Raneal were badly hurt too, but we got to them in time. They're inside, resting."

Martin immediately turned toward the house. "Raneal's hurt? How bad is it?" He moved to go to her, but Jesik put a hand on his arm. "She's all right, Martin. She's resting right now. If you go to her at this moment, you'll just keep her from getting the rest she needs."

Martin looked at Jesik, indecision written across his face. Jesik continued. "Please, Martin. Let her rest. You can see her when we're done out here."

Martin swallowed back the retort that popped into his mind. Jesik was worried about his sister. He hadn't caused any of this. Martin did. By going off on his fool's errand, against the advice of everyone, he'd left Raneal, Dinaala, Beka, and Jakub helpless. Now Beka and Jakub were dead, and Raneal and Dinaala were hurt. Good thing Jesik brought him over to help stop the Dark One and save lives. He was doing a bang-up job of it. More loss and pain for him to carry. What a loser.

"What can I do to help?"

"We must remove these corpses before they begin to stink and draw vermin," Jesik said, "and we need to prepare Jakub and Beka for burial."

The adventure novels that Martin favored always talked about the excitement of travel, the mysterious places, even the tragedy of loss, but they rarely showed the hard, nasty side of life. Clearing a hundred tons of crushed, bloody flesh from your front yard. Cleaning up the blood and gore inside your living room. Preparing your friends' bodies and burying them. His mind briefly, numbly touched on Amy. Who prepared her to be buried? Where was she buried?

Her eyes were open.

Martin angrily scrubbed a tear from his cheek. "What should we do with these bodies?" he asked.

Jesik paused for a moment before replying. "I think you should take care of them. It will give you a chance to practice your Touch. You weren't ready to face the Dark One, were you?" He held up his hand to cut off Martin's protestation. "I know you were trying to keep us safe. Going on your own was a foolish and dangerous thing to do, though, wasn't it? There is no question of your power. We all saw it in the Galorean Forest. But you still lack control."

He put his hand on Martin's shoulder and looked him in the eyes. "I know this is hard for you. I'm sorry it has to be this way. We have many dangers yet to face. Without you, all will be lost."

He lowered his hand and turned to Tony. "Jakub and Beka need to be seen to. Will you help me?"

Tony nodded. He followed Jesik into the house as Martin turned back to the corpses.

He reached a hand out to the bumpy, lizard-like skin of the palkin. The feel of it reminded him of an iguana, Mexico, home. He looked down at the rider. It had quietly expired while they were talking.

Her eyes were open and staring at him.

Standing among all the blood and gore on the field was definitely triggering his memories. He had to breathe steadily for a few minutes to get himself back in control of his mind. Even with his deep breathing he struggled to get past the memories. But after a few minutes he felt like he was able to open his mind to some other thought. Any other thought. What came to him was his need to clean up this mess. That meant opening himself up to the power again.

With his recent failure in the Dark One's palace, he wasn't sure he could do it.

He closed his eyes and tried to reach the place inside himself that held his power. As usual, it remained elusive. He searched and probed, glimpsing but not reaching it. It always seemed to be just around the next thought, just past that idea.

And then he had it.

Just like that it was there, a white-hot ball in the center of his chest.

He reached for it but shied back at the last second. Acceptance and desire were two different things. He accepted his power, knew it, felt it, even depended on it. But he hated it. It flitted back and forth before his inward eye. He despised it.

He overcame his revulsion and reached for it. Always the jester, full of taunting, it darted away from his grasp. He made a mental lunge and grabbed it in his imaginary fist. Suddenly his soul was bathed in flaming acid. Molten rock flowed through his veins. His mind screamed. The power flowed.

It poured out of him through his palm, a splash of lava that glowed like the sun. Agony. He rode the heartache into the palkin. He flowed through the flesh and bone, incinerating the creature from the inside out. Soon the red rage he had become saw skyline through the skin of the creature. First it came in fits and pops and then in great patches.

He knew he should release and regrab the Touch so it wouldn't overwhelm him. But he just couldn't face the pain of grabbing it again so soon. So Martin stayed in the Touch. The wave grew. He moved into one of the riders as lava sprayed from his hand like a fire hose. The rider melted. Within moments, like a smear on a mirror, he polished her away. It felt good. It felt right. Being in the Touch felt like freedom and power.

The grass at Martin's feet burst unnoticed into flame as he rode the Touch. And the wave grew. He rolled up the legs of the nearest beast, splashing over it like a wave in a kiddie pool for demons. As it splashed over the beast and rider, each puddled, pooled, and evaporated. Martin giggled.

His eyes were open now and staring. He flowed on, a gathering storm of liquid steel. He washed over a pair of beasts, one atop the other. He stood, arms spread, glowing like the sun. His crazed laugh shocked the birds from distant trees. He was a tsunami of magma. Hell's own tidal wave. And it felt wonderful.

The air hissed and crackled against the skin of his hands. He pounded over the remaining corpses, crushing them, vaporizing them. The wave rolled on through the little fence that surrounded the house. It lifted into the air, hanging buoyant above the ground. Martin laughed. A maniac's grin split his face. He shook and twisted. He raged.

A thunderclap sounded. A fly attacked him. And then another. *Boom*, tap. *Boom*, tap. They came in rapid succession. *Boom*, tap. *Boom*, tap. Slowly he came back to himself. He let go of the light.

He stood, shaking, smelling his acts of destruction. Even a vaporized corpse gives off a stench. He turned back to the house. There on the porch stood the gunslinger, reloading his giant pistol. It gleamed in the sun. The last bullet dropped in. The gunslinger flicked his wrist, snapping the cylinder back into place. The look on the gunslinger's face when he raised the weapon was not hatred or anger or venom. Fearless, loveless, hateless—it was completely without emotion.

Martin felt good. Energized. Excited. Almost manic. It was always this way when he used the Touch. It tortured his soul. But it felt *so* good.

He watched with detached calmness as the gunslinger raised the mighty cannon. Tony; they'd said his name was Tony. *Please, Tony,* he thought through the joy, *please kill me.*

The gunslinger's thumb pulled the hammer back. Martin smiled. The barrel, now aimed directly at Martin's head, stopped moving. Jesik was running along the porch toward the gunslinger. Looked like he might make it. Martin chuckled. *Boom*, zip. Something buzzed past his ear. He didn't flinch.

Jesik stood in front of the gunslinger, holding the man's gun-hand up and pointed away from Martin. *Looks like he made it,* Martin thought. *I guess I get to suffer through at least another day.*

Martin's grin broadened. He raised his hand to point at the pair, now arguing on the porch. He turned inward and sought the bright ball. He reached for it with his mind. The fire licked at his soul. He felt the edge of sanity. Ran the fingers of his mind along it. Savored its freedom. And turned back. He lowered his arm and stopped grinning. With a massive exertion, he let the Touch go.

"I see you took care of the corpses." Jesik's voice came to him, dreamlike and disconnected. "I suppose I should have expected my grass to get burned." He continued with a smile. "But I could have hoped for you to leave my roses and fence."

Martin finally looked around at the destruction he'd wrought. The grass of the yard was smoldering. A great patch of bare earth where the roses had been was now black, smooth, and glass-like. A huge section of the picket fence lining the yard was gone. Not knocked down but vaporized. With the smooth black ground and large gap in the fence, it looked like a driveway.

Martin closed his eyes against the pain in his soul. He'd lived for this. To save this world. She'd died for this. To get him here. Jesik had killed for this.

Now Micah, Dinaala, and Raneal were hurt. Beka and Jakub were dead. His soul wailed and begged for release. Once again he crushed it down, knowing that what he felt didn't matter. He opened his eyes and stepped toward the house.

Jesik and Tony were talking in strident words about "destruction" and "control" and "killing them all."

It didn't matter.

It never mattered.

Martin would do what he always did: the best he could.

Ignoring the men he walked past them into the house. He paused when he saw the room. The destruction inside it was amazing. The ancient blackwood desk lay in a broken pile of sticks and splinters. The harpsichord was crushed. Broken chairs, pictures, and knick-knacks were scattered around the room. Someone, probably Jesik, had started the cleanup, as the one clean corner of the room attested.

Martin walked through the refuse and down the hallway. First door on the left. Raneal. Martin had been through this doorway before on a couple of lonely nights. Raneal couldn't put things right, but she had a way of putting them into perspective.

She was lying on her side on the bed with her eyes closed.

She was covered with both a quilt and that giant crocheted doily she'd been working on since he'd arrived. He ran his hand along it, feeling her leg underneath. He wished he could love her the way she deserved but knew it would never be so. He also knew that she accepted it. She loved him anyway.

Sometimes it made him sad, how lonely he was. And pathetic. And yet she had lived almost twenty times as long, without love. Without hope. Now, with Martin here, she had both and neither.

"Hello, poppet," she ventured through closed eyes and gritted teeth. "You're a bit late. Did you have a nice day?" She grinned just a bit.

"Passable, I guess. I made a new friend." He took her hand. "Looks like you were busy while I was gone. I can't leave you alone for a minute without you getting into trouble, can I?"

"I guess you'd better not leave me alone anymore."

He just looked down at the hand he was holding. "How bad is it?"

She smiled. "I can't fix myself. Never could." She shifted positions. "Jesik used himself up along with that new fellow trying to do it. At least they stopped the bleeding and some of the pain."

She rolled on to her back. As her face came off the pillow, he could see the suffering. Her face, once so smooth and quick with a smile, was a bright pink ruin of scars. The hair on that side of her head was gone. As was her eyebrow. When she finally opened her eyes, her left was bloodshot, gray, and sightless.

She saw the look on his face. "Am I hideous now?"

She laughed and danced. He felt a complete fool. Two left feet. The music pounded out the beat for them. The caller sang out the do-se-do. She grinned, showing perfect teeth. Her hands were warm in his. She spun in a tight circle. Her red and blue plaid skirt brushed his leg as it spun out. Her beautiful hair caught the light as it spread wide like a blonde wing, wrapping her head. Her hair splayed out. It splayed out in a bright red sunset. In the bright red blood. Her hands were cold.

"No." He offered his best false smile. "Just hurt."

"It won't be long before I can't be healed." She turned away from him. "That's the way it works, you know. Over time your body comes to accept the new you. The scars become part of you. If you have them for too long, you'll have them forever."

A single tear rolled down her good cheek. He looked at her for long moments. A single tear from his eye joined hers. He made a decision. He bent and kissed her forehead, released her hand, and gently smoothed it down along her leg. He turned away.

"Martin, wait ..."

He turned back.

"Martin, you know that if you ask it of him, he will do it. Despite the Dark One. Despite everything. He loves me. And he loves you. And he would do it. He would send you back to your Earth." She took his hand in hers once again. "But it would kill him. You know it would. None of us can survive what's coming without you. It's why you're here. You can't leave now. Especially for something like this."

She squeezed his hand. "Oh, love. I know you want to help me. But you can't." She brought his hand to her cheek. "This? This is just a face. And it has seen many sunrises. And yet may see many more, if your God is willing and the Dark is destroyed. My need for beauty has long passed me by."

She looked away. She didn't say what was really in her heart, but he knew. "I'm tired now. Please let me rest."

He carefully laid her hand on her thigh. His fingers lingered on the back of it. He turned and walked out.

Loneliness threatened to crush him once again. Tears spilled down his cheek. He walked up the hallway and heard breathing through one of the nearby doors. He paused, looking into the sparse room. Dinaala was lying on the bed. He stepped in. She was sleeping. He placed a hand gently on her brow. No fever. Under his fingers he felt the swirling chaos that was the Touch. She was strong. And getting stronger. He didn't know how he knew these things, but he did. His senses seemed to be getting stronger as well.

He had a sudden urge to drain her. It would be easy. She was asleep. He could just reach in and take the Touch. Pull it out of her. It would taste good.

Horrified, he jerked his hand away. Sometimes his own nastiness took him by surprise. Another great reason to hate himself. He stepped back from the wounded girl's bed. He looked around at the room he had so recently slept in, with its white walls, narrow bed, and nearly empty dresser.

Got to find a new place to stay.

He turned and walked away from the second victim of the flood he could have stopped but didn't. He passed a third door in the hallway. This one held Micah's small, tired frame. His breathing was deep, his sleep sound. But his skin was pink with a flush. Martin sat down and put his hand on the boy's head. It was hot but dry.

The boy woke at his touch. "Martin? Did you get him? Is it over?"

"No, Micah. I'm sorry. He's still alive. It's not over."

Micah looked down for only a moment. The bright, sunny child came flooding back. "I got stung by a duur wasp, but I stomped it!" Micah's sheet tented and fell as he mimicked the action. Then he looked down again. "But I got sick. Is Mom out there? I'm kind of thirsty." He tried to sit up. "Woah, dizzy."

"It's all right, you lay back. I'll bring you some water." Martin stood. He paused for a long moment, looking at the boy. He left the room, heading for the kitchen. Obviously Micah didn't know his parents were dead. Would they be alive right now if Martin had done his job?

He stepped into the shattered living room. In his mind, the battle that had raged in the small house played out in slow motion.

Riders come in. Beka and Jakub are talking with Raneal. Activators feed. Regulators flare. Raneal is thrown back up the hallway by the blast of fire that turns Beka to ash. Jakub runs at the riders. He bursts into flame. Raneal crawls back to the living room, her hair and clothes on fire. Dinaala is pinned to the wall by a spiker. Brave little Dinaala sees Raneal. She feeds. Raneal flares. Riders die. But Micah is already gone. Dinaala keeps feeding. Raneal puts out the flames on Jakub's body and on herself. She crawls to Dinaala. Bracing herself on the wall, she stands. She Touches the girl and eases her pain, pulls out the spiker and lowers her to the ground. A pool of blood slowly oozes out across the floor. Her hair fans out in the pool of blood.

Tears streamed down his face. Destruction surrounded him wherever he went. Everyone he loved died. He was a pariah. The very specter of Death. He needed to leave.

He walked out the front door.

"… too damn dangerous! Do you see the yard? Are you a fool?" Tony made a sweeping motion with his arms. Martin stopped on the porch, unnoticed and unwanted.

"I know the risks, my friend." Jesik was calm despite Tony's adamant protestation. "He is very powerful. And not yet in complete control of that power. But he is a good man. Even if he doesn't yet see it."

"I've seen mortars, grenades … hell, I've even seen Volkswagens from a distance. But I've never seen anything like this." Tony's face was nearly as red as his hair. He turned back to the blackened swath of grass.

"What's a folks-wagon?" Jesik asked.

"It's like a cannonball that ships shoot. It's so big it weighs as much as a car."

"A car … you mean the wagon you came here in?"

"Yes. Imagine that whole thing smashed down into a ball and shot from a ship. The damage it can do is devastating, but nothing compared to this." Tony looked around.

Martin followed his gaze. The ground was torn and buckled in great chunks.

"Did you see it? It looked like it was boiling." Tony turned to look at Jesik. "And did you see his face? Damn! It sends chills down my spine … 'maniac' comes to mind. All teeth and crazy, bugged-out eyes. And glowing. He was *glowing,* for God's sake."

"Calm down, my friend," Jesik responded. "It wasn't that bad."

"Are you kidding me? I swear to God it looked like he wanted to *eat* me. *Alive.* Damn! That creeped me out."

Martin stepped off the porch. It was all true. He knew it. He walked across the ravaged yard. Both men jumped as he passed between them, his long strides carrying him toward the open hole in the fence

"Martin …" Jesik began.

Martin neither slowed nor turned. Tony was right. He *was* vile. And not just based on his powers. Powers that could be used for nothing but destruction. No, in the core of his being he knew he was useless. Granted a power he had no control over, he was a danger to himself and those around him. It would be better for him to be alone. At least the people he cared about would be safe. And he wouldn't be causing them any more pain.

He could hear Jesik's quick footsteps coming up behind him.

"Martin, where are you going?" Jesik asked, matching his stride. Their feet crunched on the crusty, blackened surface soil.

"Micah would like a glass of water," Martin responded.

"Those things Tony said …" Jesik took Martin's arm and stopped him. He looked Martin in the eyes. "They're true. I won't lie to you. These things you can do, these powers, they are terrifying and dangerous. And you are destined to kill. You have a dark side. All of these things are true. But they aren't the only truths about you. There are other truths, as well. You are a good man. You love. You care. If you didn't, those other truths wouldn't hurt you."

"You're wrong. I'm not a good man." Martin nodded at Tony. "His truths are the real me. Good for nothing but the destruction of myself and those around me."

"No one can know what you're going through. The Prophecies don't speak of these things—these times, these hard lessons. The pain we all suffer and endure. They tell of only two things: light and dark. Survival and destruction."

"And what if the cure is worse than the disease? Everywhere I go, everyone I love suffers and dies."

"You can't blame yourself for that. You didn't bring this death along with you, carried in your pocket like some trinket brought back from a long journey. Death comes to everyone in his own time."

Martin ripped his arm free. "What do you know about it? You weren't ripped from your world. Your fiancée didn't die right in front of you. Your friends dead. Your family dead. And now the whole world thinks I'm some kind of messiah. Here to free them from tyranny and pain. That's not me! I'm not that guy. I don't have it in me. I'm weak and scared and mean. And I don't want to care anymore."

"I know you're suffering. Believe me, I know. And I wish I had answers about why these things are happening. I just don't know. The Prophecies don't say. Elas could see but not interpret. He saw life. He saw death. He saw actions taken and hands stayed. But he did not see hearts broken. He saw victory and he saw defeat. He saw Darkness and he saw you."

Martin clung to his anger. Jesik's eyes looked like they held compassion, but Martin knew they hid the truth. Jesik was a good man, but if he felt anything for Martin besides contempt, he was naïve. They held each other's eyes in that tableau for a time. Martin broke it off first, opting to look at the ground.

"Where will you go?" Jesik asked.

"To do what needs to be done." Martin turned and started back toward the hole in the fence. Without looking back, he said, "Micah still needs that water."

He felt Jesik staring at him. In a few strides he'd reached the road. He looked down at the scorched and shattered bit of ground at his feet. He saw only Darkness. He turned west and began the next leg of his journey down a lonely road. He didn't look back.

Traveling Man

Thom patted the neck of his dappled gray horse as he bent to check the buckle and blanket. He straightened up, reached into his bag, and pulled out a stiff, root-like vegetable that looked like a cross between a rutabaga and a pickle. Damn goofy place. Didn't even have carrots. Ah, well. It had other benefits that outweighed the lack of carrots and bowling. It had …

Fazha straightened up from her stooped position just in front of Thom.

… nice scenery.

He leaned forward and held the root out for the horse. Bilbo sniffed a time or two. His lips grabbed on to the veggie and pulled it into his mouth one crunchy bite at a time.

"Well, boy, enjoy that while it lasts. We'll be on the road for a while."

"Fazha!" Spider burst into the barn through the door. "We've gotta go. They're coming!"

"Go!" She was moving before she finished speaking. "We're right behind you."

She guided her piebald out of the stall. As it cleared the gate, she gracefully pulled herself into the saddle. "*Come on!*" she shouted at Thom.

Damn! Keep your mind on business! Thom pulled the gray's reigns. It followed amiably enough.

Five years ago he'd never been on a horse. As he mounted, he couldn't imagine traveling this world any other way. He patted the big animal's neck again. "Let's go, fella."

The horse started moving. Fazha was at the big door, waiting to go through, but the stable boy was nowhere to be seen.

Thom's sensitive ear picked up the sound of a scuffle outside the door.

"I told you, there's nobody here but us. The damn stable boy's run off or something. There's nobody back there!"

The door started to move. Fazha reared her mare. The piebald's front hooves stomped against the big door, slamming it outward.

"Ooofump." A pained grunt came from behind the door as it flew open. A guardsman in a chain-mail shirt was lying sprawled on the ground. Two others stood off to one side, swords drawn and pointing at Spider. A third guardsman was leaning nearly nose-to-nose with Spider, his sword pressed into the thin man's throat. Spider was backed against the barn.

Fazha shot past the stunned man with Thom hot on her heels. A half dozen mounted men were scattered in front of them. One unfortunate fool made the mistake of moving his mount into Fazha's path. Her mare was no passive passenger pony. She was a mighty war horse, trained to fight and kill with or without a rider. Fazha had told him early on that Tan'aana—probably translated from the Ancient tongue as "The Pissed off One Who Treats Others Badly but Is Good to Have on Your Side in a Battle"—had saved her life on more than one occasion.

The piebald reared up as it came upon the guardsman. A powerful fore-hoof crunched in the man's breastplate, throwing him through the air. Somehow Tan'aana and Fazha both looked graceful even with the odd bunny hop Tan'aana had to make to keep her momentum. The maneuver was amazing to behold. Any other time he would have stopped to marvel. As it was, he urged Bilbo into a full gallop and thundered after her, risking only the briefest of glances at the bent and broken body of the unlucky guardsman.

The other side of the group was even less fortunate. Thom rode through them, humming the theme from Bonanza—*Dum didi dum didi dum didi dum didi DA DA!*

Men and horses flew in all directions, victims of a wedge of Touch that moved in front of him, like the cattle guard on a steam engine. He pounded through the newly formed gap in the blockade.

A twinge of guilt ran through him at the thought of leaving Karf and Spider to the guardsmen. A quick glance back at the barn told Thom they would make out just fine.

Spider was standing on one of the guardsmen, judo-throwing another at the squad leader. The leader's horse, its rider trailing from a loose stirrup, clattered up the cobblestone street toward town. Karf held another downed man by his feet, and with one mighty swing blasted the last three mounted men from their horses.

Thom turned back to the road ahead and urged his mount on. Bilbo took the hint. His hooves thundered against the ground. The wind drew streams of tears from Thom's eyes. His knees flexed with the familiar rhythm of Bilbo's gate.

Tan'aana was no slouch either. She flew along beside him. He turned toward Fazha and grinned. She grinned back.

Brown and gold leaves swirled into the air as the two horses flew along the road. Thom hoped the owner of the lonely farmhouse would be okay. Had he known how close the Duke was behind him, he wouldn't have risked their lives. Now he had another victim on his conscience. Crap. He hoped that, sometime in the not-too-distant future, he might be able to make it through a single day and night without bringing harm and ruination to anyone. Wouldn't that be great? Oh well, he always had tomorrow. In fact, given their general direction, and his (as yet undisclosed) destination, he was likely to have plenty of opportunity to avoid creating new victims. They would be in hard country for weeks.

The road they had chosen was little used and in ill repair. With no nearby towns to the west, only farmers used this road. The cobblestones quickly gave way to smooth packed dirt. Their mounts' hooves tore chunks out of the hard earth, leaving a trail behind that a monkey on crack cocaine could follow.

A crosswind blew tiny leaves into his face. He shook his head, coughed one out of his throat, and spat to clear his mouth. He and Fazha rode hard and in silence for nearly an hour. No clocks here and he could always tell what time it was. How did that work, anyway? It was another of life's great mysteries.

A stone bridge came into view as they rounded a long, lazy right-hand curve. Much wider than the trail, it looked to be fairly well made from smooth-hewn cobblestones. But it was careworn and hadn't been cleaned or repaired in generations. It was maybe thirty feet long, with a fairly steep rise to it, likely more for run-off than for structural strength.

Just as Bilbo's hooves clattered onto the bridge, Fazha suddenly drew reins and slowed to a walk. The horses were panting and wet with sweat. She turned to Thom. "I think this is far enough on this road. We should cut across country to the south from this point. It'll take us to another road that travels east and west. It heads much farther to the south, but with the heat on this road, I don't think that's a bad thing."

"What about Karf and Spider? How will they find us?"

"They know the routine and the land. They'll assume we've taken that route. The Duke won't. There are other, much more direct routes to the barony. He'll assume we've taken one of those."

"Won't it be pretty obvious what we've done when they see hoof marks leading up to the bridge and none leading away?" Pointing out the obvious was one of his more useful talents. Even if no one else seemed to appreciate it. Fazha, for instance. She just gave him the stink-eye.

"No," she replied, "because you're going to twiddle your finger or wiggle your ear or whatever it is you do." She mimicked each action as she said it, ending the whole spectacle with a goofy, cross-eyed stare, her tongue lolling out of her mouth.

Thom guffawed. "You know, for a super-tough-hunter-killer-Amazon-warrior-princess, sometimes you act like a five-year-old." He dismounted. "I mean, this is serious business."

He closed his eyes and let his Touch flow out and across the bridge, feeling its way along. Fresh scuffmarks magically appeared, stretching across to the road beyond. He marched them up the road where they quickly passed out of sight. Six black crows scattered from their carrion meal as the horseless hoof marks rushed past them. He pressed on for nearly a mile. It took only a few seconds.

As he brought his Touch back to himself, he paused for one quick swat on Fazha's bum. Her eyes flared wide as she jerked in her saddle. She glared at him. Fortunately, his mischievous grin got him out of trouble once again.

She turned serious. "Once we turn off of this road, we're going to be out of contact with people for a quite a while. I'm not a strong Activator—"

Right and wrong, Beautiful. I can tell how strong you are.

—"nor are Karf or Spider. Will your jars hold out long enough for us to get to the barony?"

"Let's worry about that when the time comes." He turned Bilbo off the side of the bridge and walked him down the embankment to the river. He felt a twinge of nostalgia as he looked at the underside of the bridge. So much of this world was covered with those weird Templar roads that it pleased him to see one made in modern times, with stones and hard work.

Bilbo affably stepped into the stream, water lapping against his legs. He had a sweet temperament, this horse. Once Tan'aana had entered the stream, Thom reached out with his Touch and erased their departure and descent from the road and embankment. They splashed their way along for a quarter of a mile or so before Fazha turned to a relatively gentle slope on the western bank of the stream. Once they'd cleared the bank, she signaled a break. She slid from the saddle …

Ho man … close your eyes, dude.

… landing like a ballet dancer. Thom shook his head. He had gone for almost an hour without thinking about her. Crap. He really had to get a hobby.

He dropped far less gracefully out of his saddle. He unsheathed his canteen and followed her back down the bank to the stream. She found a spot where the stream burbled along over some stones and dunked her canteen into the chilly water. He turned his eyes and his mind away from her and collected his thoughts.

The Duke caught up fast. Too fast. Something was wrong. The Duke had no way of knowing when Thom had headed out of town. Three days. Leave just enough of a trail to lead the Duke to the right road. Lead him toward the barony. Then turn north. That was the plan. Not the one he'd told Fazha, of course. That would have to wait. But it was still the plan. Now he had this detour to the south to contend with. It was taking him further from his objective. Now he'd have to wait until the Duke's men passed him by going west and then skirt around behind them and head north. He was going to have to cut from Fazha or share the truth soon.

But not yet.

They climbed back up the bank and walked back to their horses. Bilbo was happily munching on the low grass that grew between the trees. Thom affectionately patted his neck. He pulled himself up into the saddle, drawing a nickered complaint from Bilbo at the shortness of his meal.

"I know, fella. But we've gotta get moving or the Duke might make a meal out of *you*." Bilbo tossed his head and moved in behind Tan'aana as she headed deeper into the trees.

It was several hours later before the trees started thinning. Thom could hear and smell a camp. In a clearing ahead someone was cooking the day's meal. Fazha didn't even pause. She brazenly rode Tan'aana right out of the trees and into the camp.

Thom closed his eyes and shook his head. He gave a heavy sigh and followed her. As he cleared the trees, he could see that she was dismounted and talking to Karf. She gave a quick hug to Spider and turned back to Tan'aana. She expertly pulled the tack and saddle, freeing the piebald to roam the clearing.

"Looks like a clear night, so we'll be sleeping out. That'll get us off quicker in the morning."

Thom followed suit with Bilbo. He didn't bother tethering the dapple. Bilbo may not have been the Albert Einstein of horses, but he knew a good thing when he had it. He'd stay right there with Thom. Unloading Bilbo took a few minutes. While his hands performed their tasks, he spread out his Touch and laid down a weave over the entire clearing. He felt his companions moving about on it.

This deep into the woods the sunset came early, even in a clearing. After helping clean up after the meal, Thom pulled out his bedroll and laid it out in a hopefully knot-free spot of grass. He put his saddle behind his head and began filling his pipe. Soon he was blissfully puffing on the glowing bowl. He hadn't yet woken his companions with screams but only because he hadn't yet slept in their presence. Three days. Somehow, in this crazy place, he didn't need as much sleep as he had at home. It was just like with food. One meal a day was more than plenty. He could have, and had, survived for months at a time on one meal a week. But soon he would need to close his eyes for an extended time. He only fretted on it briefly. When the time came that he could hold out no longer, he would tell them what to expect. In the meantime, he would sit and pull on the pipe.

Hours slipped by. As they had done each night, his companions all drifted off to sleep. He smoked. He thought. But mostly he played with the Touch. He could feel each of the others as they slept. They didn't know it, but he could even sense their sleep. The first night Karf had lain awake for two hours, feigning sleep, before he finally drifted off. One other way his talent came in very handy.

And he could feel Fazha. Everywhere she touched the weave it left a tingling sensation. He swore he could almost smell her through it. Damn. He had it bad. What was he going to do about her?

Karf was in love with her. For Spider it was a different feeling. More brotherly, but still love. She had that effect on people. She had that effect on him.

The funny thing was the why of it. It wasn't her beauty, although a blind man would be stunned by it. No, it wasn't that. And it wasn't her physique. Again, perfect. But not the source of his feelings. No, it was everything else. Her utter competence. Her sense of humor. The goofy faces she'd made earlier. And the way she smelled. She didn't smell pretty. She just smelled *right.*

Oh, yeah. He was screwed.

The next day proved uneventful and saw them safely to a new clearing. This one had the convenience of a nearby creek. After they got set up, Fazha decided to take a dip.

"Alone! I'm going alone. You men can stay filthy for a bit longer. A lady needs her privacy." She grinned as she grabbed her bundle and headed for a secluded spot along the creek.

Thom exchanged glances and devilish grins with Spider as she rounded the tree line.

Whomp!

Suddenly, the stars came out as Thom's face crashed into the dirt. *Damn, should have put that weave down. I'm getting sloppy.*

He stayed where he fell, unmoving. Karf, all muscle and burl, scooped him up like a sack of grain. Damn, that had hurt. Karf carried him away from the creek toward the tree line, with Spider trailing along behind them. Thom hung totally limp, knowing he'd have to play it carefully if he was going to beat both of them. He heard voices in the trees. Oh, crap. The Monster was here. The trap was sprung and Thom's suspicions were confirmed.

He did a quick inventory. No weapons. He was in the hands of one giant. About to be handed over to another giant. At least ten people in the mix. And, judging from the spin the world had going on, he had at least a minor concussion. Did that sound about right? If he'd been a gambling man, and of course he was, he would have put his money on the crew collecting him. Then again, playing the long odds had worked out pretty well for him in the past.

"Is he out?" the Monster asked.

"Yep," rumbled Karf. "He's a rag doll. I thought for a second I'd killed him, but I felt his breath."

He tumbled to the ground in a heap as Karf dropped him. *Not* trying to catch himself when he fell took practice. Thom was an expert. He needed a few seconds on the ground to get a feel for his surroundings and how many men were involved.

Sching.

Somewhere steel was being drawn. Close, but not in this group. They hadn't heard. A light footstep crept through the trees. Fazha. She'd come back too soon. Now she was going to get herself killed trying to save him.

In the blink of an eye Thom went from prone to standing. In the next, he became a whirling dervish of fists, feet, knees, and elbows. He smashed one guard's nose with his forehead. He had to engage as many of them as he could so Fazha wouldn't be overwhelmed. He really wished he could see her elegant dance but had to focus or he'd be dead. His first furious assault netted him two downed foes and a sword. After that it was all about the dance. As usual, he got nicked up quickly, letting his opponents underestimate him. But with this crowd he had to shift into skill quickly just to stay alive. They were good. Much better than the two the Monster had brought last time.

Another went down with a slashed throat. Using his companion as a diversion, the Monster grabbed Thom in a bear hug and started crushing him. The sudden move cost Thom his sword but not his life. Touch flooded into him. He let it flow through him, strengthening his ribcage and muscles. The Monster's eyes grew wide as Thom slowly flexed, opening that beastly grip. Thom slammed his hands under the Monster's ribcage, depriving him of oxygen at a critical moment, dropping him to his knees.

Thom felt Spider's dagger slide into his back. He held his breath and spun, jerking the weapon out of Spider's hand. It clattered on the rocky ground. Thom's elbow saved Spider's life. It shattered his cheekbone and ended the fight for him by knocking him unconscious. Thom used a small, simple weave to pinch off the flow of blood from this new wound. It was relatively minor in the grand scheme of things, so he put it out of his mind. He turned back to where Fazha had engaged the group.

The fight was over. But Fazha was on her knees next to Karf's body, cursing quietly to herself. Thom rushed over to her. She was covered in blood. Most of it wasn't hers, but she'd gotten a fair share of slashes. A dozen bodies were piled around her. He'd far underestimated their numbers. The Duke wanted him bad. She looked at him with sorrow on her face.

"How could they do this to me?" Tears were streaming down her face. She turned and punched the dead man.

Thom kneeled beside her and held her. She cried into his shoulder. "They thought I'd be at the stream for a while and they could just turn you over for the money. Like I'd just let that happen. We've been friends for so long. How could they do it? He made me kill him! Why?"

Thom knew why. Karf had been jealous. Thom had seen it the first night but had assumed it was under control. He had been wrong to trust Karf without reading him. Another mistake and someone had died. Several someones.

Dammit! And damn Jesik and his damned Prophecy!

"I'm not feeling so good …" Suddenly Fazha went limp against his side.

Thom looked at her face. She looked like a ghost. She was losing blood. He reached out with his Touch, wishing for the hundredth time that he was a healer. Unfortunately for Fazha, healing was far down his list of skills. He laid a weave over her and immediately found the wound. It was a deep gash on her thigh that had severed an artery. He used the weave to apply pressure to the wound. The bleeding stopped, but he had to continue the pressure while he searched for any other life-threatening wounds. The rest of her injuries were superficial, so he focused on the gash. He bent the weave into the wound and wrapped it around the artery like wire mesh, strengthening and supporting it. He'd have to leave it there and continue to focus on it for a day or two, until the artery could heal enough to support itself without rupturing. He then used the weave to pull the gash closed like superglue. She'd have a thin scar, but she should live through it. He threw a new weave around the nearest canteen and pulled it over. He coaxed her into just enough consciousness to sip from the canteen before she drifted back out again.

Now that Fazha was stable, he had to get them moving again. Spider and a couple of the guards were still alive. Unless Thom wanted to become a butcher, the Duke would soon know they had gotten away. It wasn't in him to kill defenseless men, so he tied them up and rifled through their supplies for anything he and Fazha would need. He saddled up Bilbo, intentionally leaving off all the supplies. Bilbo would be carrying two, so Tan'aana would carry everything else. Assuming, of course, he could get the bitch to do anything at all.

The horse, nonchalantly chewing on some grass, seemed relatively passive as he approached her. Apparently, she didn't know that Fazha was hurt because Fazha was the only thing this horse cared about. He moved in a little closer with his hand extended.

"Ho, Tan'aana …"

Clack.

Thom jerked his hand back at the last instant as her teeth snapped closed less than an inch from his outstretched hand. That was it. Thom threw a weave over the horse, holding her still. Then he stomped up to her. "Listen here, you crazy bitch! Fazha is lying over there on the grass dying and I'm not gonna fight with you while she does it. So we are going to reach an agreement right here and now. When she is better, you can go back to the snotty, rotten crab you normally are. Until then, you will behave yourself or spend all of your time tied up like this. Get it?"

He let his Touch flow into her and settle her mind. She calmed immediately and stopped struggling against his weave. He kept the weave in place while he saddled and loaded her up. And when he finally released it, she was mostly docile. Of course it was the Touch and not the words that got through to her. But it always made him feel better to express himself when he was upset.

He gently picked Fazha up and carried her to a fallen tree. Stepping up on the tree, he called to Bilbo. The brilliant dapple walked straight to him and stood, waiting for him to mount up. Man, was he a good horse. Thom stepped over Bilbo's back and settled himself with Fazha in his lap. He threw down another weave to support her and keep his back from tying itself in knots. How did those cowboys in the west do crap like this without the Touch? He didn't know but intended to ponder it while he made time away from this place.

He tossed a small weave around Tan'aana's reins and pulled them close enough to grab. Once arranged, he set off through the woods to the east, hoping to swing around behind the Duke's patrols and head north.

A stream of water rolled down inside the back of Thom's shirt, along his spine, and into his pants. Stupid hat. It was supposed to keep the rain off his head and neck. Instead, it just pooled it until there was enough to tip the brim down, sending a fresh stream inside the collar of his duster.

Of course in this downpour a coat didn't really matter much. At least the blanket and weave he was maintaining over Fazha were keeping her dry. But he was miserable and tired to his bones. He needed to find shelter soon. He was physically exhausted after three solid days of travel. The horses were spent and he needed to stop using so much Touch or he would soon burn out. One weave to keep Fazha from bleeding out, a second to keep her warm and dry, and another to scout ahead for the easiest path through the heavy woods were draining him. The weave he'd laid out in front of them reached only a hundred yards or so. But it was far enough to sense the cave ahead.

With the heavy downpour and densely packed trees, it was hard to see anything. If he hadn't had the weave to guide him, he would have simply forded the small river and gone on. Instead, he followed it north to a broad pool, formed by a waterfall that crashed down a cliff beyond it. It fell from an amazing height that was obscured by the heavy rain. Thom got a face full when he glanced up the cliff. *Damn rain.*

He couldn't see the cave through the waterfall, but he knew it was there. Perfect. He moved the horses into the stream and began to pick his way around the pool, careful to keep the animals in the water. The waterfall was thundering into the pool with bone-jarring power. As they approached it, both animals shied back, fearful of the cascade. Thom pulled the scouting weave back and used it to ease both animals and coax them behind the torrent.

The cave opening was wide enough for the horses to pass through single file. Their hooves crunched and clacked on loose, flat stones that littered the bottom of the cave. Once inside, it opened out into a nice-sized condo: a single, large room with a vaulted ceiling about thirty feet high and stalactite artwork for decoration. Was the one pointing down called a stalactite or a stalagmite? Whatever.

It was dark as night inside, but he had already explored the entire cave with his weave and that it was uninhabited, with the exception of the creepy crawlies that he could always feel but chose to ignore. *Why no bats?* he wondered briefly before realizing the obvious—they couldn't get out through the waterfall.

He pulled Tan'aana over closer so he could dig one-handed into his pack.

This was incredibly awkward. As much as he loved holding her in his arms like this, he really needed to put Fazha down. But there was no way he was going to do that on this rough and tumble cave floor. He needed to do some remodeling. He didn't know how much he could do, but he knew he could at least make a smooth spot for her to lie on. *Damn thing should be in here. Got it!*

He pulled a small, white crystal from the pack. He let the smallest trickle of Touch flow into it, igniting a small bright glow in the deepest recesses of the stone. It slowly built in power until it was bright enough to see by. Now that he had a little light, he could scan the cave with his eyes. The stone continued to brighten. Soon it would hurt to look directly at it. He tossed the stone out into the cave and caught it with his weave, raising it to a long stalactite (or stalagmite, whichever it was). He wrapped his weave around the stone pillar. A bit of pressure all around, but more on the bottom, a bit of heat to soften it and push the light bulb into the socket, and there it was. An overhead light fixture. It wouldn't take much Touch to keep it lit. Fazha could probably even do it. If she ever woke up.

All right. Time to make the bed. He moved the weave from the ceiling to the floor of the cave. A small stream of water ran down the center of the cave, so he chose a likely spot next to the stream, opposite the place he and the horses were presently standing. With a little heat and pressure, course and jagged stones softened and smoothed out into a wide, slightly cupped shape. As a measure of how tired he was, he used his free hand rather than a weave to throw Fazha's bedroll down on the smoothed-out space. He steadied himself with a weave and slid down from Bilbo's back. His boots crunched on the stony floor as he crossed to the bedroll. One last weave to dry it out before he gently laid her down.

He checked her head with the back of his hand. She still had a fever. Damn, he wished he was a healer. What to do, what to do? He pulled her pants, sticky with damp blood, off her leg and checked the wound. It was puffy and red. The artery seemed stronger now, but the muscle and skin around it were pretty inflamed. He slowly tightened his weave, making it smaller and smaller. His heart raced as he briefly questioned what he was doing. Delicacy was not his forte. But he had to clean out the infection or she would die. Smaller still. And there. He could feel the weave moving into her muscle. At first he struggled to distinguish the healthy tissue from the infected. Then he felt it. The invaders were coated in white blood cells. She was trying to fight them off. He wrapped his weave around them and pulled them out through her pores.

This time the water dripping down his back was sweat from his exertions. As he came back to himself, he flung the disgusting goo his weave held out into the waterfall. The thought of it sent a shiver down his spine. Fazha was breathing easier. He checked her artery one last time and then let go of his weave. He got out his canteen and coaxed a bit more water between her lips, setting the canteen next to her when he was done.

A new shiver, this one unrelated to creepy crawlies or gooey stuff, told him the cave was too cold. He sent a final weave up to the ceiling and heated up half a dozen of the long black spikes until they glowed red. They would give off plenty of heat for at least a few hours. Lastly, he made a bug-free zone around the smooth spot by heating a ring around the space till it glowed cherry red. Not much he could do about the flying bugs, but the crawlies wouldn't cross that line for a *long* time.

Of course he had to take care of everyone else before he could rest. So he shuffled over to Bilbo and pulled his saddle and blanket off. Tan'aana was too tired to fight even without a weave, so he was able to pull off her tack and saddle without injury to himself. He dug into Fazha's bag and found some hard nuggets for the horses to chew on, filling a small, foldable bowl with enough to last them a day or so if need be. He set it out for them on the "horsey" side of the stream. For water, they could drink from the stream. Now everyone had everything they needed for the short term. Good. He was tired. Bone tired. He tossed his soggy bedroll on the ground near Fazha and collapsed onto it. He dragged a dripping blanket over himself. He didn't bother drying either one off. He was out in seconds.

Smack!

Thom's head rocked to the side onto the hard stone floor, and his face stung like the devil.

"You bastard!"

Smack!

He'd be concussed in a second if she kept this up. Come to think of it, he wasn't thinking too clearly as it was.

Fazha was standing over him, wrapped in a blanket. She turned away, looking at their bags. He guessed she was looking for something to stab him with. In hindsight he realized it probably would have been a good idea to put her pants back on after he'd cleaned out the infection. Oh, well.

Smack!

Thankfully she hadn't found anything to stab him with yet, so he might have time to defend himself. Of course that meant he'd have to be able to stand, or even move. Neither of which seemed in the cards at the moment.

So he decided to explain the situation in a clear, concise, thoughtful, heartfelt expression of his honorable actions and intentions. Unfortunately, it didn't come out quite the way it was intended. "Unnnggh …"

Smack!

"You absolute bastard! I'm out of it for five minutes and you take advantage of me like this!" She turned around again. "Where's my damned *sword*?"

"Three days …"

"What did you say, you pig?"

"Three days …" His lips were parched and cracked. He dry-swallowed. "You were out for three days." Damn, his face hurt. "You were bleeding to death. I closed the wound, but it got infected." He pointed with his chin. "Look at the blood on your pants if you don't believe me. They're over there in your bag with all of your pointy toys."

She moved over to her bag and dug into it, pulling out her pants. The second pair she looked at had a slash at least nine inches long, running down the inside of her pant leg. The entire leg below the slash was stiff with dried blood.

"Your sword's in there too, if you still want to stab me." He closed his eyes so the cave would stop spinning. "At least it would get rid of this headache."

He didn't know anything else for a while.

Rayne's Song

A long, wet lock of black hair, whipped by the turbulent wind, lashed against Rayne's face. Cursing, she swept it back out of her eyes. She'd let it get too long again, dammit. She needed to cut it more often. The ship lurched sideways as another great wave slammed against the prow. Another string of curses slipped through her lips, but she refused to drop her flow and grab the handrail. The ship had to get out of the southern islands before word got to the crest or they'd be cut off from the open sea. She guessed that she had three days, at best. So she had to push on, storm or no storm.

Kevin whimpered at her feet. She maintained her flow but risked a glance down at her greatest ally. He was the only dog she'd ever met who had sea legs. He was male and showed it in his smallish frame and loving demeanor. But anything trying to attack her would find out he was more than they bargained for. To defend her, he could be as vicious as any bitch she'd ever seen. Right now, however, he looked somewhat the worse for wear. The ragged wind she was calling up to move the ship was mercilessly bashing it about. And even with his well-worn sea legs, he was staying hunkered down at her feet to keep from toppling around on the deck.

Kevin wasn't the only one suffering on this sprint through the stormy southern islands. Several of the seasoned crewmembers were bent over the railing even now. Most kept their hair short for this very reason, but one or two would regret not tying her hair back before coming on deck. Rayne suspected there would be a rush to the cabin boy for cuts as soon as the ship was safely out of the crest and through the Spikes.

How she would navigate them she didn't know. But best to leave that worry for a time when it mattered. Just now, they had to live to reach the Spikes. She gritted her teeth as she snatched her flow across the bow to a wave that suddenly crested before the ship. Grappling the crushing pressure of the water, she pulled the wave to heel, sliding it down the portside and directing it against the stern. The ship leaped forward, tossing crewwomen aft like besotted drunkards.

Damn that pathetic Wavemistress! How could she let herself get killed? And crushed between the boat and pier for, Goddess's sake. Idiot! A good Wavemistress could have kept this trip smooth and clear.

Even as she formed the thought, she knew it was a lie. Sailing smoothly and clearly through the crest during storm season could be managed only by the best Wavemistresses. And it would take at least a week. Only Rayne's great power could whip the wind and channel the waves to guide the little ship around all the way across the Bataan Sea and through the crest in so little time. She was loathe to admit it, but had the Wavemistress lived Rayne still would have had to drive the ship this way. But at least the Wavemistress could have helped steady the ship rather than leaving it all to Rayne.

She glanced down at the chaos on the deck below and marveled. Standing calmly in the midst of the crew, sick yet working, was Gaien. Tossing ship, crashing waves, and crew shoving past him seemed to have no effect.

Rayne had little use for most men. They were smelly and hairy, squeamish and squeaky, weak and useless in a fight. But Gaien was an uncommon man. Like Kevin, he was slighter and smaller than most women. And pretty. But underneath that pretty exterior was a strength she grudgingly admired. Rumor had it he had almost died twice at the hands of his previous owner. She was a cruel woman who had used her men for her amusement but beat them mercilessly when they displeased her. Apparently he had resisted her attentions, been beaten near unto death, and when he had recovered, resisted again. That took steel tits. He was much tougher than he looked.

Now she was tasked with getting him to Ravenscroft alive. He was the queen's new consort. How he went from slave to queen's consort was anyone's guess. She knew the obvious reason: his voice. He could sing like no one had for three hundred years. She shook her head and turned back to the energy flows she was weaving around the ship.

He was so small. How could he reach such powerful bass notes? They had made her chest rattle. And such sweet highs. She had heard him only once, just as the ship left port. He was angelic. She tingled slightly at the power of the song she remembered. It was a "safe passage" ballad, at first quiet and thoughtful. But as Gaien sang on, the song grew in power and scope. It rang out across the dock, the quay, the entire bay. Images came unbidden to her eye: raging storms, booming cannon fire, screams of crewwomen in blood rage, battling from ship to ship. And as the song crested and fell it still somehow carried to everyone across the wide bay. The images changed. Peace again: ships returning safely to the haven of port. The crewwomen were returning safely to their homes and men. She cried anew at the memory of it.

So that was the obvious reason. But how did the queen even know about him? He was unique: a loner. He didn't hang about and chat with the other men over tea and biscuits. He didn't spend his time caring for the village children. The cruel bitch who owned him hadn't even known he could sing, let alone create the flows that imagery demanded. Somehow the queen had known. And sent *her*: Rayne, Elite of Eight, Knight Apparent, Scepter of Rema'ada, to retrieve him. Why? What about him could be so important that the queen would send *her*?

And now they were being chased by a Rast. She had fought a Rast once. All her strength, skill, and power had meant little in the face of that monstrous malice. She had marked it, marked it, and marked it again, wound after wound and it had never slowed. She had been very lucky. She'd just been in its way. After its massive paw had crashed into her side and she plowed through the wall, it had gone on its way, an implacable hunter seeking its prey. Her side still ached when the weather changed. She felt the pressure of this Rast's malice dogging her trail behind her.

Kevin's growl dragged her back to the present. He stood low to the deck, hackles raised and teeth bared, looking at the deck below. Three of the crewwomen were circling Gaien, swords drawn and flashing. One lay dead at his feet.

Rayne's mind struggled to make sense of what she was seeing. Why were the women attacking Gaien? As that question slipped into her mind she caught the eye of one of the crewmembers. Fear flashed across the woman's face, followed by hatred and rage. Rayne knew instantly what was in the woman's heart.

Mutiny.

She stood for seconds longer than she would freely admit, transfixed by

Gaien's graceful movements. He danced like a Battlemistress. The crewwomen's slashes and thrusts met air more often than not. Those who made contact found only steel. In each of Gaien's hands was a ten-inch dirk.

Entlear jumped into her hand and she leaped to the deck below. She had never failed on a mission yet, by Goddess. She'd be damned if this was the first time. She would get Gaien to the queen alive. Her off hand guided a whip-like flow across the face of Aedna, the crewwoman farthest away. The bitch had been her friend for nearly three years. Damn! Aedna's face splashed red with blood and she jerked back from the pain. A shocked look crossed her face. She stumbled and sank to the deck. As she fell, Gaien's dirk slipped free of her ribs. One more step and Rayne was into the fray.

Entlear bit deep into the side of the nearest crewwoman. The woman moaned in pain but kept her feet for one more repost. Rayne's flashing attack was so swift and sure the crewwoman collapsed silently to the deck before she even knew she was dead.

Flashes of black, growls, screams, and splashing blood told Kevin's tale. Gaien bent to pet the grinning hound as the dog licked the last of the crewwomen's blood from his muzzle. Her death had been neither swift nor silent but was never in question. Kevin was a good hunter.

Rayne's heart nearly skipped a beat. When Gaien reached for Kevin's head, she was certain she was going to face the lasher's whip. Kevin was sweet with her, but no one approached him without Rayne's approval or Kevin was likely to rip off a body part. But not only was he not aggressive toward Gaien, he was actually *leaning into* the man's leg. His head lolled at an odd angle, tongue out and panting while Gaien scratched his chin. *No one* scratched Kevin's chin.

She had always been proud of Kevin's sense about people. On three separate occasions, his raised hackles and low, rumbling growl had saved her life from a would-be assassin's blade. For a few tenths of a second, anger flashed through her. *What the devil? He wins one little fight and loses all good sense. What does he do? He just flops against the first pretty face he sees.*

But the anger quickly passed. Kevin was the best friend she'd ever had. He didn't deserve her ire. Besides, this had never happened before. Maybe it was just the closeness of the ship, the waves, the fighting they'd all been involved in. Any one of those things could be muddling Kevin's mind.

Speaking of minds, where are the others?

A sudden horrifying thought occurred to her. She walked aft as quickly as the tossing ship would allow. Ducking low, she stepped through the doorway and down the stairs into the crew quarters. Hopefully four other women were down there asleep in their bunks. As her head cleared the doorframe and her eyes adjusted to the dim light, the smell hit her: coppery blood and other, far less pleasant smells. Nothing moved in the dark and closed space under the stern deck. Four lifeless faces stared up from their bunks; gaping wounds ragged and bloody, ran just below each chin.

She was in trouble.

Rafael was a small, nimble sloop, designed for maximum speed, minimum crew, and not much cargo. But even a small sloop required *some* crew. Rayne couldn't handle the flows that were keeping *Raffy* afloat and manage the rigging, rudder, and sails. Not to mention going high into the rigging if anything let go. They were dead in the water. Probably literally. Any one of the half-dozen or so vessels following closely behind would easily outgun him. Besides the three-inch slide lock, *Raffy* carried no guns. The slide lock was flexible, its standing rod designed to fit neatly into the cleat moorings on the railing, but it would do very little damage to another ship. And it required someone to actually fire it. She had visions of galleons and schooners with six-, eight-, and ten-inch guns raining cannonballs, lead shot, chains, and all other forms of nastiness on a foundering *Rafael* and his hapless human cargo.

She turned and quickly climbed back up to the main deck. Stepping up onto the slick wood, she approached Gaien, who was still scratching Kevin's chin.

"Well, little man, it looks like your *Song of Safety* back at the bay didn't do much good," she said.

"You're still alive, aren't you?" Gaien shot back, grinning from ear to ear.

"This is *really* not a good time to be joking." She gritted her teeth. "We're now in rough seas without a crew, on the deck of a sloop that was barely keeping ahead of the pack even with everything I was doing! We have no adequate weaponry to repel borders, no guns to fend off other ships, and no one to stand between you and one of their Battlemistress's longswords. So if you think this is a funny situation, you'd better get your head on straight and help me think of a way out of this."

His reaction had truly amazed her. She was the definition of "walking hard." Her tongue was frequently her best weapon. She'd brought grown and battle-hardened women to their knees with far less reprimand than that. But *he* just kept right on grinning. He was either crazed or stupid. Probably both.

What the hell was she *doing* here? She'd spent her whole life avoiding just this kind of crap. Then she met the queen. A charming conversation, a flirtatious turn of the head, the briefest suggestion of something more, and *oh, if you could just do this one little thing for me* … shit. Now she was going to die on the raging sea with this pathetic little psycho-singer. And there wasn't a damn thing she could do about it. On top of all of that, *Kevin* was going to get killed too.

That shook her to the core. *No* damn *way is Kevin getting killed out here*!

"All right, little man! Get your shit together and get downstairs. We're going to get ready for some company," she growled.

At first it looked like he was going to do just what she said. *First time since I met the little rat.* But instead of heading downstairs, he simply bent over one of the dead bodies. This one had been Kevin's kill. The woman was lying helter-skelter on the deck, twisted at the hips and shoulders. But her neck was disastrously mangled. Her head lolled backward, allowing her now-dead eyes to focus on her shoulder blade. Gaien bent at the knees and grabbed her sailor top and belt. In one smooth motion he flexed, twisted, and released. The carcass went sailing out over the handrail and into the crashing waves.

Rayne stood stock still, shocked at the power she'd just seen. How could this tiny little person *lift* so much? She was so surprised by this near miracle that she just stood and watched as he tossed two of the others over as well. When the fourth was gone, he turned back to her.

"How long do you think it will be until the first of the other ships gets here?"

What was that? He was actually talking to her. Directly. Without being asked. And *demanding* answers. What in *the hell* was going on?

"Look, I can take care of the other ships, but I'll need your help to do it, okay?" he said, looking at her earnestly. *Yep, definitely crazy.*

"All right, here's what I need you to do." He tried again. "Do you think you can just keep the ship steady for about ten minutes when they first come into view?"

She replied that she could, for what little good it would do. Just as the words were leaving her mouth, the first of a trio of ships materialized through the misty air. She climbed up to the aft deck to gauge the skill of the captains. A schooner and two galleons. Damn, they were big. And fast. They must have had at least three Wavemistresses each to get that kind of speed from those behemoths.

"Okay, do it now," Gaien said. "*Please.*"

Somehow she had relinquished command of the situation and could not bring herself to wrest it back. She drew in a couple of deep breaths and held the last. Then she pulled in a flow from the sea. She pulled another from the air. She wrapped them, flipped them, coiled them, pulled, and whipped. While her hands were playing an invisible little boy game of skip rope, her mind was sorting through hundreds and thousands of strands of energy, seeking those that were pulling the sea and winds into such a fury. By tens and twenties, each bit of chaos was absorbed into one of her flows. There were so many. As she pulled more and more into her control streams, her control slipped. The chaos shredded her streams. The feedback was horrific. She'd never attempted to control so many chaotic strands before. Her temples throbbed with the effort. Still she went on, her hands moving like she was cracking whips in a circus. Suddenly the pain in her temples eased and she had the streams banding again.

Kevin was leaning against her leg. He had joined in her efforts, lending his strength in a way only he could. She'd never really understood their bond. He wasn't her familiar, that coconspirator of ancient wizarding crimes. No, he was her friend. And she needed him now.

Slowly the boat stopped pitching and rocking. At the edge of her reach she felt the ragged energy hash that threatened to leak back in. Now that the boat was steady, she dared look away from the railing and back at Gaien.

He stood perfectly still on the aft deck, looking back at the rapidly approaching ships. He tipped his head slightly back and began a song. Because she was already looking for strands of energy, she could see the power that his voice carried: hundreds, thousands, tens of thousands of strands. She had never seen so many held by one person. They sprayed off him like fireworks.

Then she heard him. It began as a low rumble in her chest. She heard his notes rise and fall, but the words made no sense to her. He got louder. The deck of the ship started to vibrate. Rise and fall, rise and fall, the song rolled on. She wondered if she'd be able to keep her footing. Seconds stretched into minutes. Even with Kevin's help her streams were starting to weaken against the ever-present onslaught of chaos.

Boom!

Splash, dapple, dapple, *splash*!

The schooner was gone. Debris, human and otherwise, rained down on the water.

The long galleon next to the schooner was called *Merced.* But now, only the *ed* was visible. The rest of his name was lost, along with a significant chunk of the foredeck, his prow, and eight cannon on his portside. She could see crewwomen scrambling about, trying to figure out what had happened. And there, skewered to the mast by a torn piece of the schooner's decking, was Aleetha, Prime Wavemistress of the Brigade. Two other Wavemistresses were scuttling here and about. They worked feverishly to try to stabilize the boat and hold the waterline over the massive hole that had been created by the blast. Dozens of Activators sent streams into each Wavemistress, giving them the Touch needed to secure the boat against the sea.

Boom!

Splash, dapple, *splash*, dapple

The song had rolled on. Wavemistresses or not, *Mercedes* met the same fate the schooner had. The rumbling in Rayne's chest was almost unbearable. The air was thick with the weaving of the song. Stream upon stream flowed out of Gaien's mouth. She could just make out the name *Ballista* on the third galleon. All three of *Ballista's* Wavemistresses were urging him into a wide turn.

Boom!

Dapple, splash, dapple, *splash*!

And *Ballista* was gone as well.

The deck stopped shaking. The rumbling in Rayne's chest slowly died down. Gaien's voice faded away to nothing. That was the moment she realized he hadn't breathed once during the long minutes of the song. How long had it been? Ten minutes? Twenty? She didn't know, but no one could sing for that long without breathing. *No* one. Suddenly he slumped like a rag doll onto the hard wooden planks.

She dropped the streams and rushed up to the aft deck. She dropped to her knees and gently rolled him over onto his back.

"Did I get them?" he asked.

"You got them, all right!"

"Good. Told you I was worth something." He checked out again.

Kevin bumped Rayne's leg as he padded nearer to Gaien. He bent low and licked the man's face once, twice, three times. Gaien smiled but didn't wake up.

The next few minutes were a blur of activity for Rayne. The wind and rain abated, but the sea continued to crash mercilessly, so she was forced to spend some effort keeping it at bay. The real challenge here was in attending to the things right in front of her while still keeping a portion of her mind focused on the energy the storm and sea were swirling around the little ship. But now that the immediacy of the pursuit had passed, she didn't have to focus so hard on driving the ship forward. She turned her attention to the little man lying on the deck.

Practicality and honesty forced her to admit he had done something amazing. Three ships completely destroyed. Not just destroyed but blown to pieces like straw in a hot wind. How could he generate that kind of power in such a weak little body? And without any Activators. She looked at him. Like most men, he seemed pathetic. And yet he had shown courage and strength, character and toughness. What was she to do with this little fish now? He looked so delicate; so *mannish*. She tried to see what the queen saw in him. How could the queen be attracted to *this*?

Power. That was the key. Rayne decided the queen wasn't really attracted to him. If she knew what he could do, she was certainly after his abilities. A man who could sing machines to death was an *incredibly* powerful weapon. Through him, the queen could put together a terrifying force of destruction.

So he was a tool, little more than a slave. The queen was cute and all, with her brooding smile and flashing eyes. And Gaien was just a man. But no one deserved that life. Rayne was suddenly certain the queen knew all about Gaien's power.

And if she knew what Rayne could do, Rayne would be in the same boat.

Not funny, Rayne, not funny at all.

She reached out and touched Gaien's throat, feeling for the beat of his heart. It was strong. She pulled her attention from the sea to glance at his energy.

Blackness.

Blind. I'm blind.

Rayne's mind leaned briefly toward panic. Wait. That's not right. It's not all black. She turned her head to the side and realized three important things. First, she was lying on her back on the deck and wasn't sure how she had gotten there. Second, she could see great blue and white waves rolling alongside the ship. Third, the back of her head was *pounding.* And something else was still wrong. She couldn't really "see" energy.

She couldn't see any energy.

Never in her life had she felt so blind, so empty, so lost. It was all darkness.

Stop it! You're not some weak little man breaking down when things go wrong. You're a woman, *for Goddess's sake! Snap out of it!*

She sat up. As with all things, she would face whatever had happened head on.

Steel tits! I've got steel tits, dammit!

She shook her head to clear the throbbing.

Wait!

There was a flicker. The mighty sea was calling to her. She could feel it. Its energy brushed up against hers, beckoning to her to seek it out, to look, to find. She did. And she found it. There all around her, the eternal sea was moving and flowing and curling.

And she could see it again.

Slowly, slowly, slowly, she started to feel the comfort of other energy patterns again. She could see Kevin, comfortable, kind, and powerful. She could see the boat itself, sturdy and waiting. She could even see where the bodies had recently lain, giving off the last energies of life. They were stains on the deck. Almost, but not quite, background noise. Most would not have been sensitive enough to feel them at all, even if the bodies had still been there. But Rayne was not most people. Her energy skill was extreme, her experience broad.

And yet there *was* a black spot in her vision. She couldn't see Gaien at all. It wasn't that he was weak or powerless, because all life leaves a mark on the energy around it. If he had just been weak, she would have seen *something.*

This was a black hole in the energy plane. He had no energy at all. It was like she was looking right through him. No … she was looking *around* him. The patterns curled, buckled, flowed, and rippled around the space he occupied. If she closed her eyes, he wasn't there at all.

Just as she was getting to her feet, the boat heaved mightily and she had to put her hand down to keep from crashing back to the deck. Gaien's energy was a mystery to be solved another day. She bent and listened for his breath. Even and steady. *Good enough. He'll live.*

Once she was certain that Gaien wasn't in any immediate danger of death, she left him where he was, Kevin lying against him for warmth, and she slipped below deck to clear out the bunks.

It was a sad duty. These were her friends. They had been good, hard women, strong and capable. They deserved to die in fair combat, not have their throats slit in their sleep. She had never been a great singer, but the passion of the moment overwhelmed her. So for each woman she sang a short song of passing, hoping their spirits would accept her blessing for the heart behind it. Her voice momentarily broke as the last song rang against the metal lamps hanging about the little cabin. She lowered her head and stood quietly for a moment, contemplating the capriciousness of death.

With that done, she pulled the first woman from her bunk, carefully laying her on the narrow deck space between the racks. The body was just starting to stiffen. Rayne had to hurry. This job would get much tougher when rigor made the bodies into planks. She folded the woman's arms across her chest and heaved her up like a sack of grain. The stairs were steep and narrow, and Dunella was heavy. Even releasing the flows she was using to keep the ship stable and using her energy to help navigate the stairs, Rayne was huffing and puffing by the time she gently lowered Dunella to the deck. She stood for a brief moment, hands on her hips, breathing deeply.

Kevin growled low in his throat. He didn't move away from Gaien, knowing his charge was defenseless. But his voice rumbled and his hackles stood up.

She reached out with her energy again to stabilize the sea before the ship started to take a beating. Something scraped at her senses. The tumultuous sea, ever-present in her mind now, was behaving oddly. A disharmony was rolling through it behind the ship. The energy of the sea had a pattern to it. Like its waves, the sea's energy had an ebb and flow. Rising and falling, sometimes swirling, it always moved in harmony. Now, off their stern on the portside, energy was flowing outside the sea's pattern.

Something was coming. And it was strong.

Rayne's movements were always fluidly graceful and she always carried sharp things with her. Now she moved to meet this new challenge, and two of her blades leapt into her hands as she flowed up the steps to the stern deck in a rush.

Just as she set her foot on the deck, a monstrous wave crashed against the portside of the ship, tipping *Raffy* precariously to starboard. Her foot made contact but didn't find purchase. The wet deck slid out from under it in slow motion. Rayne felt her balance shift away from her. The deck was rapidly approaching her head.

A common mistake among young fighters was the *hand-out*. When someone inexperienced was taken down, she frequently put a hand out to stop herself from hitting the ground. Broken fingers, broken hands, broken wrists—all were common results. They went along with loss of weapons, loss of combat, and potentially the loss of life.

Rayne was no novice. Reflexes, honed through years of single combat challenges, pulled her chin and left shoulder down. She hit the deck hard, right on the place in her shoulder where the muscles were apart and the bones came together. Lightning shot down her arm, sparking all the way to her ring finger, even as she let her momentum carry her hips over the top and bounce her back to her feet. Fluid grace. And her sword and dirk had already changed hands.

Damn! Gonna have to fight righty for a few days.

She climbed the few steps up to the poop deck and moved toward Kevin and Gaien so she could defend them if the need arose. She turned to face the oncoming threat.

Could Rast swim? If so, she and her ship were in trouble.

The twisting of the sea's flow grew ever closer. It slid up the portside of the ship and a great wave rose along with it. The wave crested above the portside cleats and cracked open. Like a giant bubble bursting, the wave crest splashed loosely on the deck, followed immediately by three soggy, bedraggled women.

While they were still spluttering and gathering themselves, Rayne wrapped stream after stream around them, binding them tight. And as was her habit, she sized them up before talking to them.

Two were obviously strong Activators, judging from the feel of their Touch—wide, clumsy streams that left resonant patterns wherever they moved. The ornate binding collars they wore told her they were owned by a Regulator. Despite the rarity of Regulators, their dependence on Activators made it hard for them to acquire enough wealth to buy much more than a home and some land. Owning an Activator was far beyond the reach of any but the most power Regulators.

That added to the third woman's mystery. With two strong Activators in thrall, she had to be special. Rayne hadn't spent enough time this far south to familiarize herself with all the Wavemistresses in the southern fleet. She knew Aleetha by reputation. She was the strongest Wavemistress in the south. Maybe she'd survived when the *Ballista* went down. Or it could be Magda, Aleetha's number two. In either case, she was dangerous. Not only were they each a powerful Wavemistress, they were trained in Martial Touch. And all three were strong enough to feel her. She needed to be very careful about how she used her power.

One of the Activators reached to the sea for a stream. Rayne snapped it off with little thought. All three women's eyes went wide. Few Regulators knew how to sever an Activator and even fewer could do it without an Activator of their own.

"Who are you?" Rayne demanded.

I am Nareesa, Wavemistress of the *Merced*."

Snap!

A small streak of blood welled up on the cheek of the Wavemistress, raised by the lashing stream that Rayne had whipped across her face. To their credit, none of the women cried out at the sudden attack.

"Let's start again, shall we? And this time we'll leave the lies behind. Who are you?"

The Wavemistress clenched her teeth and began again. "I am Magda, Second Wavemistress of the Southern Reach."

"Much better," Rayne said, moving over to the women. Like a lover, she reached up and gently brushed the woman's wet hair back from her eyes. "See how easy it works when you cooperate?" She searched the woman's face and eyes. "Now why were you following me?"

The woman clenched her jaw and held her tongue. Damn. Rayne had little stomach for questioning prisoners. Despite being a battle-hardened warrior, she loathed hurting people. Battle was a dance, with give and take. This was different. This was just hurting someone who couldn't defend herself right up until she broke. And she couldn't bring herself to do it.

"All right. I have no time for torture," she said. "And I've taken too much of my attention from the sea as it is." She turned back to the bow. "So I very quickly have to decide what to do with you." She looked over her shoulder at the Wavemistress. "Do you want to die?"

The Wavemistress raised her eyebrows. "No, of course not …"

Rayne stepped close to the woman, her nose only inches from the woman's face, and looked deeply into her eyes. "You have one, *and only one*, chance to live. I do not have the luxury of restraining you while I guide this ship. So you can *help* me, or you can die right here and now. Which will it be?"

The woman looked at the Activators. They looked back, imploring her with their eyes. She looked down for a moment and swallowed. "We'll help you."

The women were suddenly free to move. Rayne took a small statuette from a pocket in her overcloak. She tossed it to one of the Activators. "Fill that." She always kept a couple of half-empty jars in her pockets as an explanation for her power. It saved on questions and the need to eliminate the curious.

As the Activator called up a stream, Rayne took out another and handed it to the Wavemistress before turning away. "Use this to calm the ship and get us moving northward, toward the Spikes." The Wavemistress raised an eyebrow. Rayne turned back. "I have a job for your Activators. They need to clean up some people who chose to *not* help me." Rayne hated to dishonor the dead with a lie but knew she needed to establish some degree of control through fear. Her reputation would fill in where this cleanup project left off. She hoped the dead women would understand. And that she would live long enough to make amends.

Reconstruction

Aleks stirred the steaming mush around in the pan. He'd searched the cabin for food and found only a bag of grain. Shaped like tiny little eggs, they looked like a cross between oats and rice. He had felt around inside one with his Touch and decided it could work as porridge. The steam rose up from the pan, filling his nose with the sweet smell of corn and buckwheat. The water he'd boiled the grain in was nearly gone, so he pulled the pan off the heat. He set it on the counter next to a twisted blob of metal—his first attempt at using his newfound gift to heat the cereal having gone a bit awry.

He poured his porridge into the bowl he'd found. He looked into the bowl for a few seconds, wishing he had found something he could have flavored the grains with. No raisins. No brown sugar. No maple syrup. Nothing. Not even salt. Oh well, beggars can't be choosers. He picked up the spoon he'd found in one of the drawers and carried his meal to the cabin's lone table.

At some point during the long night he'd woken in a puddle of the girl's vomit. He'd cleaned himself and the mess on the floor up and then moved the girl to a mat in the corner of the room before he went back to sleep. He'd slept for hours and woke with a dry, pasty mouth and an empty stomach. Neither of his wards were awake yet. Actually, he wasn't entirely sure they'd ever wake again. But they were both breathing easily and neither had a fever. That was about as much as he could hope for right now.

He raised his spoon to his nose and breathed in a large waft of the steam coming off it. There was that sweet corn smell again. *Okay. Here goes.* He took a few grains into his mouth and breathed across them to cool them off. As he bit the grains, his tongue was flooded with the flavor of sweet cornbread and honey butter. He chewed that first bite ever so slowly, savoring the flavor flooding his mouth. He attacked the bowl. All too soon he was stuffed to the brim, unable to consume another bite. He was shocked when he looked down into the bowl and found that most of the grain was still there. He couldn't have taken more than a dozen bites. He leaned back in the chair, lifting the front legs off of the floor.

"Did you enjoy your breakfast?"

Aleks almost toppled over backward but jerked himself upright, slamming the chair back onto all four legs. Once stable, he turned and looked at Donte, who was now facing the countertop. He was stunned to see him up and around so soon. Especially after he'd been so close to death.

"I see you had some trouble with the stove." Donte turned to face Aleks, the blob of metal in his hand. "I have a bit of a shortage of pans ..."

The simple statement was so matter of fact, so mundane, that it calmed Aleks's mind and helped him accept the reality he was in, for the moment. He looked at the blob. He held out his hand to Donte, who obediently passed him the lump. Once again his mind took him where his eyes couldn't. He opened the valve in his head and let a small trickle flow into the pan. As with the recent healings, he flowed right into the object. Light, shape, planes, angles, connections: there was a structure here. It was a latticework that formed the material. Deformed and twisted, the structure was damaged. He pressed and shaped it, making it into its true self. He stretched it where it needed to be stretched, folded where it needed to be folded. Within a few eons, he was done. The latticework was right. The way it should be. The way it was meant to be. He pulled himself back from the metal and turned off the valve in his mind. Donte hadn't aged a day while he was working.

In his hands he now held a brightly shining, cherry-red pan. It was feather light, had slightly curved sides, and a strangely foamy handle, making it a perfect saucier. The color slowly faded to black. Even though the glow had faded, heat waves poured from the pan as it cooled. Aleks walked the pan over to the countertop. Using the method he'd worked out earlier, he got some water flowing into the sink. He put the pan under the water to cool it. Somehow he knew it didn't need tempering. He'd already done that inside the metal. Steam billowed out of the sink, making him wonder how he could have held on to the pan. He looked at his hands. They were pink and clean like fresh new skin—no marks or burns.

He turned back to Donte. "How long did that take?"

Donte looked at him quizzically. "A few seconds?" It was more question than answer. Aleks shivered. He was certain he'd worked on the pan for hours or days.

Sounds of movement came from the corner of the room. Aleks and Donte both turned to look at the girl lying there. Still asleep, she had shifted on the mat, pulling the blanket up to her chin.

"I don't recognize this woman," Donte said. "Who is she?"

"I thought maybe you could tell me," Aleks replied. "She didn't give me her name before …" He trailed off, unwilling to relive those events.

"Most of what happened is a blur. But I think I remember seeing her leaning over me."

"She did most of the healing on you before the accident."

"Accident?"

Aleks flushed red. "She asked me to help you, but I didn't know what to do. I didn't know how to do the things you two do, so I tried to give her some energy so she could help you." He looked away from the girl. "Something went wrong. She screamed 'too much, too much' and slumped over against the wall. You looked worse than she did, so I looked after you. Then I looked after her." Aleks couldn't remember the last time he had cried, but tears flowed freely down his cheeks at the memory. "When I looked into her, her brain had been … damaged."

"Damaged?" Donte moved over to her and looked at her face. "In what way?"

"It was …" Aleks struggled to say it. "Crushed." He walked over beside Donte. "Almost all of it."

Donte brushed the girl's hair off her face. From his pocket he pulled the small bear figurine the girl had used earlier and laid a hand on her shoulder, concentrating.

As Donte used the energy from the bear on her, Aleks felt something in the room shift. He still didn't understand how he was feeling these things. It wasn't a sight or sound. The best way he could describe it was an itch. However it worked, the sensation was strong.

The itch continued for only a few minutes. Donte leaned back on his heels. He turned his sunken eyes on Aleks. "As I mentioned before, I'm not a great healer. My skills work more on the emotions than the body." He looked back at the girl. “But I can’t see anything wrong with her. Are you sure about what you saw? Wait, what am I saying? You’re the Great Builder! Of course you’re sure.”

Aleks struck up his courage. “I … I tried to help her. I was very tired after helping you. I couldn’t believe how tired I was. Anyway, I wanted to make sure she was okay before I rested. So I looked into her and saw the damage. I tried to put it all back together but just didn’t have the strength to do it.” He stared off into the distance. “So I kind of … made her own body rebuild her brain. I don’t know if it worked right because she hasn’t woken up yet. I just hope I didn’t make her into a vegetable or something.”

Donte’s head jerked around and he stared at Aleks with his wide, cadaverous eyes. He slowly stood and backed away from Aleks. “I’ve read everything ever written about you. I knew you could shape the land and make one animal into another, but none of the writings talked about you turning a person into a vegetable.”

“What? That’s not what I meant, you loony! I didn’t literally turn her into a vegetable. I just meant I hope I didn’t permanently damage her brain.” Aleks shook his head. “Good Lord, you’re a wonder.”

“What will you do now, my lord?”

“Wait, I guess.” Aleks rested his hand on hers and watched her breathe for a few moments. “It doesn’t seem like there’s anything else we can do. And please don’t call me ‘lord’ anymore. It creeps me out. How about if you and I sit down over a cup of tea while we wait and you can tell me where in the hell I am?”

“Let me see if I have this right,” Aleks said. “I’m in a world where people can do magic.” The glowing ball he had created was bobbing and weaving over their heads. He held up his hand at Donte’s protest. “I know it’s not really magic, but it’s close enough for me.

“And we use this magic to do just about everything. Everybody has their own specialties, like healing or making stuff.”

“Not exactly,” Donte interrupted. “Most people can’t do any of those things. Most people, maybe nine out of ten, *move* energy. They’re called Activators. They can send energy into other people or into objects that were made by the Templars. The people who *can* do 'magic' are called Regulators. They can shape the energy that an Activator sends them and make it do things. *Those* people usually have specialties, like healing. Most of them can do basic shaping and crafting. But only a rare few have the ability to create complex things or heal the grievously injured. Like what you did for me."

"And the Templars were people who could do both?"

"Yes. They were wiped out in a monstrous war more than two thousand years ago. The Dark One made sure of it. He's the most powerful Templar that has ever lived. Like most Templars he has the ability to craft and shape amazing things. But his *specialty* is draining the life force from others. In the war, he sucked the life out of thousands of warriors and destroyed *all* of the other Templars so no one could oppose him.

"Doing it almost killed him. He was vulnerable in his weakened state, so he fled north to recover. He has been up there gathering power and creating an army of monstrosities ever since. Soon he will sweep across the land and enslave us all. After two thousand years, any who might have opposed him are scattered or long dead." Donte looked intently at Aleks. "Until now.

"The Prophecies are being fulfilled. The Templars have once again returned to Freia."

"Unnnhhhh …"

Aleks spun to look at the girl, who was stirring. She sat up, eyes wide. She opened her mouth impossibly far and screamed. The sound reverberated off every hard surface in the tiny, one-room shack.

Aleks smashed his hands against his ears. His brain was splitting. Through squinted eyes streaming with tears he could see Donte was suffering as well. The scream went on and on. Thankfully, no one can scream without breathing. Eternal moments after it started, the scream stopped while the girl sucked in a huge breath. "Heeeeeeeeeeeeeeeh …"

Aleks leaped the short distance to the girl, nearly tackling her. He wrapped his arm around her back and clapped his hand over her mouth, pressing her head against his shoulder. She screamed into his hand. Every nerve and fiber in her being was taught and her body quaked with the strain. Her hands came up and grabbed his arm like vices. She didn't try to pull his arm away. She just clung to it with all her might. The second scream faded away. She sucked in another huge breath, through her nose this time.

Aleks leaned his face down against her cheek and slowly let a bit of himself flow into her, calming her. "Shhhhhhh …" he breathed into her ear. "Everything is going to be all right."

The next scream was weaker and faded quickly to nothing. The tension left her body and she relaxed her grip on his arm. She leaned her head into his cheek and closed her eyes. Within seconds she was limp in his arms.

He sat with her for a time, rocking her ever so slightly and whispering just how okay it really was. Eventually her breathing deepened and became regular. He sat there a bit longer. Then he gently laid her back down on the mat, tucking the pillow under her head. He looked at her, so young and frail, as she lay there. He brushed the hair back from her face. You couldn't call her plain, exactly. Maybe just further from perfect than most folks. He immediately felt a bit mean for thinking it. Who was he to judge? He wasn't exactly Johnny Depp.

Truthfully, she would never be considered a classic beauty, but she wasn't unattractive. And something about that didn't seem quite right, but he couldn't put his finger on what.

A Long Walk

Martin stank. No two ways about it. He stank to high heaven. And he was hungry. And he was miserable. It was just what he deserved.

He walked. Step after miserable step. The walking was easy. He stayed on the road heading west from Jesik's house, so it was smooth and clear. With no bushes to push his way through or gopher holes to step in, he made great time. He had no idea how far he had traveled each day. He just walked until he couldn't walk anymore. Then he lay down in the road until sleep came and wished someone would run him over.

Now, five days into his trek, he wondered for the thousandth time why the hell he had walked off *without taking any frickin' clothes or food! What an idiot!* Which always led inevitably to him wondering how he had survived for five days without any food or water.

Something had happened during or immediately after his visit with the Dark One. He had changed in some fundamental way. Sure, he was hungry. But he hadn't eaten in five days. He didn't think he'd gone five *hours* without eating before in his life. And how was it he could go to bed exhausted, sore, chaffed all over and sunburned but wake up each morning fresh? He'd even stumbled late in the evening of the second day, straining his ankle. In the morning the pain had been completely gone.

Oh well. At least it gave him something to think about other than …

Her hair fanned out in a pool of blood. She moved. She slowly turned her head toward him. Her face was ravaged by scars and her eyes were white, dead, and lifeless.

… his memories.

He looked at the road ahead. In the distance it curved up into the foothills, disappearing behind the first low rise. Judging the hour of the day by the sun, he guessed he could make it to the curve in the road before sunset. It looked like he'd be spending the night off the valley floor for the first time since seeing the Dark One.

Movement in the air caught his eye. A lone black bird winged its way south across the bright blue sky. How was it that he'd gone five days and seen so few living creatures? Twice a flock of birds, heading south, had flown ahead of him. He hadn't been here very long, but it seemed odd for them to head to warmer climates in the springtime. Even in this weird place. Maybe they could sense the growing storm in the north and were fleeing the Dark One. Or maybe the cooler air he'd been feeling the last few days meant something more than a change in the weather. This more recent bird disappeared behind the snow-covered peaks that rimmed the south side of the valley.

He scanned the land ahead as he walked, searching for any other movements. Low grass, blotchy brown and green in color, covered the valley floor. The grass was occasionally broken up by a small bush or tree. But the only movement he detected was from the gentle breeze that occasionally tussled the grass. It was like the valley was dead. He wasn't even swatting insects. Something was definitely wrong.

He walked. Step after miserable step.

Something caught Martin's eye as he neared the low hills that framed the west end of the valley. Movement! On the hillside just beyond the foothills a small herd of animals was grazing. They were a long way off, maybe a mile, maybe more, but he could see them clearly. Nearly everything he knew about animals came from the Discovery Channel, but they looked a little like goats.

Suddenly they all stopped moving. In twos and threes they raised their heads and perked up their ears, swiveling them back and forth. The Discovery Channel documentaries would say they had sensed a predator in the area. Then, almost as one, they all turned and looked directly at him. No. They weren't looking at him.

They were *staring* at him.

It was intensely unnerving. He looked behind him to see if something was sneaking up, but he was alone on the road. He looked back at the herd. They broke and ran, banging into each other and bounding over the brush. What brush they couldn't leap over they crashed through. This wasn't a group decision to move on. It was terrified flight. And he was the predator they were fleeing.

Just that quickly he had his answer as to what was wrong in this valley. It was *him*. He was the reason there was no life here. Everything was avoiding him.

Great. Now even the animals knew what he was.

He walked. Step after miserable step.

Soon the ground on either side of the road began to slope upward, growing into foothills. A bit farther on the road began to rise and curve to the north, wrapping around the first hill and into a slight valley that climbed upward. Trees, short but thick and full of leaves, lined the east side of the valley. The west side was a mangled mass of crushed bushes and broken saplings. The herd had come this way, seeking the shelter of the trees.

The light was dimming rapidly as the sun slipped behind the higher hills to the east. He walked on for a bit. The trees on the west side grew thicker to match their counterparts to the east, and on both sides they grew taller. Soon, broad branches were stretching over the road, forming a canopy. The darkness had grown deep and ominous. The only thing missing to make a scene out of a horror film was the oppressive music.

Unfortunately, Martin had been cast as the monster.

Eventually he grew tired enough to sleep. Following his new pattern, he lay down right where he was. The day of walking had been long and he'd spent most of it lamenting. And yet sleep was slow in coming. Eventually, though, it found him where he lay.

Retrieval

Tony rubbed the soft cloth along the Ghost's barrel. The weapon was ancient, worn smooth from ten thousand uses, and utterly beautiful. Bright silver with a grip made from mother of pearl, it was perfect. It was a blend of delicate mechanical grace as the hammer rolled the cylinder into position, and brutal power bucked in his hand when each round was fired.

Soon the Ghost was oiled and polished clean. He gently laid her back in the box. Then he picked up the Darkness. The twin of the Ghost in every mechanical aspect, the Darkness was as black as night with a grip made of ebony.

There was something about weapon care that helped him find serenity and clarity. Even in this time of absolute turmoil and chaos, this simple act could bring him to a place of peace. And the cool breeze that brushed across the front porch of Jesik's little house didn't hurt.

His thoughts percolated but didn't interrupt his work. He dripped some oil onto the rag and slowly worked it forward and back along the barrel. He opened the gate and removed the spent cartridges. He carefully placed them in the cardboard box with the others. He glanced at the rounds he had left: eight in this box and a fresh box of fifty in his duffel. If the last two days were any indication he'd be out of ammo in short order. And it was unlikely he'd find anyone to load his empty shells. He didn't even know if he could use the black powder cylinders nestled in the box. He'd need black powder and percussion caps for that.

He finished his ministrations on the Darkness and laid her gently back in the box. He decided to worry about running out of ammo when that time came.

As he was snapping the latch on the box closed, he felt Jesik approaching. The door opened and Jesik stepped out onto the porch.

Brow furrowed, he approached Tony. "It is time for us to go," he said.

"Go?" Tony raised an eyebrow.

"Yes. Raneal needs help. We must go and get it for her."

"I'm not going anywhere until I get some answers." Tony leaned back in his chair.

Tony had never met a person who so fully expressed Zen philosophy as Jesik. He was the walking embodiment of calm and peace. In conversation, while working, even in battle, he seemed unflappable.

In an instant that image was shattered.

Wham!

Jesik slammed his fist on the table, making the box jump. His face was a red mask of rage, his eyes wide and bloodshot behind his round spectacles. "*Raneal needs help and we're going to get it!*" His voice thundered. "*Now!*"

Tony's blood boiled. His mind roiled. This was the fucking end. He'd been patient for two days while one crisis after another came and went. Capped off by that nut-job Martin. Tony wanted to jump up and smash the table. But his face was as cold as stone. He stared into Jesik's eyes. Thirty seconds passed. Then a minute. He simply stared. His men called this his Death Trance because it captured his victims and bound them before he lowered the boom on them. At one time or another everyone in his battalion had been subjected to the Death Trance before serving latrine duty or running messages all day in hundred-degree weather.

In truth, the Death Trance *was* intimidating. But it was actually a device he had gleaned from his sensei and cultivated over the years. *Don't speak until you are calm enough to be in control of what you say.* Of course this had the advantage of making the person he was talking to ill at ease. That was really just a bonus.

Another minute of impasse and Jesik slowly began to breathe and relax just a bit. It was subtle, but Tony was an expert in picking up on these clues.

The impasse had given him enough time to calm down and clear his mind. When he finally spoke, both he and Jesik had returned from the precipice.

"All right. We'll go get help for Raneal." Tony's expression didn't change with his words. "But the others come with us. Everyone."

Tony held up his hand at Jesik's unspoken protestation. "They are obviously in danger, particularly Micah. And we can't protect them if we aren't all together."

Jesik was naive, particularly where Martin was concerned. But he wasn't stupid. He nodded.

"And when we've gotten Raneal the help she needs, we *will* have a conversation about what is happening and why."

Jesik nodded at this comment as well.

"Now, I have an errand to run before we leave."

Jesik raised his eyebrows at that.

Gravel crunched under the tires of the RX7 as it rolled off the "paved" section of road and toward the barn. Dinaala fed the wagon enough to pull the little sports car across the last few hundred feet and through the open barn door. They stopped the wagon once the RX had cleared the entryway. Tony pressed hard on the brakes to stop her before she crashed into back of the wagon. Without power, the hydraulics took extra effort.

They had made the trek out and back in fewer than four hours. Tony had done most of the pushing from the RX, feeding the wagon from there. He still didn't understand how it worked and he still lacked fine control, but the added weight of the RX had worked in his favor. It had been a relatively smooth ride back.

Tony climbed out. "All right. Let's get her untied and get everyone loaded up into the wagon." He looked at Jesik. "Unless you plan to use one of those gates you've been hiding from me."

Jesik paled but held his ground. "First, I haven't been hiding anything. With the exception of yesterday's combat, I simply have had no call to use one. In any case, we cannot use either the wagon or a gateway to get to our destination. The road does not go where we're heading, and opening a gateway at our destination would alert the Dark One of our intentions and call his wrath down upon us before we're ready."

"So it's horseback then?" Tony replied, sizing up the mares in the nearest stalls.

"Again, no." Jesik shook his head. "Where we're going is far too dangerous. Taking these beautiful beasts with us would be akin to murder. No, most of our time on this trip will be spent on foot, I'm afraid." He took a pebble out of his pouch. "But I do have a gateway that will take us to the last village between us and our destination. That shouldn't give away our intentions and it will get us most of the way there, cutting weeks off our journey."

"Why are we doing this?" Raneal came through the barn door and stomped over to confront Jesik. She repeated her question. Actually, it was more of an indictment than a question. Fortunately for Tony, Jesik was the recipient of her wrath. "I told you I was fine. Physically, I am no longer injured. My vanity is no excuse to take these innocents into the Deep. How will we fight your precious battle if we're all dead?"

Jesik took her hands in his. "We have to go into the Deep anyway. Aleks should be here by now. It's time for him and me to enter the Forbidden City and speak to Her." He looked deeply into her eyes. "But know this, my sister. You and I have walked Freia's soil together for more than four hundred years. I love you. I would walk through the gates of the Dark One himself to put things right for you."

"But the children …"

"Are much older, more mature, and far tougher than they appear, and you know it." He released her hands. "Besides, Tony's right. We can't leave anyone behind here. The Dark One has twice tried to retrieve Micah and failed. You know as well as I that the Dark One punishes the living for the failures of the dead. The next group he sends will have the stink of pain and suffering on them. They will be much more dangerous than the last group. Micah and Dinaala *cannot* be here when they arrive."

Jesik smiled and raised a hand to forestall Raneal's final protest. "I've sent a message bird to Trin asking her to check on the horses every day or two until we get back. She'll do a fine job. Marequette will be fine. Now stop arguing and go pack before I take you over my knee."

She took a deep breath and flashed a tentative smile before turning toward the door. She stopped at the frame and turned back. "I love you too, Jesik. And thank you."

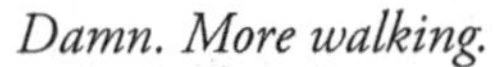

Damn. More walking.

Tony adjusted his pack straps into a slightly more comfortable position. His face never showed his discomfort, but that didn't mean he didn't feel it. He stopped himself before he could get wound up. It was time to reframe his thoughts. He looked at this ragtag bunch. Two kids, two … had Jesik said *four hundred years?* He must've misheard that. Jesik looked like he was in his early forties. *Four hundred years?* It boggled the mind.

Jesik looked at him. "Do you have everything you want to take with you?" He pulled a stone from his pouch and held it in his upturned palm. It was a tiny, four-sided pyramid, glassy blue-green with deep purple striations in it. "We'll be coming into a village shortly, so you'll have a chance to pick up anything else you might need."

Tony thought for the tenth time about what he might need. It was impossible to tell. Jesik had been cryptic about the place they were going, only saying it was extremely dangerous. Along with K'Tichnam, Shinyuu, both pistols, and all of his ammo Tony was carrying some miscellany he'd found in his car. When he'd set out from the base a few days ago he hadn't planned on doing any camping, so he had little in the way of gear.

Tony nodded at Jesik. "Let's go."

Jesik looked at the pyramid. It split along the upper three sides at the apex and blossomed. As each side folded flat, a complex tangle of gold string trapped inside was released. It quickly unwound into a small loop. The loop expanded rapidly, forming a ring several feet across.

Jesik dropped the now-flat triangle to the ground with the ring, now an oval, standing straight up like a vanity mirror. It continued to expand. Tony saw a very different landscape through the loop. Outside the circle the valley was as flat as ever, with distant peaks framing it. Through the ring a rocky cliff rose straight up. Lichen and small plants clung to the face of the cliff. In front of it were incredibly tall trees forming a canopy high above the ground. If he was back home on Earth, he would have guessed the place was somewhere in the Amazon. He hadn't been there, but he'd seen enough pictures to get a sense of it. What he could see—and smell for that matter—definitely seemed like rainforest.

If it had been a rainforest on Earth, it would have been bad enough, with giant, poisonous bugs, snakes, and other critters that could kill a person. But this was a strange land, with crazier, more dangerous creatures than on Earth. And even crazier people. And all sorts of other risks he didn't know about yet. Whatever was on the other side of that hole was probably very interested in seeing him and his companions dead.

Tony didn't hesitate. As soon as the ring was large enough for a person to walk through without stooping, he stepped through. If something over there *did* want them dead, he wanted to be the first one to meet it.

Hot Pocket

Thom's eyes snapped open, but he resisted the urge to jump up and grab his sword. He couldn't have picked it up anyway. Besides the rude awakening Fazha would have gotten as he tossed her aside, the arm she'd been sleeping on was completely numb.

Wait. *The arm she'd been sleeping on?* How had that happened? Last thing he remembered was rinsing three days' worth of crap off of himself and his clothes and then laying himself back down to rest.

Alone.

Fazha hadn't even been in the cave at the time.

He looked down at her. Damn, she was beautiful. He closed his eyes and his mind against that thought.

Shit. He came back to the thing that had roused him. There were people outside the cave. *A lot* of people. And they were coming around the pool, moving stealthy. *Dammit!* There were Regulators in the mix. Strong ones. And plenty of Activators to make them a problem.

Okay. What to do?

He gently shook Fazha, lamenting the bad timing of their guests' arrival and his own bad breath. She kept her eyes closed and told him to let her sleep; school was over for the summer. He shook her again and slipped his arm out from under her. This time she came awake. He held his finger to his lips and pointed to the waterfall. She looked at it for a brief second and then jumped up and started gathering their things for a quick getaway.

Fortunately, the sound of the waterfall covered any noise they made. He looked around the cave for anything that could be used to tactical advantage.

Of course he knew the cave intimately, having shaped much of it himself, and knew there was nothing here he could use. He put the saddles on the horses and tied down the packs. They were ready to go. But to where?

He had only seconds to decide. So he did.

He raised one hand toward the mouth of the cave and the other toward the back wall. He knew he had to mask his power, or anything he did now would be for naught. His Touch slid out across the floor in each direction. A few feet from the entrance it slid up the wall to the ceiling. The ceiling of the cave turned red. Then it softened and drooped just a bit. He pulled and pushed at the rock. It shifted. He poured more energy into it. Long spikes stretched down across the entrance of the cave, dripping onto the floor. Within seconds the drips piled up into spikes, reaching up toward their brethren. When they met they became pillars and then columns. A minute later each had widened enough to touch the columns on either side.

Sweat was pouring down his face. He tugged at the rock, spreading it out and thickening the wall. He left fissures at the bottom so the creek they were camped around wouldn't flood their little chamber.

He looked toward the back of the cave. It was now several feet farther back. The ceiling, where the river of rock had flowed from back to front, was now smooth and shiny. He looked at Fazha. In the red glow of the hot rocks, with her tight leather pants and unkempt hair, she looked like a sexy demon temptress. He shook his head. They *definitely* needed better light.

He sent his Touch into the glow stone that was still stuck in the ceiling above their heads. Just as the red glow dulled and faded, the glow stone's bright white light flooded the chamber.

Fazha was staring at him, slack-jawed and wide-eyed.

"By the Maker!" She looked back at the newly formed wall. "I could *feel* it. I could feel you doing it. How … what … you didn't … so much …" She trailed off into stunned silence.

"Speechless, eh?" He grinned. "Didn't think I'd see *that* in my lifetime."

That snapped her back to the here and now. He couldn't have her thinking too much about how strong he really was.

"Uh …" Fazha began. "I'm not one to question the great and powerful Thom, but didn't you just make a wall of rock across our only exit, smart guy?"

"Yep. But fortunately, that's not our only exit." He looked at the back wall of the cave. "We're going that way."

Thom sat down rather more suddenly than he'd intended. Actually, truth be told, he sort of collapsed onto the hard rocks.

Fazha rushed over and squatted next to him. "You *have* to rest, Thom!" She mopped his brow with one of the small squares of cloth she'd cut from her ruined pants. "By the Maker! Do you want to kill yourself?"

He knew she was right. He couldn't even open his eyes to look at her. But he also knew the truth. He might have killed them all. They had only so much air in this little chamber. Two people and two horses would use it up very quickly. It was already getting hard to breathe. During the last couple of moves he'd tried to find the oxygen in the rocks so he could release it for them. It was a bit hit or miss. He bought them some time, but it cost him some forward progress. It was a catch-22. Now *that* was a depressing movie.

"Can I ask you a question?" Fazha asked.

"Well, since that was a question, I guess you can."

She hesitated before continuing. *That* made him nervous. He opened his eyes. She was kneeling beside him. He looked up into her face. Her brow was furrowed as she struggled to control her emotion. Her long, straight hair framed her face.

Oh my God, she's beautiful. And I'm an idiot.

"How are you doing this?" With the question out there, she finally allowed her fear to show. "I mean, you're reshaping a mountain here. And there's no jar in the world large enough to hold that much power. So … I mean … you must be …" She turned her eyes away from him.

"Are you the … you know … um … the *Dark One*?" The last was barely a whisper.

He couldn't help himself. He was too exhausted to control himself. The laughter boiled out of him. Tears streamed down his face. He knew he was in trouble. He could feel her eyes boring into him. She was getting pissed.

But he couldn't stop himself. After everything they had been through over the last few days and all the effort he had put forth on the cave, his mind and body needed the release. He laughed and laughed.

Smack!

His teeth rattled and his ears rang from the slap. That would snap a guy out of anything. "I guess you're not worried anymore about my being the Dark One." He rubbed his cheek.

Her smile didn't touch her eyes. "I heard you were supposed to slap people when they got hysterical. Now please tell me just exactly *what is going on*. If you're not the Dark One, then what the hell are you? And if you could do all of this, why didn't you just … I don't know … squish them or something?"

Chuckles still threatened to bubble out of him. He took a deep breath. It was time to level with her. She deserved to know the truth. "Okay." He lay back and looked at the ceiling. "We don't have time to go through the whole thing right here and now. But I'll give you the gist and fill in the rest when we're out of here, okay?"

Somehow it was really important to him for her to be okay with all this. She nodded. Brilliant girl and very practical. He liked that about her. Of course he liked just about *everything* about her.

Focus, dammit, focus!

Sweat dripped into his eye. Damn, it was hot in there. "Have you ever heard of the Prophecy of Darkest Days?"

"Who hasn't?"

"Well, that prophecy talks about the possible fall of the Dark One and a cleansing that would follow, right?"

"Okay."

"Well, it says that the only way any of this can come about is if the Templars return to Freia."

"Okay. So you're saying you're a Templar." The disbelief in her voice cut him just a little.

"Sort of. The prophecy doesn't say that the Templars will be 'reborn.' What it says is that the Templars will *return*."

"So now you're saying that you're a Templar from more than four hundred years ago who has somehow come to our time?"

"Nope. What I'm saying is that I'm not from around here." He took a deep breath. "I'm not from anywhere here. I'm not from Freia at all."

She frowned. There was a bit of snarl in her voice. "All right. If you're not going to be serious then I don't want to know! You can just keep your damned secret." She stood up. "Now I think I'd like to move on. If you don't mind!"

He sighed. Damn. Why did *no one* believe him? He struggled to his feet, walked over to her, and took her by the arms. "Look." He dodged right and left before finally getting her to look him in the eye. "I *am* being serious. I might joke around with you, but I'll never lie to you." Looking at her beautiful face he knew that for the first time in his life those words were absolutely true.

"A man named Jesik brought me here against my will five years ago." He released her arms. Now he was going to end up using up a bunch of their minimal air on this conversation. "Like I said, I'm not going to go into too much detail on this. Let me just say that most folks don't know just how detailed that prophecy really was. It called for someone to snatch a few people from Freia's sister world, Earth, so they could fight the Dark One when the time came."

She looked horror-stricken. "He just took you?"

"Well, I've had some time to get over it. I don't blame him. He was trying to save his world. He had to make some hard choices. He really is a very sweet guy. A bit pompous, but a sweet guy. Besides, I wasn't amounting to much over there anyway. I can do a lot more good here."

He turned away from her, toward the back wall of the chamber. "I really should get us moving before we run out of air."

He'd told her he wouldn't lie to her, but there was no point in telling her the full truth about his future. At least not right now.

He looked at the stream running down the center of the cave. He'd been following it upward for several hundred feet now, simply opening the channel for them to pass and then closing it behind them. But he judged that he needed a steeper angle to reach the top of the cliff before their air ran out.

"Do you know this area very well?" he asked her.

"How would I? You brought me here while I was unconscious and kept me in a cave for three days." She grinned at him. That lightened his heart a bit. At least she didn't think he was the Dark One anymore.

"So you've got a lot of three-hundred-foot-high waterfalls in these parts, do you?" He arched his eyebrow. That look usually charmed the ladies.

"Well, if I knew which parts you brought me to before we got to the waterfall, I might be able to help you."

"Okay. So how far up do you think we've gone?"

"I'd guess maybe two hundred feet, more or less."

That was about what he thought. They were about two thirds of the way up. The horses had been skittish at first, but he had calmed them with the Touch. Now they were just tired and sluggish. They had to be urged to move.

And the heat in the chamber was oppressive. If they strayed away from the stream, they'd lose even that little bit of cooling. Well, there was no other option but to go on. Time to go.

He took a deep breath and focused his mind on the back wall of the chamber. It slowly started to glow. It grew brighter and brighter. Within a few seconds it started to flow, splitting and sliding away from the back of the chamber. Behind them the chamber slowly closed up. As the chamber moved along, the floor steepened. Now they were working to go uphill. Minutes passed. Or maybe it was hours. Who knew?

A splash of cold water on his face set Thom into a sputtering cough. He blinked a few times. Everything was kind of odd. He was looking at a stone wall that curved over him and became the floor. He was lying on it. It was hot. Why was he lying down? There was a bright light nearby. How was there a bright light nearby? He wasn't lighting it. He turned his head. Bad idea—one of those *bad ideas* he'd been having a lot lately. The pain stabbed through his temple. Damn. Another hangover without the fun of the drinking.

Fazha was sitting near him with a canteen in her hand. The glow stone was sitting on a rock by the horses. "Are you okay?" she asked. Her voice carried a bit of a tremor in it.

"What did you hit me with?"

Her smile was more compassionate than sarcastic. That was not a good sign. "The floor." She mopped his brow with her ever-present cloth. "It was just what I had on hand."

"Where are we?"

"Again, you ask me that like I would know."

"How long have I been out?"

"About twenty minutes. I was worried that we might run out of air if I let you rest any longer."

"Good call." He sat up. The cave danced and undulated. Nausea came up, but he handled it.

Let's just suss this thing out a bit.

He closed his eyes and let his Touch flow into the ceiling. He felt fissures and veins all through the stone. Further, further. There. The stone loosened. Mud. Silt. Water. They were close. Maybe another ten feet up. He reached farther out in their direction of travel. The dirt rose up and became rock again. He went up. Suddenly there was nothing. He was out. At least his Touch was. This was it. Thirty more feet at his current angle and they would be out. As he brought his Touch back, he scraped some more oxygen out of the rocks, bringing some less stale air into the cave. He opened his eyes.

"It's not much farther. We just have to go about thirty feet in that direction." His head sagged. Then his shoulders. Fazha grabbed him before he could fall to the ground. She put her arm around his waist and draped his arm over her shoulder, giving him the support he needed.

"Okay. One last go. Let's get out of here." He breathed deeply several times and then sent his Touch back into the rock wall in front of them. It slowly parted. They moved along, he and Fazha, with the horses stepping along behind them. They slowly edged along that way for a bit.

Cool air suddenly swirled into the chamber, refreshing him. Oxygen. He *loved* oxygen. One last blast opened the cavern wide enough for them to walk up and out, into sunlight.

Breath after breath.

The four of them stood there in the cool breeze just breathing. He had done it. They were out. Not only that, they were at the top of the cliff. Surely it would take the Duke days to make his way up there. Thom opened his eyes and looked around.

Beside them was a large rock outcropping, furry with lichen and tiny bushes. Fortunately, he had missed it by a few feet or they would have had to go another twenty feet before reaching the air.

The cool, cool air. It came from the strong river that fed the waterfall, tussling his hair as it passed. The river passed to their left in a wide arc, meeting up with another, wider river. Together they headed on for a half a mile or so before plunging over the edge of the world.

Wait. Another river? He turned back to the sweeping arc on his left. He detached himself from Fazha and walked upstream, around the outcropping.

As he came around the huge stone, he saw the wider river splashing against its base. There the river split into two wide arcs, the one on their side of the stone and its twin on the other side.

Damn. He had brought them up out of Freia and onto a friggin' island.

Winds of Change

Even the windows across the stern of the ship couldn't brighten Rayne's cabin. She pursed her lips and listened to the droning story the woman across from her was sharing. Some of the details were important: how many ships had been sent, how each ship carried at least three strong Activators for each Wavemistress, and how the Rast was indeed aboard one of the ships. But, as with the other surviving Activator, the majority of the conversation was less than useless. Neither woman had any idea who had sent them or why.

Suddenly, a new sense of movement tickled at her mind. The ship was turning. Rayne stood and turned toward the door to her cabin. The woman, her name was inconsequential and lost to Rayne, cut herself off in midword. Nonplussed and a bit pale, she stood as well.

Rayne strode to the door, her movements a perfect match to the roll of the ship on the waves. She jerked the door open and flowed up the steps onto the deck, the nameless Activator following behind. She could see the Wavemistress and the other Activator on the forecastle, the wind rifling their short hair. Rayne could just make out the tips of the Spikes off the portside of the ship. If they kept to this heading, Ravenscroft, the northernmost town in the Southland, would soon appear on the horizon. Ravenscroft. Her home. And the place where her queen awaited the delivery of a silly little man.

"Why have you changed course?" she called as she crossed the main deck. She had to raise her voice to be heard over the wind and the water.

Both women turned to look at her. They stood still, waiting for her, heads slightly bowed in respect. When she had climbed the few short steps up to the forecastle the Wavemistress pointed to port. "We've nearly reached the

Spikes, so it's time to turn eastward if we are to reach Ravenscroft before the trailing ships catch us up."

"We're not going to Ravenscroft," Rayne said simply.

Condescension flashed across the Wavemistress's face. "Mistress"—she began her lecture—"we must make for Ravenscroft, even if you are intent upon following the Spikes to the Western Lands. That trip is almost three thousand miles. We're not provisioned for that kind of excursion."

Rayne smiled. She loved it when people underestimated her. "Continue north toward the Spikes." She gestured northward with her chin. "Come get me when we're within a league of them."

The Activators looked perplexed. The Wavemistress looked bemused but nodded with a small bow and turned back toward the prow. The sails fluttered, shifted, and turned across the wind. The sky slowly slid across the forecastle as the ship's heading arced back toward the north.

Rayne turned away from the women and step-slid down the short stairs to the deck. Kevin and Gaien met her at the foot of the steps. Kevin was his usual wiggly self, hopping side to side in his ever-present joy.

She frowned at Gaien. He smiled back. Such a flowery face would have melted other women. It raised an annoying tickle at the back of her mind. And Kevin was spending a lot of time with this *man. That* was disconcerting. She took a deep breath. She knelt to get face to face with Kevin. He smiled and licked her. He was always so happy. At that moment she realized she hadn't done anything to care for him in days. Gaien had taken on the jobs of feeding and cleaning up after him. That made her uncomfortable for some reason.

She looked up at Gaien. "Watch them."

He nodded and made his way up to the forecastle.

She ruffled Kevin's face and neck for a few more seconds and then headed back to her cabin. Kevin followed.

It never changed. Of course it didn't; it was a map. Rayne continued to stare at it. In truth, she wasn't really looking at the never-changing image. She was thinking about the Spikes. If her plan failed, they were doomed. *Raffy* was making good time, but there were a lot of ships behind him and they were making good time too. Not to mention the Rast.

Some things were going in her favor, though. The women's arrival was fortuitous. She didn't think she could do what needed to be done alone. And they were relatively fresh, so they would be strong when they needed to be. Lastly, they knew nothing of her plan, so they had no idea how to cause her grief. Just in case, she made sure Gaien was with them every minute Rayne was occupied. Despite his mannishness, he'd shown himself capable, both physically and energetically.

Energetically. That posed an interesting question. What was it with his energy?

Never mind. There were other pressing matters to consider. Would her plan work? No one had ever tried it before, so there were no guarantees. And she had to find the right spot at just the right time for it to all come together.

She kept coming back to that thought. No one had ever tried it before. At least no one who had survived. But no one had her power, either. It would work. It *had* to.

A loud knock on the door roused her from her musing. The door opened a crack and one of the Activators poked her head in. "Sorry to bother you, Mistress, but we're approaching the Spikes, as you ordered."

"Thank you." Rayne nodded. "I'll be up shortly."

The woman ducked back out and closed the door. Rayne waited a few minutes before following. It was better if the women did not detect her anxiety. Complete confidence and control. That was the key to success here.

As she stepped onto the deck the sight of the Spikes almost took her breath away. They were absolutely amazing. A line of pillars atop a two hundred-foot-high cliff framed the sky. They rose hundreds of feet above the top of the cliff and ran for three thousand miles across the ocean, from the Northern Press to the Western Lands, completely cutting the Northern Sea off from the Southern.

The cliff cut across the ocean like a plate standing up in a bowl of water. In front of the ship huge waves crashed against the cliff face. And at the top of the cliff, on the north side of the Spikes, the sea brushed against the feet of the pillars two hundred feet higher than on this side. The Break in the World had done more than raise mountains. It had split the seas, forever separating them.

She stepped up onto the forecastle. Kevin, Gaien, and the women were all staring at the mass of rock before them. *Raffy* had drawn very close. The massive cliff hung oppressively over them.

"Mistress," the Wavemistress said, "I don't mean any disrespect, but what are we doing here?"

Rayne felt the anxiety boiling beneath the woman's veneer. Rayne didn't blame her. There was just a wrongness to the cliff. It wasn't natural.

But she ignored the question for the moment.

She looked up at the base of the Spikes, hoping to find just the right pair. It was nearly time. She could see trickles of water slipping between the Spikes and tumbling down the cliff face to the sea below. The moons were pulling the tide higher on the north side. Each day was twenty-five hours long, but only during two of those hours were the moons pulling the tides high enough for the falls to form. Within a few minutes powerful rivers of water poured between the Spikes and crashed to the sea below. It looked like hair gliding through a giant comb.

Dammit. She didn't have much time.

They would have to move fast to make it before the falls stopped, but they could just get there in time.

She turned to tell the women where they were going. Something to the south caught her attention out of the corner of her eye. Sails. A lot of sails. Dozens of them dotted the skyline.

The others turned to follow her gaze.

"Mistress—" one of the Activators began.

"Nata!" the Wavemistress snapped, silencing her. She turned to Rayne with great dignity and gravity. "Mistress. You have not treated us badly. I am a fair woman. I am tasked with retrieving this ... *man*." The last was more snarl than word. Her contempt for Gaien was palpable. She continued. "I do not wish to kill you. If you will give up now, I will ensure that you and your dog are treated with dignity and exiled to the north in the Ravenscroft gondola."

Rayne turned from the ships to face the Wavemistress. "I appreciate your offer. But I think I'll arrive in the north via alternate means." She turned back to the prow. "Now I want you to give us all possible speed toward the west. Stay at least three hundred feet from the cliff."

"Why? The cliffs go straight down forever here. There are no rocks or shoals to hit."

"Just let me worry about the whys and do what I say."

The Wavemistress took a deep breath and called on both the wind and the sea. Within seconds *Raffy* was racing toward the pillars she had chosen. She looked back at the ships. *Raffy* pulled away a bit. In short bursts, he was amazingly fast. They traveled along in silence for a while, the cliff rolling by to starboard. The waterfalls were so powerful, Rayne could feel and taste the spray they made.

"Mistress ..." one of the Activators said.

Rayne raised an eyebrow. This was interesting. The Activator was feeding the Wavemistress a huge stream of power, yet she was able to talk? Maybe there was more to these women than Rayne had suspected. "Yes?"

"If they catch you and we are aboard, they will kill us."

"I know. I don't intend to get caught."

"But we can't keep this pace up long enough to outrun them all the way to the Western Lands. Not to mention we don't have enough food and water."

"That's far enough. Turn us to the south."

The women looked confused, but *Raffy* began a smooth arc to the south.

Rayne continued to face the cliff as *Raffy* moved away. *Soon. Soon. That's it.* "All right, now turn us around and head straight toward the cliff."

Raffy shuddered as both the current and wind died. Rayne turned and looked at the women.

They stood gaping at her. "What?"

"Turn the ship around now and sail directly at the cliff as fast as he can go." If they were going to rebel, this was the moment. She focused her energy and then took that opportunity away. "*Do it now!*"

Backed by her energy, her voice struck them like a gong. They all jumped. The Wavemistress reluctantly accepted the energy the Activators fed her and pulled the schooner around in a tight arc. Within a few minutes they were flying toward the cliff.

"Your destination is that gap in the Spikes," Rayne said, pointing to the pair she had chosen.

"But, Mistress," the Wavemistress said through teeth clenched tight, "we'll be crushed against the cliff!"

"Just do as I say."

Rayne gathered in the energy of the sea. She bound one chaotic flow after another. One by one she organized them into a single wave, growing under *Raffy*. The sea began to swell, building in pressure. She closed her eyes to better concentrate.

"Unh …" The Wavemistress faltered. Not realizing where it came from, she'd tried to pull on the rising swell to move *Raffy*.

"Just guide us to that spot," Rayne snapped. "I'll move the ship now."

The women started making low moaning noises in their throats. She didn't dare open her eyes to see how they were doing. The swell was growing rapidly now behind and beneath the little ship. *Raffy* picked up speed. The swell grew. Kevin leaned in on her leg, lending his strength again.

"Keep the wind in his sails!" Rayne cried over the rush of wind and water. "If we founder now, we're all dead!"

She needed to know how high they were. She opened her eyes. More. She needed more. They needed 200 feet to reach the top of the cliff and they had no more than 170. She closed her eyes again and pressed for more. A low thrumming sound filled her ears, so low she almost couldn't hear it. Gaien was singing. The strands she had pulled in and bound grew. They expanded, *thickened*. One of the Activators was screaming. *Raffy* was accelerating faster than he'd ever gone before. The crest of the mighty wave was kicking foam over the poop deck. She felt that most of the little ship was out of the water, hanging in the air above the wave. She opened her eyes.

They had the height they needed, but the gap she had chosen between the pillars looked tiny as they sped toward it. *Raffy* was a skinny little ship, but even his narrow beam was too wide for most of the gaps in the Spikes. This one had looked wide enough before they were screaming along at a hundred knots, riding a massive wave to their own doom.

"More to port, more to port, *more to port*!" she cried.

The Wavemistress was pale and covered in sweat. Both Activators were sitting on the deck holding their heads. Before Rayne could react, Gaien stepped to the nearest woman and slapped her hard across the face. She lowered her hands and looked around and then started feeding the Wavemistress again. The new influx of energy got the Wavemistress going again as well. *Raffy* shifted to port.

"Yes! That gap, *that gap*!" Rayne cried. Now that Gaien's song was fueling the wave, Rayne could risk touching the wind. The Wavemistress would have to thread a needle at a hundred knots. Maybe she could help.

She snatched a flow of air and bound it to another. She added more, braiding them into a short, powerful gust. She wrapped it around one pillar and then added another to its partner, creating buffers of wind on each side of the gap. A person caught in one of those gales would have been flung five hundred feet.

The Wavemistress's eyes were wide now. Rayne hoped she could sense the funnel Rayne had created.

Raffy's prow edged to starboard and then back to port as the Wavemistress lined him up. The Spikes were coming fast. And the gap looked impossibly small.

The Activators were screaming. The Wavemistress was screaming. Gaien was singing. *Raffy* screamed as well, when his sides scraped the two pillars. They passed in the blink of an eye and a roar of thunder as ten million gallons of seawater slammed into the cliff face behind and below them.

Raffy lurched and dug his bow in deep when the crest of the wave he rode met the strong waterfall current. All his passengers were flung hard toward the forward rail when his momentum stopped but theirs didn't.

Rayne heard more than felt her ribs breaking. One of the Activators missed the rail completely and flew out into the northern sea. She was immediately sucked away, dragged between two pillars on the portside and flung out over the southern sea. Even her screams were lost.

Impossibly, Gaien had grabbed the rail *and* Kevin before *Raffy*'s sudden stop. They were now lying together on the forecastle. The Wavemistress and the other Activator were screaming and holding on to each other. The torrent had grabbed Raffy and was starting to pull him back toward that monstrous drop. Rayne snatched at the flows in the sea and pulled several of them to task. It wasn't much, but it was enough. *Raffy* stopped sliding backward. Rayne struggled and pulled in some more. She was so tired.

Now was the time for steel tits. She pulled in more, driving *Raffy* away from the edge. One hundred feet. Two hundred feet. She was so tired. Three hundred feet. The drag on *Raffy* eased up more with every foot she moved him. At five hundred feet she dropped the flows and let the wind work to keep him away from the edge.

Rayne sat for a minute and breathed. The screaming slowly died down as the remaining women gathered themselves. They sat crying and holding each other like a couple of men. But she couldn't judge them too harshly. Even strong women like these could take only so much.

And she was incredibly thankful that Gaien had grabbed onto Kevin. Once again the little man had done something unexpected and heroic. He almost seemed feminine.

Rayne turned back to the Wavemistress. "I'm truly sorry about your friend," she said with all sincerity. "I didn't know our landing would be so rough."

The Wavemistress looked up at Rayne. She gathered herself. "Are you a Templar?"

And there it was.

The question Rayne had dreaded since she had gained her powers. It was the question she hadn't even dared ask herself. No Templar had been born for more than twenty-five hundred years. What right did she have to even think it possible? But there it was.

And it wasn't the only question on her mind.

Now for the big one. Why had she done this? Why had she taken them through the Spikes? The queen was waiting for Gaien in Ravenscroft. Rayne had tossed aside her mission. She had thrown away everything she stood for. She had betrayed her queen. And she had *shown her power to others*. For what? What had possessed her to do these things? She didn't know.

But in her heart she knew she had done the right thing. Somehow she knew that if Gaien had gone to her queen, or been captured by the Magister of the Southern Reach, the world would have greatly suffered. She didn't know how she knew, but she knew. Gaien had to be kept safe and kept in the north.

She looked at the Wavemistress. "I'll offer you the same arrangement you offered me," she said. "If you agree to say nothing about this trip, I will land at Devil's Reef and let you go free to take the gondola back down to Ravenscroft."

The Wavemistress took a deep breath and looked at Rayne. "I have allowed you to escape with this man. I am no longer welcome in the Southern Reach. I have no intention of ever returning there. I would be honored to travel with the first Templar born in twenty-five hundred years." She looked down. "If she will have me."

"I am not a Templar."

"No one but a Templar could have raised a wave two hundred feet in the air. And you have taken no Touch from the Activators during all of this. If you are not a Templar, then what are you?"

"I don't know." Rayne breathed deeply and sighed heavily. "And I don't know where I'm going. But you're welcome to come along with me." Pain shot through her side as she stood up, snatching away the deep breath she had just taken. She stood for a moment to gauge her pain.

Kevin and Gaien were both standing when she reached them. They were fine. She looked at Gaien and wondered again what the hell she was doing.

What she *did* know was that she'd better check *Raffy* out and make sure he wasn't on his way to the *bottom* of the northern sea.

"If it's any consolation, I've failed in my mission as well. I've taken Gaien north."

Making Scents

Three days. Aleks had been trying for three days to get Alice—what he'd taken to calling his ward—to say something. Anything. So far he'd had no luck. In fact, he'd had very little luck getting her to communicate at all. She didn't grunt or make hand gestures or even nod.

He'd had great hopes when she finally woke up. After the screams from her previous awakening, he'd been sure she was somehow ruined inside. When she woke this time she simply sat up and looked around the room. Her eyes darted everywhere, never really landing on any one thing. Until they'd found Aleks.

He'd sat there for a few minutes, unable to move.

Donte broke the silence. "Are you all right?" he'd asked, slowly moving toward her. "I'm Donte, and this is Aleks."

She hadn't even acknowledged that he was talking to her. She just continued to stare at Aleks. They'd tried for more than an hour to communicate with her. The only thing they'd managed to do was get her to eat some porridge. It was the same for the next three days. Her eyes never left Aleks for more than a few seconds at a time. Aleks just wished he could communicate with her.

The now familiar smell of sweet corn overpowered the smell of sweat, blood, and pine that filled the room. He took great, huge breaths to gather in as much of the aroma as he could. It was beautiful. He would've thought that after five or six days it would wear on him. He couldn't even eat *pizza* six days in a row.

But this porridge was different. It was the elixir of life. It was "oh my God" good. He took in another huge lungful of air. Delightful!

But wait. There was another scent under that fabulous smell. It was faint. Much more faint than the sweat, which was everywhere. Donte's sweat, Alice's sweat. Even his own sweat permeated the room. And under that was the blood. It was still in the wood of the floor. There was the varnish or lacquer or whatever they'd preserved the wood with. And there was the wood itself. The building was deep, rich, and ancient. The chairs were from young, nutty trees. He smelled the wind that had blown across their branches.

What the hell?

He smelled the wind that had blown across their branches?

He was losing his fucking mind. No two ways about it. He took another deep breath. There it was again. Roses. This tree had been growing near roses.

Damn. He was truly fucked up.

And there was that smell again. Waxy. Wooden. Acidic. And something else. Stone. It came from the kitchen. Carried to him along with Donte's melancholy.

"Is everything all right, Donte?" Aleks asked. What? Melancholy?

"Yes," Donte replied without turning from the stove.

"Uh huh. Why am I not convinced?"

Donte finally turned and looked at him. His eyes were even deeper set than usual, making him look more like a skeleton than a cadaver. "I have done what I was asked to do," he said. "I waited and waited."

He carried the three bowls of porridge he had made to the table and sat down opposite Aleks. Alice came from her mat to sit between them.

"I long to return to my great love, but I can't. I have to remain here with you until you go to the Forbidden City. But you don't know anything about that. So how can you go there?" He seemed so lost.

"I'm sorry," Aleks began. "I know we've talked about this a hundred times. But I just don't have a clue what you're talking about." He took a deep breath and caught that smell again. It was coming from a cabinet in the lower left corner beside the stove, the second shelf up.

"I want you to tell me about the prophecy again." Aleks grinned at Donte. "But first, I want you to tell me about this great love of yours. You've never mentioned her before."

"The *Repository*," Donte said. He had a faraway look in his eyes. "More than five hundred thousand books. Stacks and stacks and stacks. There are scrolls in there dating back ten thousand years. It's beautiful. And so … *full* of knowledge. I've spent three lifetimes in that place and still don't know one percent of what it contains. If I live another thousand years it still won't be enough for me to get my fill."

"You've lived *three* lifetimes? Okay, wait. How long is a"—he made quotation marks in the air with his fingers—"lifetime?"

Donte finally focused on him again. "What?"

"How long is a *lifetime* here?"

"Oh …" Donte paused for a second. "I'd say most people live around eighty years or so."

Aleks was floored. "So, you're *240 years old?"*

"Hmm … let me think. I think I'm more like 270. Let's see, if this year is … and I was born … actually, I think it's 272. It gets hard to remember after a while."

"How is that even possible?" Aleks was trying to wrap his mind around a man who had lived for almost three hundred years, but that smell was so … "What in the hell is that?"

"What?"

"That *smell!* It's like wood and wax and paint and …" Aleks pointed. "It's coming from that cupboard. It's been bugging me for an hour."

"*That* cupboard?" Donte looked confused. "Well, nothing really."

He got up and walked to the cupboard. "There's nothing in here but pencils and paper." He took them out and brought them back to the table. "I use these for journaling. When I spend a lot of time alone, journaling keeps me sane. But I haven't needed them since you've been here."

Aleks picked up one of the pencils. That was the smell. Stone. Graphite. Wait. It shouldn't be graphite. This world was different. So graphite should be different. But it was the same graphite as Earth. He was sure of it. He hadn't had this sense of smell on Earth. And yet he somehow knew it to be true.

With his new eyesight he looked into the pencil. He saw stringy tendrils of wood fiber, bound together in a complex and chaotic pattern that somehow managed to stay together, firm and strong. Looking deeper, he saw the latticework of the stone that made up the central core.

He pulled back out of the wood. These things were a bit waxier than he was used to, but they would certainly do the job. He put pencil to paper, and for the first time in months he allowed his mind to flow onto the page.

Aleks had always been a natural artist. What he saw in his mind somehow made it through his hand and directly onto the page. He paused in his drawing and looked at his sketch. Stone buildings were stacked almost haphazardly atop each other along a tall, stony cliff face. In the center of the stack was a massive curved building with huge windows and three spires rising up the face of the cliff.

"Oooooh!" Donte's moan startled Aleks out of his reverie.

As Aleks concentrated on his drawing, the silence in the room had crept up on him.

He turned to look at Donte, who stood wide-eyed, staring at Aleks's drawing. "Is something wrong?"

"That's it! You've drawn it." He reached out a bony hand as if to grasp the buildings on the page. "You've drawn the Repository."

Stepping Out

Light sparkled and danced on the surface of the lake. Martin watched the dazzling show for a long time before making his way through the trees and down the bank to the water. He didn't pause at the edge of the lake or bother to check how warm it was. He walked across the stony shore, straight into the lake's chilling embrace.

His lips were chapped and his throat parched. His guts ached to be filled with water and food. And yet he didn't drink. Instead, he simply let the water wash over him. He walked farther and farther from shore, the water rising higher up his torso with every step. Soon it was at his chin.

Not much farther.

He tipped his head back as the water rose up his face. Now he was bobbing in the water. It splashed over his face with each step. He closed his eyes and walked on, snatching quick blasts of air between dunks.

Just a bit farther.

He was deep enough now that he had to pop up occasionally to catch his breath. Deep enough. He completely relaxed and opened his mouth. With a single powerful exhalation, he blew all of the air out of his lungs. It would all be over soon.

I'm coming, Amy.

Her seatback pressed against the roof. Her hair was fanned out below her, draped in a pool of blood. She turned her dead eyes to look at him. Her mouth opened in a silent scream.

I'm coming …

His body screamed for air. He opened his mouth. Water poured in and down his throat. His lungs filled up and he knew he was dying. Something told him he should be coughing or in spasms or something. He breathed out, feeling the water pass out of his lungs. He breathed in again, water flowing through his nose and mouth. It felt strange, thick and heavy, not like air at all. And it took a lot of work to move it. But move it he did.

The pressure in his chest was incredible. His ribs and throat ached with each new breath. He was breathing the water.

Fuck! I can't even kill *myself right.*

He slowly let himself sink to the lake's silky bottom. With his eyes closed, he relaxed into the soft silt. It was the most comfortable place he'd lain in weeks. Sleep closed over him.

When he woke hours later, he thrashed in confusion, trying to grasp where he was and what was happening. Within a few seconds he remembered his failed suicide attempt and calmed himself. Resigned to go on, he tried to get his bearings. His half-asleep thrashing had raised a thick cloud of silt that made visibility impossible. Unfortunately, his breathing of the water went on unabated, even through the thick, chunky silt. He sighed heavily. At least it would have been a sigh on land. This was more like a gurgle.

He shuffled his feet around, seeking a firm footing. Within a couple of minutes he scuffed his shoes across a large, round boulder buried in the silt. He squeezed both feet onto the rock and kicked hard, shooting up through the silt. Within a few feet he was clear of it. He saw light above him at the surface. The bright ball of the sun rippled and wiggled.

Off to his left a patch of darkness caught his eye. It was a large black shape on the surface of the water, blocking the sun's rays. It was the hull of a ship, sliding through the water toward him. It was still a ways off but would be above him in a matter of minutes.

The part of the ship above the surface was also rippling and wiggling, so it was difficult to make out the exact shape. But below the surface it looked exactly as he imagined pirate ships would have looked: long wooden beams sweeping elegantly from the front to the back, a thick beam curving down the length of the ship forming the keel. Strangely, there was no rudder to steer the thing.

As he neared the surface, he saw three spikes reaching up to the sky. Each had a slashing, triangular sail stretching out to the side. He felt great waves of energy and strange currents flowing around the ship.

Now he had two questions: How had this huge ship gotten up into this mountain lake? And what should he do—approach them or simply let them move on by and go about his business?

He thought he should let the boat go but couldn't. This was just too weird to let slip away. He kicked and stroked powerfully for the surface, trying to make sure he would get there ahead of the boat. Ship. Someone had told him once that when a boat got this large it was called a ship. He didn't know exactly what the rule was, but he was sure this one qualified.

His confidence was high and his curiosity piqued as he broke the surface. The fact that he was a monster had *briefly* faded from his mind.

Until his head broke the surface.

Then he started coughing, gagging, and sputtering as his lungs worked to clear out the water and muck he'd been breathing in favor of the air they preferred. He vomited a torrent of brown and green fluid.

Sonofabitch! Other superheroes get cool powers. I yak up lava and lake water.

When he'd finally cleared his lungs and was able to breathe again, the boat—ship—had slid alongside him. Over the rail, three stern-looking women, a smiling young man, and a growling black and gray dog were all looking at him.

"Um ...ahoy?"

— The Road Less Traveled —

Tony's left arm hung limply at his side. Fortunately, the demon had attacked from behind the small party. If it had attacked Jesik and Raneal rather than Tony and Dinaala, the fight would have had quite a different outcome.

Since they had entered the dark forest just after dawn, they had been attacked in turns by a wide assortment of animals, spiders, and even some of the plants. The start of it had been a small group of creatures that looked a bit like spider monkeys. Except these monkeys had needle-like teeth, bright red eyes that glowed in the dark, and three-fingered hands that ended in long, sharp talons. And they coordinated their attacks.

The first batch had dropped from the trees onto the party just as Tony, walking flank, had stepped out of the daylight that stretched a few feet into the trees. The attack was quick and vicious, leaving Jesik and Micah with deep slashes that Raneal quickly healed. Tony dropped three in rapid succession with the Ghost and the Darkness. Dinaala cut down two others. She was swinging K'tichnam. The wicked axe glowed white fire and shattered the nerves of some of the monkeys with her scream. The others vanished up into the trees as quickly as they had come.

Since that first attack they had encountered spiders three feet in diameter that shot poison-tipped harpoons of hardened webbing from their spinnerets—K'tichnam had sliced through the line as Tony was being dragged into the trees. Raneal had stopped the poison and healed the wound. Then came a puma-like cat of some sort that didn't quite get to Micah before the Ghost took it down in a snarling pile of fur, fangs, and claws; lizards that flicked razor-sharp venomous tongues at them; and a nasty little cactus that fired poisoned thorns. Most of the animals had pulled back after the initial attacks left so many dead on the forest floor.

The one fortunate thing about this place was that because it was so dark in the trees, little vegetation grew there. With nothing more than deadfall to trek through, they moved fairly quickly between the trees. As they made their way along, avoiding the cacti and clearing webs from the trail, several large but stealthy creatures paced them on both sides, staying just out of sight. They were larger than the puma but moved with surprising stealth, never stepping on a branch or twig and breathing quietly as mice. Tony could feel their energy, their venom, their rage. The creatures that were stalking them, and in fact everything in this forest, wanted not to eat them but to destroy them, to rip them apart. Tony was fairly certain this was the most horrifically violent place in the universe.

It was just after the second monkey attack—this one far better coordinated, with some monkeys throwing spears from the sides while others dropped from above, but far less effective: the monkeys lost six and the party was uninjured—that the demon dropped out of the trees on them.

Tony and Dinaala had each dived to the side, instinctively splitting up and dividing the monstrous beast's attention. It was at least seven feet tall and powerfully built. It shrugged off Tony's six remaining rounds with no effect. At least two of the slugs had simply bounced off its head. Tony slid both guns into the nifty holsters that Micah had made for him on the way to the forest and drew out Shinyuu. The ring of the blade as it slipped from the scabbard drew the beast's attention more than the gunshots had. It turned toward him just as a barrage of bizarre objects smacked into its chest. Jesik was throwing everything he had—short of his gates—at the beast: a ball of razor blades; long, curved knives; a white-hot ball that splashed flames all across the beast when it hit; and a small rock that detonated with a massive concussion when it touched the thing's head. Each of them thwacked, smashed, splashed, and boomed off the creature with little effect.

It took it all in stride. In fact, it took it all in *one* stride: one mighty step that brought it face-to-face with Tony. It raised its monstrous hand and swung a death blow at Tony's head.

Just as it began the stroke of death it howled in pain, stumbled to its left, and looked down at the severed tendon on the back of its left knee. K'tichnam screamed in glee. Dinaala backpedaled, trying to get out of the way and then threw herself backward onto the ground as the massive talons slashed across her ribs. That's when Tony cut off the tip of the creature's left wing and all of its head. That one distraction was all he'd needed.

Unfortunately, like everything else in this damned place, the dead demon did something Tony hadn't expected. It swung its arm back in a sweeping blow that tossed Tony like a rag doll, snapping his collarbone like a twig. It collapsed after that.

Tony had refused to let Raneal heal him, knowing it would take too long and they needed to get out of this infernal forest before nightfall, when all manner of new horrors would come out and try to rip them apart. Instead, he knelt on the forest floor and called them to gather around for a brief rest.

Tony glanced at each of them, making sure he had their attention. "We have to keep moving, so I'll keep this brief," he began. "Can you each feel the animals around us?"

Jesik and Raneal seemed to understand, but Dinaala and Micah looked at him in confusion.

"See if you can feel the Touch, like when you"—he pointed at Dinaala—"feed someone or when you are fed by someone. Can you feel it then?" They both nodded. "Use your senses and see if you can feel that same sensation, but much lighter, right now."

They each closed their eyes and within a few seconds were nodding.

"Now, do you feel ripples in that energy?" They nodded again. "Do you feel how those ripples are different sizes?" Nods. "And they're moving all around us?" Nods again. "Good!"

He stood up and indicated that the others should do the same. He nodded at Jesik to start down the trail again but kept talking. "Let's keep it slow and steady, Jesik." He took up his position at the back of the group. "Can you all feel that gathering of creatures ahead of us?" Nods all around. "They've been doing something up ahead since before the demon dropped on us."

Instantly all four of them tightened up, afraid of the impending attack. "I think they're almost ready. I expect the large creatures flanking us to rush out and drive us into that trap. Fortunately, ambushes are set up for attack rather than defense. If we attack the ambush, rather than just running into it, we should be able to get through it okay. Jesik, do you have any more of those throwing blades you used on the demon?"

"Yes, but I'm not really very good at throwing them. I could hit the Talmo d'k Tal, but I don't think I could hit anything as small as one of the Shulu d'k Tal with them." Jesik nodded at Micah. "He could, though. Micah is amazingly dexterous. Aren't you, Micah?"

"Sure," Micah said with a grin. Jesik handed him several coin-like objects. Micah turned to Tony. "I can reload for you."

With one useless hand, Tony hadn't been able to reload. He pulled the Ghost out and handed it to Micah. Then he dipped his hand into his pocket and pulled out a handful of shells. "Please hang on to the empty cartridges," he said to Micah. "Maybe I can find a way to reload them."

Micah nodded.

"All right, everyone," Tony continued. "Up ahead of us the monkeys have hung a large log over the trail—can you feel it up there?" Everyone nodded and kept walking. "Can you feel the vines they have tied to the front of the log? They're planning on swinging it down the trail to smash us."

Worried looks crossed Micah and Dinaala's faces. Jesik and Raneal probably wore the same expressions but were facing up the trail at the moment.

"Here's how we're going to break their ambush ..." Over the next few yards of trail he laid out his plan. When he was sure everyone had it down, he had them step up their pace and move into the trap.

Just as Tony had predicted the large animals on their flanks moved into the trail behind them, growling and snapping with huge, fanged jaws. Jesik called them lopers, but the thought that came to Tony's mind was "hellhound." He and Dinaala kept them at bay so the party could continue into the trap. As the trail wound around a giant tree trunk and straightened into a wide path leading to bright sunshine, the lopers moved in closer, snapping and snarling.

Tony called out, "Are you ready, Micah?"

"Yessir!" came the confident response.

"All right," Tony called to the rest of the group. "Let's go!"

Tony and Dinaala turned and ran behind the other three. When they were thirty yards from the opening into daylight, a huge tree trunk, covered in two-foot long spikes, began a ponderous, sweeping arc toward them. Micah's hand flashed forward, releasing the two disks in a single throw. They flew straight and true, slicing cleanly through the pair of vine clusters that had held the ten-ton tree. Rather than arcing toward the little party, the newly freed tree fell straight down and slammed into the trail with a body-shaking thud that almost tossed them from their feet. In the trees, a chorus of furious howls ripped through the darkness.

They ran straight at the spike-covered tree. They weren't out of the woods yet. It blocked most of the trail between two other large trees. But Tony had thought of this as well. Dinaala fed a huge stream of Touch to Micah and suddenly a ramp appeared before them, leading right up to the top of the spikes on the tree. The group stepped up their pace to a full sprint. The monkeys shook the trees in rage but stayed put rather than face the deadly group.

The lopers, sensing their prey was about to get away, howled and tore off after the group. As the lopers neared the bottom of the ramp, Tony was just following Dinaala in a broad jump over the spikes. And then, when the lopers were preparing to leap after the group, the ramp made a shuffling sound and disappeared.

As he landed hard on the ground beyond the tree and the woods, Tony heard squishing thumps. The lead lopers were crashing into the spiked tree trunk.

A hail of spears flew from the treetops, but no animals followed them into the sunlight.

The small group moved out of range of the spears and then paused for a moment to catch their breath. Jesik pointed to the scrub plants that grew along the ground, warning the group to avoid them if they could. Now that they were out of the forest they just had a two-mile walk to Donte's cabin. He suggested they keep moving so they could reach it before sunset. The team wearily tore their feet free of the little vines that were starting to wrap around them and trudged forward.

They made good time and were soon looking at a small cabin in the distance. Two men and a girl were standing on the porch, waving to the group. Jesik waved back. To the right of the cabin, a few hundred yards away, was a large lake with a rocky bank and—

Tony blinked for a minute before he could put a name to the object he was seeing … *a cigarette boat? Here? No way …*

He was just about to point it out to Jesik when a horrifying sound snapped his attention back toward the cabin. It was a collection of the worst sounds of a car wreck: screeching metal and breaking glass.

Everyone stopped in their tracks. The Ghost practically jumped into Tony's hand. He wished he'd let the team pause long enough for Raneal to heal his injured shoulder. No help for it now.

The air between the small party and the cabin began to bend and warp. Ripples, like the rings from a drip into water, drifted off into the air. Something was tearing a hole in reality and coming through.

Deep Thoughts

Thom's mind reeled and rolled. He was screaming and shaking. He got the screaming under control, but not the shaking. It was quite forceful, almost violent. Then the dream and sleep both slipped away. The shaking didn't.

He opened his eyes to find Fazha, her eyes red and puffy, her long brown hair in a tangled halo around her head, and her shirt in chaos—in a word, beautiful. She was kneeling beside him, roughly shaking him by the shoulder.

"Wake up, Thom! It's just a dream. You're okay." She stopped shaking him when she realized he was awake.

He cursed under his breath. His dreams were back. He was surprised to realize he hadn't had one in all the weeks they'd been traveling together.

"Hello, sunshine," he said as he gathered his wits about him.

"Are you okay?" Worry was etched across those exquisite features.

Damn. He really needed to get his mind right. "Yep! Right as rain." He sat up, stretching. "What time is it?"

"Oh no! You don't get off that easy, mister. What the hell was that all about? One minute you're sleeping like a baby, the next you're thrashing around and screaming like a banshee. What were you dreaming about?"

He reached out with a nearby stick and poked the coals in their fire, causing them to flare up and light their little campsite. Then he looked at her for a long minute. She was so strong, so powerful, and inside she had such a sweet, broken heart. She was without a doubt the toughest person he had ever known. So why was he so afraid to take this strong, capable, powerful woman with him into the Deep? She had already demonstrated a hundred times over that she could take care of herself.

But in the Deep, it didn't matter how capable you were, how strong, how competent. In the Deep, it really only mattered how lucky you were and how fast you got out.

And he was in love with her.

He could at least admit that to himself. It didn't matter that he'd hired *her* to protect *him*. It didn't matter that she had done as much as or more damage to their pursuers than he had. There were only two things that really mattered.

First, he could not imagine putting her in the amount of danger that would come in the Deep. Second, he could not imagine going on without her.

He really needed to come up with a plan because they were camped just at the edge of the "safe zone" surrounding the Deep.

Damn Jesik for making him care about all this prophecy shit!

He looked into her eyes and saw something he'd never seen there before; something that made him want to caress her face and pull her mouth to his. But he didn't. Instead, he stood up and started pacing.

She stayed on his bedroll and watched him as he strode back and forth in the light of the campfire.

She needed to know. She needed to know the truth about everything, about the Deep, about the Dark One ... about *him*.

So he told her.

Her eyes grew wide when he talked about the Deep and the horrors that lurked within those dark woods. Robert Frost would have gone screaming down any path he could to avoid them. Lovely they were not.

Her face grew pale when he talked about the Dark One, of the things he could do and his plans for enslaving the people of Freia.

When it came time to talk about himself, he paused for a moment of reflection, trying to decide what he should include. She waited patiently, intently focused on his face and what he was telling her. She was so beautiful he had to swallow the bulge in his throat. He decided he needed—no, he *wanted*—to be completely honest with her. What he had or hadn't shared with anyone else didn't matter. She deserved it. And he wanted it.

With his decision made, he trudged on. He talked about where he'd come from. He talked about the family he had left behind five years ago, his twin girls and his pending divorce. That took some explaining. The Touch made it so unlikely for people who weren't compatible to join as a couple that divorces weren't needed here. He talked about the job he'd had as a data analyst. That took even more explaining. After a few minutes of trying, he told her he'd been a scribe and moved on.

He'd already told her about most of his time on Freia, so he was almost done with his story. He was coming to the part he most dreaded.

The Prophecies.

He swallowed again. He tore his eyes from hers and looked at the ground. He was sweating. He started talking. The words tumbled out of his mouth. He couldn't tell if he was making any sense. But he had to get it out.

When he was done, he once again raised his eyes to hers. Hers were brilliant and ferocious. A single tear broke free from her eye and slowly rolled down her cheek.

She pulled in a deep breath. "You silly, silly man. All this time I wondered what was wrong with me. Why you would look at me like you do, but never ..." She shook her head and rose, gliding over to him like a feral cat stalking a mouse. She took his face in her hands and kissed him fiercely. He was transported. He was alive only for this. He couldn't breathe. Time stopped. And for that eternal instant he felt nothing but her lips, her hands, her breath on his cheek. And on his chest he felt the brush of her breast through their shirts.

After the eternity passed she broke the kiss but stayed within inches of his face. "I don't care about some stupid prophecy," she said with utmost sincerity. "You can't die. Because I'm in love with you, you idiot. I won't let you die."

She leaned back a bit, looking at his eyes. Thom's uncertainty must have shown on his face.

She sighed, her eyes bunched in frustration. "Look," she said, "I don't believe in fate or prophecy. We make our destiny every day. But let's say that there's some merit to this. Let's say the Dark One does have plans to come down here and crush us all under his mighty fist. If that's true, I want to live my life to its fullest before he gets here."

His heart fluttered at that thought. Could he really live his life before he died?

"Besides, let's talk about this prophecy thing." He nodded for her to go on. "You've talked a lot about all the things you have to do. In all of them, you say you are alone. Your friends aren't with you, right?"

"Yep. I'm the lone wolf, riding alone, in a wolf pack of one." Again, no reaction. She'd never seen the movie. That said, not many folks back home had seen *Mystery Men*.

"So how do you explain me?"

Stunned, he couldn't get his mind around what she was saying. "Huh?" His eloquence knew no bounds.

"Maybe I'm wrong, but I assume that our shared adventures have had some impact on you, right?" She cocked her head and pierced him with her eyes, daring him to say she wasn't important to him.

"I … uh …" Brilliance. Absolute brilliance. Damn he was good.

"So if my being here is meaningful and the prophecy talked about so many other details of your life here, why didn't it mention me?"

"Wait … um …"

"Right. Because the prophecy can be changed. If it couldn't be changed, what are you doing here anyway? The prophecy says, 'The Dark One will do this and that, if you don't do something about it.' So obviously you can do something about it. You can change the prophecy."

His mind tumbled around with that for a few seconds. Could he really change the prophecy? Could he really survive this? And if he could, what would his life hold then? Could he go home? Could he just do that? And go back to what? Here he was something important. He'd developed talents, skills, and abilities that weren't even physically possible back home. Sure they didn't have pizza and their coffee sucked. But they had pretty good tobacco.

And *she* was here. He could stay here with her.

He looked at her beautiful face. He reached up and stroked her cheek, slid his fingers into her hair, pulled her until their mouths met. He was lost. And he was blissful.

When he woke, the sun was cresting the horizon behind a jagged mountain ridge, a stunning red-gold display. Fazha was breathing deeply, relaxed against his side with her head on his shoulder. They fit together perfectly, entwined in his bedroll. He moved to kiss her forehead. She whispered a gentle sound of contentment when she felt his lips. His skin tingled all along his side where her silky skin touched him. He didn't want this to ever end, so he closed his eyes and listened to the sounds of a forest morning.

Birds called to each other amid the branches. Squirrels chittered at the birds to get off of their property. Bugs and small animals crawled across his weave. He'd stretched it out for more than a mile in every direction. A few short weeks ago he never would have dreamed of trying to stretch a weave that far, especially not in the forest, where so many little creatures tickled his attention.

But these weeks with Fazha, their shared peril and need had stretched him far beyond anything he had experienced alone. Maybe it was his desire to keep her safe. Or his desire to stay with her. Or maybe she just made him better. Whatever it was didn't really matter. What mattered now was that he loved her. And she loved him. And he was content.

When he woke for the third time that morning, Fazha's arm was wrapped possessively across his chest. He grinned but left his eyes closed.

"Mhm …" he said, "a few kisses here and there and suddenly she thinks she owns me."

She kissed his shoulder and gripped him almost painfully tight. Damn, she was strong. Then she crawled her way up to his face to kiss his mouth. Hard. He saw stars for a few seconds.

How is it that she doesn't have sleep breath? Incredible.

"I've owned you for weeks, silly man!" She laughed. "I just decided it was time to let you in on it." She pressed her cheek to his, her hair making a halo over them.

After a few more minutes of deep, rich contemplation made up primarily of passionate kissing, he started moving to extricate himself from her and the bedroll.

"I don't want to get up," she said, clinging to him.

"My love"—his heart fluttered again as he called her that—"I could stay in bed with you for the rest of my life …"

"Okay!" She immediately accepted his offer.

"But maybe we should wait until after we've kept the Dark One from burning the world to the ground before we retire to bed for the duration."

"Fun-spoiler!" She let go of him, flipped off the covers of the bedroll, and stretched languidly next to him.

It took everything he had to retain his resolve in the face of that vision. He closed his eyes, took a deep breath, and gritted his teeth. He was going to make Jesik *pay* for what he was going to miss that morning.

On a positive note, he thought as he was lacing up his boots a few minutes later, he would get to keep seeing that image in his mind's eye for the rest of his life. Mmmm … what a happy life it would be.

He got his bedroll and their few remaining provisions together and tied them into a makeshift pack that he could carry.

"So … why exactly," she asked as she saw him donning the backpack, "did we sell our saddles and most of our gear?"

He walked over to Bilbo, who was chewing contentedly on a small bush beside the trail. He affectionately patted the horse on the head and gave him the last carrot he had squirreled away.

"Because I won't take Bilbo or Tan'aana through the Deep."

She looked at him in shock.

"The Deep is tight, dark, and very dangerous. They wouldn't be any help to us in there. In fact, we'd have to work extra hard to keep them alive.

"Don't worry. Bilbo is much smarter than he lets on. He'll lead Tan'aana back to Jesik's house and wait for us there."

Thom patted the gray's head again. The horse was intently looking at him. Bilbo nudged Thom quizzically with his head. Thom hadn't been exaggerating when he said Bilbo was smarter than the average horse. He hadn't intentionally messed with Bilbo. It just seemed to be a natural extension of Thom's Touch. He visualized Bilbo as an extremely intelligent, capable, and healthy companion. And Bilbo was. Thom hadn't noticed at first, but over the years it had become apparent that Bilbo had not only grown smarter after living with Thom, but also was actually regressing in age. He looked like a young, fresh, unbroken stallion rather than the old, broken-down dapple gray that Thom had bought for a song three years ago.

"Hey, buddy," Thom said as he scratched behind the horse's ears, "I know you want to go with me. But I need to you take care of Tan'aana for Fazha."

Bilbo looked dubiously at Tan'aana.

Thom leaned in close. "Look, pal, you gotta help a guy out here. I just got a good thing going with Fazha and I don't want to blow it by letting something happen to her friend. You gotta be strong here. You gotta be the man … er … stallion here and take Tan'aana back to Jesik's place. I'll meet you there in a few days. I promise."

Bilbo's large left eye searched Thom's face for a few more seconds, and then he nodded and snorted acceptance.

"Wait! You think your *horse* is going to lead Tan'aana to Jesik's house because you *asked* it to? You really are crazy, aren't you?"

Bilbo stamped his hoof and snorted at her, expressing his indignation. She held up her hand, letting Bilbo know she respected him.

"Okay, okay," she said, "maybe he is smart enough to get them there. So why aren't we going with them? Wouldn't that save us from going through this Deep you're so leery about? And isn't Jesik the guy you want to give the treaty to anyway?"

"You're right. It would definitely be safer, and Jesik is the guy. But it would take way too long to take the path they'll use. Bilbo will bring Tan'aana through the northern Kalik forest, skirting Lake Marlish and then straight across the plain of Laree. That will take at least three weeks for just the two of them. If we go with them, it would take at least an extra week. We'll be at the outer edge of the shallowest part of the Deep by this evening. Tomorrow we'll go through. We'll meet Donte on the other side and he can open a gateway to Jesik's. We'll be there before bedtime."

Fazha looked down and was quiet for a few minutes. When she looked back up at Thom, her acceptance was clear on her face. She walked to Tan'aana and hugged the horse, a gesture that seemed to be in direct opposition to the temperament of the vicious beast, which glared at Thom as it nuzzled Fazha's shoulder. Fazha slowly fit Tan'aana's bridle over her head and secured the straps.

When Fazha stepped back from the horse, Fazha's eyes were clear and she was smiling. Thom knew she trusted him. Dammit. She made everything so much harder by just being amazing. He knew he had to send the horses. He knew she trusted him and would let him do it, even though it hurt. He felt like an ogre.

He walked over to Bilbo and whispered in the horse's ear. The horse shook his head again, snorting with angry eyes. Thom whispered something else and laid his hand on the horse's neck. Bilbo nodded and leaned against him. Then he turned and walked to Tan'aana. Bending his head low, Bilbo took her reigns in his mouth and led her off the trail and into the woods. Tan'aana tried to look back at Fazha, but the pull on her reigns kept her following Bilbo. Bilbo never looked back.

It was nearing sunset when Thom and Fazha stopped at the edge of a long swath of barren land a hundred yards wide that stretched across the hillside. When they stepped out into the swath, they saw the long stripe curving and arching along the terrain, off to the horizon in both directions. The woods they had stepped out of were green and lush. Tall, stately, palm-like trees were mixed with bushy, twisty trunks and giant, lacey-leafed trees. If they had traveled any higher into the mountains, these lush trees would have shifted completely to evergreens. But here they were playing together nicely, forming a thick canopy overhead. The ground below the trees was open and spongy with lichen and fallen leaves.

Across the swath things were dramatically different. The trees were massively large, tightly packed, black and ominous deciduous monsters. Black bark, black leaves … they even seemed to have black air flowing and weaving between them.

"What the—" Fazha began.

"Shhhh!" Thom held a finger to his lips. This drew a sharp look from Fazha, so he pulled her back into the trees and whispered an explanation. "The things in there can hear us from a mile away, and maybe smell us from farther than that. We need to be as quiet as humanly possible. We can't go through it at night and we can't sleep here in case something comes out."

"It looks pitch black in there right now. Surely anything nocturnal would be moving around in there any time of day or night," she said.

"No …" A tear formed in the corner of his eye at the memories that hovered behind them. "At night it gets worse. Much worse." He shook himself to clear the memories and free him for what he was about to do. He hoped beyond hope that she would forgive him.

He kneeled down and slipped his pack from his shoulders. "Besides," he continued in a whisper, "I think I have an idea how we can get to the other side without risking ourselves. I've been thinking about it since we came out of the cave onto the island in that river."

As she knelt beside him, he sketched out his plan. She nodded her understanding. As he finished describing everything, he pulled the treaty from his pack and handed it to her.

"I'm going to leave the pack here. We need to take just our swords and the treaty. I want you to carry it so I can focus on what I'm doing." He stood up.

"Now remember, when I tell you to run, you have to go as fast as you can and don't look back. I don't know if I can even do it, but I guarantee that I won't be able to hold it for long. If you look back, I might bump into you and drop my Touch. Then we'd both be dead."

He took her shoulders in his hands, looked into her beautiful, chocolate-colored eyes, and said, as seriously as he could muster, "What I'm about to try is incredibly risky and I don't know if we'll live through it.

"I love you. And I trust you with everything I have and everything I am. I need you to promise me you'll make sure Donte gets that treaty to Jesik no matter what happens to me."

She balked and tried to pull away. It must have been a half-hearted attempt because he maintained his grip.

"Please, Fazha. I don't know what will happen to me, but I want you and our baby to be safe."

"What?" This time she did jerk free of his grasp, and her response was far from a whisper.

He smiled at her and put his hand on her belly.

"Last night we got pregnant. While you were sleeping, I was awake, looking at the stars through the trees. All my senses were on high alert. I could feel it happening inside you."

She grabbed his head with her hands and kissed him so powerfully it almost pulled him off his feet. He rose up and lifted her from hers. She wrapped her legs around his torso and her arms around his neck. She pulled her mouth from his and pressed her face against the scruff of his two-day-old beard (which no doubt had gray streaks through it by now). Her tears left wet splotches on his cheek. He could feel her shaking with sobs.

He wasn't sure what to do. He had never imagined seeing this terrifying fury of a woman sobbing against him. So he just held her and loved it.

After a few minutes she released her grip and lowered herself to the ground, looking him steadily in the face. She was the one gripping his shoulders this time. He hoped it hadn't hurt as much when he did it to her.

"I will make this promise to you. But only if you promise me you will live to be with me and raise our child together."

"I ca—ouch! Okay, okay, I promise," he stammered, wincing under the pressure of her grip.

"Then I promise to take this silly paper to Donte and make him give it to Jesik, if I have to drag him there to do it." She smiled and kissed him tenderly.

He basked in the glow of that kiss. "All right," he said, "let's do this."

He took her hand and stepped out into the swath, his eyes searching the other side for any evidence of movement. He saw nothing.

Of course that didn't mean nothing saw them.

He had her stand in front of him and face the other side of the swath. He raised and spread his hands in the universal symbol of Doing Really Momentous Things—not because it would help but because it seemed like something one should do under the circumstances. He pulled in his weave and began to gather all the strength he could. He focused his mind and his might on a pinpoint ten yards in front of Fazha. Then he stretched his energy and tweaked it, pushing and pulling the pinpoint. In his mind he saw another pinpoint a few hundred feet from Donte's shack on the other side of the Deep. Like saltwater taffy, he stretched and pinched and pulled at the points until they were connected by the tiniest strand of his Touch. Then he pulled the two points together and stretched them out, making a small hole out of them.

Sweat poured down his face, and his arms shook with the effort he was putting into it. He opened his eyes as he smashed reality out of his way and pulled open the hole between those two points. The air rippled like drips on a glass of water and shrieked as it was shoved aside. Ten seconds—or possibly an hour—later, the hole was large enough for Fazha to run through.

"Go."

It was as much as he could manage to say through the strain.

Fazha ran.

She ran *fast.*

In fact, she was more of a streak than a person running. Last fall's leaves and clods of dirt flashed into the air as her feet tore along the ground. She covered the ten yards to the hole and was through it before the dirt started raining back down. She slowed and turned back just as the hole collapsed with the sound of a car crashing through a plate glass window.

"N—" For the briefest of moments her scream cut through that horrible sound. Then it was cut off. Only silence remained.

"I'm sorry, my love. I couldn't take you through that place." He dropped to his knees, completely spent.

He could hear movement in the distance ahead of him. Something, possibly many somethings had heard the horrible sound and were coming to investigate.

He couldn't raise a whisper to defend himself, so at least it would be quick.

"Well," an amiable voice said from behind him, "hello, Thom. Was it you that stirred up all that ruckus? You look like hell. Here, let me help you up."

Thom felt his arm being raised up and a shoulder sliding under it. He turned to his benefactor. It was Martin, of all people. Where the hell had he come from? Another shoulder slid in on the other side. This one was much lower to the ground. A kid he'd never met, maybe twenty years old or so, was holding up his other side. A dog jumped and hopped at the boy's feet. Other voices sounded behind him. He thought they might be women, but he couldn't tell. And he didn't care. All he cared about was that Fazha got through. And that darkness seemed like a great escape at the moment.

But as he slipped out of consciousness, one troubling thought slid across his mind. Just how crazy were Martin's eyes? He looked totally unwound. And then darkness came.

Message Delivered

Tony winced at the ear-shattering screeching that came from the tear in the air. Even though he was walking away from the blackness and misery of the Deep, he could see it through the torn hole in space that floated in front of him. His thumb pulled back the Ghost's hammer without any input from his mind. He raised the weapon, pointing it at the hole, waiting for something to charge through it.

"*Nooooo!*" A woman's scream came from somewhere beyond the hole. In that instant the hole disappeared with the sound of a thunderclap and crashing glass.

Now that the hole was gone, he could see a tall woman wearing a leather jacket and breeches who hadn't been there a few seconds ago. She was beautiful, with long, golden-brown hair and brown eyes the color of Swiss chocolate. She was clutching a roll of paper in one hand and sported a long sword at her waist.

"*Thom! Thoooooooooom!*" She screamed at the space where the hole had been. She fell to her knees amid the carnivorous weeds, apparently oblivious to their creeping, reaching tendrils.

Tony had been standing still for only a few seconds and the weeds were already clutching at his boots when he took a step forward. He immediately sensed that this woman, while possibly dangerous, was no threat at the moment. He lowered the hammer on the Ghost but didn't put it away. He took a couple of long strides toward the woman, but Raneal was less cautious than he was and got to the girl first.

"Are you all right?" Raneal asked.

The girl looked up through teary eyes. "He left me. How could he leave me?"

Raneal, seeing the grasping weeds starting to bind her legs, urged the girl to her feet. The girl looked at her blankly for a few seconds.

"You have to get up," Raneal said, taking the girl's arm and pulling her up.

The girl staggered to her feet but swayed there, uncomprehending, until the sound of a cabin door reached them.

"Come on!" came a voice from the cabin. Three people sood on the front porch and waved the group onward. They pointed behind the group at the Deep.

Creatures were lining up just inside the tree line, away from the bright sun that was edging down on the horizon. They paced back and forth, as if anxious to have another chance to sink a fang or claw into one of them.

"We have to keep moving," Tony said. "They'll be able to come out soon." He slipped the Ghost back into its holster and took the girl's other arm, leading her toward the cabin. They could sort out who she was and what she was doing there once they were out of harm's way.

"*No!*" the girl screamed, and jerked her arm out of Tony's grasp. That was no small task. After years of his training with the kitana, Tony's grip was intense. But she did it like it was nothing. Then she started walking toward the Deep, long viney strands dangling from her pants. "Thom's alone now. The Deep will kill him. I have to get to him and protect him. I have to."

Jesik ran to intercept her, holding up both hands. "You can't go in there. The sun will be down in a couple of minutes. Alone, you'd be dead within the first few feet. Please stop. Listen to me."

"Get out of my way." She put her hand on the hilt of her sword and stepped sideways to go around him. Now she looked considerably more like a threat.

"Please!" Jesik moved in front of her and tried again. "I understand you want to help your friend, but going in there now will only get you killed ..." Jesik paused as if thinking his way out of a long, dark tunnel. "Did you just say 'Thom'?"

She paused, giving Tony enough time to slide up next to Jesik. He changed his tactic on the fly. He didn't want to shoot this girl unless he had to. But he might need to give Jesik and Raneal some extra time to talk her into standing down. He didn't pull Shinyuu out, but he set himself to do it quickly if the need to cross swords came up.

"Are you Donte?" she asked.

Her question was so out of the blue that Jesik stood blinking at her for a few seconds.

"No. My name is Jesik."

Smack!!

She had moved so quickly that even Tony could barely respond. He had Shinyuu out but couldn't have intervened. In the meantime, Jesik was flung backward by the force of the slap. He landed in a bewildered heap on the ground.

"Here's your fucking treaty!" She flung the roll of paper at him. "Thom almost died, may even be dying right now, to get that stupid thing to you. He sent me here alone, without him, just to give it to you, you bastard." She crossed the three-step gap between them in one long stride and grabbed Jesik up by his shirt. His glasses were askew. An angry red handprint glowed on his face, and blood dripped from the corner of his mouth. She raised him until her fists were over her head and she was looking up into his face. His feet dangled inches off the ground. "And you told him he was going to die because of some fucking prophecy! How dare you!" She shook him like a rag doll.

Tony was so stunned by all of this that he hadn't moved a muscle. Suddenly the tableau broke and everyone was moving at once. Raneal, Dinaala, Micah, and Tony all converged on the distraught girl at the same moment.

Tony knew he couldn't let the girl hurt Jesik. But he could also somehow tell that she was holding herself (barely) in check and wouldn't kill him. He wasn't at all sure that she wouldn't break some bones, though. So, like everyone else, Tony grabbed at one of the girl's arms and tried to pull her back from Jesik.

The girl thrust Jesik away, who landed in a heap on the ground. Then she shrugged the four of them off like she was taking off a coat. Raneal and Dinaala tumbled to the ground. Pain shot through Tony's injured shoulder as his hand was ripped from her arm, and Micah crashed into Tony's leg on his way to the ground.

The girl drew in a deep breath and relaxed somewhat. Apparently, the outburst at Jesik had allowed her to release some of what had been driving her.

She turned to Raneal and said, "Don't touch me."

Jesik spoke up. "Please, you have to listen to me. Thom is important to me too. You have to believe me. I will go into the Deep with you myself to help you find him. But we can't go tonight. We'll never make it through. Thom is very resourceful and more powerful than even he knows. He'll be okay until tomorrow when we can go and get him. Please." He dug something out of the bag that hung at his waist. "I can help you find him with this." He held up a small silver ball.

She looked at it for a few seconds before relenting. And in that instant, the fight went out of her. With her eyes closed she lowered her head in silence. Then her body started shaking. Tears streamed down her face as quiet sobs wracked her.

Raneal came up beside her and wrapped an arm around her. The girl turned to Raneal and buried her face in Raneal's shoulder, sobbing loudly. Raneal hugged her and whispered a string of soothing words into the girl's ear. As she did, Raneal looked up at Tony and motioned with her head that they should start moving back to the cabin. Tony bent to help Jesik to his feet.

Raneal guided the stricken girl, whispering to her the entire way. Tony looked back over his shoulder at the tree line as they moved. The mountains to the east were now casting long shadows across the open space as the sun dipped behind the peaks. It was going to be a close call for them to make it back before the sun fully set and that growing horde of screaming nightmares came out of the forest to run them down.

The din from the forest rose up as darkness swept across the plain. Tony could see ... things ... coming out from between the trees. Large winged shapes took flight and zoomed toward them, low to the ground to stay out of what sunlight remained higher in the air. They were rapidly closing on the group.

Tony snapped the Ghost out of its holster and fired two rounds into the tentacle-covered face of the nearest flyer. He'd aimed for one that was at the top of the ... flock ... for want of a better description. It went limp and flopped down onto the monster directly below it, bringing both crashing to the ground. His second victim followed suit, taking out a fourth creature on its way out of the picture.

It turned out these creatures weren't stupid. They flattened out into a single line before Tony could down any more, so he settled for the lead one. Two more shots and it went down as well. Tony holstered the now empty

Ghost. He glanced ahead at the porch of the cabin and gauged that they might just make it ahead of the creatures.

As he looked at the cabin, one of the people occupying it raised a large crossbow and let fly. The bolt arched over their heads and buried itself in the midst of a cluster of eyes on the right side of a creature's face. The creature folded and plunged to the ground. Two more followed in rapid succession.

Tony turned back to the porch and urged Raneal forward. Raneal turned back for a quick look, turned white, and urged the girl to look for herself.

The girl turned, sniffed deeply, and glanced at the small troupe. She pulled herself away from Raneal, shook herself, and drew her sword. Tony took an instant's glance at the glowing white blade. It looked like a torch in the dimming light. The girl gave Raneal a gentle push toward the porch fifty feet in the distance and then stopped and turned, facing the oncoming rush of horrors. More creatures were falling by the second, but the horde was far too massive for the archer to take them all down. There were hundreds of creatures.

Raneal paused. Tony pushed her toward the porch and screamed at the rest of them to get up there. Then he too turned and faced the horde, pulling Shinyuu out of its scabbard with his good arm. He and the girl rushed forward at the same instant.

Time slowed. The creatures were moving as though swimming through butter. He danced through, around, and between them with Shinyuu flicking into necks, wings, and hearts. The creatures fell by ones, twos, and threes, piling up behind him. In this moment of combat he couldn't feel his shoulder, his ribs, his knee … even the new slashes the creatures opened on his cheek and forehead were of no concern to him. He danced.

In time the horde diminished, slowed, and finally stopped. To Tony it seemed like hours had passed, but the distant howls of the dog-like pursuers bounding toward them told him it had only been a few seconds. He and the girl looked at each other. They were covered in blood and gore. They turned together toward the cabin and ran. They flashed past mountains of monster corpses and reached the steps to the porch on the heels of the others. The entire company piled through the door and slammed it shut a few seconds before the first dog-like creature slammed into it.

The door shuddered but held fast. Somehow even the windows on each side of the tiny building withstood the onslaught of the huge beasts throwing themselves against them.

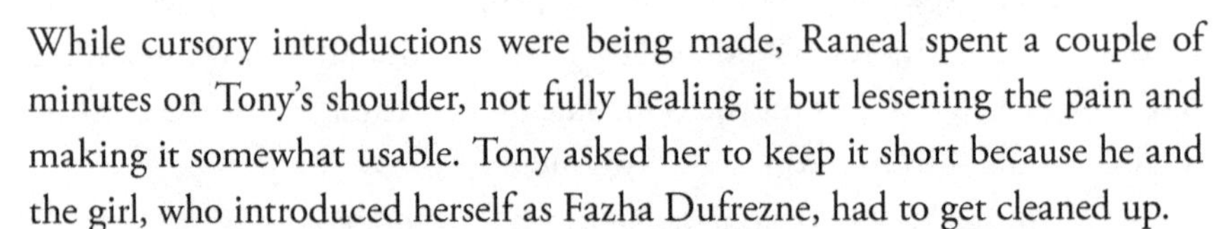

While cursory introductions were being made, Raneal spent a couple of minutes on Tony's shoulder, not fully healing it but lessening the pain and making it somewhat usable. Tony asked her to keep it short because he and the girl, who introduced herself as Fazha Dufrezne, had to get cleaned up.

Unfortunately, when Tony looked into the single bathroom at the back of the shack, he saw that it housed only a small sink and stool. Apparently, the tenants of the shack used a washcloth for their daily cleaning. He offered the small room to Fazha, who looked dubiously at the tiny space and then turned to Aleks and asked for a cloth to clean up with.

Aleks—who looked to be about five feet, eight inches or so and was trimly built, sported Levi's, a red Harley Davidson T-shirt, and tennis shoes—was obviously another abductee from Earth. Details about that and some conversation about their respective homes would have to wait for a bit.

Aleks said that in the meantime he thought he could make the cabin more suitable for guests. He stood in the center of the room and closed his eyes. The hair on the back of Tony's neck stood up as he felt the floor shift and shimmy. Suddenly, the walls simply slid apart from each other. In every direction. As they pulled apart, they stretched, maintaining their corner connections. Within seconds, the shack went from three hundred square feet to eight hundred, one thousand, fifteen hundred feet and more. The floor expanded as well, smooth granite-like stone, black speckled with blue and gold, rolled up next to the wooden slats and stretched out with the movement of the walls. As the back of the house—it was no longer a shack—moved away from the front, the granite floor stretched up to the ceiling in a succession of new walls, each fading from the black of the floor to a creamy white, with the same blue and gold speckles. Arches and doorways stretched across open spaces to support the ever-expanding stone roof.

Aleks opened his eyes and took a quick breath. The group was now standing in the great room of a fair-sized family home. A long hallway with six doorways along its walls disappeared around a right-hand bend. Aleks motioned for the group to move off the wooden portion of the floor and on to the newly made granite portion. As Tony stepped on the black rock, it reminded him of the road, hard and spongy at the same time, on which he'd driven into this crazy world.

When everyone was off the wooden flooring, Aleks closed his eyes again. The slats from the floor pulled themselves free and flopped over each other. They stretched and pinched, forming into large, flat, tabletop-like surfaces. Within seconds, twenty or more of the slats had become doors. Many of the slats slid along the hall and assembled themselves into frames on the visible doorways. They were lifted into place and stretched until pressure held them solid. The few remaining slats shattered into little pieces that became hinges, pins, and door handles. These snapped themselves onto the doors. The doors slid up the hallway, each standing up and clamping onto one of the open doorframes.

When the doors, frames, and mountings were clear of the room, the stone floor in front of the group stretched forward to fill the gap vacated by the floorboards. What had been a somewhat rickety shack was now a beautiful villa. The entire process had taken fewer than five minutes. It was renovation made easy.

Aleks turned to Tony and Fazha and said, "There are bathrooms on both sides of the hallway at this end and at the other end. Pull on the shower knob. Turn it to the right for hotter and the left for colder."

Tony took off his gun belt and pulled Shinyuu from its resting place between his pack and his back, setting them on the lone table in the room. Then he walked up the hallway and through the first door on the right. The room he entered was much larger than he had expected, with plenty of space to move around. Inside was a sink, a fair-sized bench seat, a shelf with small stone drawers, and a toilet. Each had been extruded directly from the walls. Above the sink the wall seamlessly changed from creamy white into a large oval mirror. A sizable soaking tub, separated from the room by a large, curved glass wall, filled the back quarter of the room. The tub had a stone spout above its rim and another higher up. Midway between the tub rim and the higher spout, a black stone knob stuck out of the wall.

Looking at all of the extruded objects in the room, he suddenly understood why the road had been laid down as it had. It hadn't been constructed like a road on Earth. Someone like Aleks had simply created it from the materials at hand. Rocks, dirt, and probably any plants that had been in the path of the road had been converted into the material of the road. One mystery solved.

Tony set the small pack Micah had made for him on the bench. He opened it and took out the bar of soap wrapped in a slick, waxy paper that Jesik had provided before they left on their journey. He turned to the sink. Another stone spout sat flanked by two stone knobs. The left knob was black with red flecks in it. The right one was black with blue flecks. He turned the left one. Steam rose from the sink bowl as water plunged into it from the stone spout. Tony turned the blue knob a bit to move the water from blistering to a more hand- and face-friendly temperature.

Tony washed his face. His new scratches stung as the soap cleaned away the dried blood. He gave his face a once over. His hair was too long, but there was nothing he could do about it now. His beard, on the other hand—that he could do something about. He dug into his pack a second time and pulled out a razor and a toothbrush. He used the soap to lather his face and scraped the razor over his three-day growth of beard, making sure to keep his sideburns even. Then he scrubbed his teeth with his toothbrush.

Like cleaning his gun or sharpening Shinyuu, his morning routine helped calm his mind and allow him to puzzle through problems. Tony mulled over the things Jesik had told him during their journey time and time again. Jesik could send him home but had refused to do so until the prophecy was complete. When he'd first worked that out, before confronting Jesik about it, he'd been furious. They'd had an intense confrontation about it during the long walk from the village to the Deep. Grudgingly, Tony had to give Jesik credit for standing his ground. He faced Tony with no regrets about having brought him here and staunchly refused to send Tony back.

After the fight at Jesik's house and the trek through the Deep, Tony had more hand-to-hand combat time beside Jesik than he'd had with anyone. He had developed a respect for Jesik and a new perspective about this situation. He now knew Jesik was a good man and didn't want to hurt anyone, if he could help it. He also knew Jesik was a True Believer.

Could the prophecy be true? Could Tony *really* be here to help Jesik and his group of kidnappees protect a world?

This was right out of Tolkien. The Dark One was Sauron and Tony was a hobbit. A lot of ugly things happened to the hobbits in those stories. Maybe it was better to focus on this world and its problems. With the things he'd seen and done since he got here, it wasn't a huge stretch to believe someone could see the future. But if someone could see the future and had written about it, could that future be changed? He'd always believed he was the one writing his story. That he made his own destiny with hard work and intelligent decisions.

Of course being here hadn't been in his life plans. He shook his head. There was a chink in his belief system, but he just couldn't accept he was simply a pawn to be played or lost at the whim of destiny. He let that sit for a few minutes.

Yes, he believed he had some say in the outcome of his life, even here. There may be truth in the prophecies. There may not. In his mind, the jury was still out. But he would be who he was and make his own decisions, regardless of what some dubious prophecy might say about him.

In the end it didn't matter if Tony believed in the prophecies because Jesik did. From what Tony had gathered in conversations with Dinaala and Raneal, people's talents with the Touch followed certain lines but were unique to each person. And in particular, Jesik's talent hadn't ever been seen before. It seemed the only person who could send Tony back was the one who'd brought him here in the first place. So if Tony wanted to get home, he had to keep Jesik alive or find an alternate route.

There was a gentle knock on the door. Tony opened it. Standing in the hall with a giant, fluffy white towel was little Micah.

"I thought you might want something to dry off with." He smiled at Tony.

Tony smiled back, feeling the weight of the towel. It was densely woven and very soft.

"Thank you," he said. "I'll be out in a few minutes." He closed the door, stripped off his sticky, blood-soaked clothes, and tossed them into the corner. As he stood barefoot on the strangely soft stone floor, his feet felt warm. Tony wasn't sure if it was a trick of the material the floor was made from or just another well-thought-out aspect of this new structure. He was definitely going to have to talk to Aleks once he was refreshed. And more than just a talk about Earth and the things they both missed.

The warm water was so pleasant on his skin that he took much longer than he had intended. When he finished, he pulled on some fresh clothes from his pack and replaced his toiletries, just in case they had to leave the cabin in a hurry.

By the time he rejoined the others, with his pack and ruined clothes in hand, his shoulder was becoming much less mobile and had started hurting again.

The conversation had cut off when he opened the bathroom door and stepped out.

"How are you feeling now?" Jesik asked.

"Better, now that I'm clean."

Raneal—her face smooth and pink from a fresh healing—must have intuited the pain he was in because she stood from one of several new chairs that had come into being since he left for the bathroom and moved quickly over to his side. She took the pack and the clothes from his hands.

"Micah," she said, turning to the boy, "would you take care of these for Tony, while I help him with his injuries?"

Micah nodded and took them from Raneal.

Raneal led Tony by the hand to a nearby chair and had him sit. Tony closed his eyes as Raneal laid her hand on his shoulder. He tuned in to the others' renewed conversation as she worked.

"I told you, we used a gate the last time. We didn't know what we were doing. We hadn't seen the full prophecies yet," Jesik was saying. "Aleks and I have to go to the Forbidden City alone. It's far too dangerous to take anyone else with us."

"Please, Jesik!" This from a man Tony didn't know. "You can't open a gate to send me home to the Repository, but from the Forbidden City I can get there."

Jesik replied, "If Aleks and I go quietly, we may be able to avoid the creatures in the lake. The more people we take with us, the more likely it will be for one or more of us to get killed. Donte, you are my oldest friend and I love you. But I will not sacrifice this world, even for you. I'm sorry."

Hmmm. Interesting. Donte could travel home from the Forbidden City without one of Jesik's gates. Good to know.

Raneal finished her ministrations a few minutes later. Tony tentatively stood, tested his knee and side, and then slowly swung his arm in a broad circle to test for twinges or hitches in any of his movements. There were none. In fact, he felt better than he had in quite some time. None of the little aches and pains that life had brought him were present. He breathed deeply. His outlook was suddenly very positive, and not just because he was feeling no pain.

Underneath the bolstered spirit and lack of pain was pure exhaustion. He gave a small yawn that turned into a jaw-popping, eye-watering, whole-body affair.

"Healing can be taxing on the body," Raneal said, smiling. "You had some pretty extensive injuries. You should probably get some sleep."

"Thank you." Tony bowed his head to her in respect and gratitude.

He turned to the conversation at the table. The crowd had thinned somewhat while Raneal was working on him. Dinaala and Micah had both wandered off to bed. By the sound of the conversation, it was fortunate they had.

"I can't believe you brought two kids with you through those monsters." Aleks smacked his hand on the table to punctuate his point. "What's wrong with you? Are you crazy?"

Obviously, Aleks didn't defer to Jesik in any way. Tony took an instant liking to the man.

"Aleks, there are a lot of things you don't know about this situation." Jesik was calm, even in the fire of Aleks's angry gaze. "I think now is as good a time as any to bring you all up to speed on the situation and the actions we will need to take tomorrow." Jesik included the others in the conversation with a sweeping gesture. "Please join us."

Tony, Raneal, and Fazha joined Aleks, Donte, and Jesik around the little table.

"Obviously, you each know something about the Prophecies. But only Donte, Raneal, and I know the whole of them. And some of them are confusing even to us. We simply don't have time to explain all of them to you. But I can share some details that are pertinent to this moment and go through the rest of them as we spend time together in the coming weeks.

"Before we get into the Prophecies, I want to answer your question, Aleks. You asked me why we brought children through The Deep. There are really several reasons. First, children on Freia are not always what they seem. In looking at your world through the Mirror of Forever, I have deduced that children mature at a relatively consistent rate, correct? On Earth, people are considered adults by the time they reach twenty years of life, right? Well, on Freia, children age according to their connection with the Touch. The stronger they are with the Touch, the longer it takes them to reach physical maturity. The average person on Freia takes about the same amount of time that a child takes on Earth, about twenty years. But very strong children can take longer. In rare cases, much longer."

Jesik paused to look at Raneal for a brief moment. "Raneal did not reach physical maturity until she was almost sixty years old. It took me even longer to reach my full height and weight."

"So you're telling me Dinaala and Micah are a lot older than they appear, so they can handle it, right? Well, I don't care how old they are. They're still children and shouldn't be put in that kind of danger."

"Dinaala is seventy-one years old."

The silence in the room hung for ten seconds. Then twenty.

"Bullshit!" Aleks exploded. "There's no way that little girl is older than seventy."

"If I'm right in gauging her strength, she is the most powerful Activator born since the world was broken." Jesik let that sink in for a couple of minutes.

"And I suspect that with training, she could learn to Regulate as well. Besides the Dark One and the people who have come over from Earth, I only know of two people on all of Freia who can do that." Jesik looked at Raneal, whose face was scarlet.

"What?" Donte had paled, and his head wobbled back and forth as he peered at Raneal and Jesik. "You can Activate? But that would mean you are both Templars! How can that be?"

Jesik patted Donte's hand. "I haven't shared this with you until now, my friend, because we couldn't burden you with the secret. But fear not. We're not monsters. We are just a circumstance of nature. Variations occur in every species. Like a herd of gazelles has some that are stronger and swifter than others, Templars are a part of the human herd. There was bound to be a Templar born again sometime. Raneal and I are just the result of human variation. As are Dinaala and Micah."

"So Micah is super old too?" Aleks shook his head at the thought.

"It seems that Micah is even more powerful than Dinaala. He is almost eighty. But it's not their age or maturity that led us to bring them with us. In fact, it was the very reason you felt we should have left them behind. Until they reach their full maturity, they are vulnerable."

"Wait a second." Tony couldn't get his mind around something. "Are you saying Beka and Jakub were super-powerful too? Because they certainly didn't seem that way to me."

"No, they were pretty average. They adopted Dinaala and Micah about twenty years ago. The children called them Mom and Dad out of love and respect, not family lineage. They were, in fact, the children's third set of adoptive parents."

"What happened to their real parents?"

"Their mother died when Dinaala was an infant. And their father …" Jesik trailed off for a moment. "Their father was afraid that if anyone found out who he was, the children would not be safe. So he found a suitable family to raise them."

"So you're saying he just gave them up?" Aleks's fury was written across his face. "He sounds like a coward to me."

"It was the hardest thing he has ever done." Jesik fell silent.

Tony thought it was the first time he'd seen the man out of sorts. It was a bit disconcerting. "Okay. Enough about how old the kids are and who their parents are. You said that was one reason you brought them. What are the other reasons?"

"The second reason is that I believe Micah and Dinaala are mentioned in the Prophecies. One Prophecy that talks about Tony mentions a young builder who travels with him and creates never-before-seen weapons of war. And another mentions a girl matching Dinaala's description who speaks to the dead. This is one of the Prophecies that don't make sense, so I can't tell you what it means. But they are critical to our success in stopping the Dark One. We need to protect them and teach them. So they need to stay with us until this is over."

Aleks started to protest again but kept his mouth shut.

"As far as the other pertinent Prophecies go, there are three that really matter in this moment. First, it is written that Tony and a small group of fighters will brace the Dark One at the mouth of his den. If they can hold the Dark One there, a larger force will join them and the Dark One can be stopped before he really gets moving."

Jesik looked at Fazha. "Thom is the one who will bring that larger force from the South. This second Prophecy is how I know that Thom will be all right. He has to survive for that Prophecy to be fulfilled.

"The third Prophecy involves you, Aleks. This describes you in great detail.

It then talks about how you will step through the Mirror of Forever into the past. You will become the Great Builder and wander the land for hundreds of years, creating cities and roads. In essence, Aleks, you are responsible for creating most of the infrastructure of Freia more than four thousand years ago."

"So why don't I know anything about all of this stuff I'm supposed to have created all those years ago?"

"I know this is all very confusing. As far as Freia is concerned, you lived so very long ago and created cities and shaped the land and made this valley and the creatures of the Deep. Only you knew why you did these things. All of that is part of Freia's history. But for you, this you, the one here and now, none of that has happened yet. It won't happen until you go through the Mirror of Forever and step into our past.

"This is really the most critical of all the Prophecies. If for some unknown reason you don't go back in time, then none of those cities or roads will be built. We won't be here and no one will be able to stand before the Dark One when he sweeps down from the north. Everyone on this planet will be enslaved or killed."

"No pressure then, right?" Aleks looked a little green around the gills.

Jesik nodded. "But remember. For us, all of this has already happened. So we know you will be successful. You just have to step up and do it."

Tony couldn't help himself. He yawned again, with a loud pop from his jaw. He wanted to listen to the rest of the conversation. And he *really* wanted to talk to Aleks about a lot of things. But as another yawn broke free from him on its own, he didn't think he could keep his eyes open to do it.

Instead of throwing out any of the hundred questions he had, he simply said, "Well, that was an inspiring conversation. But I'm exhausted. Is there any particular designation to the rooms, or should I just pick one?"

"You can just pick one. They're all the same," Aleks replied.

Tony thanked him, said goodnight to all, and headed down the hall. He took the first room on the right. It was as thoughtfully constructed as the rest of the house, with artful attention to detail, extruded furniture, and light in the ceiling. A button on the wall turned to set the amount of light from fully bright to completely dark. He dropped his pack on the desk and walked to the bed.

Somehow Aleks had created a mattress and pillows, along with everything else. As he lay on it, the mattress formed to his body, like an embrace. The conversation swirled in his mind for a few minutes. Was he really destined to go fight some battle he knew very little about, for people he didn't know, in a land that wasn't his own? And what about free will? Didn't he have a say in any of it?

But then his thoughts returned to what Donte had said, that the Mirror of Forever could send people to other places like one of Jesik's gates. Who knew if the mirror would allow Tony to travel back home or not? But Tony could smell an opportunity. The next morning he would find a way to go with Jesik to the Forbidden City and from there make his way home.

He smiled to himself and let sleep come.

Getting Together

Thom didn't move. He kept his breathing steady. Another of the skills that kept him alive was the ability to awaken without letting those around him know it. He often found it helpful to know what others were saying and doing when he was "asleep."

In this case, the others were also asleep. Each was on his or her own bedroll in a roughly circular bunch, closely packed around the coals of a small campfire. Everyone except Martin. He was behind Thom, reclining against a nearby tree.

Thom had no idea how long he'd been out. He remembered periods of foot shuffling between the shoulders of various people. Sometimes it was Martin and the little guy. Sometimes it was two huge women Thom didn't know. That raised some pretty unpleasant memories of his time with the queen. Ugh. The queen hadn't been huge, but the women around her sure were. Huge women. Like candy corn, they were something he'd had quite enough of in this lifetime. Come to think of it, between the Monster and Karf, huge men hadn't done him any favors recently either.

He began to wonder where they were. Without moving, Thom spread out a weave that encompassed the group and the nearest layer of forest. He would have extended it farther but the toxic feel of the foliage around them was just too strong. He felt a little nauseous as it was. They were definitely in the Deep.

"I wouldn't let the others see you do that," Martin commented.

Thom winced. Dang it! How could he see that weave? It was nearly microscopic.

"Rayne is good at hiding it, but she's incredibly powerful," Martin continued. "I think she might be as strong as you or Jesik. I don't think she'll notice it, now that it's down and all, but I get an itch whenever you lay one down. She probably will too."

Thom sucked in his breath at that, suddenly wishing Martin was whispering this information rather than casually saying it so everyone could hear.

As if reading his mind, Martin said, "Don't worry. I've kept them marching for three days without rest. So they're completely out."

"What are we doing sleeping in the Deep?" Thom hissed, turning over to face the other man. The coals from the fire cast an eerie red glow over Martin that made him look like something out of Dante's *Inferno.*

"They needed the sleep. You've lost some weight since I saw you last, but carrying your carcass around still tires a person out." Martin casually uncrossed and recrossed his legs, as if to renew circulation to his lower foot. "And it looks like the Deep has decided that I am a kindred spirit, a true monster, because the creatures and plants in here are leaving us totally alone. In fact, they seem to have a no-go zone around us. We haven't seen so much as a cockroach since we crossed into the trees."

Thom stretched. "How far do we have to go to get to Donte's place?"

"We're about halfway through. I'm going to let them sleep for another hour or so and then get them moving. We should break out of the trees around sunrise."

"Who are they?" Thom asked.

"I found them in Lake Tarks," Martin replied, as if that answered everything.

Thom waited for Martin to continue. Nothing.

"You found them at Lake Tarks, and …?"

"Not *at* Lake Tarks, in Lake Tarks. I was swimming in the lake and they sailed up in a three-masted sloop."

Thom's mind spun at that. He wasn't completely conversant with the terrain around the Deep, but he was pretty sure a sloop with three masts would require deep water access. And there were definitely no deep water rivers in the mountains.

"What the hell?" Thom asked.

"Exactly! And they had some cock and bull story about sailing it there looking for something or other. It was pretty obvious they were running from someone. The man's tiny and the women are huge. Plus, they don't have much of an opinion of the worth of men. Any ideas as to where they ran from?"

"Oh shit ..."

"Yep. I'm guessing they came zipping up here from the Southern Islands, with someone on their tails. Why they would go to the coast and buy a ship to come inland, I have no idea. It's pretty rough terrain, so a wagon wouldn't work to get them here. But why buy such a large ship to go into the mountains? All good questions that remain unanswered. In any case, they bumped into me on Lake Tarks and I told them I knew someone who could help them find whatever they were after. They jumped at the offer."

"Maybe they aren't running from something but after something," Thom said, his nerves starting to tingle. "They might not have recognized me from the way I look right now."

Martin shook his head. "If they were after you, I'm sure there would have been a lot more questions and more looking ahead, rather than behind." He nodded toward Rayne. "As strong as *she* is, whatever's after them is probably not a physical threat. But they're afraid of it just the same."

Thom nodded. Martin was far from stupid and his logic made sense. Of course, he still had those crazy eyes and the new, ever-present grin. It would probably be a good idea to separate from Crazy Eyes sooner rather than later. Hanging with nutters was a good way to get hurt.

"I figured anyone that strong should become acquainted with our little adventure. The fact that they haven't once balked at the pace, terrain, or lack of habitation on this little trek also speaks to them running from something." Martin let the last sentence hang there for a few seconds.

"Well," he continued with a sigh, "I guess that brings you just about up to speed." He started to stand up and then paused. "Except, of course, for the part where I went to see the Dark One, he sent some weird creatures after Micah, and they killed Beka and Jakub and wounded Raneal and Dinaala."

Martin stood up and started moving toward the others, presumably to wake them.

"Wait!" Thom said. "Wait.... You can't just dump all that and not explain any of it. Are Raneal and Dinaala okay?"

Martin nodded. "Yes, Jesik and a newbie got there before the bad guys made off with Micah. The newbie's name is Tony. Between them, he and

Jesik chopped up the kidnappers pretty thoroughly. I got there just in time to clean up the mess.

"Raneal and Dinaala were okay, if a bit the worse for wear. But Beka and Jakub were gone before Jesik and Tony got there. Raneal was scarred pretty badly. Dinaala and Micah didn't know about their parents by the time I left, so I don't know how they're doing."

Thom thought all of that through for a few minutes. Poor kids. He knew they were much older and more mature than they appeared, but it didn't really matter. Losing your parents had to suck. He turned his mind to the other news. Tony. He knew the name from the prophecies. Tony was a warrior. He'd guide the combined armies of the humans against the Chinon d'k Tal of the Dark One. Thom wondered if Tony knew it yet.

"What about your visit with the Dark One? I assume you would have mentioned it if you'd killed him already, right?" Thom asked.

Martin looked at him, losing his grin for the first time since he found Thom. "It didn't go particularly well." He turned back to the group and shook the tallest redhead awake.

Her hand shot out, quick as a snake, snatching Martin's throat in a grip that made the tendons stick out on his neck. Thom jumped to his feet and moved toward Martin. Martin held up his hand to Thom, stopping him in his tracks.

"It's time to get moving," Martin said through clenched teeth. If the woman's grip on his throat was causing him any discomfort, he didn't show it. The woman released him.

"You would be better served by having Gaien wake me in the future," she commented, stretching as she stood. "I'm very unlikely to kill him by mistake."

One by one she roused the others and ordered them to break camp. So she was the leader of their group. Thom thought Martin had called her Rain. Odd name, that. But the women of the Southern Islands were a bit strange.

Thom used his hands rather than his Touch to pack up his bedroll and the rest of his kit. He made it a point to stay out of the women's way. Martin might have been right that they were running from something, but there was no sense in tempting fate.

When they started walking again, the little guy, Gaien, slid into step beside Thom. A dog, something like a black border collie with a white chest and socks, padded along beside Gaien, keeping careful eyes, ears, and nose on the surrounding forest.

"Nice dog," Thom said to Gaien with his best disarming grin.

"Thanks, but he's not mine." Was that a hint of regret or jealousy Thom detected?

"And his name's Kevin." Strange name for a dog, especially here. But, Kevin it was.

"Hello, Kevin," Thom said, reaching his hand out toward the dog.

Out of the corner of his eye Thom could see the redhead tense up. Just enough for Thom to catch it. She relaxed when the dog accepted Thom's head scratches. So the redhead was the dog's master. Then why was the dog walking here with Gaien? Curious. Very curious, indeed.

The group walked on for quite some time with no monstrous interruptions. It was very strange. Thom had carried the weave along with them and felt no animal or insect presence at all. He could hear animal sounds through the trees in all directions, but none even made a feint toward the little group.

"Has this been going on the whole time?" Thom asked Gaien, indicating the forest and including Kevin in his question.

"Kevin got a little ... well ... a lot crazy when he first sensed Martin in the water." He patted the dog's head. "But after we had a chance to talk to Martin and bring him aboard, Kevin settled down a little. I still don't think he likes Martin, but he isn't trying to rip his throat out, either.

"As far as the forest goes, we haven't seen anything move in here since we walked into it. It looked all ominous and chilling. But it's been totally smooth sailing."

Something was definitely wrong. The monsters of this place should have taken the little group apart and picked their teeth with Gaien's bones. Instead, coming through the Deep had been like a walk in the park. Admittedly it was a gloomy, ominous, pitch-black park with really unpleasant shrubs and horrible smells. But still.

"Smooth sailing, huh? I guess so. I've had enough rough water lately to sink a galleon." Thom was hoping to draw Gaien out a bit and find out what they were truly about.

"I know what you mean." Bait taken.

"Oh? Did y'all run into some rough water of your own?" Thom asked, just as innocent as a Venus Flytrap. He found that a slight southern accent often put people more at ease. Why, he didn't know. But it even worked over here, where southern accents didn't exist.

Gaien started to talk, caught himself, glanced at the redhead walking up ahead of them, and then spouted the party line about their group traveling up the river with the hopes of setting up a new business in a village in the mountains.

"Uh huh ..." Thom nodded. He didn't dare use his Touch with Rayne around, so he had to work the guy old school, with words instead of juice. "Y'all seem pretty well armed for entrepreneurs. What kind of business are you in?"

"Transportation." Gaien seemed to be getting a little nervous. Obviously he didn't want trouble with Rayne, if he said too much.

Thom decided to let it rest for now, rather than push the guy too hard and lose out on all opportunities for gathering information. He changed the subject. "The trees look weird, don't they?" he said, looking up at the branches that arched over their heads. The light stones they had mounted using walking sticks were bright enough to see by, but made strange shadows among the trees. The shadows were twisting and moving with every movement of the walking sticks. It almost looked as if the trees themselves were bending and moving.

"Yeah. They look like their moving," Gaien said, with visible relief at being on a topic with no landmines hidden in it.

Thom pointed. "Look at that one. Does it look like it moved away as we came closer to it? And there, that one too."

Gaien nodded. "That one did too. And that one. They're definitely moving away." He looked back along their path. "It's almost like the forest is making it easier for us to move through."

"That sounds like a positive way to look at it," Thom said. "It looks to me like the forest wants to avoid us at all costs. Assuming, of course, that a forest has a mind and can decide things for itself."

"I guess that does sound a little crazy," Gaien replied. But he continued to walk amiably enough beside Thom, now that they weren't on dangerous footing.

They continued on through the forest with no untoward events. Thom made a couple of halfhearted attempts to get more information about Gaien and his friends, but he found that he liked the little guy, so he didn't push it.

Within a couple of hours they could make out the faint light of dawn coming through the trees up ahead. As they approached the edge of the woods, they were able to extinguish their light stones. A few minutes later, to Thom's utter amazement, they simply strolled out of the most dangerous forest on the planet. Unscathed. Unmolested. And apparently unnoticed.

It wasn't like he was expecting a ticker-tape parade or anything. But it might have been nice if *someone* was looking for him. He was pretty sure he'd gotten Fazha to the right place. By now she should have given the treaty to Donte, who would have let Jesik know about it. You'd think *someone* would have been worried about him and come looking.

He glanced at the ground as they started hoofing it toward the cabin. This was one part of the trip he had been dreading. Not particularly fearing, because this scrub brush crap could only really hurt him if he fell in it. But it was worse than walking barefoot through a patch of nettles. Ugh. *Hederus malum:* evil-weed. Of course, Donte had called it "cutie," or something like that, but Thom figured that something this rotten deserved a good Latin name.

In a night full of weird things, this one may have been the weirdest. The scrub didn't reach toward the party like it usually did, with those vicious, poison-tipped thorns. Instead, the plants stretched their tendrils as far away from the group as their roots would allow, making a nice clear path for the troupe to walk along. It was totally unnerving.

Thom looked ahead to the cabin, which was no longer a cabin. It was now a large stone house, with dozens of windows and a porch that wrapped around it. They were still a long way off, but he hoped to catch a glimpse of some activity. He was rewarded. There was a fair sized group of people standing on the porch near the door. He couldn't make out numbers at this distance, but was sure there were at least six or eight people there.

As they got closer to the cabin, Thom could make out wild gesticulations among the people on the porch. He silently cursed the fact that Rayne was there, keeping him from throwing a weave out to hear the conversation. It must have been intense because it seemed no one on the porch had noticed the troupe making its way toward the house across the field of evil-weed.

Just when he could begin to identify some of the people on the porch, a weird acoustic anomaly, either due to the shape of the terrain or possibly the fury of the person talking, brought some of the heated conversation to the approaching party's ears.

"... don't give a shit about what you *want to do! You promised to help me find him and you are bloody well going to do it if I have to break your legs and drag your wailing carcass through those fucking trees!"* Fazha was screaming at someone.

Thom could just make out that Fazha was poking Jesik in the chest. Ouch. Thom knew how much it hurt when she did that. Jesik had nearly toppled backward over the porch railing trying to get out of Fazha's reach. Several others on the porch were gaping at her. Interestingly, no one seemed to be rushing to help Jesik. It was almost like they already knew better than to get in her way.

"*Now get your shit together, because—*" Fazha stopped cold in her tirade. She turned from Jesik to look across the evil-weed at the party. Thom's heart fluttered when her eyes settled on him.

There was a flash of movement on the porch. How did she move so fast? Fazha hadn't bothered with the steps. She simply stepped up on the handrail and leaped thirty feet out onto the evil-weed. She was a streak of light moving toward them.

There was the briefest of moments when it could have gotten ugly, as Rayne reached for her sword to counter this new threat. Thom stepped up and touched Rayne's arm. "Wait! She's with me."

Rayne looked dubiously at Thom and then back to the flying woman. Fazha plowed into Thom, lifting him completely off his feet. They crashed to the ground in a heap, landing in one of several neat rectangles of ground that had no evil-weed growing on them. Thom had just a moment to ponder the origin of the bare patches. Then began the kisses. For some time after that, kissing was his only occupation.

Suddenly, Fazha leaned away from him.

"You"—her anger was almost palpable—"are an *ass*!"

He held up his hand. "Wait! Please, before you go off on me, I had good reason to do what I did."

"Let's hear it, Mr. Man. And none of your finger-waggling business! You're not getting off that easy."

"Okay, look," he said, staring deeply into her stunning eyes, "you know all of the things I've been through since I got here, because I just shared them with you yesterday, right?" She nodded. "I've got scars from them, but I survived each of those things. And I keep coming back for more. And I know I hired you to protect me, so you feel some obligations there. But I can protect myself. I can handle just about anything that comes up."

He paused and took a deep breath. "And if I watched you get hurt … if I watched you die … I would not survive it." Tears streamed down his face.

"You think I'm mad because I feel some obligation to protect you?"

"Aren't you?"

"Of course I am! But I'll get over it. I know you didn't really hire me to protect you because you're silly enough to think you can do it yourself. I know you hired me because the Duke was looking for a lone stranger. With me and my team along, you looked like a group. I get that.

"But know this, you silly ass. I am a different person than I was when I met you. Without you, *I* would wither up and die. I had no idea how empty my life was before you came into it. And now that you're here, all I live for is to be with you. So I *am* going to protect you, whether you think you need it or not. And don't you dare send me away again. Ever. Do you understand me?"

Tears were streaming down her face now too. In that instant he felt the love in her heart. He didn't care one whit who was watching and whether or not they should see his weaves. He just knew that he loved this woman to his soul and wanted to share his essence with her. He wrapped her in a very light weave, feeling every inch of her body, heart, mind, and soul. And she knew him. They kissed.

"Ahem …" came a voice from a few feet away. Thom separated enough from Fazha to glance over to where the voice had come from. Jesik, Raneal, Donte, Dinaala, Micah, and a couple other new folks were all watching them.

Raneal, smiling widely, continued. "Do you think you could finish your sex play some other time? We *are* on a schedule."

This group was getting quite large, so introductions took some time. Thom held Fazha's hand and watched the evil-weed sway and pull away from the clean patch of ground the group was standing on while they talked.

Eventually he had a vague notion of who some of the people in the group—*cadre? kabal?* whatever it was called—were. The four new people he'd come with, Gaien, Rayne, Magda and Shaulee, were still clinging to their story and remained something of a mystery. Jesik's band all seemed to intuitively grasp the significance of this subterfuge and refrained from saying anything about their own strength and their purpose for being in this forest. It made communication among Jesik's band extremely difficult. Lastly, a blonde girl who couldn't speak for herself was introduced as Alice. No one seemed to know who *she* was or what she was doing there.

After an excruciating few minutes of listening to each person dance around his or her personal story, Thom got fed up. He'd been plying his trade as a Negotiator for a few years now, so he had to live his life with a pack of lies and half-truths, but this was ridiculous.

He turned to Rayne. "All right. I've had enough of this." Rayne looked at him with confidence and a small token of disdain or superiority. Before meeting Fazha, Thom had had to touch someone to read them. Now he could do it without moving a muscle. His Touch flowed out along the ground and slid up under each of the four of them.

"I'll show you mine if you show me yours," he said.

Gaien, Magda, and Shaulee, the fourth member of their troupe, all came into crystal focus. They were all afraid. But, when Thom's weave slid under her, Rayne hopped from one foot to the other, looking down at her feet.

Rayne lashed out with her Touch, a whip-like flick of power that came so quickly Thom would never have gotten out of the way. Fortunately, Tony and Fazha both stepped in front of Thom. He never saw either of them move. Tony actually grabbed the end of the stream of energy and held it fast. Rayne's eyes opened wide. Two, three, four, a dozen more whips flashed out from her. Tony and Fazha deflected or caught each of them. The other three in her group tried to step forward and help their leader, but Thom's weave enveloped them and held them still. Thom's energy calmed the two women, but Gaien was trembling with exertion. Kevin started moving and Thom had to tether him as well.

Suddenly Tony, holding on to four or five of Rayne's whips, was hauled up into the air and flung back and forth like a rag doll. Tony not only hung on to the whips, but also started pulling himself up them to reach Rayne, who now stood alone, sword and dirk drawn. Fazha's sword was in her free hand. There was the ring of steel on steel.

And then the ground erupted in a shower of dirt and evil-weed as a foot-thick wall of stone shot up into the middle of the fray. Fazha and Tony were sent flying in one direction; Thom caught them both and set them gently on their feet. Rayne was tossed in the other direction. She managed to get her feet under her as she fell and landed in a fighter's crouch. The move looked a lot like one that Fazha would have made. It was actually quite beautiful to watch.

The guy introduced as Aleks stepped forward and said, "Knock it off!" The wall slid back into the ground. Everyone turned to Aleks.

"If you're all done comparing the size of your dicks, we've got a lot of things to do. And we don't have much time to do them." He pointed to the northern sky. The others turned and followed his finger with their eyes. An ominous black cloud was boiling in the north, covering the sky in a blanket of black and gray cotton candy. Within a few minutes the morning sun was dimmed as if in partial eclipse. The sky felt dark and crushingly oppressive.

Thom rolled his eyes. *Oh, come on. You had to pull out the ominous cloud cover bit? That's the oldest all-powerful bad guy trick in the book.*

"He's getting ready to move," Jesik said. "Soon he'll begin sweeping down from the north and crushing every farm, village, and hamlet between the Northern Sea and the Sky Wall mountains. We need to get Aleks on his way and decide what to do next."

Jesik turned to Rayne, who stood with her swords forgotten in her hands. "I can offer you safe passage out of these lands. Thom is a Negotiator. If you will agree to a binding, promising that you will not attempt to harm us, report our location or plans to the Dark One, or tell anyone else about us, I will help you return to your ship. Or anywhere else you wish to go, for that matter."

Rayne sheathed her swords and looked at her crew. For the briefest of moments Thom thought she was seeking their counsel. But she seemed not to notice or care that their opinions showed in their faces. They all wanted to go home. Rayne decided their path for them.

"We will abide by your binding," she said. "Provided you agree to a binding not to disclose our presence or location."

Jesik was powerful enough to detect Rayne's strength, and he was no fool.

"We'll agree to that. Assuming you will tell us the truth about who you are and why you're here."

Rayne's eyes grew cold. "We just came through this 'Deep' you all seem so afraid of. It was not so terrible a place. I think we'll take our chances going that way."

She turned to Martin. "We left our ship for this?" She spat the words.

Martin and Aleks both stepped in front of her as she started to leave. Rayne once again reached for her swords.

Aleks held his hands out to her. "Wait," he said. "I don't think you have all the facts."

He led the group back on to the porch. Rayne and her crew reluctantly followed but apparently were willing to listen. Once up on the porch, Aleks looked out at the evil-weed. "Do you see those bare patches of ground out there?"

Rayne nodded.

"Watch."

Bulges formed all over the yard as Freia belched out body after body. Lopers, spiders, death-stalks, palkin, those damned little red-eyed monkey things that Thom couldn't remember the name of were all being disgorged across the yard.

Even Rayne's hard eyes widened at the sheer volume of the nastiness in front of her.

"What is this?" she asked.

"That is what came out of the Deep after those guys, when they came through." Aleks said, nodding toward Jesik. "The things that stayed in the trees are much worse than these things."

Rayne looked at the creatures and then back at her crew. Her companions were obviously concerned about what they had gotten themselves into. She whispered a single word to them. Jesik and the others could not have heard it. Thom heard it only because his whisper-thin weave was still in place, bringing the word back to him.

"Rast."

Thom felt the blood drain from his face, mirroring the faces of Rayne's three crewmembers.

Before he could say anything, Rayne had turned back to Jesik and said, "We will tell you about ourselves. *After* the binding is in place."

Jesik nodded.

Thom was about to pull Jesik aside when Martin spoke up. "Wait a sec." He was looking closely at the nearest pile of monsters.

Aleks had just started to return the creatures to their graves. He stopped and raised them once again.

"Something's been nagging at me, and I can't put my finger on it." Martin stepped off the porch and walked unmolested through the evil-weed. When he got to the first pile of creatures, he grabbed one cluster of the creature's face tentacles and spread them to expose its beak.

"This is a palkin, right?" Martin asked of no one in particular. Jesik agreed, moving up to the porch railing to watch Martin as he inspected the giant beast.

"These aren't the same creatures as the ones that I cleaned up at your house," Martin said.

Jesik looked surprised.

"I saw a bunch of these at the Dark One's palace," Martin continued. "He said they had come from the Deep. The ones in your yard had different heads and no tentacles."

"You saw these at the Dark One's palace?" Jesik asked.

"Yep."

Thom was still shaken by the thought of a Rast somehow included in this mix. He wanted to know more about it. And he wanted to know now. He stepped up to Jesik. "We should probably do the binding before we have much more conversation, don't you think?"

Jesik nodded.

Thom asked Martin to come back up on the porch and turned to face the main group of people standing there. What he was about to do was incredibly serious and had to follow a certain protocol. He put all jokes and thoughts of a Rast rending people aside for the moment.

"All right. For those of you who've never been through a binding before, here's how it works. I will touch your hand to get a sense of your Touch. Then I will ask permission of you to perform the binding. It's very important that you give that permission, both out loud and in your mind. I won't perform a binding on anyone who doesn't give permission. So if you don't give it, the binding will fail.

"Once I have your permission, I will ask you to state your promise for the binding, out loud, for all to hear. Then I will apply my Touch, sealing the promise. After the promise is sealed into the binding, you will not be able to act contrary to it or your Touch will be cut off until you resolve it. People have died because they refused to resolve a binding transgression.

"Lastly, once the binding is in place it cannot be removed, even by me. You will be bound for the rest of your life, or until the promise no longer has meaning. Some people have died trying to remove a binding." Of course, this wasn't strictly true. Thom was strong enough to unwind even other people's bindings. But these folks didn't need to know that.

"This includes killing the binder. If I die, the binding will remain. So don't even think about trying to off me to get out of it. Once you're bound, you're bound.

"Do you each understand how serious this is?" Thom looked to each person, making sure to get eye contact. Each nodded in turn.

"All right, we'll start with Rayne." Thom guided her to a spot a few steps away from the rest of the group. Bindings were performed quite rarely, and he felt everyone's eyes on him as he began the age-old ritual.

He stepped close to Rayne, took her hand, closed his eyes, and let his Touch flow into her. Every time he did it, it felt strange and intimate, this getting to know people from the inside out. He never delved into deeply personal things. He just went far enough to get a sense of the truth of the person. To determine if they could be trusted. This intimacy, as powerful as it was, was like a teardrop compared to the ocean of emotion he shared with Fazha.

Within Rayne, riding above all else was her sense of honor. She did what she said she would do. He felt an itch around that concept. Nearly everyone he'd ever felt had some of the same emotions. Rayne was no different. She was regretting something she had done that went against her basic sense of self and truth. Rather than show treachery in her spirit, this showed that she was far *more* likely to be trustworthy. People who were truly treacherous often felt regret about the *results* of their actions. Not about the actions themselves.

But there was something more. Something else about her tickled at his perceptions. She obviously didn't enjoy personal physical contact. With a man. That was it. She hated having a man in this intimate contact with her. He opened himself up more to her feelings. There was something more inside her. Her hatred of this contact was a ruse. She was hiding something behind all this emotion.

And then he had it. She was trying to mask her Activator from him. But he was far too strong and adept for her to completely conceal it, even with this level of emotion. She was an Activator *and* a Regulator. She was a Templar.

Interesting.

The contact lasted only a split second, but it was enough for her to know that he had the measure of her. She could be trusted.

Rayne was a bit pale and wide-eyed when he pulled his hand back and opened his eyes.

"Do you give me permission to perform this binding?"

For the first time since he had met her, Rayne seemed hesitant for just a second. Then she resolved herself and became confident again. Her answer was strong and sure. "Yes."

Thom lay a new weave over her. This one was very thin and light. Not much Touch was required for a binding. It was skill more than strength that dictated its success.

"State your promise."

"I promise to not intentionally reveal your group's location or plans to the Dark One or anyone else and to avoid bringing harm to anyone in this group, except in defense of myself, another member of this group, or another innocent person."

Thom looked at Jesik. "Is this an acceptable promise?"

Jesik smiled ruefully at the added escape clause. But he nodded.

Thom pulled tight on his weave, like a net over a Christmas tree, cinched it, bound it, and snipped it off. For a few brief seconds he could still sense the glow of the binding as it wrapped around Rayne before it faded from his perceptions.

Rayne let out a sigh. Apparently she had been holding her breath. But she looked as calm and confident as usual when she stepped even closer to Thom.

"I need to share something with you before you continue," she said. "Alone."

Hmm. This was interesting. He walked with her a few feet away from the group.

"I must tell you something about Gaien," she said when they were far enough away from the others to safely whisper to each other. "He and I have traveled together for a few weeks now. And Kevin trusts him."

She looked pained at the next part, like it was hard for her to say. "I trust him."

She turned and looked out toward the forest, over the evil-weed, as she continued. "I could feel you, when you were sensing my Touch. I have the sense that I can trust you. So I am going to share something with you that I have told no one about. I did something similar with Gaien a couple of weeks ago. When I looked at him ..." She trailed off, as if searching for the right words.

"I don't know. I was knocked unconscious. And when I came to, I was blind for a time. I don't really remember what happened, but it was extremely intense." She looked back at him. "But that's not all. There are parts of my story that I will tell you now that are different from what I will tell the others later."

Thom paused in his automatic protestation when she raised her hand.

"None of these differences will harm your friends. In fact, they may keep them alive. When we left port in the Southlands, we were being pursued by three ships. They were larger and faster than our ship and they were gaining on us. Many of my crew had mutinied and killed the rest. Gaien and I won the fight with the mutineers but were the only two left to sail the ship and fight off the others. I took us through the Crest."

Whoa. That was a scary place to sail through. Thom had been there once on his journeys into the Southland and he never wanted to go back.

"The other three ships had true Wavemistresses, more sails, and a lot more crew onboard. They made it through the Crest as well and gained on us. When they were a league away and gaining fast, Gaien stepped onto the poop deck and sang. He just sang. And the ships exploded. One by one, they just blew up. I've seen strong Regulators with a team of Activators create a building in a day. And I'm very powerful. But I've never seen *anything* like that. I've never seen the Touch used that way.

"I don't know what Gaien's purpose is in this life. I don't know if his power can be used for good in this world. But I know in the core of my being that we can't let him fall into the hands of someone like Queen Sheefa." She caught Thom's eyes.

"The two women with me are survivors of one of the ships that was chasing me. So when I share this with your friends, I will tell them that *I* destroyed the boats. I wanted you to understand that my lies are not intended to hurt your friends. And also that when you sense Gaien's Touch, you can't talk about what you find. At least for now. Do you understand?"

Thom nodded his agreement. She had a very valid point. He'd had the opportunity to spend time with the queen himself and it had been quite unpleasant. She was ruthless, heartless, ambitious, and powerful. Not a good combination. Give her a power like Gaien's and she would wreak havoc trying to take over the world.

And the queen wasn't the only person on Freia who couldn't be allowed access to someone as special as Gaien. The Magister of the Southlands was almost as bad. Even the Duke and the Baron should be kept in the dark about the little guy.

And from the things she said and the feel of her Touch, he could tell that Rayne herself was no slouch. She could be an incredible ally or a horrifying foe. The world needed Gaien and Rayne on the side of the good guys.

In fact, with this conversation, Rayne had taken a step up in his estimation of her—not because of her obvious power but because of the woman she was turning out to be. She was one brave lady. Although, now that he thought of it, she would probably hate being called a lady. That thought made him smile.

The pair returned to the party and Thom began the binding on Rayne's female crewmates, opting to leave Gaien for last. In turn, he touched each woman on the hand and flowed into her. Magda, the Regulator, was no comparison to Micah, but she still had plenty of juice. She was mostly honorable, if a bit ambitious. And she was head over heals in love with Rayne. She would be no problem.

On the other hand, Shaulee, the Activator, was stronger than she let on, devious and cunning. She tried to hide her strength and the undercurrent of her character. He let her believe she had succeeded. He trusted that the binding would prevent her from taking direct action but intended to watch her just the same.

When he was finished sensing them, each woman gave Thom permission to bind them and they spoke their promise. He bound them as he had Rayne.

Then he moved on to Gaien. Thom was grateful for Rayne's warning when his Touch flowed into Gaien. He was able to set up a buffer within himself that kept him from being overwhelmed by the Touch he sensed within the little guy. Flowing into Gaien was like stepping off Freia into the night sky. It was a vast, empty, echoing chamber of nothing. At its center was an incredibly intense, bright ball of energy. Rayne must have looked on this ball and been blown back by it. It was incredible. It was a direct connection to the source of the Touch on Freia. Gaien was somehow tied in to the very heart of the Touch. He was limitless. This was the kind of thing that could make a guy very afraid.

Except for two things.

First, Gaien's spirit. Thom could sense it within him. Like Thom, the little guy had suffered greatly in his lifetime. Thom could see the scars and lashings on the man's soul. But, also like Thom (or so he hoped), Gaien had made peace with that suffering. He'd accepted it as a learning tool that made him better. And he definitely was better. Gaien was a good man.

Second, Thom had seen this kind of power before. Once.

After Gaien's permission, promise, and binding ceremony, Thom moved on to Jesik's group—everyone but Alice, who could not give permission. Aleks took her inside to wait until everyone else was done. Thom took each in turn, binding him or her to the promise to not harm or reveal Rayne's group to anyone.

Each had his or her own flavor. Raneal was as bright and sweet as she appeared but held some dark pain she could not or would not share. Dinaala was electric. She was full of energy, life, and bravery and was as strong as a bull. Micah was a bright fire, a spark of creation. Jesik was all secrets and ancient knowledge. Donte was anxiety tempered by wisdom and age. Tony was honor, loyalty, discipline, and controlled rage. Fazha was, well, Fazha. When he sensed her, he opened himself up, as well. Mmmmmm. That had been *nice.* He'd never wanted it to end.

Lastly, he came to Martin. Thom had sensed Martin once before, in the Galorean forest, on the night of Thom's nightmares. Thom still wondered why his nightmares were of *that* forest and not the Deep, which had been much worse. But that was a musing for another day.

Thom set up his buffer again and flowed into Martin. And there it was. That same sense of vastness and space, with the brightly glowing orb at its center. Only with this one the man behind the power was mostly unstable. Thom's vague fear about the craziness in Martin's eyes was no longer vague.

Martin was not wired down real tight. Thom felt certain that Martin wasn't completely crazy. There was still a sane guy in there, at the core of Martin's being. Thom could feel it at the edges of his perception. But Martin was definitely not stable. Of that Thom was absolutely certain. And Thom was equally certain that Martin was Gaien's father.

Vision Statement

Aleks listened with the others as Rayne told them about their flight from the Southlands, their escape from the ships that followed them, and her decision to come to the north rather than deliver Gaien to some queen everyone seemed to recognize. She finished the story with a description of heading upriver to the lake, where they had met Martin, by raising the water in the river to allow their ship to pass.

Her long black cloak and red hair lay flat despite the stiff breeze. He could see that she was holding it there with some kind of Touch, but how she was doing it eluded him. She stood eye to eye with Tony and Jesik, towering over everyone else in the group, and used frequent hand gestures to punctuate the tale. It was all very convincing. And he could smell the acceptance among those around him—all except Thom. Thom knew the story was a lie but let it go on without comment. Strange.

Over the last couple of weeks Aleks had come to accept his new senses of smell and sight. He didn't understand them: How could he see inside objects with such detail? He was seeing at a subatomic level. He'd seen pictures taken by an electron microscope and they looked something like what he was seeing. Except the pictures were black and white. What he was seeing was in Technicolor. And moving. He was pretty sure he would have been grossed out about it all, if he'd seen it before coming to Freia.

And the smells. That was truly weird. The first thing he'd registered about this perception was that smells now held new meaning for him. Before, Aleks had been repulsed by some smells. Shit, piss, vinegar, and many other smells had really disturbed him.

Fortunately, that wasn't the case any longer. He didn't think he could have stayed in the house if it had. Every time someone took a crap in that place, he could not only smell it but also identify the person who did it and the last week's worth of food they'd eaten.

And how exactly did *that* work? Identifying people from their scent? He didn't know. But under the combined scents of their clothes—leather, denim, cotton, and their local equivalents—each person had his or her own unique smell. Try as he might he couldn't correlate any of their scents to anything else. They were Rayne's scent, Fazha's scent, Donte's scent.

What really perplexed him was his newfound ability to identify people's emotional state from their aroma. It was fascinating and a bit scary. He decided it was similar to what bloodhounds could do. He must be picking up on pheromones or something. No, he didn't understand how these new senses worked, but he had come to trust them.

And right now, this mystery skill was working overtime. It told him Rayne was lying through her teeth. Aleks decided not to call her on the deception. Not because he trusted her—or Thom, for that matter. He'd just met them that morning. He decided not to say anything because he trusted his new sense of smell. And in Rayne, he smelled no ill intent, no darkness. What he smelled from her was caution. It reminded him of buffered aspirin. She was lying—not to harm anyone but to protect something.

After Rayne finished her tale, Jesik gave a brief sketch of the Prophecies, explaining about the Dark One's impending assault on the rest of the planet and the small group's foretold role in preventing it. He finished with a description of the Forbidden City, lying empty and forsaken at the bottom of the lake a short walk from the cabin, and their intended actions once they reached it. If he knew how they were going to get to the bottom of the lake to enter the Forbidden City, he didn't share it with them.

He also neglected to mention that Thom, Aleks, Martin, and Tony weren't from around there. Or that they were Templars.

Rayne was far from stupid. Her suspicions wafted off her in great waves. In her doubt she was alone among her little group. Neither Magda nor Shaulee gave off any aroma of suspicion. Gaien gave no indication either.

Gaien was an interesting question mark. Aside from Micah's early teen physique, Gaien was by far the smallest person there. He was treated with contempt and condescension by Magda and Shaulee. He was deferential to

Rayne. It wasn't exactly subservience—more like a deeply held respect and commitment. Despite that, he smelled calm and confident. Aleks imagined the Dali Lama would have a similar aroma.

And for her part, Rayne did not have a high regard for men, in particular Tony, whom she had clearly taken an immediate and deep dislike to. Her disgust poured off her in waves at every interaction. But she was different with Gaien. She didn't carry any negative feelings toward him. In fact, Gaien elicited a warm and respectful aroma. It had no spice of sexual desire but instead a maternal sweetness, like honey butter on homemade biscuits.

When he finished talking, Jesik turned to Martin. "When last we talked, you had just come back from the Dark One's palace. In that moment we weren't in a position to discuss the events that transpired while you were there. Would you care to share them now?"

"No," Martin said, wearing that unnerving, ever-present grin he'd been carrying since Aleks met him. That grin went hand-in-hand with the cloud of near mania that he walked around in. That scent didn't tell Aleks that Martin was crazy. Yet. It felt more like Martin's sanity was slowly chugging its way up the long hill of the roller coaster, about to crest the peak and go hurtling down into all the twists, turns, rises, and falls of lunacy. And if Martin really was strong enough to kill the Dark One, Aleks didn't want to be anywhere near him when that sanity-coaster careened around the first bend.

"It was far too disturbing," Martin continued. "But I will give you some of the highlights. And then we should talk about those beasts.

"The Dark One was ready for me when I arrived. He knew all about the Prophecies and our role in them. But he didn't show the least fear of me. Exactly the opposite, in fact. He laughed, fed me a fine meal, and then showed me all around his palace, including the training grounds he's using to prepare his armies."

Martin paused, looking at the confused faces of the people around him. "Yes, armies. He has more than one, housed underground all across the tundra. I would guess that the group I saw had at least twenty or thirty thousand Chinon d'k Tal, maybe a thousand palkin, and hundreds of the Talmo d'k Tal. I believe there are at least four other groups."

As Martin's account of the Dark One's forces sank home in the small group, fear began to taint their sweat. Jesik looked completely gutted as he collapsed backward, leaning against the porch's handrail.

"How can we possibly stand against an army so vast?" he moaned. "Just one of the Talmo d'k Tal nearly killed all of us in the forest. How will we stand against a thousand of them?" He looked at Tony.

"It sounds like we need a plan," Tony said. "In order to plan, we need information. You said this Mirror of Forever could take us places. Can it show us things as well? Can we use it to get information about him, his capabilities, and his troops?"

The fear coming from Tony was a small thing, overpowered by confidence and competence.

"Yes," Jesik said, with little hope.

"Then we'd better get down there and see what we can learn."

"There's more," Martin said, before anyone could respond to Tony's comment. "He also took me to a room with a huge mirror in it. Then he showed me Thom and Fazha, traveling through the forest with men at arms chasing them. He showed me you and Jesik talking by a large pile of wood and he showed me Donte's house." Martin looked around the group. "He can see anything he wants to see and he knows everything about us."

Now the fear was a powerful cloud surrounding the entire group. And Aleks was contributing.

Jesik took a deep breath and collected himself. "None of this makes any difference. Apparently he too has read the Prophecies. If so, his ability to watch us doesn't matter. He already knows what we're going to do. The Prophecies are very clear and curiously detailed, wherever the information won't create a paradox. It tells us that we can stop him, no matter how large his army is." Jesik seemed not to be talking to the group. Instead, he seemed to be trying to convince himself. "We can stop him. But we have to get to the Forbidden City first." He made as if to move to the door, but Martin stopped him.

"That's not all. I'm not going to share everything he said to me, because most of it was … ugh." Martin lost his grin for a few seconds and visibly shuddered at the memory. "What I will share is that he has plans for this place. I don't mean just the planet. I mean this place. This valley. He's planning on expanding this valley until it covers everything north of the break. He wants the north to reclaim itself, to completely wipe humanity off the continent. He called it his pristine playground, where humans would not be welcome."

Aleks thought of all those hell spawn creatures spread across the land. It chilled him to the core. He didn't know much about this place, having spent all of his time in a tiny cabin in a small pasture next to a lake. But he knew those creatures. Releasing them on the populace of *any* place would be horrifying. Aleks looked around at the rest of the group. They were each as horrified as he was. A person wouldn't need Aleks's powerful senses to feel their foreboding. It was palpable.

Martin let all of that information sink in for a few seconds before continuing. "Now, about those creatures that came after Micah. I don't think the Dark One sent them.

"First of all, why would he want to take Micah? He's an incredibly powerful maker in his own right. I saw it all over his palace. He'd made hundreds of artifacts that rivaled Kitarni's best. And if what he says is true, he made the entire palace in a single day. No one's done anything like that since …" Martin paused and then nodded at Aleks. "Well, since him. So the Dark One doesn't need Micah to make anything for him. If he was trying to keep him from helping us, he could simply have killed him in that attack.

"Second, those creatures only looked like these. If he was the one who sent them, I think he would have used the palkin he's been training in the north, rather than those weird hybrids. They had no tentacles at all. And their heads looked more like a cross between a lizard and a shark, with wicked-sharp rows of serrated teeth."

"What?" Thom interrupted, growing pale and puffing out a cloud of remorse and fear. "Did you say rows of serrated teeth?" Martin nodded. "And they were how big?"

Martin shared glances with Tony and Jesik and then pointed at the ground where the huge flying creatures were buried. "About as big as those things." The others confirmed it with nods.

"Oh my God." Thom gave off a waft of fear and shame. "We have a new problem. It may not be as big as the Dark One, but it's considerably more immediate."

"I think I may have made that creature." Thom rubbed his temples. "Well, not exactly that creature, but the creature that it was made from." He looked at Jesik. "You remember when Queen Sheefa had me for those months? She's a Regulator who can generally sense the power and nature of people's Touch anywhere in the world. Fortunately, her sense is only accurate to within a few hundred miles, so she can't find us directly."

Aleks caught a sudden draft of bitter fear with an undertone of creamy relief coming from Rayne. Maybe Rayne realized just how close she'd come to having her own cell in the queen's castle.

Thom continued. "But she knows Templars are back. She found me, caught me, and was able to hold me because of a Regulator she had on hand who could create bindings. But I managed to mask some of my power from her, so she underestimated me and I got away. While I was working my way free, she had me do things." Thom paused for a second and shook his head, as if trying to free himself from his memories.

"One of the things she had me do was add wings to a small lizard that lives in her land. It had a wedge-shaped head and rows of serrated teeth. It took weeks, but I managed to shift the creature into an eight-inch-long winged terror. She must have taken what I'd done and made someone else grow it to monstrous size.

"The bad news here is that she must be the one who sent the beasts after Micah. If she knows enough about Micah to want him, she must know about what he can do and wants him to be her new maker." Thom looked at Micah, who was casting off acrid terror. "Don't worry, buddy. There's no way I'm going to let her get her hands on you."

Aleks put the cloak he made into the pack he'd made for himself. The pack already contained a large bag of damain, the beautiful grain he'd been eating for weeks, some toiletries he thought they might need, and clothes he'd made for Alice and for himself.

When the group discussed their plans for traveling to the Forbidden City, he'd decided to take Alice with him into the past, despite the others' protests that his mission was too important to risk taking the girl. Their assurances that they would watch over her weren't enough for him. He felt that taking her with him was absolutely the right thing to do. He was responsible for the state she was in and he wanted to make sure she was okay. No matter what the outcome.

He pulled the pack over his shoulder and tried to ignore the grain's intoxicating aroma as it shifted inside its sealed bag. He picked up the long, twisted, black walking staff he'd fashioned and walked out the door of his room, down the hall, and out the front door of the house. The quiet click of the door's latch had a sense of finality to it.

Alice sat silently on the porch steps waiting for him to emerge. Despite the excitement of the last two days, and all the people who had arrived at the house, she was still totally focused on him. That was one more reason to bring her. He couldn't abandon her and take away the only thing, besides drawing, that she had shown any interest in.

He took her hand as she stood. They picked their way through the cotie grass to the group that was assembled on one of the larger monster graves, the smaller graves having already lost their clear patches to the encroaching viral weeds.

The women and Gaien also carried their own packs and equipment. Most of the rest were carrying weapons but were otherwise unencumbered. Aleks looked from Tony in his black leather jacket, red Pendleton shirt, Levis jeans, and cowboy boots to Thom in his nondescript tan shirt and black leather breeches. He wished he'd had more time with them to talk about Earth and the things they missed. Being the only people from another world went a long way toward bringing very different people together. And he would have liked to have someone to reminisce with, even if only for a few minutes.

Then a fresh scent of chaos washed over him as Martin came out of the house behind him. Maybe not everyone could come together, even *with* that shared background.

The little group was now ready to move out. But to where?

In the distance, maybe two or three miles south of the cabin, the mountains rose steeply from the valley floor, gray-green and midnight blue against the backdrop of thick gray clouds. The hillside got taller and even steeper, forming a high cliff face as it passed by the southern end of the lake. Jesik led the team to the stony lakeshore and then south toward those high cliffs. He'd said the city was cut into the base of the southern cliffs at the bottom of the lake.

The stupid, fist-sized round stones that made up the lakeshore shifted and rolled under Aleks's feet with every step. The same was true for everyone else, so he and Alice didn't lag behind. But he thought very seriously about smashing the entire lakeshore into a long stretch of asphalt so he could quit twisting his fucking ankles with every other step. He glanced up the bank at the cotie and decided it was better to wobble-walk down here by the lake than walk through that vile scrub and end the day with outrageously itching legs.

He didn't know if it was one, two, or even three hours later …

Three, it definitely seemed like three

… that the group reached the place where the mountains, lakeshore, and cliff face all came together. Jesik, Thom, and Tony scouted around the immediate area looking for a way to move up the steep hillside and look down over the lake. Jesik seemed to think they might be able to drop from the cliff in a bubble of air, sink to the bottom of the lake, and enter the city before the Kraken could sense, track, and catch them.

Aleks interrupted their search. "Jesik, just how far below the surface of the lake is the entrance to the Forbidden City?"

"At least three hundred feet, I would say."

Aleks said, "I think we need to change our plan here. I'm sure that, with the Touch, we can safely drop from those 150-foot high cliffs into the water. But for us to travel 300 feet down into those freezing lake waters with no motors will take us quite a bit of time. In order for us to have enough air to go that far underwater, one or more of us will have to create some kind of air pocket for the team, right?" Jesik nodded. "Won't that attract the Kraken? And if the use of the Touch doesn't attract her, I'm sure the splash will. When I got here, my boat landed in that water. She was on me in a matter of seconds and was able to chase me to the shore at more than thirty knots. We'll never make it. But I think I have an idea."

Aleks pulled Jesik aside and whispered to him. "According to you, I created this whole place, right?" Jesik nodded. "Then I created it with a secret entrance. I'm certain of it. I would have wanted a way to get in and out that was easy to use and couldn't be found by anybody but me."

Aleks looked at the hillside in front of the group. Then he closed his eyes and looked inside the hillside. There it was! They were almost on top of it. Right where the three plains of the valley met—lakeshore, hillside, and cliff face—was a hallway. It was ten feet back from the stony surface they were standing in front of. A flick of a thought and the stone in front of the group melted, pulling back to the sides, perfectly extending the hallway to the open air. The group gathered before the long entrance.

"Well now," Jesik said, "that was *much* easier than the way I got in last time. Don't ask; it wasn't pretty."

Aleks caught Donte's shudder out of the corner of his eye.

The group started filing into the hallway. Aleks gently slid his hand into Alice's and took the lead.

As he passed Rayne, she whispered an aside to him. "What an interesting group. It seems that one can hardly swing a cat o' nine around here without hitting a Templar."

Aleks whispered back, "It takes one to know one."

As Aleks stepped into the hallway, lights came on along the ceiling. They looked like they had been seamlessly inset into the stone. One odd thing was that these lights seemed perfectly normal. For Earth. What made them strange on Freia was that they did not need to be fed the Touch to function.

The walls and ceiling were the color of sand, with gray, black, and blue speckles mixed in. The floor was flat black and smooth as glass. The lights cast everything in a slightly bluish tint. The hallway was quite long and swept off to the right.

The space was ten feet tall and wide enough for the group to walk three abreast. Aleks put Alice's hand on his shoulder and started down the hall, letting the others sort themselves out behind him. As they walked, Aleks's tennis shoes and Alice's soft-soled boots made almost no sound, but Tony's cowboy boots echoed loud thumps off into the distance.

Aleks walked casually up the hallway, letting his vision flow ahead of him. The first trap was positioned just at the former end of the hallway. A person using Touch while walking through the space would trigger an ultra-thin line of force, like a monofilament, to whip back and forth across the hallway, slicing anything within range into bits of meat. He disabled the device with another flick of the Touch before moving past it.

Over the next hundred feet he disabled a dozen other traps, some Touch based, others purely physical. They were spaced at random intervals in the floor, walls, ceiling, and even floating in the air across the hallway. Each was keyed to be triggered by different things: sound, movement, Touch, temperature, heartbeat. Each was successively more deadly than the last. And even he didn't sense the last two triggers. He just knew instinctively they were there and found the active mechanisms behind the wall. He was sure the others felt him working, but he didn't bother explaining what he was doing. And none of the others asked him, which was convenient, as any break in his concentration could have cost someone his or her life.

As they passed the last trap, the curving hallway came to an end in what looked remarkably like a large, split-door elevator. There was a single black button midway up the wall to the right side of the doors.

Aleks searched the button and surrounding area for traps but found none. He used his Touch to depress the button, just in case there was a physical trap he hadn't picked up on. Nothing happened. He waited. Still nothing happened.

Just as he was turning back to the group to see if anyone else had any ideas, the doors to the elevator opened. Either it was the slowest elevator in the universe or it had a *long* way to go to get to the hallway.

The compartment the doors revealed was huge. It was easily the largest elevator Aleks had ever seen. He quickly checked it for traps and then stepped inside. Apparently, it had only one floor to go to because there were no buttons inside.

When Aleks didn't plummet with the elevator into the depths, his Earth brothers followed him. However, the Freians required a little coaxing to step into the strange room. The whole group fit with plenty of personal bubble space left over. A few seconds after Shaulee, who'd required a direct order from Rayne to overcome her doubts, had stepped through the doors, they slid closed and the elevator started moving. This set off a short cacophony of exclamations and a grabbing of people or walls among the Freians. But the calm assurances of the Earthlings, and the lack of instant death, settled them down pretty quickly.

The elevator traveled down for long minutes. Many long minutes. Aleks was certain that the group had aged by the time they stopped their decent. In an elevator deep underground it was difficult to tell, but Aleks felt sure that the orientation of the elevator had changed on the way down. The elevator had been facing east when they entered it. Now it felt like the doors were facing west. Strange. Then the doors slid open, revealing a city street.

Aleks was stunned by what he saw. It looked like some giant had taken a mixing bowl and turned it over on top of a scene by Thomas Kincaid. Above the city was an arching roof that stretched off into the distance in all directions. At its highest point the ceiling must have been at least five hundred feet from the street. The street was obviously designed for foot traffic. It was narrow and had grass and tall trees running down the center of it, trees whose branches almost touched the five- and six-story buildings on either side.

Under the canopy of the trees, gaslight poles were spaced two to a block along both sides of the streets. The buildings were right out of nineteenth-century Europe. They had brick, stone, and iron facades, stacked tightly together, with signboards above each doorway calling out a pub here and a haberdashery there. Women's clothing and shoes. The general store. It was all there.

Before any of the group could move, Kevin shot out of the elevator, his nose to the ground, smelling everything and marking trees, buildings, and light poles. He would definitely need to drink a lot of water if he intended to continue that level of communication.

Aleks stepped out of the elevator onto cobblestones and was struck by the magnitude of what he was seeing. The span of the roof was monumental. How could anyone have possibly created this place? Even with all the marvels of engineering on Earth, could they keep a billion tons of dirt and rocks from crushing a roof this large?

And it was completely deserted. Not a person was evident anywhere.

The tree-lined street made a T directly in front of the elevator. To the right and left the side streets followed the arc of the wall, curving back behind the buildings on either side of Central Avenue as a nearby sign identified the road in front of him.

He was surprised the air smelled sweet and fresh, not at all stale or closed up. He doubted that the trees, as impressive as they were, and the grass would be enough to account for the freshness of the air. But maybe without any people breathing down there, they were enough. Of course if there were no people breathing down there, what were the trees breathing? He took notice of the air: plenty of oxygen for people and plenty of carbon dioxide for the trees. He smelled ash, maple, and oak. He smelled myriad flowers and bushes. He smelled ivy growing on some of the buildings. He also smelled the fescue and moss. A lot of moss. This was coming from high up on the walls of the giant dome. He hadn't noticed before because he hadn't been looking for it. But the arching wall of the cave was covered in a wide, green swath of lichen. *That* was producing the air he was breathing.

He stepped away from the elevator and walked left along the wall. He could see that the roof got close to the nearest building as it arched up and away, but a gap did exist. The light from the ceiling was diffused across a wide area but had a central source as well, presumably to mimic sunlight above ground. It even hurt to look at the "sun." This place was a marvel.

Jesik stepped up next to Aleks. "Amazing, isn't it?" he said.

"It's awe-inspiring," Aleks agreed. He let his eyes follow the curving road around behind the first row of buildings. Another street branched off from the arc, parallel to Central Avenue. It had its own rows of buildings, grass, and trees. The backs of the Central Avenue buildings and those on the next street were separated by a narrow alleyway.

Looking farther down the curving street, Aleks could make out one more off-shoot before the road disappeared behind buildings. "How many people could live here, do you think?" he asked.

Tony stepped up beside them. "Major cities in Europe get about ten thousand people in a square mile. You couldn't put up a skyscraper here, but there aren't any farms, either. So let's say you can get about half that. Looking down the street there, I'd guess this space is fifteen to twenty square miles. That would give you between fifty and one hundred thousand people."

"Looks like none of them are home," Thom said. By that point the rest of the group had joined them and were also gawking at everything in sight.

"How would you feed that many people? And get them supplies?" Martin asked.

Aleks said, "Well, I haven't needed to eat much since I got here. And if there were Templars in the mix, they could probably make anything you needed. Maybe that's who ran all these shops."

"This is a fine conversation, but I think we should make our way to the Mirror of Forever now and get our travelers on their way," Jesik commented. He set off up Central Avenue with the rest of the group in a loose pack behind him.

Aleks turned to look at the elevator behind them and was surprised to see no evidence of it whatsoever. It seemed to have disappeared from the face of the wall. He used his Touch to look again and saw the space behind the wall. The elevator was still there, but only the most talented or gifted could have seen it. Interesting.

Each building they passed was unique, with its own architecture and flair of design—more iron, less iron, more polished marble, or more chiseled stone than those around them. But each drew from the same city and era. Which seemed truly odd, since London didn't exist on this world. And construction here was based on an entirely different model that didn't have the same materials or issues that Earth had. It was almost like this place had been built by someone from Earth.

"You did," Jesik said, looking at Aleks.

"What?"

"You were wondering who built this place, weren't you? At least, that's what I wondered the first time I came here. If that *is* what you were wondering, and then I believe the answer is: *you* did." Jesik looked up at the high ceiling and all around him. "I can't be sure, of course. As far as I know, you didn't tell anyone about it and you never brought anyone down here. So only by going through your travels will you understand how and why you built this amazing place." Jesik paused for a moment. "Assuming I'm right, that is."

They walked on in silence. After they'd traveled ten or eleven blocks—Aleks had lost count—Jesik crossed to the right side of the street and turned right on Main Street.

Aleks chuckled to himself. *Of course it was called Main Street. Why not? If you were creating an underground city on an alien planet, wouldn't you name one of the streets Main Street? Wait. I guess I did.*

Several blocks ahead of them on Main Street, Aleks could see a massive building. It looked to be nine or ten stories tall and spanned the street and a city block to either side of it. This building was the first thing Aleks had seen that touched the mighty domed ceiling. In fact, it looked like the dome had been molded around a much taller building, obscuring the view of the upper floors. A long set of steps curved around the front of the building. From this vantage point Aleks guessed that an extensive courtyard fronted the edifice.

The building seemed to be Jesik's destination because he didn't pause to look at anything on either side. He just kept his long stride moving in that direction, never looking to see if the others kept up.

Aleks and Tony were keeping pace, but the rest of the group seemed to be traveling at their own speed, gawking at everything around them. And Kevin was bounding along the fronts of the buildings, sniffing and marking and then darting ahead, but always keeping within sight of the group.

Fifteen or twenty minutes later Aleks came out from under the trees and had his first unobstructed view of the building. The road they had crossed coming out of the elevator continued to follow the dome around the city but straightened out and crossed in front of the steps. The curving steps stretched from the wall of the dome, out and across a full two blocks and back to the dome. The building itself, a red brick and gray stone affair, looked like it was a block deep at the base and stretched at least four hundred feet from side to side. Rows of large arched windows spanned the building above a giant wall of glass that curved up from the ground in a graceful arc.

The courtyard must have been huge, because the building's facade was set back at least two city blocks from the top step of the long, sweeping stairs. And it should have an excellent view of the city because the top step was two stories above the ground.

Aleks followed Jesik up the steps. But when he neared the top step, he paused in his tracks. What immediately came to mind when he saw the space was a picture he'd once seen of a Greek theater from ancient times. At the top was a wide sidewalk curving around in front of the building. Beyond the sidewalk, the entire courtyard had been carved out in a wide arc. The sides sloped steeply down and were filled with bleachers, row after row of them, dropping not only the two stories back to the road but also an additional three stories into the ground and curving all the way around to the building on either side of a wide stage five stories below the sidewalk. This entire courtyard was a giant amphitheater.

Looking down a nearby staircase gave Aleks a sudden case of vertigo. Fall down those stairs and you'd be lucky with a hospital stay, rather than a visit to the morgue.

The bottom of the building's facade was cut out, forming the backdrop for the stage, with the large wall of glass as the capstone. Seats made of the same material as the road were spaced along each neat, half-circle row wrapping around the stage. This thing could seat thousands. Tens of thousands. Maybe even the entire population of the city.

Jesik had stopped at the top and was looking up at the glass face of the building when Aleks came up beside him. Jesik said, "From what I can deduce and the documents I've found, this seems to be the administration building for the city. It's where I found the Mirror of Forever. We need to follow this walkway around to the entrance, there in the middle of the building." Jesik was pointing at a tiny door on a narrow ledge above the amphitheater's backdrop. Dark shapes dotted the ledge, but their purpose wasn't clear from where Aleks stood.

The group had joined them at the top of the stairs with a chorus of oohs and aahs. They made their way along the wide sidewalk. It took ten minutes for them to circle around from the street side of the bleachers to the "ledge." The ledge was thirty feet wide and covered in beautiful bronze sculptures of children dancing and people walking here and there. The sculptures were both highly stylized and detailed, with flying hair and swirling coats, but nearly featureless faces reminiscent of impressionist paintings.

The group made its way through the artwork and over to a pair of glass doors at least ten feet tall and six feet wide. Jesik grabbed one of the four-foot long door handles and gently pulled. Two thirds of the door swung out and a third swung in as the door pivoted around an inset hinge. The glass was at least an inch thick. The door must have weighed five hundred pounds or more. Yet Jesik was able to pull it open with almost no effort. Like everything else here, the door was a marvel of engineering. If Aleks was indeed the one who had created this place, he would have needed a *lot* of practice with the Touch first. And, he supposed, a reason for doing it.

The lobby was immense. Light pouring through the glass wall behind them splashed across what looked like an acre of shiny, creamy yellow marble floor. Great long slashes of colored stone, lapis lazuli, carnelian, amethyst, and onyx swooped and flowed across the space, breaking it up and giving it a more organic feel. Three staircases led up from the floor of the lobby to platforms on the second floor.

The staircases on the right and left side mirrored each other in wide, sweeping arcs that curved out to the sides and back in, coming to the lobby floor a hundred feet apart.

Deeper into the lobby the third set of stairs was thirty feet wide at the top and bottom, smoothly narrowing to fifteen feet wide in the middle. All three sets of stairs appeared to be made the same way. Each step was rich, red wood and seemed to float on air, with no visible means of support. A brass and silver handrail flowed with the edge of each staircase. Additional handrails hovered over the center of the straight staircase. Beyond the stairway the lobby's back wall was made entirely of the same rich red wood as the steps and covered in large panels of artwork.

"The Mirror of Forever is in the royal chambers, up those stairs," Jesik said.

"I guess we should go on up," Aleks said reluctantly. "But I wish I had more time to look around in this place."

"I'm sure you'll get ample opportunity in the future," Jesik said with a vague smile.

The group made their way across the lobby to the central staircase and climbed to the large central landing. The landing was framed on three sides by walls that climbed three stories before reaching the ceiling of the lobby. Each of these floors had windows that overlooked the landing and the floor below. A floating handrail, identical to those lining the stairs, was the only thing that spoiled the view of the lobby from the curvy front edge of the landing. The other two landings were set against two walls at each side of the lobby, a floor higher than the central landing. A large desk was positioned in the right rear section of the central landing at an angle to the staircase, obviously meant to house a receptionist. In the left wall of the landing, and within direct line of sight of the desk, was another elevator.

Jesik walked to the elevator and pressed a round brass button on the wall. As they waited for the elevator, Aleks said, "I suppose there's another entrance for the handicapped?"

"Handicapped?" Jesik asked.

"You know, people with disabilities."

"I don't understand." Jesik frowned.

"You know, people who can't walk for one reason or another," Aleks prompted.

"People who can't walk for one reason or another are taken to a healer so they can regain the ability to walk. Don't you heal the injured where you come from?"

Aleks thought about this for a second "We don't have the Touch there, remember? We don't always have the ability to heal the injured. Sometimes people are hurt so bad they can no longer walk and there's nothing we can do about it. So we do the best we can by giving them wheeled chairs to move around in."

Jesik looked horrified. "I had no idea. In all of my viewings of your world, searching for you, I assumed people in those wheeled chairs used them by choice." He looked away.

Thom stepped up to the two of them and took Jesik's arm. His face was closed with anger. "You can choose to look on our world with disdain and horror over the challenges some of us face if you want to. That's up to you. But remember this. In our world, we help people who have challenges rather than throw them away. I've seen some very ugly things done to people in *this* world that would *never* have been allowed in ours."

Jesik looked at Thom for a few moments and then at Aleks, Tony, and finally Martin. He nodded, acknowledging that he could not fairly judge a world he did not understand.

At that moment the elevator doors opened, allowing the party to enter. Old hats with elevators now, no one required a direct order to step through. While more cramped than the spacious one that had brought them all down to the city, this elevator was still large enough to accommodate the entire party. A dozen buttons in two columns were neatly lined up on the right side of the doors. They were topped by a thirteenth button centered between the columns. Jesik pressed this button. Aleks felt the flow of Touch that came from Jesik as he pressed it. The top floor must have some form of access control because everything else that they had seen in the city—lights, heat, and the other elevator—had operated without Touch. The doors closed and the elevator began to move.

"How did you get the elevator to move?" Aleks asked Jesik.

"What do you mean?" Jesik asked, the scent of confusion coming from him. "I fed it as usual. Why do you ask?"

Interesting.

"If we're heading to the royal chambers, they should be access controlled. So you shouldn't be able to get the elevator to go there unless you'd been approved. I wonder if any of the rest of us could make it work." Aleks paused for just a moment, lost in thought, and then waved as if trying to clear his mind. "It's really not important, I just thought it was odd." He spoke as much to himself as to Jesik. Alice took his hand again, but whether it was to set her mind at ease or his, he wasn't sure.

A few minutes later the elevator slowed and came to a rest. As soon as the doors parted, Aleks caught a whiff of something that tickled at his senses. It was a scent he was familiar with but couldn't quite place. That made him uncomfortable. Even though he'd had his heightened senses for only a short time, he had increasingly come to rely on his ability to identify even the most innocuous scent without a thought. As he peered out of the elevator, he kept his mind working on the mystery.

The doors had opened on a living space that belonged in the Guggenheim Museum or the Museum of Modern Art in New York. Glowing orbs hung at seemingly random heights and spacing from thin, straight cords, casting the room in rich, golden light. All the walls were straight up and down, but gracefully sinuated horizontally, giving the room an organic feel. The right wall was of the same red wood they'd seen in the lobby. The remaining walls were made of stones, light gray and rough to the touch, decoratively placed atop each other. The floor was a winding, twisting band of highly polished clear crystal over river rocks. The combination made it look like they were standing in a fast-moving stream.

Sunken into the stream was a lovely living room arrangement with sofas and comfortable chairs designed in groupings of four and five. The steps down to the living room were shaped like tiny waterfalls, adding to the illusion of running water. The right and left walls of the room continued their curves, meeting up with a large flat section on the back wall. This flat section was an inverted version of the glass front of the building. The jet-black pane of glass began six inches from the sunken river floor and curved upward, growing ever wider until it met the ceiling.

As tempting as the comfortable chairs and calm atmosphere of the room were, the group had business to take care of. Jesik led them around a curving corner to the left and up a short hallway. Several doors in the hallway were closed, giving evidence to more living quarters that could be explored when one had more time. Soon enough Jesik reached the end of the hallway, where a wide spiral staircase led up to another floor. He didn't pause but started right up the stairs.

Aleks's mystery scent grew stronger. Was it a person? Yes. It was definitely a person. And one he was familiar with. But who?

Aleks guided Alice to the stairs, following her up, leading to a room that could have been nothing but a library. Like the rest of the apartment this room was configured as an organic explosion of curves. However, every wall was lined with bookcases filled to capacity with books of every shape and size. What made this room unusual was the complete lack of windows. Only one wall was flat, and it was made entirely of the same jet-black glass as the wall of the room below them. The scent was even stronger in this room. He closed his eyes and traced the scent to one particular bookcase.

When he opened his eyes again, Jesik had walked directly to that very bookcase and extended his hand. A small trickle of Touch slid from his hand toward the bookcase. It silently pulled away from the wall and moved to the right, revealing a doorway to another room.

Aleks followed Jesik into the new room. The rest of the group must have come in behind them because the small room quickly filled with people. This room was a striking contrast to the beauty of the rest of the home. It was a basic rectangle, with a white floor, white ceiling, and three white walls. The remaining wall, what must have been an extension of the neighboring wall, was also made of jet-black glass.

The room was about twenty feet square, so the whole group was able to enter and stand comfortably. Placed near the black wall was a large, gray, oval mirror with an ornately carved gold frame and stand. It was at least ten feet tall, six feet wide, and slightly tilted downward for easy viewing from the only chair in the room, which was overstuffed, made of leather, and stained with age and use. Next to the chair was a small table.

The smell was strongest in and around the chair. Suddenly Aleks had it. The smell was his own scent. He hadn't been able to identify it because he'd never had a need to identify himself before.

And in the instant he identified his own scent in the room, everything Jesik and Donte had been saying about him—his purpose and the Prophecies—all came crashing down. It rocked him so hard he had a moment of vertigo. Jesik and Alice each grabbed one of his arms as his knees buckled. They managed to keep him from crashing to the ground and gently guided him to the chair. He gratefully collapsed into its plush embrace, his mind a swirling mass of doubts, fears, and memories of the last few weeks.

As soon as he sat the gray disk flashed brightly to life. A chaotic image of grizzly creatures pouncing on a hapless pair of men running across a field was punctuated by the horrifying sound of screaming and the shriek of the beasts. The beasts—which changed in midair into large dogs—were thrown off the pair. One of the men picked up the other man, who looked surprisingly like Donte, and began to carry him. A huge flying nightmare dropped from the sky with a soul-piercing caterwaul. The men crashed to the ground. The beast took to the air with Donte in its claws. A crossbow bolt slammed into the creature. It dropped Donte. Aleks picked him up and hurried up onto a porch next to Alice. The trio moved into the house.

Aleks wanted the pictures to stop. Jesik was talking over his shoulder, telling him something about how the mirror worked and how he could control it. But he couldn't get his mind to process whatever message Jesik was trying to share. He could hear the gasps of horror from the rest of the group behind him as they saw the damage Donte had sustained. The image moved on. The Alice who was in the room with him took his hand as the one in the mirror told him she could do no more to help Donte without more Touch. Aleks was dreading what was coming but could not figure out how to stop it.

The girl in the mirror lurched to her feet. "Unnnnnh … too much. Too much, *too much*! *Aaaaagh!*"

Alice squeezed his hand hard. He turned to look at her. The disk flickered and went gray. Tears flowed down Alice's face. In his mind, he told her over and over again how sorry he was and begged her to forgive him for his mistake. But his mouth couldn't make the words. Alice pulled her hand away. He watched as she processed what she had been seeing.

And then she did just what he had been hoping she would do for weeks. She spoke. "You hurt me."

He stood up and moved toward her, his apologies and sorrow finally pouring out of him. But she turned away and stumbled into Raneal. Alice clung to the woman, who held her. For the second time in two days, Raneal calmed and soothed and comforted a distraught member of their party.

At that moment Aleks couldn't even put a name to what he was feeling. "Miserable" might have been an adequate start.

Jesik stepped up beside him, putting a hand on his shoulder. "What happened was not your fault," he said.

Aleks shook his hand off. "Tell that to her!"

"I will," Jesik said, "as soon as she calms down." He put his hand back on Aleks's shoulder and bent down enough to look Aleks directly in the eyes. "She'll be okay. We'll take care of her. But you need to go. Thom's gateway announced our presence here, so the Dark One may make an attempt to stop us at any moment. You must go through the mirror."

Aleks looked at the girl. Why had he thought she was plain? She was really quite pretty. "You're right." Aleks was suddenly sure that going through the mirror was the right thing to do. He didn't understand that feeling, but like so many of the instinctual things he had done recently, he knew at the core of his being that it was true. "What do I do?"

Jesik had him sit back in the chair and clear his mind. Following Jesik's guidance, he let his Touch flow through his mind, guiding his thoughts wherever they needed to go. This time, when the mirror flickered to life, he was looking at a sunny clearing in some dense woods.

"This must be the time and place you're destined to step into," Jesik said. "All you have to do now is step into the mirror."

Aleks nodded. He was tempted to look at Jesik and exchange some form of good-bye. Or possibly to go to Alice and kneel at her feet, begging for forgiveness. He did neither. He simply stood and stepped through the mirror into the clearing without saying a word to anyone.

In hindsight, it would have been a good idea if he'd grabbed his backpack.

Some People

Thom paid very little attention as Jesik explained to the rest of the group how the mirror worked. He had always hated lectures in school, opting for the "learn as you go" model. Come to think of it, that model hadn't worked out all that well over the last five years, often getting him into the trouble he was always having to get himself out of. But he had momentum with it, so he went ahead and ignored Jesik.

What he didn't ignore was Shaulee. He had placed a second weave on her when he placed the binding, assuming she wouldn't be able to distinguish between the two. So far she hadn't done or said anything that would cause trouble for the group. But there was always tomorrow. So he monitored the weave to gauge her state of mind while she listened to Jesik's explanations. She was going to be the first of Rayne's crew to go through the mirror. Back at Donte's place they had agreed on some destination Thom hadn't recognized. She now sat in the chair, focusing her mind to bring that destination into view.

Something tickled his weave. Shaulee wondered if the mirror would lose the place she wanted to see if she moved away from the chair. Jesik explained that staying in the chair was not required to keep the mirror on a time or location. What mattered was the focus of the person controlling it. As long as she focused she could move around the room. She nodded, focusing intently on the mirror.

She was up to something.

Suddenly, the image in the mirror moved. It veered off to the left, dragging everyone's attention with it. *Ugh.* A wave of vertigo washed over Thom. The sensation reminded him of a 3D roller-coaster movie he'd seen once. It seemed he wasn't alone. Someone behind him groaned.

Most of the folks in the room were reeling as the mirror's image snapped to a stop. Before anyone could recover their unstable stomachs, Shaulee was up and moving. She dived through the mirror into a large, richly appointed receiving room.

Rayne jumped toward the mirror to follow, but Jesik caught her around the waist before she could get there. She immediately pushed him away, saying, "We have to catch her and bring her back! That's Queen Sheefa's palace!"

Thom stepped between her and the mirror.

"You don't want to go through the mirror. It only goes one way!" Jesik said.

"And we can't have *you* end up in Sheefa's hands any more than him," Thom said, gesturing at … no one. Gaien wasn't in the room with them. Thom started looking around. He sent out a weave through the room, down the stairs, and out into the living room. Nothing.

"The binding will prevent her from doing or saying anything that could harm us," Jesik said. "It doesn't matter if she talks to the queen."

"You don't understand!" Rayne said. "The binding only prevents her from harming you! She can still tell the queen about us. And where are we? With you! The queen will know everything about this place in a few minutes. And if you don't think she's resourceful enough to find this place and get in here, you are seriously underestimating her."

"Gaien's gone," Thom said, interrupting their argument.

"What?" Rayne said, irritated with Thom for breaking in on them.

"Gaien's gone," Thom repeated, looking Rayne in the eye. "As in, 'not here now.' Gone."

"He was here just a few seconds ago." She looked around.

"Martin's gone too," Raneal said, worry etched on her face.

Thom felt intense empathy for the woman. Talk about falling for the wrong guy. Fazha had it easy compared to Raneal.

In that instant, long, thick, black tentacles erupted out of the air near the ceiling, wrapping around each of them. Thom's arms were slammed against his sides and his legs came together, bound in a vice-like grip. He was lifted from the ground to dangle in space. He reached for the Touch to fight the constriction, but the Touch wasn't there. For the first time since coming to Freia, he knew what it felt like to be fully human again. It sucked. He felt weak, pathetic, and dehydrated.

He craned his neck to see Fazha. Her face was red and sweat beaded on her brow as she fought against the black bonds, to no avail. Like the rest of them, she'd been plucked from her feet and now dangled above the ground.

Thom turned to the source of the tentacles in time to see a figure emerge from nowhere, sliding into space. The tentacles originated at his hands and feet, spreading out like some obscene cross between a man and an octopus. The tentacles coming from his feet stretched out to the ground, lowering him gently from his entry point. When his feet were on the ground, these tentacles receded and disappeared.

"Well, well, well," the man said calmly. "I see you've found the Mirror of Forever. How fortunate for me. I've been looking for it ever so long now."

The Dark One wasn't nearly as imposing as Thom had expected him to be. He couldn't have been much taller than five feet. Of course Thom and the rest of his posse were hanging like a veal six feet above the floor, totally immobilized and completely at the monster's mercy. But, still. It seemed only fair that the man should be seven feet tall, have glowing red eyes, a widow's peak, and a pointy goatee. Instead, he was a brown-haired, brown-eyed, olive-skinned man in gray slacks and a blue pullover. And at the moment, he was every bit as *terrifying* as Thom had expected.

"You're too late, Dark One! We've already sent Aleks back to prepare for you, and Martin will be ready for you soon. You will *never* control this world!" Jesik spat. "So killing us means nothing."

It was actually brave, Thom thought. *Stupid*, but quite brave. But as curses go, Jesik should have left that to Fazha. If the Dark One hadn't wrapped that black tentacle over her mouth, she would have burned the hair off his head with her tongue alone. Maybe Martin was right. Maybe the Dark One could see everything. And where the fuck was Martin right now? Shouldn't Crazy Eyes be there to vomit up some lava on this Dark Dick?

"Poor little Jesik," the man said. "You really do think it's all about you, don't you?" He moved over to stand in front of the mirror. "Where's your friend Martin, son?"

Jesik blanched at that. "Don't call me that! I'm not your son."

Thom was sure it was a typical "clean up your own mess because I'm not your mother" comment from Jesik.

But it seemed Dark Dick didn't think so. "Of course you are."

Shocked looks spread across the faces of the entire group. Could Jesik actually be *the Dark One's son?* How creepy would that turn out to be?

"Luke, I am your father." It popped out of Thom's mouth before he could stop it. Damn jokes sometimes got out of hand. A fat black tendril smacked against his face, blocking his mouth.

"Time to be quiet, Thom, the adults are having a conversation right now." Dark Dick smirked. "Now, son, about your friend Martin …"

"*I am not your son, you evil bastard!*"

That was more like it. Not a very productive curse, but it had some energy to it. Thom hoped Jesik was right, but there was a rightness—

… *and a wrongness*

—to the Dark One's words.

"Oh? Haven't you figured it out after all these years? How do you think you came to be a Templar?" Images began swirling on the mirror. "Were you just randomly born with both sides of the Touch? And your sister? How is she such a strong healer?"

Thom had no idea how he was staying so calm, especially with Fazha hanging so close to death right in front of him. But something told him that the Dark One had other plans for them than death. And anything but death would offer him a chance. A chance to get free. Or maybe a chance to get Fazha out of there alive.

Fazha. If that crazy fucker did anything to hurt her, Thom would crawl over broken glass to get his hands on the man and pull him apart by his lips. Thom had no idea what that meant, but it sounded really painful when it crossed his mind, so he was going to stick with it.

The mirror stopped swirling and settled on a stable scene. It was a library, with row after row of shelves packed floor to ceiling with books. Amid the shelves was a small open area with a few tables and chairs set up for reading. People young and old were seated around the tables and wandering between the shelves. It was a busy library. Weird.

Somewhere off to Thom's left Donte let out a low and miserable moan.

"Where is Martin, son?" The Dark One looked from the mirror to Jesik.

Jesik pinched his lips closed, refusing to answer. Not that he knew where Martin was, since the little shithead had wandered off. Jesik must have figured it would be best not to let him know that Martin was nearby.

Several new tentacles sprouted from the man's hands and threaded their way toward the mirror. Jesik's eyes opened wide as the greasy-looking strings of evil slipped through the mirror's surface. The people in the library panicked, screaming and fleeing. An old man with a long beard was too slow to get away. One of the young men standing near him rushed over and tried to pull the tentacle off the man. Another tentacle swatted him across the chest, flinging him backward into the end of one of the bookshelves with a sickening crunch of bones. Within seconds, two more of the people were snatched from under the tables and hanging in the air.

"Where is Martin, son?"

Jesik's eyes were bulging, but he held his tongue. He was made of sterner stuff than Thom had given him credit for.

"Please, stop it!" Dinaala screamed. "He doesn't know. None of us do!"

"Aaah! My granddaughter speaks. You are a brave one, little Dinaala! You make me proud. Now what is this about no one knowing where Martin is?"

"Granddaughter?" Dinaala said, momentarily stunned by what she'd heard.

"Andrus!" came a voice from behind Thom. For just a second, Thom could have sworn it was Aleks speaking.

Whoever it was, it seemed to be good news for their team. The wicked little man's eyes bugged out when he saw the newcomer.

"Let them go, Andrus." The man stepped forward into Thom's view. Good God. It *was* Aleks. Only a little older, a little grayer, and better dressed.

"Martin is obviously not here, and this will not serve your purpose," Aleks said. "I have sworn not to interfere in your plans, to aid or impede you. But if you harm them, my oath will be lifted and I *will* act against you."

"You're dead! I killed you!"

"As you can plainly see for yourself, you failed to kill me." The new Aleks held out his arms. "And you failed to kill her, as well."

Dark Dick's face went pasty white at this phrase. Here was the bane of Freian life, a man who held all their lives in his evil tentacles, looking just like any ordinary befuddled data analyst talking to a programmer.

"Tan'aana? She's alive?"

Aleks walked past him and the mirror to the large glass wall. As he looked at the wall, it slowly faded from black to gray, gaining translucency as it shifted. Soon it was completely transparent.

Through it, Thom could see a school of fish darting back and forth in the light shining out from the room they were in. They were looking into the depths of the lake. Bright lights blossomed on the other side of the glass, penetrating the water and sending the little fish darting away.

Movement far out in the water caught his eye. Something was coming toward the light. Something large. Something *very* large.

In the instant when the monstrosity came fully into view, Thom's mind decided it would be better to shut down than to try to make sense of the roiling mass of living flesh his eyes were showing him. If the constriction of the tentacles around his body had allowed him to throw up, he would have, and prodigiously, he was quite sure. Instead, he closed his eyes, hoping against hope Dark Dick would change his mind and crush Thom before that alien thing got hold of him.

"She's been here the whole time," Aleks said.

Thom opened his eyes. "You turned her into that *thing*?"

Aleks turned to look at him. As he did, a small section of the ceiling soundlessly fanned open behind him. A long tentacle, this one living flesh rather than Touch, slid out of the opening. It was covered in long, sharp hooks. The end split open, revealing a deep maw.

Tony shouted, "Look out!" at Aleks. Aleks looked at him and smiled. The tentacle waved back and forth for a few seconds before gently brushing its smooth outer skin against Aleks's face. Aleks wrapped his fingers around the tentacle like he was holding hands with the thing.

And suddenly he was. The beast simply folded in on itself and disappeared from the window. Now, standing behind Aleks was a stunning, chocolate-skinned woman. Aleks pulled off his coat and helped her put it on, covering her wet, naked form.

"Tan'aana!" Dark Dick exclaimed.

The enchanting woman glided up to him and took his face in her hands. "Let them go," she whispered, her voice a silky alto that had an untoward effect on Thom's nether regions. Fortunately, everyone's attention was focused elsewhere or he'd have some explaining to do to Fazha.

Her voice must have had a similar effect on Dark Dick because the tentacles holding the group immediately disappeared, dropping everyone in indignant heaps. If any of them harbored the stupid idea of attacking while the Dark One was distracted, they each thought better of it.

As he looked at the woman, a startling mix of emotions—love, lust, sorrow, and rage—all crossed the Dark One's face in a split second. He lifted his hand toward her. Then his eyes darted to Aleks. His face got very hard. He brushed off Tan'aana's hands and stepped back. Three or four of the tentacles that had torn open space near the ceiling still clung to the hole they'd made. Now they convulsed, lifting Dark Dick back up toward the hole. Two new tentacles lashed out at the mirror. It flew across the room and smashed into the wall, shattering into a thousand pieces.

"Remember your oath, Aleks!" Dark Dick called back as he was pulled through the hole. And then the hole was gone.

Thom sat for a split second, wanting to look down and see if he'd wet himself, but it wouldn't have been dignified. Instead, he crab-crawled over to Fazha to see if she was okay. She grabbed him hard and clung to him. He could feel her quietly shaking against him. He knew no one else could see her weeping. In her mind, only he was trustworthy enough to see it. He let his energy silently flow into her. He didn't shift her in any way. He just shared himself with her so she could feel him.

She grew a little calmer. "I couldn't do anything. I was so weak," she said. "You were in trouble and I couldn't help you. I couldn't speak and I could barely breathe." She looked ashamed. "And suddenly I was that little girl in Hexa's room, weak and defenseless."

This time it was Thom who squeezed hard. He crushed her to him and held her. He told her he was so proud of her for how strong she was. Dark Dick wasn't Hexa. No one could stand against that kind of power.

They stayed that way for a few minutes. It seemed to be time everyone needed because no one in the room moved more than a few inches or spoke above a whisper.

When they had composed themselves enough to begin moving around, Thom stood and helped Fazha to her feet. They held each other for a few more seconds, assuring each other the other was there. They turned toward Aleks and Tan'aana.

They were also holding each other and whispering quietly together. The rest of the group had turned to the couple and were all waiting patiently for them to come back from their private moment. It took a while.

Finally, Raneal cleared her throat. She was pretty good at reminding people they weren't alone.

Aleks and Tan'aana turned toward the group, their heads naturally tilting together.

Tony stepped forward and looked at the couple. He didn't say anything, just looked at them. Aleks unwaveringly returned the gaze.

Finally, Tony's eyes narrowed and he asked, "What the *fuck* was that?"

Aleks let his eyes rest for a few moments on each member group, as if reminding himself what they all looked like, before he replied. "I'm sure you all have a lot of questions. We'll sit down and go through them together. I promise to answer as many of them as I can. But right now, I think we all need a bit of rest. So I'll quickly go through the obvious ones, saving your more detailed questions for a later conversation.

"Yes. I am the same Aleksander Volovniev who stepped through the mirror a few minutes ago.

"Yes, Andrus is every bit as powerful and unstable as he seems to be. Power corrupts, and, as you saw just now, he has plenty of power. But he is not omniscient. He didn't know Tan'aana and I had survived."

Tan'aana? Wasn't that what Fazha had named her horse?

"He is very old. And over the centuries he's become rigid in his thinking. It will take him time to assimilate us into his thoughts and plans. This should afford you some time to prepare. Maybe even a few weeks.

"And, yes, I have a history with Andrus. For reasons I can't explain right now, I ..." He looked at Tan'aana, his face flashing through several unreadable emotions. "We have taken an oath that prevents us from helping you oppose the Dark One. So we can't help you prepare for what is to come." He held up his hand at the protestations that burst forth from Jesik and Raneal.

He continued. "But I am also prevented from helping *him* against *you*. To that end, I have now placed a barrier around this entire city that prevents him from returning here by the means he used a few minutes ago. You are now safe here. And you will remain safe as long as you stay. I suggest you take advantage of it while you can."

He took Tan'aana's hand and stepped toward the door to the room as he continued. "You will find guest rooms at either end of the two floors below this one, and the kitchen is well stocked with food and drinks. There are even some libations, if you're interested. Or, if you would prefer, there are many homes available throughout the city. Any and all of them are at your disposal."

Everyone in the group followed the two out the door and into the little library. Most tossed questions at them like water balloons being tossed at the cousin no one likes.

As Aleks followed Tan'aana down the circular staircase, Thom blurted out, "What happened to Martin and Gaien?"

The question was directed at no one in particular, but Aleks paused, looking back at Thom. "And *that* is a good question! They are resting peacefully in a room at the other end of the floor below us."

By the time the group had assembled at the base of the staircase, Aleks and Tan'aana had slipped through a doorway that disappeared as soon as it closed. Even throwing a weave on the wall didn't reveal the doorway to Thom. Dammit! He *hated* being in the dark about everything. And then it hit him just how tired he was. It had been days since he'd slept more than a couple of hours.

He didn't know how much of Aleks's "answers" he believed. Or even understood, really. But his instincts told him that Aleks had been both truthful and accurate about his protection around this city. Somehow Thom was certain that Dark Dick couldn't come back. And when that belief had seated itself inside him, relief washed over him.

He took Fazha's hand, turned to the rest of the group, and said, "You know, I've had just about enough bullshit for one day. I'm going to take Fazha to one of these rooms and do things with her that I should have done weeks ago." Fazha blushed brightly with uncharacteristic embarrassment. Thom led her to one of the nearest doors and pushed it open. He turned back to the group. "Don't call me, I'll call you."

Remembrance

Alex sat in his study. Shelf after shelf, filled with books of every sort, wrapped the walls. He had spent countless hours over the last two hundred years of his life in this very room, searching for and retrieving these books with his little mirror. He'd read every one a dozen times over. Some days he felt remorse for having taken them from their owners. But the shining gold coin he'd left for each book made it a little easier to stomach. He often wondered what it must have looked like from the other side of the mirror. To have a hand appear out of nowhere, drop a circa-1850 twenty-dollar gold piece, snatch a book, and disappear must have been disconcerting to say the least.

Aleks watched the group through the little mirror. Thom and Fazha had just gone off together, leaving the rest of the group to fret and bicker about the future. He hated when people argued. It ate at him. Whether it was because of the life he'd led before coming to Freia or the wars he'd seen since jumping through the mirror didn't really matter. He hated it. It made him crazy. He wanted to run away and hide again. Maybe the hiding was partly from himself. And what he could do—*had done*—when he was the one who was upset.

So here was a group of people in his home, arguing about the Dark One, about the future, about the past. Everything they were arguing about was out of their control. He wanted to toss them out of his city on their ears. But something about them wouldn't let him.

He had lived more than twelve hundred years. In that time he'd known these people for only a few days.

In fact, he didn't even remember most of them. He had a fuzzy recollection of spending a few weeks with the bony man, Donte. But the rest were essentially strangers. And yet they were very special to him. He liked them. Maybe even loved them.

He swept the mirror over the group, looking at each one in turn. It came to rest on the one member of the group he had thought about over the last twelve hundred years. Alice. A tear came to the corner of his eye. Seeing her again here and now, looking so much like he remembered her, brought his regret flooding back. He'd done some things over his lifetime that he wasn't proud of. In fact, some were horrific. But he had come to grips with all of them except this one.

Tan'aana's scent drifted to him through the smells of the dusty tomes, city stone, and lake water. As always, it lightened his mood. A gentle hand caressed his shoulder.

Tan'aana's light touch sent tingling, warm waves of pleasure flowing through him. "Will you punish yourself forever for an accident, Beloved?"

"I could ask the same question of you, my love."

She took her hand from his shoulder. "What I did was no accident. I did it with purpose and intent."

He turned to look at her. "What you did was horrible and cruel. And absolutely necessary for the salvation of mankind. And you have suffered enough for ten thousand lifetimes. I'm just glad we no longer have a need for the beast. I would gladly let the world burn before I will ever change you back into that monster again." Tears streamed down his face, but he didn't care.

She knelt in from of him. The love on her face was plain to see and he accepted it gratefully. "Each time you changed me, you were doing what you had to, what I deserved, and what I wanted." She put her electric hands on his cheeks. "But those times are behind us now. We can be together again. Not just some brief dream between time jumps, but truly together. I love you."

"I love you too, my dangerous beast."

They smiled at each other.

But he soon broke eye contact, turning back to the mirror. He was in this room for a reason and needed to continue to watch the discussion.

The group had stopped arguing about the Dark One and were now discussing Aleks and Tan'aana.

"How much do you think they know about the Dark One's plans?" Tony was looking at Jesik, but the question seemed to be for the room as a whole.

"He seems to know much more about things than he is sharing, as is typical of a man. And he certainly knows more than we do." Magda seemed to be adopting Rayne's disdain for men. Unless of course she had already hated men to begin with.

"What do you plan to tell them about Andrus, Beloved?"

Taa'nana's question was a good one. Aleks thought about it for a few minutes. "I'll tell them as little as possible about him. The less they know the better it will be for everyone."

"They'll have to know sometime, Aleks. We can't keep this secret forever."

"I know, my love. But it will need to be kept for a while. Otherwise everything we have done to minimize bloodshed will be for naught."

"You saw Andrus. He's not the same man we knew all those years ago. Must we hold to our promise? If these few try to fight him alone, they will almost assuredly die. Can't we help them?"

"You know we can't, my love. If we go back on our promise, Andrus won't settle for simple domination. He'll destroy everything to get what he wants."

"The Andrus we knew so long ago would have honored the promise as long as we did. Can you be so sure he'll settle for domination if we do keep our promise?"

"No. But we don't have any choice right now. Until he breaks his part of the promise, we *can't* break ours."

Newcomers entering the room caught the pair's eyes and brought their attention back to the mirror. Martin and Gaien staggered back into the room, rubbing their eyes and mumbling about sleeping through everything.

"It looks to me, Beloved, like you made too much of your 'sleeping gas.' They look like a mule that's eaten Loonweed." Taa'nana laughed.

"I needed to make sure they weren't in the room when Andrus showed up or all hell would have broken loose."

"As you have explained several times, Beloved. But that doesn't change the fact that you intervened when you said we must abide by our promise."

"Our promise not to interfere with Andrus did not include destroying our home, the city, or this mountain range. Nor would I like for either of us to be killed in the crossfire. They can have their war. They just can't have it here."

She leaned down and kissed him sweetly on the mouth. "You traveled four thousand years into our past on the small words of a man you barely knew, created the cradle of our civilization, taught all of Freia how to craft with the Touch, and you're still afraid to lose the woman you have had enthralled for a hundred lifetimes. You really are a wonder, Mr. Volovniev."

"If I hadn't done all those things, my love, I would never have met you, the woman I want to spend the next hundred lifetimes with." Aleks turned back to the mirror. "Now can we please focus on the plotting before us, so we know how we can help them without breaking our promise?"

"You are a sneaky one, Beloved."

"Created the cradle of civilization, lived twelve hundred years, beat back the gathering hordes. Yada yada. I've had both the time and the need to learn sneaky."

Taa'nana grinned at him and then perched herself on the arm of the chair to watch the show.

Next Steps

Quite a few hours had passed when Thom and Fazha joined the others in the Creek Room. They were rested, refreshed, and cleaned up. The room they had chosen included a bed that might have been an acre across and a tub that could have held the entire group, or so Thom supposed. In any case, each was amazing and served more than one purpose for the two of them. Thom was happier and more relaxed than he had been in a long time.

So it was no surprise to him that the group was having a very disturbing conversation when he walked in. It was simply the nature of things on Freia that he couldn't go an entire twenty-four-hour period in any kind of bliss. Stupid planet.

"We have no idea what he'll do now," Magda was saying. "Aleks said that things had changed from what he had expected. The Dark One seemed afraid of Aleks when he saw him. Might he not change his plans to avoid that fight?"

"We don't know," Jesik responded, looking more bedraggled and dejected than Thom had ever seen him. "The Prophecies did not mention any of this."

Tony said, "How reliable are these Prophecies? Can they be trusted?"

Jesik lifted his hands and shrugged.

Donte said, "We have read every Prophecy Elas has ever written. And we have spent hundreds of hours at the Mirror of Forever. Many of the things that have happened today were not shown to us in either case. You weren't in any of them." He waved his arm toward Rayne, Magda, and Gaien. "Or you, for that matter." He nodded to Fazha. "I don't know what this means ..." He trailed off.

"It means that we can't trust the Prophecies to guide us," Tony said. "We have to go on what we *know* to be true and on any educated guesses we can make. One thing I can tell you is that I was prepared to use that mirror to go home today, regardless of what Jesik or any of the rest of you had to say about it. Your fight wasn't mine." He held up his hand at the look of horror that crossed several faces in the group. "But that was before that psycho-freak trussed me up like a Christmas ham. When he was holding us, I could feel it in him. It was like being caressed by an oil slick of lunacy. I wanted to wash my mind afterward."

He shook his head like he was trying to dislodge an unwanted urge. "I can't just walk away and leave this place to him. He needs to be stopped. And if the Prophecies can't be trusted to tell us how to do it, I think we need to make our own plans."

He looked around the room. Jesik was still distraught and Donte looked confused, but Dinaala and Micah were paying rapt attention to Tony. And the rest of the group was listening alertly. This guy could work a crowd.

"The first thing we'll need is intelligence," Tony said.

"Men are not known for such things," Rayne replied with a small smile.

"Funny." Tony's face was hard as stone. "I mean information about the enemy. We need to know as much as we can about his capabilities. What does his military look like? How well trained are they? What capabilities do they have? What weaknesses? Will he use land, sea, air? How will he move his troops into position to attack? What does the terrain look like?"

"Does it matter?" Jesik jumped to his feet. "You saw what he did to us. And that was just him! If he has his whole army behind him, he is unstoppable. He'll crush and enslave the world, and there is nothing we can do about it."

Tony stepped over to Jesik, and very quietly but with infinite authority, he said, "Sit down."

Jesik complied.

"Let me make this very clear," Tony said to everyone in the room. "Until we know exactly what we are facing, we can't plan what to do. But remember this. If his army is large and powerful, it has to be led. It has to move. It has to eat. And sleep. It has to share information among its leaders. It's awkward and cumbersome, slow to move and adjust. It can be disrupted. It can be mired down on land or cast adrift at sea.

"We, on the other hand, are small and agile. We can be stealthy and devious and disruptive. And we're far from weak. You three brought a sloop hundreds of miles inland. You"—he pointed at Thom—"punched a hole in *space*. And you"—he pointed at Jesik—"brought four people here *from another fucking planet!* So let's stop whining and feeling sorry for ourselves. Okay, we've lost faith in the Prophecies. That's a tough break. But we're not dead and we haven't lost this war. Not yet.

"Besides, if the Prophecies can't help us, they can't help him either. He didn't know about you three. Or you, Fazha. So he doesn't know how powerful we really are.

"From this moment on, we go to ground. We move in secret. We hide our power at all times and we gather as much information about him as we can. When we know more about him, we will be able to plan a strategy for overcoming him.

"Remember what it took for each of you to get here. It seems to me that overcoming the impossible is what we do best."

Thom wanted to stand up and cheer. At least a little. But he was a Negotiator, after all. It was his job to remain impartial and unemotional in situations like this. So he was quite delighted when Fazha stood up for him.

"Tony's right!" she said. "I'm tired of hearing all of this Prophecy garbage anyway." She looked around the room. "Now who else wants to kick that fucker's ass for him?"

Obviously Thom's foul mouth had really rubbed off on her. Oh well, her passion was definitely sexy. He stood up. "I'm not letting you out of my sight, so I guess I'm in," he said, smiling at her.

"You were a given." She kissed him on the cheek. "And your magic fingers will definitely come in handy. Now, who else is in?"

Dinaala and Micah jumped to their feet, followed by Raneal, who took each of their hands in the universal symbol of maternal connection to a loved one.

When Gaien stood Kevin jumped up as well, causing an irritated look to sweep across Rayne's face. She rose to stand by the dog, casting a look at the smiling canine that clearly said, *I can't believe you'd take their side in this.* Magda jumped to Rayne's side.

Eventually, Martin stood as well, saying, "What the heck?"

That left only Alice, sitting alone on one of the couches. Thom didn't know if she even understood the ramifications of their conversation, as she hadn't said a single word since her comments to Aleks in the mirror room. A tear ran from each pretty eye as she sat looking at the ground near her feet. Maybe the new Aleks would be willing to watch over her after the rest of the group had gone to battle the Dark One.

The group talked long into the night, brainstorming ways in which they could gather information about the Dark One and his armies. They agreed to split into thirds.

Donte, Thom, and Fazha would travel to the Repository to see what augury options might be available. Raneal, Jesik, and the "children" would travel to the Southern Reaches to seek out a mirror rumored to be somewhere on the Southern Islands. Rayne, Tony, Magda, and Gaien would travel north with Martin in an attempt to scout the Dark One's domain and gauge his capabilities. They would all rest for a day or two before setting out on their various missions.

It was at this point, when the group had moved on to several overstimulated conversations about places they'd seen and people they'd left behind, that the new Aleks decided to join them again. He walked into the room as if he owned the place. Which, Thom guessed, he did.

He walked over to the small gathering that Thom and Fazha had joined and listened patiently for a few minutes, while Rayne shared with Dinaala and Micah about the horses she had left behind when she came to the north. Rayne was saying she was sad she would never see the beautiful animals again.

"Hmm …" Aleks said. "Why would you never see them again?"

"Because I can't take Gaien back to the Southern Reaches and I won't abandon him," she said, looking slightly confused. "But you already know this."

"Yes," he replied. "Traveling south of the Break does present problems for you. However, I have another mirror that you can use to look in on your friends, if you wish. It's a much simpler mirror than the Mirror of Forever, showing only the present. However, it should do a fine job showing you whatever you wish to see right now."

Everyone stopped talking.

"You have another mirror?" Jesik asked from a few feet away, where he had been talking with Tony and Raneal.

"Of course," Aleks said. "It seemed like a wise idea to have more than one means of watching the events of the world transpire while I waited."

He took the group to a nearby room with a simple oval mirror mounted on the wall. Several chairs and a sofa were positioned in front of the mirror, with one of the chairs centered exactly before the glass.

"I do not believe anyone in the entire world knows this mirror is here. So no one will know you can see them, should you wish to look in on …" He looked at Rayne. "Queen Sheefa, for example. With that, I will return to my wife and leave you to your viewing." He turned and left the room.

"Oh my God," Thom said, to no one in particular. "Did he just give us a way to look in on Dark Dick without him knowing about it?"

"Dark Dick?" Jesik asked.

"He's not God. I'm tired of everyone acting like he's all powerful," Thom replied. "Besides, he really is a dick, right?"

"Um … yes … well, anyway," Jesik said, "in theory, this mirror should allow us to do exactly that. I think we should try it."

They spent some time getting the hang of controlling the mirror. Unlike the Mirror of Forever, this one did not project sound from the scene on display, so it sometimes made understanding what they were seeing a bit challenging. It was like watching a silent movie without the background score or dialog shots.

And like the Touch, the mirror responded uniquely to each viewer. For Rayne and Tony, the mirror responded more to their subconscious desires than the topic at the top of their mind. So they spent a lot of their time looking at the sea, horses, a trail through open woodlands, and Tony's car.

For Jesik and Donte, it constantly took them to the Repository and showed them rack after rack of rolled-up scrolls. Jesik acknowledged that the information he wanted most to understand was how the Prophecies could have been wrong and if he had missed something in all of his research.

As each took their turns at the mirror, only Thom and Micah were able to give some level of direction to it. How Micah managed was unclear to

Thom. The kid just seemed able to use any device with little or no trouble. Unfortunately, when he sent the mirror back to Jakob and Beka's house on a whim, he immediately started crying and couldn't continue. Dinaala and Raneal took him back to the Creek Room to support him and share his grief with some measure of privacy.

Thom's method was pretty simple. He treated the mirror like a person in a Negotiation. He kept his own emotions completely in check and used his Touch to guide the mirror where he wanted it to go. Within a few minutes he had the mirror gliding over the landscape north of the Deep, up over the northern range, and across the Kowlit glacier into the Dark One's lands.

Tony said, "Where are you now?"

Jesik replied, "We've just crossed over the last section of the northern lakes and are heading into the Valley of Shadow. This is the Dark One's territory."

Tony said to Thom, "Slow down. We need to see what the landscape looks like here. Can you change the perspective from straight down to looking forward? I'd like to see the elevation of the ground."

Thom shifted the view more by instinct than specific action. Now the scene was more like a panoramic helicopter shot than a satellite image. They traveled through a wide, curved valley over dense forest. A river ran down the center of the valley, leaving a sharp, black slash wavering back and forth through the bright-green trees. Soon the valley narrowed and steepened, passing between two scraggly lines of mountains before spreading out and flattening into a marshy plain. The river widened and stretched, taking in other feeder rivers and streams. Thom could make out in the distance grand castle spires jutting up through the mists that clung to the marshes across the valley floor in the early morning sunrise.

The closer they got to the towers, the larger and farther apart they proved to be. They had to be at least a thousand feet tall and maybe a mile apart. Thom zoomed the mirror closer. He waited for the castle to get ominous. Maybe it would have skulls along it or orcs lining the walls, or maybe a giant, hideous eye watching from a gruesome tower in the center of it.

But aside from the size of the place, it really wasn't bad. The spires appeared to demark the four corners of a huge rectangle. Connecting each of the spires was a tall outer wall formed from light-gray stone. Decorative carvings twisted and looped along the top edge of the wall. Leading up to the wall was a wide lane with carts and people moving toward a mammoth gate. The gate was shifted off center along the wall, toward the southwest corner of the huge structure. It stood open, even at this early hour.

East of the road entrance was another large gate. This one spanned the powerful river that Thom had noted earlier. Apparently, the river ran straight into the town, under the south wall. A small skiff was working its way out through the river gate. Thom guessed there must be a village or hamlet upriver.

As their helicopter view approached the castle—so-designated in Thom's mind because it looked just like what he pictured when people said the word "castle"—Thom started feeling a strange buzzing in his Touch. The image's progress slowed to a crawl. Thom fed it more Touch and it picked up pace again. Instinct told him he had to be careful or Dark Dick would figure out they were able to see into his place.

He cautiously moved forward. A city, nestled within the castle, came into sight as the helicopter view moved up and over the wall. Thom guessed it was three or four times as large as the Forbidden City, and in stark contrast to their temporary underground home, the castle was bustling with activity.

"Try going east a few hundred feet and then down into the ground about a hundred yards," Martin said from his seat on the sofa.

The pressure against his Touch was getting quite strong. And with the pressure, his worries about Dark Dick feeling them looking around were also getting stronger. He let everyone know about the feedback and pushed ahead.

The cobblestones grew large in their vision. Then everything went completely black. Ten seconds later they were through the dirt and inside a humongous chamber. This one was geometrically similar to the Forbidden City but lacked the buildings and bright-sky ceiling, and it lacked something else the Forbidden City had: hope.

Thom hadn't really thought about it until now. But the Forbidden City was a haven, a safety zone. It was a place people would want to call home. But the Dark One's underground lair lacked any hope at all.

Instead, it had monsters. Lots and lots of monsters. Row upon row of them marched in lock-step precision. Over their heads palkin soared and weaved, their riders pulling Touch from Activators spread throughout the mass of monsters and pouring it back out over the creatures in the ranks.

"Okay!" Tony said, leaning closer to the mirror. "Now we're getting something we can use. It looks like mostly infantry with some air support. We don't know if they can do much damage from the air, but we've seen infantry like that in action. Do you see how those flying riders are controlling the monsters? One of the things we can try to do is disrupt them during the fighting and create chaos in the ranks of that infantry."

Sweat poured down Thom's face at this point. Apparently, taking a mirror into a place where it isn't wanted was a *lot* of work. The screen wavered, faded, and went blank. "Oh, man!" Thom sighed, and everyone in the room turned to look at him. "I need a breather."

Thom got up from the overstuffed chair and made his way to a clear spot on one of the sofas. He plopped down, leaned back, and closed his eyes. Micah must have taken his spot in the chair because conversation picked up again as people began to make comments on what they were seeing.

Thom mostly ignored their comments as he rested his eyes, right up until he felt Fazha's light but electric touch on his arm.

"Wake up, love," she said to him. "It's time for us all to take a break."

Apparently, he'd worked harder at seeing than he thought. He stretched, stood up, and followed Fazha out of the room. When they got to the Creek Room, everyone else was already sitting in various places. With the exception of Micah, that is. He was stretched out on one of the sofas, snoring lightly.

Jesik brought Thom up to speed on what he'd missed during his unintended nap. "Micah got us only about another ten minutes in the Dark One's place, so we spent the rest of the hour mapping the terrain around his grounds."

Tony said, "Based on what we've seen, I have some ideas on how we can bottle up the army before they can spread out and overwhelm us. But I want to create some maps before we go any further so I can verify what I've been seeing. For that, we'll need some paper and something to draw with."

"I have plenty of paper and pencils right here," came Aleks's voice from the end of the hallway. As he stepped down into the seating area of the Creek Room, he held out a thick stack of paper and a dozen pencils for Tony to take. Somehow he always seemed to show up just when the conversation turned away from the group's plans around Dark Dick. And he always seemed to have just what the group needed. Interesting.

"It looks like you're taking a break from the mirror. Some of you look quite tired, but I know you had a lot of questions. Is this a good time for us to talk, or should we wait until the rest of your group has had a chance to get refreshed?"

"Why are you calling it *your* group?" Jesik asked. "Are you no longer part of what we're doing?"

"In truth," Aleks said, "I never was part of what you're doing. I have always had my own path to follow. And now that you're here, I will step back onto that path."

"And what path is more important than stopping the Dark One from enslaving the world?" Jesik snapped.

"A lonely but necessary one," Aleks responded.

"I don't understand," Dinaala said. "Aren't you going to help us?"

"I would help you if I could," Aleks said. "But my oath prevents it. And even if it didn't, I have other work to do that I must prepare for."

"I don't understand!" Jesik said, with more heat in his voice. "You're just going to abandon us?"

"No," Aleks replied, "you don't understand. And that's the way it must be." He sighed heavily and sat in one of the chairs. "In truth, I'm not sure my help would change the outcome all that much anyway. Now what other questions do you have for me?"

The questions were tossed at him from all sides. Aleks answered some, mostly those relating to the arrangement of the Forbidden City and the origins of the creatures in the Deep. It turned out that Aleks had created them more than two thousand years ago to guard the city from intrusion. They'd been quite successful. Until the group had arrived, only Jesik, Donte, and the Dark One had been in the city in all that time.

But as far as the rest of the questions went, he didn't really answer anything that mattered as far as Thom was concerned. Tony, on the other hand, really perked up at one topic that Aleks went on about at some length.

Wars.

Of course Tony was a warrior, so maybe ancient history intrigued him. The things Aleks was talking about now all happened before the world was broken. How that could help them slipped by Thom.

Eventually the conversation wound down. And when it was complete, all Thom had really gotten from it was that Aleks had created most of the major cities on the planet sometime before the world was broken. There had been a lot of squabbles between nations. All of the Templars had gone to war. The world was broken. The Templars were killed. Andrus went north. Aleks and Tan'aana came here. People slowly lost the ability to use both sides of the Touch. Aleks and Tan'aana had used the Mirror of Forever to see what the future held. And they had used it to jump forward in time. At first it was a few years at a time. Aleks and Tan'aana would stay in the Forbidden City for a while, learning about the status of the world. Then they would jump again. After doing this for a year or more they realized that very little ever really changed. Politics were politics. Nations grew and shrank. Sometimes people prospered. Sometimes they failed. But they always seemed to bump up against each other and fight. Aleks and Tan'aana grew weary of the constant turbulence of world politics. So they stretched their jumps to decades. And then they went to hundreds of years.

Until the most recent jump, when they realized they were in the right time frame to meet this group. So they waited. It was a little more than two years from the time they jumped until Thom's group stepped out of the elevator into the Forbidden City.

That had more or less—mostly less—brought the group up to speed on Aleks and Tan'aana. There were a few other questions that Aleks deflected or flatly refused to answer: "What do you think the Dark One will do now that he knows you're back?" And, "Why did you take an oath not to interfere with the Dark One?" And "Why did you make this city?" And "Is there anything else you can do to help us?"

Actually, that last one he did answer. "I have already done everything I can to help you, both now and in the past. For my help to help you, you need to help yourselves to it."

What the *fuck* was that supposed to mean?

Thom—and several others in the group if he was going to be fair about it—jumped all over Aleks's comment and hammered him with questions. He simply shrugged them off, saying he could give them no more information. And with that, he stood up, bowed to the group, and disappeared down the hallway amid a torrent of questions.

The group argued bitterly for a few minutes about the things Aleks had said and about what they should do next.

Tony let out a piercing whistle that immediately silenced the room. He either didn't notice or completely ignored the angry looks he got from several members of the group. "Arguing like this is getting us nowhere," he said with authority. "What we need to do now is take the information that Aleks gave us and put it with what we know and what we think we know. Only then can we make a good decision about how to move forward."

He looked at Thom. "You seem to be the best at using the mirror. Do you think you can be ready for another go after a few hours' sleep?"

Despite his usual lone-wolf mentality, Thom found himself strangely willing to accept Tony's leadership. The guy really seemed to know what he was doing. Thom nodded.

"All right," Tony said. "Let's all take a break for a few hours while Thom gets some sleep." He looked around the room. "I'm going to explore the city a bit and see what other supplies we can put together. Does anyone want to go with me?"

Dinaala and Gaien raised their hands. Kevin's head popped up when Gaien's arm moved. Rayne looked disgusted but raised her hand, followed by Magda. Martin nodded. It looked like more of a crowd than Tony was expecting.

Raneal said, "I'll stay with Micah so he doesn't wake up alone."

Jesik said, "I think I'll see what I can find in this building. We haven't done much looking around in here. Maybe there's another library that will help us understand some of what Aleks told us."

Fazha slipped her arm around Thom and walked with him back to the room they were using.

"Don't you want to go with them?" Thom asked, knowing Fazha was more of a "doer" than a "rester."

"I think resting with you is a great way to pass the time," she replied, smiling.

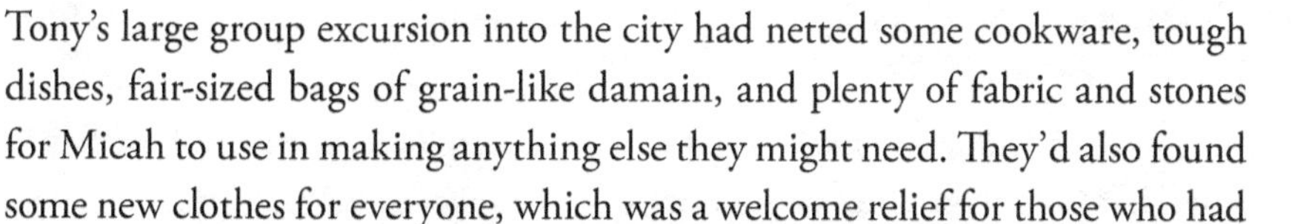

Tony's large group excursion into the city had netted some cookware, tough dishes, fair-sized bags of grain-like damain, and plenty of fabric and stones for Micah to use in making anything else they might need. They'd also found some new clothes for everyone, which was a welcome relief for those who had only the clothes they were wearing, specifically Thom and Martin.

Jesik had found a public library in the building that provided some additional information about Aleks. It seemed Aleks had been involved in a number of skirmishes immediately preceding the breaking of the world. Most of the information from that time had been lost, but the bits he could glean described a battle over territory that took place in the far north between Kamash and D'june, two city-state kings of the day. A map in one book Jesik had brought back showed the battle lines between the two warlords. It was drawn right through the valley that Tony had pointed out during their fly-over.

Tony studied the map for a few minutes and then turned page after page, looking at other maps. His expression was inscrutable, but it was obvious he was working something out. Suddenly, Tony jumped up and said, "C'mon!" He grabbed the book and Thom's arm and half dragged him into the mirror room.

He had Thom sit in the chair and said, "Can you show me this valley?"

Thom focused on the mirror and let his Touch do the walking. Within a few seconds the forested valley whizzed into view.

"Can you get closer to the ground?" Tony asked. "Along those valley walls? Right there, between those large lakes." He pointed to a spot on the mirror. "Right there! Zoom in on that!"

Thom complied, bringing that section of the landscape into clear view. The trees grew in size until they totally dominated the mirror.

"Closer!" Tony said.

The view moved in between the trees and up to a stony outcrop that jutted sharply upward through the steeply sloping hillside.

"There," Tony said, "right there! Do you see it?"

Thom looked more closely. The rest of the group pressed in as well, trying to get a better view.

"Right there," Tony said triumphantly. "*That* is the end of a shield wall! If we can fortify that wall, we can put a stopper on the bottle before the genie gets out."

"What?" Dinaala was clearly lost. Admittedly, Thom wasn't far behind her.

"If the topography matches what we're seeing here, the Dark One has to travel between these lakes and this mountain range, right? So if there's a shield wall across this valley and then the Dark One—assuming he can't make his entire army walk on water—will have to go right up this valley to get out of the north and into the rest of the world.

"Now, I'm making a couple of assumptions here. The first is that he doesn't have enough ships to move a million monsters on the sea. Second that he isn't strong enough to reshape ten thousand square miles of landscape. If he can do either of those two things, we have a whole different war to fight. We'll definitely need to know more about his capabilities before we go too far with the shield wall. But at this moment, it gives us a chance."

Tony had Thom zoom the mirror around the landscape of the north to ensure that his understanding of the terrain was accurate. Then he drew some pictures of the area and detailed his plans to the group.

A lengthy discussion ensued in which everyone expressed themselves quite loudly and with little regard for logic or military strategy. Finally, Tony corralled the group with another whistle and dished out assignments for preparing to leave the Forbidden City.

One thing about the assignments struck Thom as odd. When Tony gave tasks to the Freians, he sent most of them off immediately, while he, Thom, and Martin were left behind in the mirror room.

After the others left, Tony looked at Thom and said, "There's something else we need to see, while no one else is in the room."

Martin looked as confused as Thom felt.

Tony asked, "Can you get us a satellite view and zoom out? Like, way out?"

Thom nodded and shifted the mirror. The view pulled back until a long, thin pie slice of land, wrapped by water, could be seen. The tip of the slice was bent to the east and a massive mountain range ran the length of the eastern edge of the slice, leaving a narrow strip of land between the range and the sea.

"According to the map in this book, and my compass, that's north, right?" Tony said. Both men nodded. "Zoom out more."

The view zoomed out farther, finally showing the break slashing across the southern edge of the pie slice, like someone had trimmed off the outer crust. When it reached the eastern edge of the pie slice, it curved and followed a narrow strip of land to the south. The strip widened and widened and then spread out into another continent.

Oh my god!

Thom's brain struggled to reconcile what he was seeing. He heard Martin suck in a breath. Tony simply nodded.

"That's what I thought," Tony said. "We didn't go to another planet. That right there is the Gulf of Mexico. Their southern land is our North America. See how the break cuts across the northern edge of South America and then runs up through Central America and along the west coast?"

The three stood looking at the image for long time before anyone said anything.

"There are two moons," Martin said. He didn't sound like he was questioning what he was seeing.

Thom was trying to get his mind around it too, and he had a stable mind to do it with.

Tony nodded. "And north is south. This must be an alternate universe. One in which the rules of physics are slightly different. The poles have flipped one extra or one fewer time here than on our world. And this Earth must have picked up a second moon at some point."

"That's why most of this place is so familiar!" Thom said. "I've wondered for years why most of the animals, plants, and people are so much like those on Earth." So many weird anomalies suddenly made sense. Not the least of which was how Fazha had gotten pregnant by an alien. Sci-fi movies showed it all the time, but come on.

The three of them stayed in the mirror room for quite a while, sitting in silence and looking at the mirror's image of a world that was so familiar and yet so different from their own. Eventually, people started returning from their assignments gathering supplies. Thom wiped the mirror clean before any of them could ask what they had been looking at.

They piled their various travel packs on the floor and had a final round of conversation about their next steps. Then they hugged one another and got set for Thom to show them their target destinations. Before each person left, Jesik gave them a gate stone that would allow them to return to the Forbidden City when their tasks were done.

As Thom was guiding the mirror to the location that Tony and his team would jump to, Aleks walked back into the room.

"Alice can stay here with us for the time being," he said, looking kindly at the woman. A strange expression crossed his face as he looked at her, but it vanished as quickly as it had come. Poor Alice. She had been led everywhere and had spoken to no one, including the new Aleks, since the incident at the Mirror of Forever. "She'll be safe with me."

With that, the group said their good-byes and good lucks. Then Aleks waited patiently as one by one each person stepped through the mirror. Soon Thom and Fazha were the only two left to go.

Thom pulled up the last location. He watched Fazha go through and was about to step through himself when a new question crossed his mind. He turned and looked at Aleks. "Your wife's name is Tan'aana, right?"

Aleks nodded.

"What does it mean? You know, in English."

Aleks's smile radiated love. "It means 'the one who brings sweetness and light.'"

Of course it did. Only Fazha would name her obnoxious beast of a horse something like that.

Thom picked up his pack and sword, turned, and stepped through the mirror after his beloved.

CPSIA information can be obtained
at www.ICGtesting.com
Printed in the USA
LVHW021101041119
636249LV00002B/225